The Chain

A Story of Faith Seeking Understanding

ANNA RIST

The Chain

*A Story of Faith
Seeking Understanding*

 Angelico Press

First published by
Angelico Press, 2017
© Anna Rist, 2017

For information, address:
Angelico Press
4709 Briar Knoll Dr.
Kettering, OH 45429
angelicopress.com
info@angelicopress.com

978-1-62138-259-1 paperback
978-1-62138-260-7 cloth
978-1-62138-261-4 ebook

Cover Image: *The Temptation of Adam and Eve*
by Br. Bernward Schmid (1994), on the
outer portal of Seckau Basilica, Austria
Cover Design: Michael Schrauzer

to Gay, Maydie, Rose,
for memorial,

and for John,
who kept me at it

AUTHOR's NOTE: Thanks are due to Beryl Connolly who enlightened me on aspects of life in the country that today is Zambia and to Leonie Caldecott and Father Aidan Nichols o.p. for reading the novel in an earlier version and encouraging me both to improve on it and to seek publication.

CONTENTS

Tout comprendre est tout pardonner
(To understand all is to pardon all)

Traditional French saying

PREAMBLE

The Undeparted

RETURNING through the City to the Bank station that to-be-remembered day of 1936, and what should beguile Edith's journeying but reminiscence of a past both immediate and more remote. Casting back behind that morning's brisk walk through a March chill suspending smokes already rising from many a grate and many a steam locomotive: remembering days when one had to remove and re-tack the false hems that protected one's skirts from mud and the mix of rainwater and equine manure... Though her generation had come to expect material Progress, its manifestations left Edith largely unimpressed: she would live to view men on the moon with equanimity undisturbed. Moral progress might have astonished her more.

Remembering that morning's encounter with last night's birth, and so much that lay behind it...

They had hugged and kissed and cried. Until Edith, turning to survey the room, began, "Veronica, my precious!"

Thus, as she had planned, did Edith greet the Vessel of this solemn event, this ushering-in of a new generation. The name given in baptism was written in heaven; Edith shunned "pet" names and familiar abbreviations. The exception was Ron, given the impossibility of calling him "Aaron", which he so plainly disliked and which anyway had *not* been given in baptism...

Her newly-travailed daughter responded affectionately as, relaxing in her mother's warmth of greeting, she turned her face up to receive and return her kiss:

"Darling Deedie! How lovely that you've come just in time!"

"Yes, though I waited it seemed an age. They said you had visitors, who I guessed... You look to be quite comfortable here."

"Utterly luxurious, thanks to you—and of course Ron!"

"Who of course has seen her...?"

"Yes, last night, and again this morning. He thinks she's really pretty!"

Reassuring—for Ron, being Jewish, would, she thought, have

hoped for a boy. And newborns, even girls, were, everyone knew, not pretty but red and wrinkled.

"Surely...!" Edith had begun, but thought better, adding:

"But let me have a peep at the little precious!"

"There's not much to see of her at present. You can try lifting the blanket a little, only please don't wake her."

...Moving over to the cradle... Uncovering a little more of the smooth, dark skull just emerging from the white coverlet... dark lashes on a creamy cheek... Softly breathing "The darling!"... Tip-toe-ing back to the bedside to pronounce in hushed exclamation:

"Why, I do believe she is—pretty, God bless us! And her, the little precious!"

"In my day" (This phrase, which Edith knew amused her daughters, ever conveyed a hint of reproach to modernity.) "In my day only the poor went into hospital to have their babies. My mother was always by for my *accouchements*; I would have hated her to be away—especially the first time!"

Remembering—though in time Edith would conclude that memory had conflated more than one visit—how beyond this her daughter's day there lived on that earlier Edith felt by even those of her grand-daughters who scarcely remembered her as standing behind them all—and not only in that Faith by her embraced, to be mediated by their mother with a gentle assurance more persuasive than their father's cut-and-dried dogmatics, but also in the propriety in speech and manners that were only a lesser legacy of her who here so readily stepped into the foreground of shared memory...

Eldest of a country doctor's fourteen children, and having to make her way in life, that former Edith had accepted the position of housekeeper to a respectable widower with two motherless children —and by the time she herself gave birth to the child christened Edith after her, had become generally known as wife to her former employer and stepmother to her former charges.

Another daughter followed, to be christened Elizabeth. "Edie" and "Liza," as they were known, were sixteen and fourteen when the family began to experience hard times, the father taking first to drink and then to laudanum—culminating in an overdose accompanied by a note he left accusing a certain Father Dyer of alienating his wife's affections by persuading her into the Catholic Church.

Except she was not his wife according to law, and though law by now might have made that good, still that could not be without a stigma and publicity both parents shunned. What Law enabled was the bestowal of their father's surname on Edith and their natural children and for some years all continued smoothly to outer appearances. But beneath appearances conscience did not cease to disquiet the mother until, dissatisfied with counsel sought within the Methodism in which she had been raised, and long fascinated by a Catholic past evoked in the romances of Walter Scott, she one day ventured into a "Roman" church: there to experience such peace as would draw her to return and soon to seek out its pastor.

Father Dyer had listened sympathetically but was in no two minds: so long as John Hislop's lawful wife was living, Edith and he could not be wed in the eyes of God. If, as was soon the case, Edith desired to become a Catholic, they might for the sake of their children continue to dwell in the same house, but with "separation of bed and board"—and more crucially the former.

All too predictable had been John's reaction to Edith's proposal for this re-ordering of their arrangements. There ensued the domestic storm from which their shocked daughters learned what all had contrived to keep from them: their mother and father were unmarried—were, in the phrase which did not fail to strike a shudder to the core, "living in sin." Their half-brother and half-sister, Walter and poor feeble-minded Hester, were their father's only legitimate children.

For a time the parents lived on uneasily under the same roof—at least when the father was home from travelling on behalf of the shoe business of which he was junior partner, when after a hasty supper he would repair to the pub and she be abed in the same room with their daughters before he could return, they would hope not inebriated. The laudanum he first obtained under prescription, later under the bar of his "local"; this tended for a while to keep things sedated in the house, but the footwear wholesalers were losing custom. It was on one of his business journeys that he had been found moribund in his hotel bed, having attempted the criminal act his letter attributed to the Romish priest's interference. His presumed wife being contacted, her father hastened to the scene, possessed himself of the note and prevailed with the attending physician to present the matter as accidental overdose. John, by now addicted, would spend much of his remaining life in and out of an institution and refusing the proffered visits of his family. After he was released and occupied the ground-floor flat of a house in Surbiton, Edith could console herself that she had visited him weeks before his death, taking her own impressionable eldest with her.

At the outset of the drama she and Liza, made wary of their father's moods and drinking, had rallied to their mother, electing to enter the Roman Church with her. Walter, having once finished an apprenticeship to his father's occupation, would follow them. The old doctor, besides contributing to their provision, found for Hester a place in a genteel asylum where he could keep an eye on her; it stretched his resources, but he was a generous, kindly man and afflicted by his eldest child's aberrant circumstances—worsened, as he saw it, by her turn in religion.

After he died, mother and daughters were reduced to supporting themselves as best they could: Edith could recall all three sitting assiduously to the making of paper bags in a cheap lodging in the East End—until their priest-mentor persuaded the Mother Superior of a Belgian convent school to take both girls to round off their education; in addition, Edith would instruct in English and Art and so be put in a position to relieve their mother. In this she had acquitted herself well enough that, with the first year's ending, the Mother Superior proposed that she "try her vocation" in the convent. This invitation being firmly declined, Mère Thérèse was persuaded to furnish the headstrong young Englishwoman with a recommendation to an Austrian family seeking a governess, and replace her with her more docile-seeming sister.

From there on, much of Edith's eighteenth and nineteenth years had seen her pass into positions ever farther afield, as English governess to households in which her looks earned her little favour with the mistress even where they did not find too much with the master, until she reached the confines of Russia, being received into the extensive and very Catholic household of a Polish nobleman, where her breeding and intelligence recommended her to the Princess, mother of the two young princes, Edith's charges. In this well-ordered *milieu*, where she took precedence before the house servants, as they before those ex-serfs working the wider estate—and once her first month's salary had enabled her to be provided with suitable footwear and warm clothing—Edith had endured a Russian winter not unhappily, for the Princess proved kind. But she still yearned for her mother, and having saved up a little money, asked leave to make the arduous journey home.

She had intended to return to this not-unhappy though remote situation, but the assuaging of her homesickness induced her to linger long enough for Father Dyer—ever-conscious of having been in some sort instrumental to their shipwreck—to draw attention to an advertisement in the Catholic press: a companion-secretary was required by a French lady of impeccably Catholic credentials—and through inquiry he learned (though did not divulge to his protégées) that "Madame Rigg" was by this means seeking a suitable wife for her only son, "suitability" implying an unimpugnable Catholicity and ladylike breeding accompanying looks and disposition such as to please the young gentleman.

Indeed Edith appeared a likely candidate—provided only the circumstances of her birth were not viewed as obstacle, and they should initially go unmentioned; Father Dyer had ever stressed that, these circumstances being no fault of her parents' children, and all being comprehended in the merciful Providence of God, they should in no way consider themselves diminished by them. Wealth, it transpired, was inessential, Madame having already acquired it by shrewd French business-sense backed by French social assumptions which, as Edith would come to realize, even suggested its lack in a daughter-in-law to be an advantage: appreciation of her good fortune would surely incline the chosen one to deference to her husband and, standing firmly and financially behind him, her mother-in-law. As daughter-in-law, Edith had come in time to divine how, beneath an imperious manner, Madame Rigg felt herself undervalued: her good—even, she liked to claim, noble—French descent going unappreciated in her father's heretical and semi-barbarous country, to which her parents, staunch Catholics, had retreated before France's anti-clerical laws; where in consequence she and her sister had been reared in genteel poverty—Madame's English would all her days be marked with the accents of the East End—and where paucity of Catholics had obliged her to be married, as she considered, below her station, to a scion of obscure but obdurate recusants from a provincial town. Conveniently, that same England had latterly furnished married women with the power of financial independence: those, at least, who had inherited means or the determination to acquire them. A series of stillbirths and infant deaths—interpreted by her husband as rebuffs to his family's devout expectation that he would continue a modest but proud line tracing its Catholicism back behind the English Reformation—left her wounded but unvanquished; rather they stimulated her redoubtable business talents to found the fashion-house on which she bestowed her name as "Madame Rigg."

In the event, the survival of one son promised fulfilment of the father's prayers that the Rigg name be in him continued—as of the intention of Madame that her exertions and their rewards should devolve upon René, the heir thus triumphantly secured, and for whom a wife was now sought to continue the line and secure the interests of both parents. And René promptly obliged by accepting to be in love with this handsome and demure specimen of a sex hitherto represented only by "The Mater"—so at his public school he had learned to refer to her he had hitherto called "Maman"—and her self-effacing sister, Tante Geneviève, who was married to Raoul, another émigré cousin, and mother to his thus doubly cousin Léon.

His father was never "Pater" to the young René, but "Papa"; the French term had become *de bon ton* in England from the years of the Empress Eugénie's sojourn at the court of Victoria. That René himself would become known to the family he would found as "Pawa" was characteristically the upshot of his upbringing and of a long battle to be called as he had called his father: further to be greeted daily by his children as had been required of him, by a mother punctilious in lip-service to the paternal authority while it remained in place, with the formula "Good morning, Papa." But the English middle class had abandoned Frenchiness and the young generation, aware that their friends used the colloquial "Daddy," persistently evaded this requirement, providing for their father one more evidence of the excellence of his own upbringing at his mother's hands, as of Edith's own failure in complaisance toward himself: controversy that had seemed endless until a lisping Veronica evolved the "Pawa" on which even he had by then been thankful to compromise.

Veronica resorted to their childhood term.

"Oh, Mumsie, it *is* a comfort to have you here now, even though you could not be when... Then do you think that old way was better, dearest Mumsie?"

...Standing back, her hand resting on the recumbent shoulder as she surveyed her...

"Yes, with the long labour you had, you poor darling! But no, it was better provided everything went well, but think of Grandma Rigg, losing two at birth who perhaps might have lived with better care! Your father, too: assumed dead: set aside while they attended to her! Only later was it noticed he was still breathing—it prompted them to call him René. In those days there was more anxiety about the mother than the child—and with good reason. Mind you, the way she treated him sometimes, you might have concluded she wished he *had* died then—though I know I should not say that!"

"Poor Pawa! And poor Grandma Rigg!"

"Indeed—and though she has certainly been a bane to me, she must have suffered much and we cannot judge; perhaps it was going through all that that made her hard on others—and so set on making a success out of something."

"Doesn't it sometimes seem things go back for ever in families— like a chain! Or like the Furies, you know."

Though Edith had little acquaintance with the troubles of the House of Atreus, their brother's friendship with the Greek airman they called Andy had prompted her elder daughters—withdrawn from schooling with the nuns of the Sacred Heart just as they had begun to thirst for a wider cultivation—to stretch their small salaries to the purchase of Professor Murray's translations of Greek dramas as they came fresh off the Oxford University Press; these they passed on to their younger sisters. All had been admirers of the personable young pilot: not least Veronica, for whom Edith thought he had shown a certain predilection.

She had been better acquainted with the presuppositions of Veronica's next question:

"Mother—Deedie—do you think that could be what Original Sin is?"

"Partly, I dare say"—cautiously—"but you shouldn't trouble your head about such things at such a time." She should not have been speaking as she had and added,

"It's all water under the bridge and we won't go into past griefs when we're so happy that your baby's arrived safe and healthy, the little precious! I hope she *will* wake up soon and let me see her properly; they don't give visitors enough time here. Meantime I can see you! You're looking a little pale still. I hope you're eating well."

"O yes, though the food's nothing special—not up to *your* joints and puddings!"

"At least it's a rest for you, darling, so do take full advantage, won't you. And we know, dearest child, you don't much care for cooking— though I'm sure you've learned a lot since those early days…"

"When you and Freda brought dinner round in a taxi, you were so afraid Ron might starve—or might think he would—I mean, I could manage toasted cheese or scrambled eggs even then! But his mother's a real Jewish cook; he must be enjoying that, at least, now he's back with her, though of course…"

"Yes, how are things going in that quarter? Is she pleased about Baby?"

The widow Keller had received news of her son's marriage to a gentile with lamentations impelling the busy housewives of Whitechapel to arm themselves with chicken soup, schmalz and suchlike products

7

of their daily toil and hasten to witness her anguished avowals that her only solace was her Abe had died before this calamity came upon his family—interspersed with threats to end her days forthwith with her head in the gas-oven.

"Pleased enough, I think, and Ron's going to bring her tomorrow. It's her first grandchild—even though not a Jewish one; you have to have a Jewish mother to be Jewish and she's stopped telling Ron I'll have to 'turn,' as we've both made it clear I shan't! So I don't see why she'd be more pleased if it was a boy, but I suspect Ron thinks so, and we were going to have him—you know, circumcised: only not like in the Bible, but you can have it done by a proper surgeon. Of course it costs a lot, so from that point of view it's a good thing…"

Steering away from these somewhat distasteful particulars, Edith observed,

"The important thing now is for you to recover well: get some colour in those cheeks and put some flesh on these thin arms. Is Baby feeding well?"

"Yes—only she's hungry before the time is up."

"Then feed her more frequently."

"You're not supposed to. I asked Sister when she did the rounds yesterday and she said, 'Well, Mrs Keller, I can't prevent you doing as you please with your own child, but if you'll take my advice you'll stay with four-hourly feeds if you don't want to make a rod for your back.'"

"That seems absurdly rigid with a newborn…"

"But it's scientific! Agnes gave me this book by Doctor Ruby King…"

"Truby. I've heard of him and I've no time for such notions. A mother does best following her own good instincts, her heart…"

"I know, you dear Deedie!"

Feeling her mother wax indignant, Veronica had taken her hand and pulled her down to kiss her cheek again.

"You were always soft with us and if it wasn't that I want to give Elaine the best start and the very best upbringing, to break that chain, you know…"

"If it's a chain of sin, only love will break it."

"But if it's—ignorance? I mean, if we *know* more now, it must be more loving to do the right thing, mustn't it? Isn't Original Sin partly ignorance?"

"Partly, I suppose. But it would be rash to think the instinct of mothers and nurses—the instinct of women throughout the ages—less reliable than a Doctor Truby King in the twentieth century."

"But Science only started quite recently!"

"Science will need grace to direct it if it is to do good—to build up God's world and not destroy it. We saw destruction enough in the Great War, about the time *you* were born, and let us hope our little girl will not see another!"

…bethinking to add,

"I don't believe it's knowledge that counters sin; rather understanding, perhaps. At all events you can take it from me that a half hour or so early can't make any difference; a routine is desirable, but these are early days and your little one needs to be helped to adjust…"

Aware that she was hardly being marked, she had changed the topic…

"I take it you've quite decided on Elaine?"

"Yes. Don't you like it? Pawa says it's the same as Helena. She *is* a saint, isn't she?"

"Yes, the Emperor Constantine's mother, who went to the Holy Land and found the True Cross. Why *not* Helena? Or Helen?"

"I don't like Helen—too *femme fatale*!"

"'The face that launched a thousand ships'?"

"Yes. Besides, Helen Keller's that blind and deaf girl—and there's an awful poem we read at school: 'Dust has closed Helen's eye'."

…both of them viewing Leo's rigid corpse, coffined, draped in the flag before his military funeral…

Her daughter saying:

"Because we both love Tennyson—you know: 'The Lily Maid of Astolat'"

…recovering herself, demurring,

"She too was rather—*fatale*, as I recall!"

To receive the unforeseen reply:

"Oh, but she was a maid! Doesn't that mean a—a virgin?"

The word out, Veronica had broken off, her face and neck turning pink; this was still un-broached ground between them. As diversion and to restore cheer, Edith said lightly,

"I dare say the Lily Maid or Helen of Troy herself was no finer baby! What about a second name?"

…hoping the answer might be her own, her mother's…

"Winifred—for Freda, of course, but also for my friend Winnie who's going to be her godmother. There's a Saint Winifred, but I don't know much… There's a well, isn't there? We read a poem about that at school, too."

"Indeed yes, Holywell, in Wales…"

On safer ground, she had expatiated on Holywell: place of pilgrimage, visited by Catholics even during the Elizabethan penal laws when to go there in secret became a badge of defiance, as well as a supplication for better times. "René and I went there after your birth—to give thanks and to pray for a son."

"And instead the saint sent you another girl!"

"Let us say, rather, God did—and so we called her Winifreda. And now it seems she has obtained the redoubling of His gift in your little Elaine Winifred!"

Rising, walking softly round the bed to lean a moment over the cradle, contemplate again the tiny form within, its breathing hardly stirring the lacy knit shawl, of Ron's sister's workmanship, which covered "it"—Being so still—seeming precarious, as hovering yet on birth's brink...

"Elaine Winifred," she had repeated: "two very English names for—for her. You'll have her christened soon, won't you?"

"Oh yes. Ron's agreed to that. Of course he doesn't think it's particularly urgent. You couldn't expect him to believe people who aren't baptised are damned or anything, could you, when none of his people are—baptised, I mean! Besides, she's strong and healthy, so there's no hurry."

"Even healthy babies..."

She had broken off, unwilling to strike a note of alarm. She resumed,

"We can't believe a just God damns unbaptised people—'If they follow the light they have' is what I've been told."

"Jews too?"

"My dearest Veronica! Why, of course it applies to everyone—perhaps specially to Jews, who know the true God though may only know Him fully in the hereafter. As indeed is the case with us all..."

Implications for Ron becoming involved, she began again: how little Elaine was called to be Christ's in this life, to be Catholic "through your faith—our faith—and now your Catholic marriage. To be born and to go to God: that is all that truly matters in life—though perhaps it's easier to see that from where I am..."

...breaking off as pressure of past griefs was vented in a sigh, she ended,

"My great solace is that my two little ones are with their angels guardian and, as I often think, watching over us. Praise be that I had a Catholic *accoucheuse* for little René, who baptised him just before he expired, naming him for his father but surely inspired by God, for he was no sooner born than reborn!"

Had she gone too far? Her daughter leant over to extract a packet of cigarettes from her handbag beside the bed and held them out to her mother.

"Do they allow you to smoke in here?"

"They don't much like it—and I don't have a light. Open the window a bit."

Edith had lifted the sash a little, noting that the day had brightened somewhat, as she placed a cigarette between her lips and produced from her own bag a small petrol lighter.

"And if—like Pawa, if he *had* been born dead... It happened to a woman here, poor thing! Can *they* be baptised? And miscarriages?"

"Yes, they should receive conditional baptism, in case... We don't know when the soul leaves the body. But let's not worry our heads about that now."

Still trying to rein in the conversation before obliged to enter upon Natural Bliss and Limbo (Herself a convert, Edith sometimes wondered how years of convent schooling could have left her daughters so vague as to Church teaching), she had mustered her habitual bright assurance into smile and voice to say,

"Your little darling is well and strong, for which we can thank God, who is over all, and 'not a sparrow falls...'"

Then the two had smoked in silence, for both knew this meant that Leo too had died "fortified with the rites of Holy Church," as was stated in black and white on his memorial card with Jesus showing His Sacred Heart and the prayer for remission of "whatsoever sins he through human frailty hath committed." It meant that a priest had been called in time to ask in his ear for some sign— even the motion of a hand—betokening repentance for those sins, including this culminating one of suicide, and to pronounce God's absolution over the head too broken to receive the Viaticum: to anoint that head and the shattered limbs of the hope of Riggs and Lumleys, his parents' one surviving son. And though the coroner had given his verdict with the usual formula, "while the balance of his mind was disturbed," they took comfort that, from the all-important standpoint of eternal verity, the disturbance surely had been such as to cancel the crime. The young man had been suffering from a fever, probably exacerbated by wine crassly supplied with his last meal in accord with military protocol for officers—as well as from mental anguish over the woman he had engaged himself to marry: a divorcee whom his family viewed as about to seal their surviving son's own divorce from the destiny into which he had been born as hander-on not only of the Rigg name but of their Faith. A letter from her had been found, received that morning, breaking off the engagement in a few crudely wounding sentences.

And there was—if possible—worse. Edith could not but believe her presence would have rescued him from desperation—perhaps even regained him for the Faith–had she been informed of his illness. Magdalen, the sister closest to him in age, from childhood his trusted confidant, alone had known of it, and Edith, as culmination of her grief, would have to struggle to forgive this most aloof of her daughters for keeping it from her.

No speculation, no regrets, nothing could change the fact that the son she had fought to keep by her as a child—hope of Riggs and Lumleys, her triumph over them all as summed up in her mother-in-law—had flung himself from the high window...

From watching a slight stir in the cradle, Edith returned softly to the bedside and stubbed out her cigarette. Reseating herself she bethought her to ask,

"Pawa's already seen her?"

"Yes, this morning. He came straight after Mass. He brought this for baby."

Veronica reached down into the handbag, this time bringing up a small black box she passed to Edith, who opening it held up a frail corona of geranium-pink corals.

"And he gave this for me." From round her neck she produced an oval medal, slipping over her head the chain on which it was suspended.

"It's all in one piece"—turning the chain about—"no clasp, just a long chain: silver, quite heavy."

"I remember it: the Miraculous Medal. See" (turning it over): "Our Lady on one side—on the other the Cross."

"There's some writing round the edge."

"Yes: 'O Marie conçue sans péché originel...' It's been abbreviated and I can't make out the rest but you'll know it in English."

"'Mary conceived without sin, pray for us who have recourse to thee!'?"

"Yes. Our Lady is said to have appeared to St Catherine Labouré, a nun in Paris in the early part of the last century, when the Church in France was being persecuted anew. The French Orders who taught you and your sisters took refuge in England around that time. I like to think it was reparation for the English religious and priests who had been driven out, often to France, in the sixteenth and seventeenth centuries."

Edith touched the medal to her lips, then weighed the whole in her hand before passing it back to Veronica, adding, "It was his mother's —and I believe her mother's, Clothilde's, who will have brought it with her from France when they all were obliged to leave."

Grandma Rigg had departed life two years previously, assisted by the prayers and benisons of many a cleric whose ambition to rebuild the Catholic Church in England she had materially furthered before being bankrupted by the combined effects of War, Depression and the incompetence of her son.

"He had the medal specially blessed. I put it on because I was feeling rather down, but I'd better take it off before Ron and his mother come."

"I don't know that you should hide your faith from them," Edith protested. "Remember that night soon after you were married..."

"Do I remember! Poor Ron, it was neurotic of him," (She must have caught that word from Agnes). "But his mother was carrying on so, and his brother—who I tried to be nice to, but he actually *said* we could never have anything in common—horrid little man!"

"Hush, child! Upsetting yourself is bad for the milk and besides, we must try to understand. We must seem so—so well set up in their eyes, though we know all is not as it may seem, alas! But by a real Christian example I believe you will win your husband over in time."

"I don't honestly know if I want to, Mumsie, or not till I'm too old to have children. It might lead to too many—like you!"

"No, child, not too many! If ever I thought so, then God knows, but I wish all had lived! As Magdalen used to say when I complained—God forgive me!—'Come, Mother, which of us would you be without?'"

Her daughter laughed at this familiar reflection... Who might well surmise it was Magda herself, coming so hard on Agnes' birth, that her mother could have done without—or Freda who had followed close on her own, and was "the youngest-born," as they would tease Deedie, chanting, in delighted parody of Scott:

"Their mother answered them in scorn,
'*You* are not the youngest-born!'"

In sober fact, Freda had not been the last-born... But if God gave children, as was unthinkable to doubt, He surely allowed people to make mistakes—though the Church seemed to hold that He allowed them in everything *but* that! She had concluded with that favourite of René's sayings:

"God writes straight with crooked pens."

Again a silence, until Veronica picked up the hand that still bore the gold ring placed on it, alongside that with the five diamonds that had sealed the ill-starred engagement, and stroked it with the hand that bore her own gold band and that topaz encircled by brilliants Ron had picked up in the East End from a dealer in antiques.

"You poor Mumsie, such hard times as you've had! We definitely shan't be able to have many, not unless Ron does better than this clerical job."

"At least it's a steady occupation, as your father never had."

"True, and he's going to start evening-classes to qualify as an Inspector, but it doesn't look as if we'll ever be rich—unless he can succeed as a writer."

"Remember the Roman Matron Cornelia, who said her children were all her jewels!"

The reference was a favourite with Edith, perhaps brought to mind by the rings they both were contemplating.

"Meaning boys, no doubt! Deedie, is it true Pawa said 'Another girl!'? Ag told me…"

Agnes, as Edith expostulated, was over-inclined to take amiss everything her father said and did—and for that herself must bear some of the blame, adding,

"We know he has suffered and is blind to many things, but he was quick to bring Baby a present; perhaps we should let that speak for him."

Taking from the breast pocket of her elegantly ruffled blouse the little timepiece inherited from her mother-in-law (another silver chain!) and having consulted it, Edith, standing again over the cradle, buttoned her coat and drew close under her chin the fox-fur terminating in black snout and glass eyes. Drawing on her gloves, she kissed the fingertips, to touch them to the faintly stirring white-wrapped form within; finally sketched a cross in the air above, murmuring, "God bless you, little Elaine Winifred; I hope you and I may become friends. And goodbye—God be ever with you, my blessed Veronica! And you *are* blessed; remember that!" …had stooped to kiss and trace a cross on her daughter's brow—just as a nurse's head appeared round the door to announce the end of Visiting.

Her thoughts occupied with all that had passed, Edith took occasion for the detour offered through this history-laden area of the City and down to its River: arrived at the Bank, continuing on, observing the Monument, crossing St Paul's Churchyard, passing before the Old Bailey, making for Blackfriars Bridge, from where to look down on Thames' ever-fascinating current; Edith was keenly aware of the river's role in the national history that for her had been a lifelong romance, nourished by her Catholicism and, reinforced through her husband's family, extended into France. How many this lively brown artery below had borne on its scaly back as it lapped so lovingly up and through London, to turn and run swiftly and inexorably back down to the sea! From Julius Caesar to Thomas More—and many a royal pageant, from Tudor to Hanoverian! In her mind still her words so recently spoken: "all water under the bridge." Though was it—that past that seemed to cling and shadow one, did it ever slip away like these turbid waters, away to be lost, assimilated into the seas and the great oceans that seemed to promise forgetfulness—or eternity? Or God, to whom in the end one must entrust all, as she reminded herself.

Then how many had ended obscure lives in those eddies which she could not view without a shiver—because so they must have swirled around Barnes Bridge, upstream from here, when her father's first wife—no, his wife—had leaped, clutching their baby son, dragging by the hand her young daughter…

They had been rescued and the attempt put down to childbed fever, avoiding charges of attempted suicide or child-murder; but Minnie's madness had continued in alternations of brooding silences and paroxysms which led her to committal to Bedlam, her daughter to her life of amiable imbecility brought to its ending by the influenza-outbreak at the close of the Great War. To which the elder Edith also had succumbed—and her daughter wiped away tears as memory revived the loss of the mother who had been her support through all trials.

Nothing changed the fact that, with Minnie living on, Edith's father and mother remained unwed—and by the time she died their tragedy had been consummated. One must not wish it otherwise, and though Edith saw ever less of a Liza bent on advancing her family's fortunes, ever less sympathetic to what she viewed as histrionics deplorably public, she knew that both of them alike continued to feel their illegitimacy—however they had been counselled of their priest to make peace with this as sober fact and with the past. Only that this new birth seemed to confirm there *was* meaning; while this standing and gazing upriver brought so much to mind: poor crazed Minnie had proved to their father a sullen, unpredictable onus from the time she entrapped him, younger than herself, much as another woman would entrap the son of that untimely pregnancy, only in poor Walter's case it had been with pregnancy's simulation—as unscrupulous women did... Here Edith reproved herself. Who was she to judge the shifts of all-but-destitute women, who herself had married for security and social advancement?

She sighed again at the questions that were like the water slipping incessantly under this bridge—history done and gone! What use to ponder a sorry tale, keep dragging a heavy chain: chain symbolized, as Veronica had felt it, in that round her neck, linking her through Grandma Rigg to their forebears... That brought back that other thing Veronica had said, about the House of Atreus and Original Sin: had said with the acute sensibility of the newly delivered mother, making way for new life, a new beginning—but for that Chain! Therein lay the meaning of baptism: birth anew, regeneration...

One use such a tale might have should she find leisure and summon up purpose. A story emblematic of our need for redemption: a novel—it had occurred to her before, but the subject matter had seemed too tangled, too fraught with emotions to be tackled as sometimes it seemed it might. Instead, and to fill the interstices of her chaotic life with writing, she had drawn on the reading for which her sojourn in the Belgian convent had provided the resource of a few well-vetted French books, among which the Letters of Madame de Sévigny had engaged her fancy. Determined reading, issuing in writing, had kept alive a romantic sensibility that might not have survived the ordeals of her marriage; on her late move to Shepherd's Bush she had come across the ribbon-tied bundles of ruled foolscap covered edge to edge in her laboured longhand—her schooling had made no concessions to left-handedness. She intended to revise and some day to seek publication for this novel, set in the lush court of the *Roi Soleil*...

Here Edith left sighing to shake herself mentally into the present. A shock to them it had been, Veronica's secret marriage—and to a Jew, and René had reacted predictably to this news of his favourite daughter. Yet even he had made his peace with accomplished fact: even come to like Ron, perhaps recognizing in him one in whom trust could be reposed—a good deal more than in some of the men whose attention they had attracted, her tall pair: the dark and thin, the fuller-formed and fair, alike in their height and their gaze of grey-blue innocence. Innocence, she felt uneasily, that might have evaporated of late; something had occurred with the younger in Venice: seduction, she thought only attempted, but distraught on her unscheduled return, the child closest to her, the baby she had saved from her infant sister's fate, had turned rather to Veronica, unswervingly protective of the younger and, their mother sensed, experiencing some remorse for having carried off the quarry: the image was apt, for in their searches for likely men they had hunted as a pair.

Nor, given her own history, had she discouraged daughters thrown upon their wits—as arose, she recognized, from their having no secure place in British society: bred to ladylike expectations, yet with truncated education and means and lacking the father's support that should have opened paths for them had René's blooding at school not left him indignantly repudiating social ambition that could be construed as snobbishness or common worldliness.

There had been their acquaintance from Hamburg: he might even have prepared the way for Ron by regularly averting to Jews as the authors of all Europe's ills and notably those of his Fatherland. Her girls were friendly with a Jewess, Rachel, who occupied—doubtless more competently—Edith's old position as companion-secretary to a Grandma Rigg grown surprisingly fond of her, as were they all. Naively expecting to confound their new acquaintance's prejudice, they had invited both to tea, but even as the introductions were made, Helmut Ritter had bowed slightly and stiffly, thereafter had sat monosyllabically silent throughout the pouring and passing, had made early his excuses and not been heard from again—to much wonderment but nobody's undue distress.

And her daughters, Edith could reflect, were not alone in consorting with the numerous foreigners one encountered in London these days. Liza's Teresa—so lacking in that prudence characterizing mother and elder sister—she too had become "entangled," and with a German Jew whose child she was even then expecting. Whatever the shortcomings of the creed in which they had been reared—accidents, they held, of time and place or of men's inability to penetrate the Divine Wisdom—they all accepted from it the preciousness of each person, together with a detached view of the assumptions or presumptions of their fellow-citizens. Had not St Paul written that the Jews would come to accept their Messiah before His Second Coming?

Not that she expected her son-in-law's conversion to wait upon that! Ron had not long occupied that status and, still cast off from his family, was living in Edith's house while he and Veronica looked for a flat, when he had been taken ill one night with chest-pains alarming enough that they had sent for the doctor. Someone—Winifreda?—had proposed sending also for Father O'Shea, and to this Ron assented—being, it seemed, in a frame to overlook pique at the Irishman's shaky grasp of his name on the occasion of their Church wedding.

By the time his sister-in-law returned in the doctor's car, the pains were receding and were shortly banished: more, it seemed, by medical reassurance than by the prescription for which Winifreda—her sister being in no condition—rushed on her bicycle to the duty chemist. The priest was left undisturbed that night, Ron's anticipated baptism deferred—for Edith felt sure it must come—albeit from that point of view it had been perhaps less than helpful that Ron's mother had "come round"; cast off by his kin, Ron might have remained the more disposed to align himself with his wife's family and all they stood for. On the other hand, it was desirable that Mrs Keller senior should accept her daughter-in-law, and Veronica had set herself with admirable tact to win her over. If only she, Edith, had been as forbearing with *her* mother-in-law!

She turned from the river and this time her sigh was almost a groan as she remembered the ill-omened return from a less-than-happy sojourn on the Riviera, to begin their married life. While she might have been a deferential employee, she was far from submissive by temperament and less sensible than Madame Rigg had anticipated of obligation to herself and her son for the establishment to which they were raising her, a penniless, almost unsupported girl. Madame had taken for them a flat hard by her house in Princes Gate; in it Edith had arranged their numerous wedding-gifts, which included some of her mother's relics of better days and furnishings supplied by Madame together with some handsome antique pieces, fruits of her penchant for auctions and sharp eye for a bargain. All too vividly recalled, that day she and René returned from their wedding-trip—both of them thankfully and in hope of settling into a better beginning—to find Madame had re-ordered all!

Three weeks had better acquainted the bride with his mother's ascendancy over her husband. Fuelled by indignation, she restored her arrangements—leaving for ensuing years to ponder whether a modicum of tact in approving something of her mother-in-law's preferences might have mollified that matriarch. As it was, their married life took off in a storm that left her and the furniture unmoved, René sulky and inclining to the side of The Mater.

Here Edith's recollections were interrupted by the exigencies of descending the steps to the Underground and finding her way to the westbound platform, where they resumed on a less painful note. She had survived the ebb and flow of fortune, of births and deaths, even the latest and most cruel. Madame Agnes' Business had been bankrupted, but its foundress—nothing if not a survivor—had emerged from the wreck of her life's ambition with honour, contriving to pay off creditors whose gratitude was engraved on a massy silver tray; strangely René had left this with her, perhaps in recognition that her common-sense practicality had led to The Business living on under the modest name—still bearing witness to its author—of A. Lumley and Company, and with the modest function to produce overalls and suchlike serviceable items.

Madame Agnes had departed this life unknowing the presumed male heir would shortly follow her. After his mother's death, René had blundered on before turning all over to his wife, content with the small allowance that enabled him to follow the life of religious observance coupled with renunciation of worldly goods to which the more charitably-minded of his family wondered if he were not "really" called—or could have been without those aspects of his destiny owed in the main to Grandma Rigg. He continued to tenant the attic flat high over premises which still bore the fading legend, "Madame Rigg and Company"; there he conducted the solitary life that best suited him, drawing his old-age pension, shopping for his few wants on his way back from daily Mass at Farm Street, tinkering with old bicycles and sewing-machines—even an old car—and seeing few visitors apart from a sympathetic priest with whom to discuss matters religious and old Mr White who inhabited the flat below and had become a convert under the influence of Mr Rigg—to which name René had reverted, perhaps for its simplicity, perhaps as marking his disjunction from herself; perhaps too in filial recognition of his father, regarded as the Missing Link.

As for his mother, to do her old enemy justice, financial integrity had in the end been more important to her than the money she had pursued for the independence and power it gave a woman for doing good as she saw it. But if Edith did not feel entitled to sit in judgment on conjugal failure, her elder daughters had no such scruples. Magdalen, prone to classicising, would evoke a Nemesis upon Madame when, she entering on cancerous decline, The Business she had built devolved upon the son she had dominated. Agnes, having turned for redemption to Freud and his following, diagnosed in their father an unconscious drive to destroy the life's work of the mother in fearful dependency to whom he had set himself from childhood to be a model son.

Never having had time for psychologizing, "Yes, dear, you may be right" had been the extent of Edith's response to reasonings she noticed left Agnes' contempt for her father undiminished. Though it was likely enough—she, now hurtling underground inside the swaying red and green Tube carriage, admitted to herself—that even while he maintained this deferential role towards his mother, her dominance over his father, as over himself, should have formed his rigid outlook on marriage and the female sex. That women should receive only so much education as would fit them to be devoted and devout wives and mothers he had only found confirmed in herself, whose education—encouraged and paid for by her poor father at a City Guild school—had, he concluded, equipped her with just the sort of godless learning that rendered wives opinionated and rebellious to that head to whom St Paul had decreed they should submit. Nor had her sojourn in the foreign convent and subsequent postings across Europe undone the harm, but rather contributed a delusory breadth to an already reckless independence.

Edith sighed again, recalling a line of argument she had been unable to refute without confirming. She had had no option, she told herself again, but to accept the unhappy consequences for her four surviving daughters, even while she sorrowed over *their* truncated schooling, for which her means had allowed her to make small compensation. The Sacred Heart nuns had pleaded that Agnes—a paragon regularly first in her class—and then Magdalen, less industrious but of a penetrating intelligence—should stay on to sit the School Leaving Certificate; they offered to keep them on minimal fees. One year beyond the legal school leaving-age was allowed before, turned fifteen, each was withdrawn and set to work in The Business.

Later a shop had been tried in Bayswater under the name of "Miss Rigg," for the elder pair to manage while living in the small flat above; this experiment lasted for only the time it took Agnes to arm herself with a Pitman's shorthand-typing certificate and find a position as secretary to a Benevolent Society for the handicapped. With a colleague (Marg., a "common" name, Edith considered, suiting a rather "common" girl), she had set up in a flat in Hammersmith and over the doorbell affixed a stamped metal strip which read: "Miss M. Baxter and Miss A. Lumley," thus ridding herself of the hated name of Agnes Rigg and defying, as she saw it, father, grandmother and all their works: from which, once she had put sufficient money by, a course of Psychoanalysis should finally deliver her.

This she was currently undergoing, as Edith understood—for Agnes had detached herself from her as well; also that she had been introduced by "Marg" to courses from the Workers' Educational

Association; the Socialist organisation represented another *défi* of her father, unquestioningly Conservative out of Catholic loyalty—so in English history contested—to sovereign, country and the memory of the Duke of Wellington, hero of a fight more significant even than Waterloo: that for Catholic Emancipation! She herself, despite some small exploits in the Women's Suffrage Movement, had in this one respect conformed to her husband's family, departing from her father's allegiance to Grand Old Man, William Gladstone.

Magdalen continued in what was salvaged of The Business, though it soon bored "Miss May," as she had become known since the "Miss Rigg" venture. Rather than the secretarial course customary for young women of limited means, she had elected to take drawing classes and soon acquired a circle of smart friends to withdraw her too from the household of mother and younger sisters. Of these, Winifreda had begun to show the signs of an erratic mind of her own, while Veronica continued outwardly conformable: still the only of their children to straddle the fault-line between the parents. With the decline of The Business, the younger girls were soon drifting through a series of underpaid secretarial positions. It was easy to see how marriage beckoned as the way out: had it not so beckoned for herself?

Lancaster Gate, Notting Hill: names bespeaking the solidity of the imperial capital. Beyond Holland Park Edith rose to alight and walk, still pensive, through quiet streets.

For a few precious years she and her "tall little pair" had lived happily together, making up somewhat, she thought, for their having been sent, too young, to boarding school. Periodically restlessness would set in; one such time had seen Winifreda's ill-starred venture to Venice as Companion to the titled lady... It had been then that she and Veronica took the walking holiday in the Welsh Border country...

Like all their excursions, it had been in part with an eye to meeting unattached men; and sure enough there were two young men in their group. Jess Lewis, who had newly given the world some aesthetic musings on London life, she had been more immediately drawn to; not only was he a published author but of fairer complexion and more British-sounding name than his friend Aaron Keller. Only she soon discovered he was married and to an Irish girl who had taken their baby on a visit to the Emerald Isle: a propitiatory one, as Edith guessed; the baby would have prompted the marriage, as happened with Irish girls far from home and not always falling in with situations in families such as hers (she reflected with charitable smugness, remembering Biddy and successive Irish nursemaids).

The happy coincidence of authorial interest had left Jess's friend, whom he called Ron, and her daughter free to discover their own coincidences.

Veronica had begun it as they walked a few paces behind on paths through the undulating green countryside.

"How odd that we both have the same name! I'm called Ron, too."

"Really? Didn't I hear your mother call you Veronica?"

"Mother always uses our full names, but at school I got called Ron or Ronnie—by my friends, that is. Veronicas always were."

"I wouldn't have thought there were many."

"In convent schools there are. Though Veronica's not even a proper saint, only it's said that she wiped Jesus' face on the Way of the Cross; there's the Holy Face on a cloth somewhere."

"You don't say!"

"*You* probably don't believe that!"

"Probably not. But you haven't explained…"

"No, well my parents wanted to name me Teresa, after the Little Flower, because, you see, they went to Lisieux—that's in Normandy —and, I mean, after that… Well, after that I was born, but in the meantime my cousin was born and named Teresa—I think they'd been to Lisieux too. That's my Aunt Liza and Uncle Raoul, though we don't see them any more… You see…"

She had stopped, conscious of having said too much and "Not quite," he said, gravely enough that, encouraged, she continued,

"You see, the Little Flower's full name is Saint Teresa of the Child Jesus and of the Holy Face."

"Really? I didn't know saints had such long names."

"She was a nun, you see. She entered Carmel at age fifteen."

"Carmel? That's a mountain in the Bible, isn't it? But I see! They called you Veronica because of the—the Holy Face."

"Yes. Veronica Rose."

"It's a beautiful name—poetic. Is Rose a saint's name?"

"Yes, Rose of Lima. She scarred her face—tore it with her nails so no one would want to marry her."

"That surely isn't a holy thing to do—or so I'd hope."

"I know. Saints are different."

Pause again, then

"I take it you're Catholic. I'm Jewish. Your Jesus was a Jew, you know."

"Yes. But Jews didn't accept Him. Though some did," she added, not to seem impolite.

"And we've been made to suffer for that. We're still suffering for it."

"I know. Teresa—my cousin—is expecting a baby—with a—a Jewish man who's left her and gone back to Germany, because his father's furious, and he's very rich… They're hoping he won't let her down."

"Gosh!" (Edith had winced but excused the expression: the young man, who had seemed well enough spoken, perhaps did not realize it was near-blasphemous.)

"Gosh! I hope he gets back, because, you know, there are rumours… But there do seem to be rather a lot of Jews and Catholics having babies together! Jess there—his wife is Irish and I suppose Catholic. They have a baby, otherwise Eileen would be with him."

Edith heard her daughter laugh nervously at the turn the conversation had taken and was framing a pretext to intervene when Veronica, properly avoiding the baby-theme, resumed:

"Yes, the Irish are all Catholics—all the Irish in England, anyway, which is most of the Catholics. We're English—and a little bit French."

"Really? How interesting—Ron! Or should I say Veronica?"

"Don't; it's such a mouthful! But perhaps you'd better say Ronnie, or it'll be too confusing. My sisters call me Vee."

"Then, Ronnie—or I know: how about Vee-Ron? You see, I'm Aa-Ron. We're called after dead relatives, not saints. I was named after my mother's Uncle Aaron in Lithuania, but I don't like the name—too obviously Jewish."

"Yes. Like Veronica's too obviously Catholic. We seem to feel the same about our names—and, you know, Catholics and—Jewish people (Edith again approved her daughter's delicacy; somehow "Jews" didn't sound proper from non-Jews) are a bit alike. In England Catholics don't belong either, you know. Perhaps that's why…"

She had broken off this artless sentence and Aaron Keller had merely said "Really?"—to Edith's relief, who had been responding to Jess with polite assents to his literary theorisings, but at this point had her attention engaged by questionings she could not ignore—and suspected were intended to free Aaron to pursue the promising acquaintanceship on which Jess as well as she had been listening in. Though both would observe that the name-play persisted for the rest of the holiday, she had not been privy to the delight of Jess's friend, nor perceived how that happy inspiration had turned Aa-Ron in Vee-Ron's conceit into a master of wordplay.

A Jew had, of course, scarcely been her idea of eligibility, but then neither had her own experience inclined her to the desirability, so emphasised by the Church, of a Catholic marriage for her daughters. Magda's recent match, eligible in worldly terms, had been a decided jolt: not because he was Protestant but because he was divorced—and in circumstances strikingly similar to those of her own father; only divorce was no longer regarded as barrier to a second union as it had been in her parents' time—or only by Catholics. Jews, she believed, made dependable husbands; this rather refreshing young man was unwed and her poor girls had few opportunities, despite her constant prayers—indeed, had felt their disadvantages unfairly multiplied, for as if their Catholicism were not handicap enough among the wider reaches of middle-class England, their family's situation had further restricted the tight circle of their co-religionists.

Then there was their exceptional tallness in a society in thrall to the cinema's portrayal of petite and clinging females. She herself, born to a generation that still admired the statuesque in women, was proud of her pair and had contrived occasionally to take them to a theatre or restaurant (never both) where they might witness a little Society and hope to attract notice, fashionably dressed out of the resources of The Business in accordance with the precepts of her youth: blue silks for dark-haired Veronica, pink for blonde Freda; herself less tall would sweep majestically in ahead of them in a crèpe-de-chine to match the still-brown hair under the velour hat, its half-veil softening wrinkles the hair belied. Like a mother duck introducing her brood to the farmyard: so she saw it but kept this fancy to herself, recalling as it did that favourite of nursery days, the Ugly Duckling, with whom her "little" girls, in whatever feathers, too readily identified...

For now, she told herself, she hoped to have steered her small clutch into haven. Not but what—she reflected as she took the Yale key from her purse and turned it in the lock—calm waters were liable at any moment to be upheaved. This latest upheaval, of Veronica's pregnancy and sudden marriage, was tiding over, becoming assimilated to the life of mother and the sister remaining under this blessed roof; the adjective was suggested by her dipping two fingers in the small porcelain stoup on the right-hand wall as she passed into the hallway: stoup that ever brought to mind René reaching for it to lustrate one or more of the band of rebellious females a crossed destiny had allotted him.

Crossing herself with the blessed water and opening the door into her sitting-room, where weak sunshine sat placidly on the blue carpet, Edith reached for the packet of Weights and the matchbox that lay on a table just inside. Then it was into the kitchen to light the gas under the kettle for tea...

PART I

"To the Third and Fourth Generation"

I

A SATURDAY afternoon in late June, and so much had happened in the preceding twelvemonth, it was like being newly-weds again—or in their case un-weds, reflected Ron, but did not venture to voice the notion. They were sitting in deliciously prolonged ease—Sabbath ease—this he ventured to joke—on the still-new sofa, its shape suggestive of giant matchboxes under the discreet surface patterning in beige and green. Two similarly constructed armchairs and a "dining suite"—glossy square table, two chairs drawn stiffly up to it, the two disposed about the room displaying their seats' also greenish upholstery. That filled most of the narrow room, but a metal-framed bay-window allowed space for the odd piece out: the solid, inlaid chest that was one of the past triumphs of Grandma Rigg's auction forays, now transferred from Veronica's old home by way of wedding-gift.

Sitting not quite cheek-to-cheek, and as near hand-in-hand as permitted by the cigarette they were puffing turn by turn, husband and wife could survey, beyond the net curtains of their ground-floor flat, the Close, still lit by an afternoon brilliance only a little blurred by city airs and the haze spreading above and before them from the curlicues of their combined exhalations.

"Well, Vron, my girl, isn't this quite like old times!" suddenly declared Ron from a mouth still smoke-wreathed, and stubbing the half-fag firmly into the chromed ashtray between them on the sofa, he turned to seize both her wrists and draw her to face him.

"Careful, Ron!" she admonished and struggled, but he held on laughing. The slowly westering sun slid warm patches of light across the carpet of small coloured squares that brightened this otherwise drabbish room; sitting there, Ron could watch its progress from square to square across what was to him symbol and reminder that his mother had "come round"—enough, at least, to be persuaded into providing this wedding-gift. Persuaded by his sister Jane, backed by Ben, now her husband, who having inherited the thriving rag-business founded by his father, had been happy to pay out a handsome share.

And though he felt constrained to concur in Veronica's demurrals at the carpet's vivid hues, secretly Ron approved the choice. It was Vron had insisted on the "tasteful" upholstery of what he referred to

27

as their "lounge-suite" (And though she protested that was vulgar, she failed to meet his challenge to find another collective noun for it); still, he knew she also was relieved at what it signified, while for him it was glad evidence not only that his childhood bond with his younger sister held, but that it was reinforced by the alliance with their eligible neighbour—the newly wed pair refusing to share in his mother and brother's shock—rippling out in the gossip of neighbours and a wider Jewish community—at his "marrying out." Evidence too that Jane—hitherto always quietly compliant with their mother—had been emancipating herself ever since betrothed to Ben ("Engaged," they and everybody these days said, but Ron's ventures into English verse had thrown up "betrothed," and so it was the more poetic word that came to mind as he contemplated the carpet and what it stood for). Massive as his name suggested, and outspoken with it, Ben Grossman had, like himself, small time for atavistic prohibitions aimed at preserving the Chosen People from adulteration by the *goyim*—and which in the *stetl* from which their forebears issued had consolidated Jews' liability to persecution. What mattered was to engage with the British society into which their generation had the happy chance to have been cast, unite with its underdogs, gentile or Jew, destined to be the Chosen of the March of History.

Socialism was the creed of most of their tight community, and Ben was by now a candidate for the East London Borough Council to service on which his bride's late father had risen. Avram Keller, Ron was conscious, had blazed for his sons a trail the father, himself an immigrant, could hardly hope to follow further, but he had made it plain he anticipated his descendents' honourable participation in the new and free society to which his mother, on her widowhood, had so resolutely brought him away and out of the reach of an Austrian army which maintained among its traditions the making of life especially hard for its Jewish conscripts. Arrived in London aged fifteen, quiet, industrious Avram—Abe, as he was soon known—had served apprenticeship as a tailor before marrying Esther, of a generation that had grown up speaking in the accents and embedded in the world of the East End. With her dowry added to his meagre savings, Abe had set up his own small business and become a solid family man when the World War pitted Poland's overlords against his new protectors. His elder son had acquired a scholarship to the local Grammar School, a respected charitable foundation, and so it was to its Headmaster that Abe had turned to inquire how he might contribute to the victory of the nation whose citizenship he had proudly acquired over that which had the more recently oppressed his tribe.

"I understand you are a tailor, Mr Keller?" had been the response of that august person: "You could perhaps make uniforms for the troops?"

And so he had, setting aside other ambitions for the duration. The war over, he had turned his energies to the fashioning of a fairer world, or at least of the immediate neighbourhood, being elected Councillor and in time Alderman, after which term he had returned to work in the obscurity of his tailor's shop much as his father had done back in Kazimierz. Ron found few anecdotes of him to relay to Veronica, rather more of his mother: most notably how she had slipped a certain ring into her pocket when Abe came courting, and how she would laugh and toss her reddish mane at one of his rare teases: that sandy hair betrayed the penetration of Lithuanian Jewry by Vikings! Though she would continue to protest it was the Scandinavians had converted, either way they all knew this remote *goy* pedigree gratified her. "Litvaks" of the second generation viewed themselves as superior to the new wave of Jews from Poland, and Esther's family had arranged a match with one of their own; but whether it was Abe's tease did it, or his quiet persistence combined with a sober idealism, Ron's most salient memory of him summed up both. Provoked at the family meal by his wife's harping on—on what, they had forgotten, but Esther inherited her fair share of the contumacy of Hebrew women since the Matriarchs—Abe had laid hands on his plate as though about to hurl it; but even as they all caught their alarmed breath, he changed course, inverting plate and contents on his own head in a gesture more eloquent than words.

The family had made shift to survive the Depression. Ron left the Grammar School where he had been accepted in the wake of Izzy and the pair of them sold socks in Petticoat Lane to those who could still afford the most basic of clothing. Abe had seen his firstborn's debut in a law practice before, some three years since, himself departing this life prematurely in his sleep, as had his father before him. Ron had not shown the competitiveness of the industrious Isidore; this, with some plausibility, he attributed to artistic sensibility. Now, despite his mother's ritual plaints as to the infidelity of Jacob—interspersed with declarations that her only solace lay in her husband's being no longer living to witness their disgrace—he privately felt satisfied his father would not have been inconsolable at his following, as it were by a short cut, where himself had led the way: out of the ghetto and into the wider English society.

So it was that on that Saturday afternoon of June, this couple's younger son, released from the morning's stint of largely male gossip with feet up in the Council's office, sat basking again in contemplation of the momentous step he had with such ease accomplished in the generational shift from underdog to respectability. Resting a head of curly black hair, already thinning at temples and crown, on the shoulder of his wedded (nay twice-wedded!) wife—pose the more readily adopted in that she was half a head taller than him—he believed himself romantically in love; and what is romantic love without the belief in it? He believed it was he, rather than his brother or new brother-in-law, who had, as he put it poetically to himself, "o'erleapt the barrier of their tribe."

Part of Ron Keller knew that his Vron (as by now he called her) had picked up with him, a Jew with little to offer but devotion and dreams, because of the constricting effects of her own family's troubled background. But if there was calculation on both their parts, both too were seduced by that "romance," and the daring overstepping of boundaries her people drew tight, his deemed absolute. He saw himself as "o'erleaping" East London to embrace that refinement hitherto encountered chiefly in heroines of literature, but now in her manners, her regular, even aristocratic features, above all her speech: Ron, gifted with an acute ear, had tuned in to variants in the enunciation of the English language that was his prized maternal inheritance, and opted for the diction of his schoolmasters rather than the Yiddishly tinged whine of the Cockney prevailing in their tight circle. With that ear went too a melting baritone voice in which he would break into snatches remembered from forays to the "gods" at Covent Garden, as well as English airs learned at school, with preference for the melancholy: "Tom Bowling" and "Down Among the Dead Men."

Izzy, via an external degree from London University earned while assisting their father with the tailoring, might have fetched up a solicitor, but Ron had learned—from his friend Jess even before Veronica—to regard him as a Philistine: immune to music and poetry, irritated by his brother's claiming of them as a superior preserve: claiming and also declaiming: the better-known works of the English Romantics could be heard out loud in the Kellers' narrow house on Robert Street, until the parents, alerted to the contrast in the brothers' reports, had approached the Headmaster with the complaint that Aaron wasted time writing poetry. The resulting interview provided the only one of Ron's rare anecdotes from which any of his teachers emerged with credit—and indeed they appeared to have allowed his passage among them to be fearful and devoid of much intellectual gain. Instead of admonition, the Head had asked to see poems of his writing and, Aaron evading further questioning, had dismissed him with "Make sure, boy, you keep it up!"

The narration of this triumph of finer feeling over Philistinism could only evoke in Veronica, coming of people who took for granted the cultivation of the arts, sympathy for the poor boy who had had to defend his discovery of them, and who confided in her his unappreciated feeling for beauty in all its forms—most lately in her under-appreciated self. With all this in his favour, Ron had had but to write some stanzas to her and she had fallen a conquest—the more easy since, not long before they met, he had had some slight recognition: two short stories had appeared in collections of new authors, allowing him to dream of being welcomed into the left-wing circles surrounding such names as Shaw and Spender.

Veronica, for her part, had conceived the notion that her more rooted and schooled love of literature would second and refine his for this alluring prospect. Neither was equipped or much disposed to assess the outlook in the world of letters for a talent so little tutored and supported only by a passionate sense that poetry pointed to a Beauty freed from the pettiness of daily life—and more specifically from the religious framework with which his mother surrounded it and to which his brother subscribed. If Ron was by instinct a Platonist, he would never know it, for a lingering self-doubt combined with indolence to dissuade him from "heavy" reading—or, indeed, extensive writing; already he had come to excuse it as lack of time left by that clerical post which the fresh memory of Mr Alderman Keller had secured for him from Hackney Council, and which in his dreams would give way to entry into recognition of his literary talents. Poetry would remain for him as he met her in her Romantic exponents and their imitators, whose cadences and conceits he absorbed and reproduced and which simply *were*, for him, Poetry—as those chosen spirits who gave utterance to them simply *were* Poets. Beyond these, he made room for one or two of the best-known passages of Shakespeare. Of his own century he revered Housman and some of the War Poets, paid homage to Yeats and Eliot and ignored Pound, being made uneasy by rumour of his anti-Semitism.

He had let go her wrists and placed an arm round her shoulder, still drawing her to face him as with emphasis he repeated,

"I *said*, Vron, my girl, isn't this quite like old times!"

Ron's second apostrophe was met with the outrush of a sigh that caused his mobile mouth and the dark eyes behind the tortoiseshell-rimmed spectacles to describe a rightward grin and him to add:

"Glad of a little respite from being Mother, eh?"

"I certainly am, and I think I deserve it, with all the nappies and the feeds—and the nights. Yes, it is blissful just to sit and enjoy our home for once!"

"And me, I hope!"

"Yes, of course, dear Ron!"

"And we'd better make the most of it, as it's only until they come back. Come on, give Hubby a kiss!"

She backed slightly to bring her face level with his and let him plant on her mouth his loose-lipped kiss, which always left her, annoyingly, wanting to wipe it off. Restraining the urge, she kissed him primly, which always amused him. He laid a hand on the knee protruding from her fashionably brief tunic.

"Careful, Ron; I can see them coming round again."

"They" were their infant daughter and Vron's elder sister Agnes who had volunteered to wheel her round and round the tree-shaded Close which rendered the Finsbury flat so particularly attractive and quiet for London. Ag had said she needed exercise and could read as she pushed.

"As they will be doing for the next half hour!," he mocked. "Forget about them; we can't be seen through the curtains, can we? Anyway, we're married—couldn't be more so, between the State and your Church! How does it go? 'For better, for worse, for richer, for poorer...' I like that."

They fell silent, both unwilling to complete the quotation, until its unspoken end prompted her to ask,

"Though couldn't you give me a 'bill of divorce,' like it says in the Bible? I mean, isn't it in the Old Testament? It's in the New, because we did it at school."

"That's true. Jews can give their wives a bill of divorce; it's called a 'get.' But I think you'd have to have a Jewish marriage to 'get' one—if that doesn't sound too Irish!"

The supposedly paradoxical Irish being a safe butt, they laughed, but Veronica had a serious purpose or two.

"Perhaps *not* having one would make it all the easier?"

"What's the point of speculating? You know I'm not going to do it and all that's nothing to me. I didn't ask to be Jewish!"

"And I didn't ask to be Catholic—and have no divorce!"

"Well, you can stay with that bit of your Church's teaching, and I'll join it that far. Of course (His tone became teasing again), good

32

ground for a Jewish divorce might be a wife's resisting her hubby's—advances!"

The free hand moved up provocatively under her thigh.

"Not, surely, if it's in front of her sister and the baby!" She removed the hand and held it, turning to him to add,

"While we're on the subject, I'm a bit concerned, now I've started her on the bottle…"

"I've told you, you can leave all that to me."

"But, Ron, you know the Church…"

"I don't belong to the Church—luckily for you, or rather for us both—and I don't accept it can interfere to make us have babies like your mother did."

"But, Ron! If she hadn't, I almost certainly would not be here!"

"True, and the world would be the poorer, or certainly my world would! (He kissed her again and she squirmed uncomfortably.) But so what? Here you are and we're going to enjoy our lives, which is difficult enough with one baby—even though you know I'm devoted to the little blighter!"

"I do know, you old softie! Except when she keeps you awake at night."

"We seem to have stopped that. Old Art at work, he knew a thing or two more than the books, when he said to just let her cry one night and she'd learn you don't give in."

"Oh but that night was awful!"

Veronica shuddered. She had hidden her head under the blankets, held down by Ron's arm to stop her obeying the instinct to rush to those wails, less angry now than desperate-sounding, from the slip of a bedroom to which their daughter's cot had been removed.

"But it worked, and now we get some peace and quiet; we're entitled to that at night, surely!"

"I still wonder what the neighbours must have thought."

"They must think it's nice and quiet now. She's hardly cried since, not at night."

"That may be because I'm giving her the bottle more. She could have just been hungry…"

"Well, she's satisfied now and so are we, and so are the neighbours, if they matter that much; they must know that babies cry! But there you go, worrying about babies and more babies—which God forbid, at least for now!—when this is our only bit of time to ourselves. Tomorrow you'll be off to your Church—Lucky for you I don't belong and can mind Elaine! Then dinner at your Mother's and our weekend's gone…"

"You know, Ron, seriously, going to Mass isn't going to be easy for me if we're going to—practise birth-control."

"Well, ask Father O'Shea about it. Isn't that what Confession is for? And not a bad thing, if it teaches young women to submit to their hubbies, as you say they used to tell your mother. Only in this case the hubby is a bad Jew, eh?"

"Oh no, Ron; I'm sure they don't think like that!"

"I'm sure they do in Poland, where my father came from. Not that there was much chance there of Jews marrying Catholics. Business was all that ever brought them together. Money always talks! Here it's different, but I reckon only because the Church doesn't have the power."

"I know, Ron; terrible things have been done in the name... Deedie says it's because power always corrupts and Lord Acton said that, who's a Catholic and a historian, though Pawa says he's a Modernist."

"Well, I'm a simple man; I just know right and wrong when I see them."

Veronica wondered if it was as simple as that, but having broached the difficult topic needed to press on with it.

"As a matter of fact I did talk about it—birth-control, I mean, and not to Father O'Shea, because he knows us and he's Irish, but to Father Johnson, who Deedie knows and he said it wasn't a mortal sin if I didn't consent."

"Remarkably tolerant of him, leaving all the sinning to me! Still, as I suppose I'm damned already, one may as well be hung for a sheep as a lamb, so that's fine by me; I'll do the sinning and you'll be spared the pregnancies!"

"Oh, Ron, don't! Of course you're not damned! St Paul says 'The unbelieving husband is sanctified by the believing wife.' It's because we're 'one flesh,' you know; we learned that at school."

"Ah, that's more like it; so sex is a good thing, is it—according to the Church—and did you know that if a man and woman have sex, our religion—Jews, I mean, regard them as married, like us even before...?"

"I'm not sure 'one flesh' means—you know, *bodily* relations—not exactly," Veronica broke in before he could mention their—anyway her—original sin; then feeling herself beginning to blush, she added hastily, "Anyway, Father Johnson isn't like that at all. He's an English priest, a convert and educated—a moral theologian. That's why I went to him. I knew what Father O'Shea would say."

"And can they both be right?"

"I suppose not—though in a way I think they can. No, I don't quite understand how, but I *feel* they can. We're not meant to understand everything, just have faith in God—that is, in the Church…"

"Which tells you different things?"

"That's not the Church, that's—just different priests, who are human and can get things wrong."

"You're telling me they can! Father O'Shea got my name wrong all through our wedding, calling me Aaron Killer, or that's what it sounded like: 'Christ-killer' was I suppose what he had in mind!"

"Oh no, Ron! But it *was* bad of him."

"You could tell he didn't like me, anyway."

"I think he might have taken Keller to be your second name—like I have Rose."

"Then he should have found out properly—and at least he could have pronounced it right. He didn't call you Veronica Clumsy-Pig, did he?"

Ron's reference to this corruption of their surname by jeerers at her and Freda's convent school earned him a wan smile from his wife, which was as far in mirth as she would be found. He went on,

"I wonder if it didn't—What do they call it?—invalidate the marriage!"

"Oh, Ron…"

"Well, don't let that worry you because, after all, it was to please your parents and so far as I'm concerned we were married already. That's something else I fancy they've got wrong, because didn't he explain that it's not the priest who does the marrying but we do it?"

"Yes. We learned that in Catechism. The consent of the parties makes the marriage."

"So there you are; we already consented in the Registry Office, at least I know I did, and I thought you did too."

"Of course, Ron; you know I did. But I was glad it was put right with the Church."

"Even though they get a few things wrong—and what they're surely most likely to get wrong is something your priests have no experience of, and that's marriage. I must say your reasoning doesn't seem as logical as mine. *Could* that be because you're a woman?!"

The hand darted again. Veronica shifted a little and smoothed down her skirt before observing sententiously,

"Logic isn't everything; that's a mistake men make. Pascal says 'The heart has its reasons which the head wots not of.'"

"What's not of what?"

"Wots: W-O-T-S. It's Old English for 'knows.' We learned that at school. Pascal was a Catholic philosopher. Pawa likes him because he was French—though he doesn't like all French philosophers; he'd think some of them much more likely to be damned than you, because they *were* baptized, you see, and they started Atheism."

"Ah yes, Voltaire. We have *Candide*, on the bookshelf there; I bought it at a W.E.A. sale. You should read it; it's quite short."

"I don't know that I'd like it. I had a peek at your Renan's *Life of Jesus*, really because Pawa said it was blasphemous—and it is—shocking. But you're not an Atheist, Ron!"

"I've told you, I'm an Agnostic: someone who doesn't know, who thinks we can't know if there's a God or not."

"In that case we probably all should be Agnostics, because we don't *know*—except perhaps some of the saints."

Ron laughed. "Well, if you believe those saints—I suppose that's what you call faith."

"Yes, I suppose so."

"Anyway, to come back to babies and the making of them—which, if I may say so, is a most delightful invention of God if that's who's responsible—and I reckon we Jews have got that much right at least, because for us marriage and babies is tops: none of this celibate stuff! Only we don't go for making them regardless, or most of us don't; there *are* some Orthodox who are a bit like Catholics for that, but most of us prefer to follow common sense. However, to come to the point—and this has spoiled our afternoon for long enough—I take it you told Father Johnson you didn't consent to birth-control?"

"I told him I didn't want it, that I'd prefer—abstinence."

"Which I take it you told him I wouldn't?"

"Yes, of course. I don't think he was surprised. Even good Catholics—men, I mean, like my father—don't seem able to practise it."

"Or don't want to, which no one need be surprised at. Because if there's one flaw in God's delightful invention of sex, it's that horrid men want it much more than nice women!"

"Not the babies they don't!"

"True enough. We're back to the babies, which we both admit can be inconvenient. So what does Father Johnson propose we do about it?"

"He didn't. He just said if I didn't want birth-control—if I'd prefer abstinence—I just had to tell you, but not force it on you—abstinence I mean—as that could be sinful."

"Ah, good man!"

"Yes, and I was rather surprised because I'd heard a wife should refuse a husband who offers—sex—with birth-control. That's what I was afraid Father O'Shea would say if I asked him. But perhaps that's Catholic husbands."

"There seem to be many advantages in marrying non-Catholics!"

"I think that's rather what Mother thinks—and quite a lot of Catholics."

"I can well believe it, because something seems to have gone pretty wrong here. Still, it doesn't have to bother us, because you've told me, haven't you? Like he said."

"I suppose I have."

"Well, I consider myself told. And I've told you. So now you won't be committing *your* sin but leaving it to me who don't know any better—and I don't, that's certain. Though after all, a bit of sinning spices things, doesn't it? Or so you've seemed to find in the past! So is that okay?"

"Don't say 'okay,' Ron; it's American. I suppose it is—all right. Because there's some sin in almost everything we do, anyway. The Church…"

"Come off it, Vron! I've heard enough about the Church's dismaller teachings for now! After all this there's no chance of sinning this afternoon, dash it, and I suppose it'll soon be time for Elaine's bottle."

"Yes, and I said I'd have tea for when they came in. But Ron, we've not wasted the afternoon, really, because I'm glad I've told you. And we've time to finish the cig."

"Pass me my lighter, then."

She reached over to the chair on the back of which he had carefully hung the blazer he had bought for his Church wedding, because she liked a blazer and the suit his father had made him when he turned twenty-one was needing letting out. She gave him the square metal lighter; he opened the top and flicked at the cog until a small flame sprang, placed the half cigarette between his lips, lit the end and sucked until it glowed. Then he snapped the lid down, handed her the lighter and leaned back while she replaced it in the inside breast pocket; she had learned to be careful with his possessions.

"The rest is yours," he said, passing her the cigarette. Moving close up to her again he laid his head on her neck and slid his freed hand round her waist. Both were conscious that things did not feel the same and, except for her puffing, were silent, she thinking on her private resolve that her marriage should be a success—meaning all that her parents' marriage had not been—he made uneasy by a feeling he had lately that she kept herself at a certain distance from him emotionally and physically. But perhaps that was to be expected still so close to the birth.

So they sat, preoccupied while ostensibly watching out of the window for Agnes to come round the Close again, wheeling the high pram she had helped them buy out of her salary; after all, she said, what was left over from rent and food would only go on books and she could get those from the public library. For clothes, as everyone by now understood, she professed contempt, reiterating that having quit the fashion shop known as "Miss Rigg"—and cast off that very name to be known as plain Agnes Lumley—she need only dress respectably and could stop wasting time and money on all that fuss. So she had two tweed suits and three long-sleeved blouses, lisle stockings, sensible shoes, and for another half-century would part her hair in front and turn it up over a ribbon in one horseshoe-shaped "sausage," as she called it. As a concession to the summer's day, she had folded the suit-jacket over the pram handle.

"I think Elaine's awake," remarked Ron, watching them take another turn.

"Then we must get a move on."

Veronica stubbed out the cigarette and led the way into the small kitchen, where she took the loaf from an enamel bin marked "Bread," the butter from the terracotta cooler. As she spread and cut, Ron filled the kettle and lit the gas under it.

"There's boiled water in the measuring-jug in the larder," she said, "so if you'd be a dear and get the feed ready, we can stand it in a saucepan to warm for when they come in."

She paused, saw-knife suspended and, as if coming to a resolve, said, "Ron!"

"Yes, dear girl?"

"I just wondered, do you blame my father for all those children? I mean, as a man do you?"

"What, that he couldn't—abstain? No, of course I don't."

"I think Mother thinks it's rather that he wouldn't—that he was insisting it was her duty to have them. Because as a Catholic he should have been able."

"I don't see why Catholics should be any better than the rest of us poor males. Anyway, it's not so long since many people had as many children as that—in the days before Birth-control. Wasn't your mother's mother...?"

"Yes, the eldest of fourteen. And they were Protestants. *And* her father was a doctor!"

"Perhaps that's how they all survived—or did they?"

"I think all but one. They mostly emigrated to Canada."

"Actually, I like your father; he may be odd, but he's interesting, and he even seems to quite like me."

"Oh he does—he calls you 'Sonny.'"

"Yes, it's flattering, though I know I can never replace—what he, what all of you have lost."

This was no more than the truth and they were silent again until the slices were all arranged around the flowered pot, into which Veronica had spooned a discreet quantity of jam before placing it there in the centre of the big bread-and-butter plate. Meantime Ron measured out the Ostermilk into the glass jug and set it in a pan of water over a low gas. She said,

"Thank goodness Elaine can take a bottle! Freda couldn't stomach it and nearly died when Mumsie couldn't—feed her herself. Then the doctor said to give her the juices from a piece of raw steak, and that saved her. I think that's how she and Mother became so close, from nearly losing her. Ron!"

"Yes, love?"

"I hope we'll have at least one more. A boy would please your folk, wouldn't it? And also Pawa—even though…"

"Always provided we don't get another girl! And not quite yet awhile. Elaine came a bit early and now we're entitled to some life to ourselves."

"If we can get it! And I'd need some help in the house—if we had a house."

"All that takes money. Perhaps if I could publish a book of stories…"

"Yes, you might get to write for the newspapers."

They had been over this ground before.

By four-thirty, a leaf of the square table had been extended and the whole covered with the *broderie anglaise* cloth that had been Freda's wedding-gift. Three matching napkins had been placed beside three small china plates, florally patterned like the big bread-and-butter one in the middle, and the cups and saucers set out, each with its teaspoon, on the oblong tray, with the round sugar-bowl and milk-jug: the tea-set had been Agnes' gift and the spoons were from the canteen of plate presented by Ron's office. The culmination of this elegance was the Limoges cake-stand from Magda, now crowned by the sugar-dusted round of a Victoria sponge.

No sooner was all in readiness than there came the expected short ring at the door. Veronica opened to her sister, who entered the small vestibule with a finger to her lips, leaving the door ajar before hissing,

"She's awake! You might like to have her bottle ready before she realizes she's hungry!"

"It's not due till five," murmured back Veronica. "We can have some tea first. The kettle's on."

"No, thanks. Tempting though it is, I like my tea in peace. Besides"—Agnes had stepped inside the room and surveyed the tea-table—"It would be a shame to interrupt tea when you've arranged everything so nicely. Is the bottle not ready?"

"It can be in five minutes. It's still too early."

"You know, I'm beginning to be sorry I gave you that book by that doctor. I just thought it was the up-to-date thing, but… After all, savages carry their babies about with them and put them to the breast whenever they cry."

"But Ag, surely…! We're *not* savages, and children have to learn…"

"They can learn later. And my reward for over an hour of wheeling is a peaceful tea! Listen, she's beginning to fuss. Not surprising if she *is* hungry after that long airing!"

"Ron, dear, could you warm that bottle!" Veronica called in her best wifely tones, and added to her sister, "We can give you a 'cuppa' first if you're dying for one."

"No, thanks. For now I'll have a cig. Will you join me?" She extracted a packet from her leather shoulder-bag; she scorned handbags.

"Not now, thanks; it's not long since we—I—had one, and we're trying to cut down. Was Elaine good?"

"Good as gold. She likes looking up at the trees and after a bit of that she fell asleep for about half an hour and then woke up and did some more looking. Very good for the eyes."

"Yes. I was afraid she had a squint, but Doctor Martin said it was too early to tell, and her eyes do seem straight now, and turning darker, I think, to match her hair. Only she seems to be losing that. I hope she doesn't go bald."

"Babies do; you did, for one. But they don't stay bald. Just don't fuss over her is my advice. We were all too fussed over, at least I know I was; it's most insidious with the first. I'm sure we grow best left to ourselves as much as possible."

From beyond the vestibule and open front door, intermittent squawks could be heard and the creaking of the pram's springs.

"Ag, you should be the mother! With your experience, I'm sure you'd do it far better!"

For Veronica this was a rare disclosure of her misgivings, but Agnes had been closer to her in her growing years than their over-burdened mother and could be more easily confided in than anyone, Ron not excepted.

"Nonsense, you're doing perfectly well! Just don't fuss the child. Somehow I don't think motherhood's in my life-line. I'll just be a maiden-aunt—or if not maiden…"

She broke off, grimacing deliberately. Her sister knew enough to suspect that Ag might not be "maiden" since she had begun to frequent free-thinking circles of literary people and Socialists, who, she reflected as she tested drops from the bottle on her wrist, would have no objections to that "birth-control" that had made "free love" quite the fashion.

The squawks had turned into a fitful crying, convincing Veronica it was near enough to feed-time. She returned with the bottle, to meet Agnes who, having soon extinguished her cigarette, was carrying the baby in at the front door.

"She's sure to need changing after all that time," she said, and proceeded into the bedroom. Veronica followed with the bottle, calling to Ron,

"We'll feed her in here. Why don't you stay and read the paper! And then be a dear and make the tea."

Ron sensed that the sisters wanted a chat. That was all right with him, enabling him to have another smoke and a look at the *Daily Herald*, which he still took, though Vron wanted him to change to the more respectable *News Chronicle*. Agnes was decidedly his favourite among his sisters-in-law; you could have a sensible conversation about politics or literature with her and she was a good support for Vron with the baby.

In the bedroom, Agnes laid a piece of rubber sheeting on the bed and, while her sister removed the sodden towelling nappy, picked up a dry one up from the pile on the little chest of baby-clothes to wrap the bottle. Another she folded cornerwise, and catching the flailing legs slipped it under the puckered pink buttocks. Veronica applied Vaseline, then removing a large safety pin from her mouth, succeeded in passing it through the wodge of thrice folded corners.

"Damn! I've pricked myself!"

"Better than pricking her! Dip the pins in the Vaseline; it makes it easier."

"What a good idea! I so hate doing this—and I suppose I'll be doing it for a good few months, at least. That'll be the next thing: potty-training!"

Taking up the baby she seated herself on the stool before the mirrored dressing-table and advanced the rubber teat protruding from the towelling. There was sudden quiet, broken only by small sounds between the rubber valve at one end and the mouth at the other of the boat-shaped feeding-bottle. Agnes, looking round the room, observed,

"I see the wardrobe went in all right!"

The wardrobe's imposing lines and elaborate veneer matched the dressing-table and stool, as also the bed's head- and foot-boards and a lesser cupboard with shelves, known as "the Press." They had treated themselves to this massy bedroom suite "on the never-never," not envisaging that its largest item would resist all attempts of the delivery men to take it via the narrow passage into the bedroom of their first home. It had had to be stored while they flat-hunted again, and Ron had not hidden his exasperation: the suite had been an extravagance indulged because his wife had fallen for the triple-mirrored dressing-table. However, it had worked out "providentially" (as she put it), this quite new Council flat being in every way superior, so that by now they could laugh off the *im*providence of finding a flat to fit the furniture. It amused their friends but had occasioned weeks of strain.

"Yes," she replied briefly, and there ensued a silence enhanced by small sucking and bubbling noises before she added,

"But, Ag, I wanted to tell you, while Ron's not here, about last Wednesday, when I took Baby to see Mag after The Business closed. She had offered to do a drawing of Elaine, but now I shan't ask her, because—because I said, 'Don't you think she's pretty?' and Mag just laughed and said, 'I expect she'll grow into a fat Jewess!' Wasn't that horrid of her!"

Agnes pursed her mouth, then herself laughed mirthlessly.

"Charming! And why 'fat,' pray? If she takes after her father, she'll not be fat—even leaving her beanpole mother out of it! But don't you think it's possible Mag might be a teeny bit jealous—miffed at you being a mother before her? I know she told Deedie something about them being happy and all they lacked was a child; she may be beginning to wonder if they'll have one. She's thirty-three and he's a good bit older, and I suspect... He doesn't look a fathering type, does he? So prim and set in his ways..."

"Ag, what *do* you mean?"

"Oh, nothing in particular, only—time will tell! I know *I'm* jealous of you! Ron's by far the nicer husband to have: *so* much more interesting and—alive—than that stuffed shirt Hilary! And it puts our dear father so delightfully on the spot, having to choose between a Jew, who by his and even the Church's reckoning *is* his son-in-law, and a toff who isn't!"

"But I don't think Pawa disapproves of Ron. I suppose he did of me getting pregnant, though he's not said so, or not to me. After all, he has said often enough we're a Church of Sinners..."

"You may be; I'm not: neither a member of his Church nor—particularly—a sinner! I'd advise you to drop all that if you want a chance of a happy life! Did I tell you what our father said about you: that the one daughter who had never grieved him was married to a ...?"

"Yes, you did. Don't tell me again, Ag. I'm sure he was upset—shocked. But he's been really friendly to Ron since." She added timidly, "We have to remember he's had a lot to bear."

"Most of which he's brought on himself. And on Deedie—and on us! Not to speak of Leo, who do you suppose would have done what he did if he'd had a happy home and not been fought over as a child? Or had the dear Church telling him—through Pawa, no doubt—that he couldn't marry a divorcee—and that, I reckon, was a bid to throw off the Church's dogmatism!"

"But Ag, that failed. She threw him over!"

"And can't one understand it—finding what sort of family she'd be joining... And so the whole thing, beginning with inheriting the family obsession, drove him—unconsciously, I'm sure—to ...""

"No, Ag! Don't...!"

Would the void left by her admired brother's suicide ever close over? Who could ever fill it? She shook off the fleeting image of Andy, her brother's friend. Her voice trembling with unfeigned distress, she said,

"I know, Ag, and I'm sure he—Pawa does blame himself, and I know Mother blames herself—perhaps with less reason, but... We have to remember Pawa's unhappy childhood, with *his* father..."

"With his mother, rather, who turned his father into a drunk and a remittance-man! Mother's father too—who I remember and you don't: he was a good man, a kind and a just, and look what the Catholic Church did to him! As for poor Austin Bellarmine—what a name! Did *his* parents realize Bellarmine used to burn heretics!"

"But Ag, don't you think...?"

Veronica broke off. She knew so little History and Agnes would scorn any suggestion that excuses might be made even for the sainted Cardinal.

"I mean, he couldn't help his name," she finished lamely.

43

"No, poor man! And did you ever hear our father put in a word for him? No, it was always The Mater this and The Mater that, who could do no wrong. A fine dance the pair of them led us when I was young: one as bad as the other! I agree both husband and son must have been terrified of her; that doesn't excuse…"

"Ag, I can't bear… I mean, I'm fond of him, whatever…"

"Yes, you always were his favourite; according to him your guardian angel always kept you away from any trouble—meaning unlike Deedie or me—or young Freda. Guardian angel indeed! Your good sense might seem a perfectly adequate explanation!"

The baby had slackened her sucking on the bottle and Veronica sat her up and patted her back as she had learned to do. She was trying to remember, but couldn't—not much—and privately she thought her guardian angel might indeed have been keeping her out of trouble in those childhood days that were not so distant. But unavoidable and unforgettable had been one terrifying row when their father could be heard raging at their mother and Freda had hidden on the stairs and with all her small force brought a picture—the back of it, fortunately—crashing down on his head. Veronica could still hear the glass shatter and with it the shattering of all hope for peace among those she loved. It had hardly harmed him physically— thank God!—but she felt the blow to his self-respect, his pride, and knew the fear that henceforth her beloved, her too impetuous younger sister, could never appear to him as other than an unnatural child. And though one could not say he had dealt harshly with her— Freda shared no more than the rest of them in the deprivations occasioned by his rigorist views and chaotic life—yet from that day a distance was between them.

"Ag," she said, watching the small, mobile face again suck on the rubber teat, "You know about dreams and I had such a bad one the other night. I woke Ron, shrieking out 'Elaine, Elaine!'" She shuddered slightly and the bottle slipped from the baby's mouth. It groped for it frantically.

"Steady on, old thing!" Restoring bottle to mouth, Agnes put an arm round her sister's thin shoulders and felt her still shaking. "Let's go in the other room to finish off and we can talk in there. I take it Ron knows about your dream?"

"Oh yes. He can finish feeding Elaine; he likes that."

"Ah, Jewish men are real family men! You can't imagine our father giving a baby a bottle, can you?"

Indeed Ron took the now flailing bundle with much gentleness, "winded" it with expertise, insisted on going to the kitchen to warm the bottle, then seated himself and tested the milk on his wrist before returning the teat to the eager mouth.

"Have a cig, Vee," said her sister, producing them with a box of matches from her bag. She waited until Veronica was drawing gratefully on one before saying,

"Now tell me more."

"I was with the—with Elaine in a building that was vast and empty, and then somehow I was outside and she was inside and I couldn't get to her. I was shut out and I started crying and calling…"

Agnes lit her own cigarette and sank back in the big armchair, crossing her legs and blowing out smoke: every inch the elder sister. Judiciously she said,

"That's an easy one, Vee. Obviously it's the Church. Taking over your child and shutting you out. A barrier between you and—life."

"How do you mean, Ag?" Veronica's voice was still tremulous, partly from awareness that Ron was listening.

"What I say! Didn't Ron—didn't you both have to promise to bring her up Catholic, otherwise they wouldn't marry you?"

"Yes, but…"

"Well, if it had been me, I wouldn't have given them the chance. You were married already, weren't you? But they have to take over and get a hold on you and your children…"

"But of course I wanted her baptized."

"Yes, that's how they get at you. Otherwise she might go to Limbo, forsooth—a pretty fable, Limbo, and says a lot for a God who is supposed to be just, let alone loving!"

"But, Ag, Limbo…"

"Yes, don't tell me! I know all about Limbo being 'a state of natural bliss'! They've made *that* up because in the old days Limbo was part of Hell and people began to take exception to most of the human race going there—even the less awful parts—merely because they hadn't been baptized. But I won't argue about theology; psychology is enough for me and that's what dreams are about. In any case, Elaine has been baptized. Freda told me about it. She and your friend were both godmothers and there wasn't to be a godfather until Pawa put himself forward…"

"I suppose we should have thought to ask him."

"Are grandfathers usually godfathers? No, he must have decided it was Providence asking him to step in and take responsibility for your child's Catholic upbringing."

"No, Ag, I'm sure not. At least, what he said afterwards was that even though he was old to be her godfather, he would hope to be allowed to look after Elaine from heaven one day, and that she would help him to get there."

"I reckon that's giving her a rather tall order, poor mite! But she's your child and Ron's here, who might have *some* say in it. Don't, for heaven's sake, let her be bamboozled as we were! The sooner that chain is broken the better!"

"But you can't undo Baptism!"

"Maybe not, and I've nothing against Baptism. Not in itself: a charming ceremony if no more. It's all the propagandizing that follows, anyway for Catholics like us, or rather like you if you don't get free of it. That's what needs undoing."

"But Ag…"

"Oh I know it's not easy; they get a hold over us young. Like the Jesuit—wasn't it?—said: 'Give me a child of three years…' But it can be done, as I know. Some *can't* free themselves, it seems, ever, so just don't let it take hold with your child!"

The subject of this advice had fallen peacefully asleep on her father's lap. He rose to carry her to that slip of a bedroom that was now hers and place her in the basket inside the high-railed cot with nursery rhymes round it which Freda had spotted advertised second-hand on a card in a newsagent's window. Veronica made the tea and carried the heavy pot in to place it on the waiting tray, then removed the cloth from the plate of neatly sliced and buttered bread. In a few minutes they were all three seated at the table, she poised for the pouring rite that not long since would have been for Ag, in their mother's absence, to perform. First the milk in the small jug did the round of the cups, then the strainer was placed on each in turn and the steaming tea poured through it.

"Bread and butter first!" said Agnes, grimacing as she passed the platter, in mimicry of a succession of nursemaids: Biddy who had had charge of her and Magda and Leo in their nursery days in the seclusion of Princes Gate, and successive Irish girls: all devoted to Madam, as they called Deedie, though each less grandly caparisoned as the addresses declined through Bayswater to Kilburn: the succession ceasing by the time—which followed on Deedie's heroic efforts with The Business—they had fetched up in Shepherds Bush with its handy connections to the West End.

"And jam!" exclaimed Ron, plunging his knife into the flowered pot to heap it lavishly onto his bread.

"Excuse Ron, Ag," said her sister archly, "He's still not used to this. Tell Ag, Ron!"

"That's right! It was butter *or* jam when I was a boy," said Ron,

"Usually jam and straight from the jar, not all lah-di-dah like this—which is okay by me," he added hastily, "but we were hungry youngsters and my mother wouldn't have had time even if..."

Realizing from his wife's frown that he had said "okay," and further was talking with his mouth full, he took refuge in a defiant second knifeful of jam. Had they been alone, she would have expostulated but now merely said,

"Mind you, they had wonderful food! I can't think how Ron didn't grow fat on it, like his brother. I'm afraid he won't grow fat on my cooking, though I am trying, aren't I, Ron?"

"You are, dear—trying!" (wrapping the retaliatory barb in comic emphasis to allow its sting to pass) "and—"

"It's not my fault..." began Veronica, but broke off in time and, mindful of a resolve formed out of past observation of her parents' war, contained her grievance. It was *not* her fault that she had been taught French and the piano—Would they ever have one?—and needlework, at which she was so bad, but never cooking, because—presumably—the nuns assumed she would have someone to cook for her! Ag was quick to fill in the awkward pause with,

"I'm afraid we're none of us much in the way of cooks, Ron. Our mother always hated it too..."

"That's not quite fair on Mumsie, Ag. She never liked it, but she did it just the same—She always said that—and not badly either! I think she assumed we would pick it up as she had to."

"Plain English cooking for husbands who would expect no more. She never reckoned with Jewish immigration!"

This passing as a compliment to the immigrants, they could leave it at that and, the bread-and-butter plate being emptied, Veronica drew the cake-stand toward her and picked up the knife which had been her father's characteristic gift to them: an impressive steel blade set solidly in a dark bone handle.

"I'll have none of this stainless steel; it never really sharpens," he had said, presenting it. "This blade will stay sharp if you whet it occasionally. You know how, Sonny? I'll show you. And I'll ask you thrippence for it."

Ron had been mystified by this last, but produced the required three-penny piece and Veronica explained later: "It's a sort of superstition, I suppose; anyway an old custom, because if you give someone a knife it might suggest you mean them harm, so you sell it to them."

He had asked, "Is it a Catholic superstition?"

"No, an English one, which is almost as important to Pawa. He likes to keep up old ways."

"Yes, like the watch-chain. And the collars. Thank God I don't have to wear those stiff ones!"

"*Please*, Ron, don't say 'Thank God!'; it's—exaggerated!" She had stopped short of saying "blasphemous"—which would amuse him—or, worse, "vulgar," and she adopted a more emollient tone.

"I'm thankful, too, that I don't have to starch them! Of course, Mother used to send Pawa's to the laundry—like most other things."

"So do you my collars—though not to be starched."

The detachable white collars that were the badge of the non-manual worker were indeed itemized with the sheets, pillowcases and handkerchiefs to be picked up weekly by the laundry-man. That was about all they dared afford, so she washed the shirts, rubbing them on the washboard with the underwear and her own things—on days, that was, when she didn't have to boil a pail of nappies. Most weekdays saw stretched over the bathtub a line of washing damp from the mangle; today being Saturday, she had removed the clothes-horseful from around the inlaid chest, where the sun could fall on it. Falling in love and eloping might be romantic, and getting pregnant sinful; you surely paid for it in toiling and moiling! Her mother had always had help as a matter of course, even when you'd have thought it couldn't be afforded. With mixed pride and resentment Veronica regarded her big-boned hand holding the knife and more than ever ungainly from being damp and chapped even in summer. But she only said,

"You must have learned somewhere to make this Victoria sandwich, Ag! It looks every bit as good as a bought one. You'll have to teach me."

"I will, pet, if we ever find the time. A sponge is quite simple, but it can go wrong, so it's best shown. Ron," she added, seizing on a moment when he would be appreciating her virtues as a sister-in-law, "I've a confession to make. That copy of *Lady Chatterley* that you bought—in Barcelona, wasn't it?—I'm afraid I left it on a bus!"

"Good Lord!" This expletive drew a look but no reproach. Veronica realized that was a shock and upsetting; early on he had told her of his triumph over restrictive bourgeois laws, smuggling the banned book in a plain cover and lending it out to literary friends with *avant-garde* views. Veronica had suppressed any curiosity to read it, and somehow he had felt he should not press it on her: that perhaps there was something right about the convent education, with all that emphasis on "purity," even though it could go too far and get in the way of a man's legitimate pleasures... Reining in his chagrin at the loss and annoyance at Agnes' carelessness, he adopted the arch tone of a man of the world:

"I wonder what the bloke thought who found it!"

"Bloke or gal, I trust they thought they were in luck! All this absurd censorship! You'll understand I could hardly inquire for it at the Lost Property Office. I'm dreadfully sorry. And the only amends I can make is to pay you for it."

"Don't do that. You can just teach Vron to make this delicious cake!"

"I expect it's providential," his wife said. "We wouldn't want a book like that in the house with Elaine growing up."

He hadn't thought of that.

II

In bed that night and early, as losing no time in establishing what he waggishly called "the regime of sinning," Ron soon was heavily asleep. Veronica lay restless, recalling for perhaps the fiftieth time the birth that a few weeks before had so changed her life—and not as might have been foreseen, even though in a direction she herself had charted—and for it she had felt "in her bones" that she was to pay the price! Beginning with the punishment of guilty Eve: childbirth with its pains and indignities worse even than the act of engendering. Only after prolonged labour had the child been born, in the small hours of the previous day and proved to be a girl: a pity, what with Pawa having no surviving sons and Ron's family—like it said in the Bible: "The male child that opens the womb is holy to the Lord"—would surely have been impressed had she become mother of their first grandson! But no help for it, and when it had been weighed and checked and washed they had put it to her breast, but it hadn't wanted to suck, and it seemed both had fallen asleep because she awoke to find she was being transferred to a bed and Baby soon followed and was placed in a cot alongside, in their private room under the watchful care of Day Nurse Higgs.

That book, Ag's gift: in her mind's eye she saw it lying on the bed-side table, beside the posy of anemones in its tiny porcelain vase that was Magda's gift, propped against it a little gold-scrolled card bearing, in their second sister's tall, spidery hand, a promise to "make a sketch of Baby so soon as she can 'sit' to me." Nurse Higgs had already augured peril to this delicate offering when grudgingly she had returned it that morning: flowers at night, it seemed, were Bad for Baby. To Veronica all was rather reminiscent of her convent boarding-school, and when Nurse had picked up the book and glanced into it before snapping it shut as though ridding it of dust, it recalled the Mistress of Discipline examining a suspect parcel arrived through the post.

On Nurse Higgs' erect five feet retreating through the swinging baize doors and down the corridor—starched apron creaking, crepe soles squeaking—Veronica had relapsed against the expertly positioned pillows with something of the sense of relief of a recruit obeying the sergeant's "Stand-easy!" Something too of the recruit's abiding tension.

Thank God—or anyway her mother and Ron, who between them had found the money—she was not in the ward but on her own behind that door—and here memory surveyed the room: the electric lamp and wireless set on the bedside table, the chintz-covered armchair, the matching curtains behind it, drawn back, framing symmetrically the closed sashes which excluded the sullen airs of a March morning in mid-'thirties London Town. Against that sky that appeared cast in lead, the tall vase of roses on the sill flaunted crimson, flame and baby-pink: her mother and Freda were extravagant dears, and Deedie, with her exactly right air of gentle command, had asked that they be replaced on the sill each morning, furthest away from the heating-pipes which were a feature of this up-to-date maternity-home.

Ignoring Higgs' parting shot, that with baby sleeping peacefully, she'd do well to take a nap herself until Visiting, stretching out a white-lawn-sleeved arm to pick up that book, Veronica resolved to begin her maternal learning at the beginning. Reading was what she chiefly delighted in; mercifully, once Ron had fallen asleep it never disturbed him if she read to any hour, or padded restlessly about the house, or just lay tense and thinking, as now…

It had hardly been welcome reading, rather a duty: the authoritative Doctor's expectations seemed so uncompromising, confirming her doubts of being up to it—to motherhood. She was miserably conscious of having got off to a bad start that previous evening, with Baby whimpering for a good quarter of an hour, followed by what seemed endless minutes of thin, quite unexpectedly piercing and increasingly frantic-sounding wails, before nerving herself to pick her up out of the hooded basket. It wanted some half hour to authorized feeding-time and she had waited, watching in appalled fascination the mouth grope towards the source of succour, before shamefastly untying the ribbon of her silk-and-wool bed-jacket to expose her still thin breast, to which the mouth fastened, "like a limpet," she thought, yielding uneasily to the new sensation. That recalled her brother, poor Leo, prizing these off seaweedy rocks at Shanklin Bay: and again she shuddered, whether at memory of him or of those blindly waving feelers...

The wails had brought Nurse Higgs, about to hand over for the night, who scolded her: she should have rung the bell, or better, waited until the Night Nurse should come on duty.

"But she cried so, Nurse!"

"Wind, Mrs Keller! Rub her back. Four-hour feeding should be ample for a healthy newborn and you cannot begin too soon to establish a routine."

It seemed all so much more daunting than she had realized; she did wish she had experience of babies such as her elder sisters had with her and Freda...

All was coming back to her as if it were yesterday: that yesterday of the birth and that morning after, feeling decidedly more herself and able to conceal her doubts under her more usual air of assured practicality. The baby, mercifully soon sleeping again, could not have come to any harm. She tried for a while to focus on the book, but anxieties would creep in to vie with the rational counsels of the eminent doctor, so sure he knew what it was a new mother was saddled with; it seemed as though no question need arise.

Once discharged she had persisted conscientiously in following the Truby King prescriptions. All the more because the cries had become ever more *determined*—even angry: could a young baby be angry? Saint Augustine—his *Confessions* had been one of the more interesting books available in the school Library—had, as she recalled, observed greed in babies at the breast (a wonder the nuns hadn't pasted over that passage, as they had some in the small-print Bibles they studied for Sacred Doctrine). Or was it jealousy? Anyway, sin.

The small pool of her notions wavered uncertainly between Original Sin and Holy Innocence: of this, as depicted in the painter Holman Hunt's *Flight into Egypt*, she had a print she had selected as a prize for Sacred Doctrine; come to think of it, it must be still in her school Missal, which must be still at Deedie's. Only now, lying here in a home of her own, beside a gently snoring Ron, did she recall the India paper leaves, gilt-edged between the stiff, black covers with the crest depicting the Immaculate Heart of Mary and below that the Latin motto: *Ad Jesum per Mariam*—and Mother Imelda was before her, sweeping back into her portfolio of holy pictures: the Sacred Hearts on fire with love for us, the Black Madonnas and the jewel-encrusted Infants of Prague passed over by the winner of that half-term's Catechism competition.

Nor had Mother failed to deliver her judgment—no doubt bethinking her how every situation should be improved to the greater glory of God—that the painter had done well: for a Protestant, as became plain when she added, "Remember, when you look at his picture, to pray for his conversion," adding, "And that of his family." Veronica had not much remarked the addendum until, term ended, she brought home its haul of ribbons, medals and cards gained for merits on fronts academic and behavioural to display before her mother and sisters. Then, as usual, it had been Agnes' part to supply enlightenment: the Sister of the painter's Deceased Wife had become in her turn his wife, challenging a "theocratic" law and incurring an odium that clearly should have fallen equally on Hunt himself: here Ag had seemed to be pointing to one of her well-worn themes, the prejudice against women of a Society still under the influence of Religion, while that had led on to another, the odium attaching to divorce and remarriage in general. Pondering this, Veronica could see that the connection was, as ever, Religion, and Ag meant there should be no odium: people should be free to marry and remarry as they chose.

If her sister's vehemence had left her, aged fourteen, confused and doubting as to these rights and wrongs, Ron too—she now, some seven years later, understood—would hold that there was no odium attached. At the time she had rather been struck by Mother Imelda's appearing to side with those scandalized by what—unusually—appeared to be a sin of Protestant manufacture; surely in Catholic eyes the Church of England, not possessing that Magisterium about which Sister herself had taught them, had no power to pronounce on what might make or unmake a marriage—particularly considering its origin in the Divorce of a cruel and scandalous King! She wasn't sure if Catholics could marry their deceased wives' sisters; it hadn't figured among prohibitions learned in Sacred Doctrine, like First Cousins not marrying, though perhaps like that it might need to be Dispensed. Perhaps that was it: Anglicans didn't have a Pope to grant Dispensations, so they had to stick with their laws or else change them. Had they not quite recently done so with Divorce! Which would make it much easier to be Church of England than Catholic; but then it already was!

The memory train was departing where she would not be taken—not at present, anyway. *Her* Church marriage had been "dispensed," because Ron, of course, was not even baptized, and you had to be baptized to receive any of the other sacraments; they had learned that in Sacred Doctrine. Which meant their marriage was no sacra-

ment—or could it be one for her and not for him? It seemed not—
and yet Father O'Grady had said these were "Church norms" and we
could not know God's view of it; that was a comfort—but it still left
a bad feeling, as if the Church didn't regard hers as fully a marriage,
or was making her pay a price for it. All too often their Church
seemed to be against Catholics marrying—or wanted them to be
made miserable by it: it might be to encourage them to become nuns
or priests, or to make that not seem the more miserable course,
which it surely was, for nuns, anyway: look at her friend Winnie...

No, she really must put these thoughts aside. There was always the
hope of Ron being baptized; would that make their marriage a sacrament after all? Anyway, it would be through their marriage; that
would show the Church! And they *were* married—doubly so, as he
joked, and, with a *double-entendre* she ignored, called them "the he-
Ron and she-Ron double-act." She had been so fearful of the spinsterhood to which her elder sisters seemed consigned as they entered
their thirties... Until, that was, Mag had upset them all by settling
for a divorcee—well, not all of them: Ag had been grimly delighted at
this flying in the face of their father and the Church, and even Deedie
showed herself unwilling to condemn; of course her own mother—
the cases were oddly similar—but it had been a blow to Pawa all right
and upset Freda and herself, she supposed, though really...

Well, now she was the first to have a baby, as well as the most properly married, even if things hadn't taken place according to the proper
sequence—she still squirmed inwardly at that, though what was a girl
to do...? The path to that so-coveted status had begun with pregnancy and continued with elopement: that was what it had been,
even if not to Gretna Green but only to the Hammersmith Registry
Office; after all, she was "of age" now and Ron a good bit older, as
well as more experienced... If at the end of the line Mother Church
had had to pick up the pieces and "regularize" their marriage, it at
least meant her parents could recognize it. Ron had been understanding of that...

Of course, in the circumstances she had not worn white, which
was as well as, even with a dress from The Business, a white wedding
would have been extravagant and her sisters, Ag especially, would
have thought it a lot of old-fashioned fuss. Nor had they received the
Nuptial Blessing. Not that that seemed to have done her parents'
marriage much good...

Here, as ever, presented itself an image of an image: the photograph in its tarnished frame on the mantelshelf in her mother's bedroom. In the background the porch of that church preferred for

fashionable Catholic rites and known as Spanish Place, with before it the wedding party arranged around the perfect couple: at its centre Deedie—as she might now call her in recognition of her new status—a bride younger even than herself: those clear, composed features framed by the heavy lace veil and "bangs" of luxuriant hair which to this day retained its dark colour; they related to Mumsie like a ripened apple to one still green. Or rather the other way round, and come to think of it, had the apple ever reached its promised perfection and not rather passed imperceptibly from green to sere?

That would not be a question to trouble the Deedie she knew, though she guessed it might the Edith of the photograph—albeit she, in following her beloved and namesake mother into the Catholic Church, had made profession of a Hope beyond worldly considerations. She must have learned to let her beauty go as the years and eight pregnancies exacted, while continuing to dress and present herself with decorum, impressing on her four daughters that attention to appearance that showed respect for others and for the God who had condescended to His creatures: that was about as theological as Mumsie got, perhaps from having had so much of it with Pawa...

And here Veronica's focus shifted from that youthful Deedie in bridal splendour, eclipsing the bridesmaid on her other side as much as did the hat with enormous ostrich feather that covered the blonde prettiness generally conceded to the young Liza: shifted to Pawa's leonine head looming higher than veil or feather, with beyond him his cousin and Best Man, mustachio'd Uncle Leon, beyond *him* Grandma Rigg, recognizably a younger edition of the squat tyrant hobbling on silver-topped wand, before whose imperious tapping Veronica and Winifreda had been wont to scatter; her widowhood already betokened by a tuft of black lace suspended from a satin crown—She affected high headgear to enhance her stature—and an enveloping dark mantle. As the story went, removal of these weeds for the wedding supper had disclosed a white lace dress: an offence to English decorum the more marked when at the wedding-feast she was heard to jest that she had been taken for the bride.

She it was had provided all this grandeur, and notably the dresses for the main actors, out of the fashion-firm founded upon her Parisian connections and the toils of Irish seamstresses culled from Catholic charitable institutions. The plain grey silk of the elder Edith, whose sad-visaged form, seated at the far end beyond her two daughters, balanced Madame's bold front, had been a gift. Not so the satin and lace gown in which the bride's beauty had done credit to the house of Rigg; this that chagrined bride had discovered only at her eve-of-wedding party when Madame presented her bill—for the materials only, she had been at pains to emphasize, leaving Edith to digest the objection that these had been selected with little reference to her taste or means.

As a child poring over this photograph, Veronica had exulted in its display of fashion and fortune and in the beauty of the couple, from some fairytale realm mystically connected to their actual unquiet household. She had grown to read disillusion onto the handsome face of the groom, consciousness of self-sacrifice in the bride's composed features, even before she heard the story of their engagement. Which, strangely, had not been until she reached almost the age her mother had then been; Agnes, from whom she heard most things, might have been less forthcoming on whatever could cast their father in some light of compassionate understanding.

Not that she ever wanted to believe Ag as implacable toward him as she seemed; this ten-year-older sister from the time she could remember had been on hand to fill the gaps in her mother's available attention and the comings and goings of nursemaids. Devoted as she also was to Freda, Veronica harboured a secret satisfaction that she had come off the better in the allocation of surrogate mothers, excusing it as only fitting Freda should have Magda, for both were artistic...

Now she was the mother and Elaine the first child—who might turn out like Agnes: did one turn out, or was one made...? And would there be a sister for Elaine to mother, or a brother, as she and surely Ron would hope...? She reverted to the photograph and what lay behind it.

She knew the scene by heart, as did all Edith's and René's children. As usual, Agnes' reconstruction was the most explicit: Grandmamma Edith, while not of the dark dye of their other grandmother, nonetheless in her state of penury brought on by her absurd rejection of their wronged grandfather, had been urging her daughter to quit Madame Rigg's employ—not, as professed, out of self-respect and for the avoidance of scandal, but in the expectation that this would precipitate young Mr Rigg's declaring himself.

"I thought you did not care for *me*," Edith had replied—not, their daughters suspected, with complete ingenuity—when René had sought her out to propose, on that afternoon of the first Easter Sunday of the new century.

"I was waiting until after Lent; it was not a fit time... But I had made up my mind before and I hoped—May I hope that *you* could care for *me*?"

"I can!" Edith had replied, but then, as willing to give Providence another chance, added,

"Though I have to tell you that I do not love you."

It seemed he had shrugged that off, and yet… In the consciousness of recently gained experience, their daughter pondered the hurt of that reply. Had it stood in the way of what was at that point admiration turning to love? More realistically—and putting aside the difficulty of viewing their proper Mumsie as object of masculine desire, and their larger-than-life father as subject to commonplace male passion—could one suppose that once she was possessed—the senses she inflamed cooled—left was the bitter taste of that avowal, to rankle with him all their days together? Perhaps one only need suppose he felt unable to take the opportunity half extended to him to withdraw his offer, preferring to view that declaration as some show of modesty or maidenly whim that marriage itself would dispel, rather than behave, as he might have seen it, as a cad. A gentleman could hardly go back on a proposal of marriage; in a not-distant past that had even been the law of the land… Be that as it might, the decorous feasting had scarce finished before his anger had flared, kindled by a handful of rice catching him in the face as their landau started for the station and their wedding-tour. Veronica's own honeymoon (The American word was by now "in") had been happy, with all the excitement of an overnight voyage to Norway, a country unknown to either of them, and all the immediacy of the new life growing within her; still, she had asked herself what was the lesson for her own marriage, so newly and also rashly entered upon.

The answer certainly did not seem to begin, as in the nuns' instruction, with two Catholics qualifying for the Nuptial Mass and its concluding Blessing pronounced solemnly over the kneeling couple: Deedie was fond of repeating the final words, "And may you see your children's children, to the third and fourth generation." That had seen part-fulfilment yesterday when, on visits timed to avoid a meeting, her parents had separately looked on this first child of child of theirs, this "second generation" who in some time unimaginably distant might give rise to a third…

Nor in their family—than which few, surely, could be more Catholic—were Nuptial Masses other than a rarity. Aunt Liza must have had one since she went on to marry Pawa's Cousin and their Uncle, Leon. Insignificant she might appear, but she had kept her eyes open under that ostrich feather, and soon carried off that mustachio'd Best Man—on his feet in the photograph, though only remembered in a Bath chair, which might help explain why that marriage had seemed not unsuccessful, so that even after his death her cousins had continued to move effortlessly on their mother's upward course. Watchful little Aunt Liza had secured her place in Society and from there on steered her vessel well clear of her sister's unquiet household—wherein the worldliness of these relations was a rare point of parental agreement.

At the time, she and Winifreda had been unhappy at not being bridesmaids at Elizabeth's wedding to her titled widower, Pawa insisting it was already stretching a point that they were allowed—by his Confessor's permission—to attend at all, the bride being a baptized Catholic and marrying in the Church of England, where you could be present but not take part; this nice distinction, they would notice, seemed not to hamper the bride's mother and sister from acting out the roles the Church Established assigned them.

Veronica had since been at two "mixed" marriages, but in Catholic churches, for though the Church officially disapproved, it was easier to get a Dispensation in England than in Ireland and other countries where you should have no difficulty in finding a Catholic spouse. Anglicans were baptized, of course, and even validly—though Deedie, brought up a Methodist, said sometimes the water might be sprinkled and it had to flow, like the River Jordan: it was enough for two drops to flow together, but while this seemed not unlikely, one could not be sure. Since Jews were not baptized at all, perhaps she and Ron might not have got a Dispensation if it had not been for the Registry Office wedding—and the baby. Was that why she had done it, meaning all the time to force Mother Church's hand? She didn't really know, and anyway Ag would say she must put all that aside, as she had this afternoon, and even in the maternity home, when she found her weepy: that it was like a faulty phonograph record and she must get out of the groove of all these doubts and perplexities.

More awake than ever, and feeling now agitated, Veronica got softly out of bed and padded in her slippers to the kitchen to heat herself some milk. This she carried in its mug into the sitting-room and, seating herself in one of the green-and-beige armchairs, picked up the soft white beginnings of a matinée coat she was making: a labour of love proper in a new mother, especially one hard up, and Elaine had by now outgrown most of the things friends and family had provided at her birth. Knitting was not one of the accomplishments which had won Veronica prizes at school, for while her dark hair and doe-eyed prettiness came from her mother, her elongated frame, complete with large hands with square finger-ends, came from her big-boned Frankish father. Now she worked a row laboriously with the steel needles, sighing a little as she turned them to start another row and working on painstakingly for several more, after which she let it drop idly to her lap. It was easier when she had her glasses on and though she hated wearing them, she would have to get used to it; her mother had warned she would need to wear them when the baby started to crawl, or she would miss pins and other dangers on the floor. And now she no longer needed to attract men, it wouldn't matter so much. Ron was short-sighted; anyway, she wouldn't be wearing them in bed...

The recurring image of their marriage-bed awaking further perplexities, the train went back: to that event of her new maternity: the newborn in the cradle beside her—she could see the small features, the hair wavy and dark like the lashes lying lightly on a creamy skin, not mottled and red like some newborn babies, the mouth, sucking slightly, and surely innocently, in sleep. "Like a rosebud," sentimental Freda had said, who found the new baby "so sweet"—and Veronica could see it was, except for the sucking, newly known to her so intimately. No, not a limpet with those horrid feelers; perhaps more like a sea-anemone—and now she was back in Shanklin Bay, where Grandma Rigg would take for them a villa and sit in a deckchair perusing *The Lady* or *The Tablet*, darkly shrouded and raising and lowering her parasol, while beneath three identical straw hats her mother and Agnes read and Magda sketched and their father and Leo went off to the row of changing-huts to slip discreetly into the sea in their stripy bathing-suits, and peace reigned for the duration...

Leo would not know his sister's child, his niece—not in this life...

No, not Leo; banish Leo! Would that wound—still seeming fresh—never scar over? Inexorably her thoughts passed into their accustomed round. If not their mother nor Magda, ought not her young self—favoured, she had thought, above Freda, though both had looked on Leo almost as a second father—surely they should have meant enough to him—had he had no thought for the injury they would sustain: her, Freda, all of them? But no, it had been from impulse, or from delirium—had he fancied he was launching himself skyward and carefree, as he and his friend Andy were accustomed to do in their squadron's two-seater 'planes: like Phaethon? Or Icarus? Her Greek mythology was sketchy...

"And what of the poor Pawa?" had asked Andy, whose real but unpronounceable name was Panayiotis Andropoulos. Indeed they had drawn the circle of their grief tight round their mother, as though Leo had no father—yet for Pawa there must have been the added bitterness that in Leo lay all his hope of passing on the name and line of which *his* father had been the last... Last, that was, before the "Second Spring" followed on Catholic Emancipation. Andy of course would hardly have understood all that—or had Leo told him something of it? But her Greek hero's good heart would go out to the father who had failed to earn his family's trust or much love...

But she must not think on Andy either, not now. He who might perhaps have atoned to her for her brother's loss, he himself had told her she must not think of him; hers was not a nature to stand transplanting to the rough conditions of his country, and with the present unease in Europe that could call him—could have called too on Leo—to the sacrifice of self, of life... Perhaps that had been partly an excuse, because he saw how this gawky, straggling plant was preparing to cling to him, the tall, valorous stranger. But with chagrin she had to recognize he was right; the Greece of his description sounded in many respects more backward than the land of those heroes of old to whom he had been in her mind assimilated.

No—banish Andy, who she must *not* think on—for whom she had substituted Ron... Pawa though, Pawa visiting that day and showing her how the miniature fingers gripped more strongly even than that mouth sucked; saying it was like monkeys and old Darwin was probably right that we were related to them and it didn't make an atom of difference to *Genesis* because that only required us to believe there had been an Original Human Couple and monkeys and apes were not human even if God used them to arrive at us—just as it didn't matter about the Seven Days though we now knew the Earth was billions of years old. Perhaps most babies were like monkeys: anyway ugly, as Deedie had seemed to imply on *her* visit.

Ron, too, had shown great pride when he set eyes on his scrap of a daughter, and said Elaine, the name they had decided on for a girl, was just right. So was she proud, of course, to have given birth to an unusually pretty baby—though for a girl to grow up *too* pretty might cause problems... By now Elaine was fast losing her dark hair and looked more average-baby... Then innocence: *could* a child inherit sin, as the Church taught? More, could it carry the mark of its parents' sin in conceiving it out of Holy Wedlock? At least its Catholic parent, who knew that was sinful and yet had "consented"? No, that surely was nonsense, as Ron would say if she told him these thoughts—which she had better not; as would Agnes, and pour out her wrath at the Church for putting such ideas into people's heads. It seemed easy for Agnes to decide the Church was wrong and to cast it all off; but what if the Church was right?

Anyway, the Church did not teach that, not even about bastards, who in olden times had been thought unnatural: wasn't it in Shakespeare? Even their mother, beneath all her properness, felt, her children had come to realise, the stigma of illegitimacy. Somehow it all tied in to that Original Sin which we inherited, which was different from Actual Sin; she hadn't grasped how—only seen how that innocence that seemed so palpable sleeping, even at a day old could give way to a peevish crying that was more pitiful only because more feeble than that awful night of the furious-sounding cries that had gone on and on until they tailed off in a fitful wailing as she covered her head with the blankets...

The knitting had fallen again from her hands and at last a slackness was stealing through her limbs and seemingly into her head. After all, Elaine was no bastard; they already intended to marry when she was conceived. In Medieval times, Veronica had heard, "sex"—So Ron called what she had until then only heard referred to, distantly if at all, as "conjugal rights"—once you were betrothed was regarded with indulgence. It was the Puritans had made it no better than common fornication: that too was in one of Shakespeare's plays—not one they had read at school, of course, but her sisters sometimes read plays aloud and she had been struck by one about a ruler who was a Puritan and made a law condemning to death those who continued in the older, more tolerant views. The Puritans had been new in Shakespeare's day and were Protestants, though it seemed the Church nowadays had plenty of her own Puritans: the Irish priests especially, according to Magda, who had stopped going to Church too—even before *her* marriage, that in the eyes of the Church was no marriage! Yet Magda seemed more understanding of their father than was Ag—which was so sad and went back to before she, Veronica, was born. Magda said Pawa, in spite of his English father and Benedictine schooling, was a Jansenist, which he got from his mother's side, because the French were Jansenists. It was not clear why Jansenism should have infected the Irish; only, as Magda told it, caught between them and the French, the sparse band of English Catholics hadn't had much chance and now Catholics of the revived English Church were far too self-conscious about their faith.

Still, Magda did not, like Agnes, scornfully dismiss the Church as the source of all their family's troubles, but took it seriously, at pains to understand what made it—or Her—what She or it was here and now: Veronica thought Magda would not refer to the Church as "Her"—the Bride of the Apocalypse who was also and mysteriously Mary the Mother of God, as they had all learned from school, or was it from Pawa—or from Deedie, who though a convert often seemed to know most about it?

Pawa, come to think of it, had said nothing about his favourite daughter's pregnancy, at least to her—though Agnes said he had burst out in no uncertain terms when he heard she was married to "that Jew"—with an adjective she would not willingly recall. That it undoubtedly had been a great shock she could understand, and he could be surprisingly lenient with human frailty—which he surely recognized in himself or why did he go to Confession every Saturday? That to Veronica he had said nothing could be a result of that Confessional: a warning not to antagonize the young couple; priests could be very wise—or "prudent"; Prudence was one of the four Cardinal Virtues—though Agnes of course would say it was only to keep people in the Church. Whatever the case, informed of their registry-office wedding, Pawa's one thought had seemed to be to get them married in Church. To herself she could own that she had been counting on this, and even though she had made out it was to satisfy her parents, that was more so Ron would accept to do it. Of course he had to agree to Elaine being baptized—washed of Original Sin—though not its Effects, like the crying! He was less sure about promising to bring her up as a Catholic, though Father O'Shea had pointed out that children needed to be brought up something, and Ron had agreed he didn't want them brought up Jewish, which he had thrown over for himself. Then what might he want their child to believe in? Perhaps Science, which he seemed to think was going to explain everything—though Pawa, who knew a lot of Science, said that was Modernism, a new Heresy.

Remembering Agnes' warning, Veronica picked up the discarded knitting to begin a new row, resolving from now on to think only good thoughts. She would be doubly responsible for their daughter's upbringing, for watching over that baptismal innocence, warding off those Effects—and she banished to the threshold of consciousness the thought that would next present itself: "so she does not stray as I did"; for of course she had confessed before the Church wedding, even though it was not a Sacrament and she would not be receiving Communion. Father O'Shea had urged her not to dwell upon her "error," as he called it, for which the example of a good Catholic wife and mother would make amends, and while it was right to repent of our frailties, too much self-blame would be Pride. Both, of course, had skirted round the matter of that "purity" to which sermons made veiled allusion, which the nuns had conveyed without addressing it directly—and which Agnes decried as "a load of tosh."

But if family troubles had propelled Agnes into rebellion and herself into compromise, her daughter could, should, make amends, or rather she herself could and should by giving her a good upbringing in the proper loving and peaceful home she and her sisters had lacked.

In this resolution, and by now irresistibly yawning, she crept back into bed and to sleep.

III

Edith had retired upstairs with her hot-water-bottle and her book for her habitual rest—that day, she told herself, well-earned after the baptism, which had taken place not in Veronica's new parish—where she attended Sunday Mass but avoided the priest—but in Edith's parish in Shepherd's Bush: that same church where they had been so hastily—and in Ron's view superfluously—wed. Lingering annoyance at Father O'Shea's clumsiness over his name had been sufficient pretext for him not to attend the Christian rite and the little group assembled round the font had comprised, besides Veronica, both her parents (the significance of the occasion overriding, as rarely, their separateness), her sister Winifreda and Veronica's school-friend Winnie: to both the neophyte Christian was to be entrusted as godmothers, the near-coincidence of names enabling Veronica to please both and dispense with a godfather now that any she chose would only remind her of him who should have stood sponsor to his sister's child: her brother Leo. Winifreda and Winifred had both of them brought silver chains as christening gifts: Winnie's bore a crucifix, Freda's a medal of the Virgin. The child could not be expected to wear both—or any, for some time to come, Edith reflected as she filled her hot-water bottle; both were long and Freda's particularly heavy, as marking an assumption of precedence: Edith knew her to be secretly miffed at not being chosen alone, as the aunt who would be close to the child as she grew... Dramatic had been the event that day commented on by Ag: their father's putting of himself forward as godfather. He brought no chain for his godchild, but Veronica had been careful to display his coral pinned to the baby's gown and round her own neck his mother's chain and medal.

After the ceremony, tea and cake had been duly partaken in that precious small house that was Edith's, through resolute keeping of the remnant of The Business going. Veronica and the baby were to stay the night; Ron would come over to Sunday dinner and take them home with him. So after many expressions of cordiality on

Edith's and Winifreda's part, and genuine affection on Veronica's, Pawa had left, insisting on escorting the third young woman to her train: taking, they surmised, occasion to impress on her the duties of a godparent.

Edith was feeling her heart full—as was the idiom of her day, for by this her daughters' day the mind was the preferred seat of emotion. But whether in the more or less substantial of these entities, what preoccupied her were memories awakened by sight of one of her children become herself a mother; of a grandchild baptised into that Catholic Faith she and her mother had embraced and followed faithfully where it led: by Life stirring again in a family where death had wrought much havoc.

For first—though surely she and René had assumed it worst and last—their second son had been carried off by the whooping-cough, introduced (alas!) into the house by her half-brother Walter's wife with her own sick child; the four children had all caught it, Agnes, Magda, Leo and Paul the baby, who that black night, before he walked or had words, suffocated and died.

They had kept up relations with their also bereaved kinswoman, recognizing obtuseness and not ill-will as cause of her fatal negligence. None the less were they bitterly afflicted, as was the whole family: Agnes' resentment of her father and all his works seemed to have originated at this time, encompassing the Church at which, in token of resignation to the Will of God, he insisted on increasing his family's attendance; for their eldest daughter had early picked up on her mother's grievances and marital situation: that having borne four children and lost one before she was well on in her twenties, she was likely to continue to bear, and to depend upon their erratic father for the wherewithal to rear them.

Could it have been otherwise? There had been times of fairer promise. As in far echo, Edith could hear Agnes' pure soprano gracing his stagings of Gilbert and Sullivan operas in days when she still would tolerate to do anything for him. That voice nowadays found employ in monotonous flows of scorn-laced chatter sousing the rare occasions one saw her! And the stage-productions used up moneys needed for housekeeping or for the school-fees that had to be paid off in installments and arrears. René's first invitation to her had been to *The Mikado* in Drury Lane; he regarded Gilbert and Sullivan as the height of humour, while at the same time both moral and patriotic. And she had tried to be appreciative, but though not tone-deaf—She had in youth mastered some few pieces executed on the piano in ripples of broken chords—she very nearly was to humour, whether Gilbert's or the more boisterous exchanges among her children: Magdalen anyway, and also poor Leo and Winifreda; not, of course, Agnes, nor Veronica much, though Ron had introduced a Jewish fund.

"I fear I have no sense of humour!" Edith now half smiled at how she would apologize thus, redoubling their mirth.

And she had to own some justice in what she had known Agnes remark caustically: that however their father might, in his chosen role as Pooh-Bah, carol that "family pride Must be denied," the establishing of his French genealogy with trips to Paris and other cities of France further deprived his family of the moneys thus spent, as well as The Business of his attention: fault too of Agnes' hated namesake, "The Mater," who having failed to encourage his considerable talents—even, apparently, to perceive them—had appointed him continuator of her life's investment, become the source out of which he spent insouciantly on researching his past, rather than on supporting his present family: Agnes saw this as compensating for the neglect and actual wrongs of which he would never consciously accuse his mother; retaliation too, on the delinquency he found in his wife. Alas again! For she had been indeed a source of his grievances—of his real griefs—beginning with her accepting to marry him…

"Not for nothing is this life called a vale of tears!"—how often had she heard this René's set response to felt sorrow! As his marriage and paternity seemed ever to fail him, the defections of his daughters and deaths of his sons became trials permitted by heaven, to be countered by an all-encompassing dedication to the Faith that supplied meaning to these afflictions—periodically stimulated by travel for which The Business supplied pretexts, to France or the wider continent: Rome was of course a favourite destination, Prague a more plausible, on account of the glass beads demanded by contemporary fashions "Madame Rigg"'s must be abreast of.

"The Business," thus identified by its official name with its foundress, had its origins in the unhappy failure of Austin Bellarmine Rigg—"the Meek," as Magdalen had dubbed him—to satisfy his wife's ambitions or keep her preoccupied, like Edith herself, with a family; the succession of stillbirths and infant deaths had surely sealed the wife's iron determination and all contributed to break the husband's more passive spirit.

Agnes' version—after she had herself psycho-analysed—was that René inherited that passivity, along with his mother's questing intelligence, but was checked from breaking into adult independence by the same fear inspired in the father, in the son masquerading as filial duty. But while the son might have been tied into a dependency from which he lacked the will to extricate himself, Edith had come late to question if it was not also into aims for which, left to himself, he would have had little sympathy. In the workroom it was the machines and their maintenance that attracted him—He was wont to remark he had "engineer's thumb"! In the products of those machines he had scant interest; had he dared frame an idea contrary to his mother's, might it not have been that women needed to be clothed with decorum and modesty, not in hock to worldly dictates? It seemed not to have entered his mother's head to have him schooled in any useful occupation; it was as a gentleman he was to inherit and live off her Business, doing credit to his Catholic forebears on both sides. And the beaded, bustled or sequined whims of fashionable women were what The Business had to supply in order to flourish.

The years of separation had made room for such cogitations. Yet without Madame Agnes' Business, René's and her paths would not have crossed, and nor would she have accepted him without the promise of what had been still, in the parlance of their age, "an establishment." The Rigg fashionable address and substantial style of living had combined with their Catholic credentials to seem the answer to her fervent prayers—on her mother's behalf as well as her own: had surely *been* answer, or the Almighty was a cruel deceiver! So how had it lacked the one elusive essential—the very mark of God Himself?

Not romance, for all the fairytale wedding so tinged with chagrin! She was not, and neither was René, swayed by romanticism. While she had found him indeed personable, and he been briefly dazzled by her beauty, each had viewed their union rather as compliance. With Providence rather than Destiny, and with that Duty so readily descried as the Will of God. If it had only been romance that was lacking, and not that Love which "suffereth long and is kind": the words of the Apostle Paul, read at their wedding…!

And though part of her was still tempted to wish she had never crossed Madame Rigg's threshold, that would not do; there were the children—now even this grandchild, and lives unborn—Who knew how many?—dependent on that meeting! Why Providence should allow people to come together, and even to come into being, through such unsatisfactory pairings was a mystery—yet one with the Christian God's own brand on it—of suffering, long-suffering, unstinting patience, the patience of a Griselda, patience of a saint…

Alas! A third time Edith barely voiced that sigh in the manner of her age. That Lesson read at the outset had echoed implicitly in every Mass of their life together or apart, in each shifting home where René would place prominently the altar Crucifix from the Rigg family chapel, flanked by silver or porcelain statuettes and plaques brought from Rome, Paris, Paray-le-Monial, Lisieux, in which mementos she read monitions to her and the children to keep to the path of that grace he found them devoid in: serving also to remind her he had always money for such things but she must beg it from him for shoes for the children. Until she had come to read in his waywardness that no wealth or distinction should accrue to her—nor to their children whose affections she engrossed away from him—from the family into which she had married for his worldly goods' sake rather than for his own.

As, she must recognize—did recognize—she had, and in René's dealings there was some justice, if small charity. She had told herself she was marrying him chiefly for her mother's sake—but had not that mother urged her to call off the wedding on its eve, when Madame presented her bill! Only she sensed her poor mother divided, herself borne along by a theme of self-sacrifice learned from that same mother: shallow and theatrical, she now saw, in one unprepared for the price to be paid in long-suffering!

Had that been too high a price for goods mundane but real: for a comfortable home and the reclaiming of social respect? Would René have proved kinder if only she could have submitted graciously to him and—yes—to his mother? Could she have won him to be provident, in the begetting of children as in their finances? She must have asked these questions of herself a thousand times. Nothing was beyond Grace, but she doubted she could substantially have altered him.

Here rose up the figure she had striven all her married days to suppress—but thus late on he surely could be faced: George Bartlett, René's friend from the choir at Spanish Place. Not that René had belonged to that choir—oddly, and for all his stagings of comic opera and his allegiance to the Church, she could not recall René's being in that or any choir. Agnes would of course say that his prevailing feeling toward Mother Church was the fear in which he had early learned to hold his human mother: witness his holding up for admiration how she had obliged a reluctant nursemaid whom he had bitten to "drive" him round streets in a harness from which hung a placard, "This boy bites"! She had dispatched him to boarding school at the earliest opportunity, removing him from Old Hall to Paris, away from the influence of a father seeking ever more alcoholic solace, thence—and wearing his French military-style uniform—to that English public school where he would hardly live down this appearance among the scions of "good" Catholic families whose view of themselves as gentlemen revolved around dress before even the sports to which he never could accustom himself. This, Edith contended, one could better excuse as parvenu ignorance abetting French thrift; even so, it seemed the boy had not found much understanding among his masters at that fine abbey-school, save one monk only, after whom they had named their second son. There he had learned to "scrape"—Agnes' word—on his fiddle. His voice went untapped by their famous choir…

George Bartlett was both singer and violinist. That fateful Easter Day she had been invited to spend at Madame Rigg's, and at High Mass found herself seated beside Madame in her pew, both of them following René's tall, robed figure bearing the Cross. George they afterwards encountered as they waited for René in the porch—and poor George, who lacked public-school address, had been seen off with scant greeting by Madame, who proceeded to pass comment on the shabbiness of his suit, together with some gratuitous aspersions on musicians and drink. Her sharp eyes had noted something in his demeanour to her *protégée*.

After an exceptionally lavish midday board, and so soon as his mother had retired for her post-prandial, René had ushered Edith into her office—it seemed emblematic of the businesslike way he went about seeking the happiness… The crux she had been half awaiting! Had they not prayed, that Holy Week, that she find another position to enable her to support the mother who knelt at her side, who had urged her to quit Madame Rigg's after learning that the girls in the workroom had been tattling about her daughter and their mistress' handsome son? Though the proprieties might be all that remained for their self-respect, to them they would cling! Already the curse of the dependent endowed with physical beauty had led Edith stumbling across half Europe, a too-youthful English governess prey to malicious tongues, eluding improper advances…

Here she rehearsed that little exchange, so well known to their daughters, which followed his brief declaration. Bluntly she had responded:

"I have to help my mother; she needs fifteen shillings a week."

Clumsy as a defence against an outcome she had watched coming, even gone to meet, but about which she felt still divided. He had seemed not to notice, replying cheerfully enough,

"Oh, we can do better than that. Only don't tell the Mater!"

That was reassuring, yet left her still undecided. He had shown no hint of the amorousness to which she had become wearily accustomed from men usually older and married. And apart from a presentiment of ill to follow, there was that which would need to be told, to "The Mater" as to him: the defect of her birth. This she would not reveal without consulting her own mother.

"Thank you,—René," she had begun; "You are most generous and—it makes me very happy…"

There she had stumbled, conscious of falsehood, to resume:

"I am indeed happy to accept—to be your wife. Only…"

(That ill-conceived if well-intentioned ending)

"…Only I have to tell you that I do not love you!"

Had a shadow passed over that correct countenance, never to be lifted? Edith had long given up the painful attempt to unpick the skein of misunderstandings then first begun to be ravelled. Instead, memory jumped to the unexpected sequel. As she had made for home, leaving René to follow next day to ask her mother's consent, honest George—So she ever after with compunction thought of him—had followed her to this very Bank station she was making for today, and there declared himself. He could not offer her a home as yet; besides his pupils, he sought a position in an orchestra, or if that failed would go into business; he asked only to hope for the happiness… Her prayer might seem to be receiving superabundant answer, or was Providence putting her to the test? She was eighteen; her engagement depended upon parental consent. She could have spared many a sorrow by sending René a word that might even be of secret relief to him. Then there was her position with Madame and those tattling tongues that her acceptance as René's betrothed must silence…

Again, what use to sift over these dead cinders? Held by that fate that had led her own mother, like many a girl for whom penury was excuse, to purchase a secure-seeming berth, she had replied to George—less handsome, more self-effacing than René, but whom she might with more conviction have promised to love and honour,

"You are too late; I am engaged—to René."

For a moment his expression had changed, fleeting from urgency through shock to resignation.

"René, my best friend!" he brought out, "He's one of the best—helped me out more than once. Don't mind about me! Just remember, if ever I can do you a service… I'd do anything for you!"

Even as she began to stammer, "I'm sorry," he had slipped among the anonymous crowd and was gone.

In a day of shock and despair when, albeit incredulous, she knew Leo dead, she would remember and turn to him in her bitter need… By that time poor George—who had been godfather to their first child; who had never married nor made much of his music, but lived out an unadventurous life as clerk to some City firm: whom she by marrying might have made more of—unless that was another delusion!—George had long ceased to be in his friend's confidence, René perhaps inferring, from things she had unguardedly or in anger said, that she regretted her choice—even suspecting her unfaithful in her secret thought; at any rate determined to bind her by restraints and by childbearing: no doubt he would see it in the light of his duty to protect the weaker vessel... How had she not let herself see clearly, with that "single eye" of the Gospel, cut through the web of distrust in which she—they—had been dragged through calamity after calamity?

But if such considerations might once have been useful, the time for them was long past. No longer was she, who had come through so much, the deluded girl she then had been, with her pretensions to honour and gentility! Things were as they were, and here she half smiled, remembering Ron's recounting of his parents' engagement: how his mother, in accepting her Abe, had concealed another man's ring in her pocket! Really, one could understand inveterate male diatribes against female fickleness, yet poor women had to thrive by their wits, be they Catholic or Jewish, genteel or poor immigrant! Madame Agnes too, daughter of an immigrant mother, having set out to establish herself within the tight English Catholic circles, had stood upon no niceties where she saw her advantage. But perhaps even she had learned from the long chain of setbacks she had confronted with such determination: the deaths of her babies; her husband's drinking; her son's dilettante incompetence; her daughter-in-law's bearing of daughter after daughter...

Yes, even the first of them had been greeted coolly, despite being given Madame Agnes' name, while Magdalen, less than a year later, had been received with outright disappointment. Two boys had followed, but the death of the second had riveted expectations on the fifth pregnancy, which was not long in coming—and in view of which René announced his purpose to have the young girls board at their convent school well before the confinement, their mother's state and its event being unsuited to their witness.

Edith's indignation had blazed, goading her to the ill-advised removing of herself and the three children to the home of her half-brother—and here Edith dwelt a moment on poor Walter, dead these many years, in life ever conscious his wife—that Ada through whose negligence the whooping-cough had been brought into his sister's home—was a connection his family but tolerated, after she enticed him away from his intended bride by means of those embraces which entitled the supplanter to claim—falsely as proved—to be with child by him.

Those embraces! Had any wife, had anyone, anywhere, ever been made truly happy by them? Edith had been apprised of "the facts of life" by her mother, a doctor's daughter. René had not, and the gap had been filled by schoolboy innuendo commented by priestly piety. She would not let memory dwell on their honeymoon. Out of the whole sorry business had come life continually springing, because the grain had fallen into the ground and died, as the highest Authority had attested it must. And here was arrived the first ear of the new harvest, this half-Jewish mite—Providence ever came up with the unexpected—harbinger of further scions springing on the stock of Rigg. Both sons had fallen into the ground, not to bear fruit but to perish. But four daughters survived.

Out of five—for a fifth birth had added her puny death to the tally of griefs of the young mother still unconsoled for Paul and long numb to pious assurances of having innocents in heaven. The parish priest had christened her Renata, for her father, having by his mediation reunited the family outwardly. But already René had taken to assuaging his wounded pride by the "charitable" conclusion that his wife was of unstable mind. On her decamping to Walter's, he had sublet the house; now he moved them to a cramped apartment and engaged a woman who soon made it appear she was instructed to tolerate none of her mistress' nonsense. She had escaped into lodgings, but had to appeal to René for moneys he supplied with a niggardliness he calculated would bring her to her duty. She had barely been able to feed the baby, who had caught fever…

Again, what use to dwell upon grief? At the instigation of a Madame Rigg furious at prospect of their name being dragged through the courts—for Edith had found a coterie of suffragettes to sustain and advise her—the usual interposition of priests effected a reconciliation which appeared sealed by pilgrimage to Lisieux and Veronica's subsequent birth. Scandal having been scarce averted, the most public outcome was the doubling of their impugned surname with that which Madame's English father had bestowed on the French Chevalier's daughter whose ugliness Agnes, relying on the one sepia photograph of arrière-grandmère in René's album, affirmed to have been the decisive factor in her father's willingness to marry her off to a countryman of the Iron Duke minded to renounce his nation's heresies. As had Edward Lumley—and his retort to his Yorkshire kin's charge that he had "turned his coat" was a high-point of the Lumley-Rigg narrative:

"I have but turned it back to the cut of our ancestors!" They had cut him off nonetheless.

Some suspected the Riggs of a desire to dress themselves in polysyllabic distinction; nor had she, Edith admitted to herself, been insensible to this motive, for however handy a name for a fashion-firm, plain Rigg had its ridiculous side, on which, she knew, her children's schoolfellows fixed—to have, as it turned out, their malice further stimulated; the addition of Lumley would but give rise to "Clumsy" as epithet to that "Pig" under which they suffered!

Veronica had thus been the first to be born Lumley-Rigg, and despite the new start to which all this attested, Edith's resolution had been severely tried when a few months after she knew herself again with child. Another daughter to dissatisfy the father, another mouth —this one so difficult to feed that the mother became absorbed in the struggle night and day to save Winifreda from Renata's fate. After that, and for a few years, relative peace had reigned, not unassisted by a visit paid to a practitioner in the prevention of pregnancy. External peace only; she shuddered still in recollection of the clash between revulsion and shame at the mechanics of contraception and the judgment that it was her only defence against unwanted and unwarranted impregnation. Ultimately she had tired of a bad conscience and the shifts to conceal it from him; she still wondered at his being so easily deceived by her feigning a sudden faintness, or "remembering" having eaten that morning, in order to avoid following him to the Communion rail in the state of mortal sin. For a time she had insisted they sleep apart except for the few nights when, basing herself on new and scarce-tested knowledge, she believed herself to be infertile. By the time she must face her eighth pregnancy it was René who had decamped and installed himself at his mother's, from there managing his anger with resignation and a daily walk to Mass at Farm Street; on Sundays conducting the still outraged Mater by taxi-cab to High Mass at Westminster Cathedral, to the evolving fabric of which she had contributed handsomely.

Again Edith re-lived her desperation at the onset of this last pregnancy, which had rendered her ill and desperate enough that she longed to be rid of it; this she in Confession admitted to their parish-priest, who was adamant: the taking of unborn life not only was a crime in the eyes of the law, but so grave a sin as to incur automatic excommunication. Ironic that the child should be born already *in extremis*; doubly ironic that it should be at last the son so desired by the father!

He had sent lilies, had followed with her the third white casket to the Catholic reaches of Kensal Green; then having partaken of sherry and biscuits in the flat in Bayswater, husband and wife had taken of each other a formal farewell, to bear their grief and their grievances apart, unknowing worse was to come.

PART II
Wartime

I

(1940)

MAGDALEN Lomax, born Rigg, sat upright opposite her lawful husband, as she habitually thought of him. Between them a breadth of pale oak, with a grain like shot silk, was demarcated centrally by a ring-vase her hands had potted. It held the late summer's stray flowerets of marguerite and pink, plucked by those hands from the garden that stretched eastward beyond the low windows to where a wan light was beginning to suffuse the mist.

"More coffee, Hilary?"

"Thank you, my dear. Shall I make more toast?"

"Only if you wish it, my love. I have had sufficient."

She rose to turn to the serving hatch where a portentous chromed pot, plugged into an electric socket, emitted the gulping sounds that led them to refer to it as "Belcher," after the cartoonist: one of the quiet whims that sustained their shared routine; so too had they named their sleek dachshund "Jelly" for his wobbling walk, which being short for "Jellicoe," after the Admiral, invoked a defiant patriotism to redeem his German breed; they disdained those heartless owners jettisoning dogs up and down the land on this pretext.

The sun's rays were advancing to penetrate the room; already they illuminated the disused limestone quarry set into the eastern flank of Lone Hill, protecting the house within its hollow from northerly blasts. "The Quarry" they had named this house, having chosen with care the spot where would evolve their sedate existence. His daily round: begun with raking the ashes before his bath and proceeding, according to season and the barometer, through wood-chopping, walking the dog, gardening, to dressing first their evening salad, then himself for dinner, and so till locking-up time; between times lending himself to such enterprises as should approve themselves to the vicar of Long Moreton's Norman-towered church and an oligarchy of farmers headed by him who, having inherited the mansion and park over and beyond Lone Hill, they still called the Squire.

And hers: seeing to the housekeeping, preparing meals for the two of them and occasional guests; beyond that, sketching, painting in oils at the easel set up in a spare bedroom, sitting to her sewing-machine to hem the tablecloths she embroidered for gifts, writing letters—and before all gardening. Initially she had thrown her energies into landscaping the quarry, ordering in quantities of limestone such as might formerly have been extracted from it, to create terraces, walls, a rockery, a fishpond. Then, having formed an alliance with a nurseryman, she planted out shrubs and flowers. Hilary's responsibilities were the vegetables, the fruit and the grass: that on the hillocks and in hollows that required scything, and the broad stretch of lawn that was mown, rolled, trimmed and sprinkled to a state suitable for his putting-practice; in his native Scotland he had won trophies for golf and intended to take it up again, once this War-business was over. That was how they had planned it: the agreeable, rational routine into which children born to them might in time be accommodated.

The dining-room and its furnishings were contrived, as was the rest of the house, to combine the best of old and new—like the Good Steward of the Gospel, as, from their differing confessional backgrounds, they agreed in remarking. The kitchen range provided hot water to bathroom, kitchen, laundry and a downstairs lavatory, as well as for a radiator in this pleasant dining room. A second electric point allowed the master of the house each morning to plug in the toaster's long flex and as regularly unplug it before returning it—crumbs brushed out, chromed exterior polished, flex wound round—to its place to one side of the serving-hatch. During breakfast it stood before him and he watched attentively for the moment to open down first one and then the other of its side flaps and extract from each a square of uniformly browned toast, exposing filaments that glowed red until he pressed the switch that caused them visibly to cool.

Today as every day, he closed the flaps, cut the squares cornerwise, placed the resulting triangles in the chrome-plated toast-rack. Domestic gadgets had arrived from America to replace the almost vanished servants, and The Quarry boasted a gamut of them. Most had been wedding-presents, as indeed was the house itself the gift of his family, delighted that poor Hilary was giving himself another chance and had attracted this second bride, admittedly from circles beyond their ken, but her good breeding and handsome presence evoked respect. They had hopes she would prove "the making of" a disappointed scion, lending resourcefulness where he was lacking. And importantly, though not in her first youth, she was near a decade younger than he; their clan, honourable in the lowlands, could again expect from this member a progeny hitherto so unhappily abrogated.

So his sisters had built them their hillside house, secluded yet close to habitation, at a remove from both their families, yet respectable connections of Deedie's lived over the county boundary; Hilary had accepted this as reason enough to settle far from the Lomax seat. Already, after a traditionally dour childhood, he had been cut adrift in the enterprising south, to be prepared for a role in the family business. Long Moreton was convenient by road for Reading and even Oxford, where Magda was planning to resume art-classes at the Ruskin School and to which Hilary too retained some link, having there stood the course to obtain an undistinguished degree in History. Of the need to earn a living he had been relieved at the instance of his united family after it appeared that the carefully nurtured import trade from which their substance proceeded stood to suffer at his willing but incapable hands. Once and once only, he had been entrusted with a voyage to China, trophies whereof in the form of jade green and rose platters and bowls stood on the room's tiled sills, holding lavender and petals from the summer past.

Apart from the belching coffee-pot, the only sounds in the room proceeded from Jellicoe stirring beneath the table and sighing as he replaced a patiently alert muzzle on paws extended. Then a bee's humming beyond the morn-lit east window intimated that Sunday had fairly begun. On weekdays they rose earlier, responding to Hilary's upbringing rather than to any very pressing need. He now finished his last corner of marmaladed toast, drank off the last of his coffee, wiped his mouth on the damask napkin and, rolling it prior to replacing it in its horn ring, remarked:

"The news being what it is, I take it we may expect your sister to arrive from London very shortly."

"I am afraid so: probably this coming week, as her letter of Friday envisages. At least that is preferable to having unknown persons billeted upon us."

"By far preferable."

"We must hope having the child here will not turn things too topsy-turvy! Then there is the unexpected factor of Veronica's pregnancy."

"A child may provide interest for you, my dear—indeed, for us, albeit I am less accustomed to children than you have been..."

He glanced at her, mute in the shared consciousness that she had not known pregnancy; of their being, after nearly six years of marriage, childless: a lack for a woman, even one so little given to sentimentality as his second wife. Yet he sensed, and sensed she sensed, that for neither of them was it the most important thing, or rather perhaps not the right thing. Both operated within a narrow predictability. A child, as he knew with sorrow, could entrain catastrophe. Then that bodily commerce: a necessity, even a duty, but distasteful—he felt and felt she felt.

"It will be good for the child and for your sister," he said, "Their lives, as I understand, being somewhat confining. A spell of country air does nobody any harm."

"True, my love; however, if the situation in London continues beyond, say, October—though it is hard to believe matters are so bad as is alleged—then helping them to suitable accommodation in time for Veronica's confinement will be best for all concerned. You will remember to have a word with the Vicar about those new houses at the bottom of the hill? I understand they are to be finished, even though further building is suspended."

"I hope to speak with him today after Service. But I beg you, my dear, not to make yourself uneasy on my account. After all, the little girl is old enough to be no great trouble."

"Elaine is five. She struck me as a rather moody child, more like her father than like Veronica, I would say; Jews are so temperamental—impulsive, you know. Though of course not only Jews," she added, aware that impulse smouldered too beneath her own self-imposed discretion and good sense. As she knew, it was this underlying warmth had drawn to her this disillusioned, sad Scot, and reciprocally, she had been drawn to his aloof, considerate breeding and, "I must have him," she had told herself, after he had singled her out where she towered as tall as he above the chatterers at one of those select gatherings noted by her family. Of his history she had known enough to be struck by its similarity to that of her unknown maternal grandfather, but could discount that having any relevance to her; by the 'nineteen-thirties avant-garde British society was tolerating divorce—at least in all ranks below royalty—as exotic even if not quite respectable.

Now she too rolled her napkin and placed it in its ring before rising and pushing in her chair. They stood a moment, his grizzled and balding pate level with the light brown "permanent" waves that descended almost to the collar of her severely checked shirt. She said, "I shall take the car as usual and return about midday," then hastened into the kitchen to don a bibbed apron and receive the breakfast things as he passed them through the hatch; today they would do their own washing-up, leaving only the dinner dishes for Mrs. Cox, their "char," next morning.

Some ten minutes later Magda left Hilary putting away the silver in the wide drawer below the hatch, laying out forks and spoons in sets on the baize so that any defections from their ranks should appear: thus had been detected a teaspoon she had thrown out with the rubbish—a delinquency less only than her having on their honeymoon left her engagement-ring with its three substantial diamonds in a train lavatory which Hilary, fortunately, had been the next person to use. His reproaches had been conveyed impeccably and beyond that he saw nothing in the incident. She did and, duly penitent, set herself to watch her ways.

Now she said, "Goodbye, my love," and each kissed a cheek. Finally she took the car-key from its hook beside the telephone in the hall and set out along the driveway at the far end of which their Morris Eight shared its ample garage with two outsize bicycles, a wheelbarrow and other garden implements, a stack of logs for the drawing-room fire and a broad shelf strawed for the incipient apple-harvest.

Driving into Reading for ten-o'clock Mass, she reflected that resuming Communion would mean depriving them of their pleasant Sunday breakfast. Unless she went to the early Mass and returned in time—still fasting, however cold and dark the morning! Why not leave things as they stood? Nothing prevented her from continuing their Sunday-morning routine as of today—except that if she put that to Father Dennis, the Oxford Jesuit to whom she had turned for counsel, she knew what he would say: that the main point was not even Communion, but the state of soul to receive it—to receive God himself and his salvation! Did she believe that? She still did seem to, and her drowning grasp at the Faith had brought her back to living. Not that she was worthy, any more than was anyone of themselves, but God would aid the desire He implanted: to be freed from mortal sin, from death of the soul. He would give strength for the sacrifice... Behind this train of thought hovered that maternal grandmother, gently devout in contrast to the autocratically pious paternal counterpart.

Edith Hislop—as she had been known—had left the man to whom the world assumed her married, whose children she had borne and reared: fateful decision that had entrained his attempted suicide, their impoverishment and so much besides, not least their Catholicism, and that, together with her mother's quest for respectability, was responsible for her parents' unhappy marriage and so all their births and outcomes: tale of mainly misery culminating in Leo's early death, in the marriages, irregular in their different ways, of herself and Veronica, in Agnes' bitter choice for what they called "free love," in the spinsterhood one could foresee for Freda...

After all, was it so differently from Agnes that she, Magdalen, had attempted to free herself of this entail, only to descend into a blackness from which the Jesuit had been instrumental in returning her to the world of sanity! If she had taken refuge in marriage, somewhat as her mother had, and lived a subterfuge somewhat as had her grandmother: the parallels were not exact. She had been drawn to Hilary as more than a hoped-for escape—and what a delusion on her mother's part that had been! She was still prepared to love, honour and care for him she had taken as her husband, yes, until death them should part, provided he too was willing...Hilary would be, she felt already sure. And God alone knew if that would not make theirs a true marriage in some sense beyond the reach of even the Church's jurisdiction. Of course, his first wife might die... She had been over that ground too with Father Dennis: to dwell on it would be to give occasion to sin; she must hope only for God's will. Besides, by the time that came about she would most probably be beyond childbearing age, even if... Well, they had given that a chance: given God the chance to "write with crooked pens" those too-human lines that never were entirely straight. And write what? Further bastards into her father's Catholic lineage? No, that was an unworthy notion: had not Our Lord Himself condescended to have dubious ancestry "after the flesh": Tamar, Bathsheba—even King David, and probably others in that Genealogy provided by St Matthew! Vee's children, though, were lawful according to the Church—even the one arrived too soon after that Church's solemnization; they might suffice for the continuance for which their father, so tragically thwarted of male descent, still prayed. Strange if that should be through infusion of Israelite blood but as Father Dennis liked to observe, the ways of the Lord so often were strange to our notions!

By the time Magda returned nearly two hours later, Hilary had put the shoulder of mutton she had left ready in the roasting-pan into the range's main oven and sliced the last of the broad beans from his kitchen garden. She strained the coffee remaining in Belcher into the saucepan which still held milk from their breakfast; this she now set to warm on the Baby Belling they had installed to supplement the range. She chopped the onions, potatoes and carrots of his growing for a *macédoine* and raised them to the boil with the beans before turning them with seasonings into a casserole for the oven. She rarely cooked desserts other than a wholesome spice-cake to accompany the fruit and cheese when there were visitors, but by way of a Sabbath concession to masculine weakness, a blancmange made by Mrs Cox waited in the refrigerator which occupied much of the pantry by the back door, to be served with damson jam of Hilary's own making.

Having poured out her coffee, she placed a plate over the remainder and left it on the top of the range for Hilary, then carried hers to the kitchen table and spread before her the copy of *The Tablet* she had bought after Mass. She was catching up with the Church again, something she had to explain to Hilary…

Poor Hilary, he had not realized what he was taking on with her! Nor, she was inclined to add, had she; but no, she could—should—have realized. She did not fear he would leave her; they fitted together too well, each making room for the other in this peaceful life they had evolved. She even hoped the more refined, more English aspects of her Church, as embodied in *The Tablet,* might lead him in time to convert, even though that seemed an unlikely change from his orderly Low Church habit—all unlike what her critical mind perceived as the "hot-house" air surrounding the self-conscious residual English Catholicism.

Soon she heard him enter at the front door and go straight to the drawing-room, then the clatter of the parish church's Sunday haul of brassy threepenny pieces and the odd sixpence being emptied into the japanned box he would lock away in his desk; he was a churchwarden. She poured the remaining coffee into a cup, placed two lumps of sugar, two petit-beurre biscuits and a spoon on the saucer and carried them with *The Tablet* into the long and by now sunny room she had endowed with an informal elegance, covering his sofa and chairs with William Morris tapestries of birds and flowers set amid lush blues and greens. His desk, over which he still stooped, was under one window. Hers was nearer the door and on it she had placed Pawa's gift to her— He had not called it a wedding-gift—of the altar Crucifix from the Rigg family's chapel: a relic of recusancy—like the father from whom René had received it—from the still-penal times, before the "Second Spring" had made secret chapels obsolete. Under the pedestal that supported the ebony cross, her father had, she knew, affixed a note of the Crucifix's history with a prayer "that it might bring a blessing to one or more members of my family." As she passed she cast at the hanged ivory figure a silent appeal that that prayer might assist her now, in this after-church time she had chosen advisedly.

"Coffee, my love?"

She placed cup and saucer on a walnut table beside one of the deep armchairs, then herself in the chair opposite, stretching out silk-clad legs and crossing feet so long and slim they required a biennial excursion to London to be shod.

"Dinner will be ready in an hour. Meantime there is something I have to speak to you about."

"Luncheon" was what his upbringing had taught him to call it, and she had adopted it for weekdays in place of her family's more familiar "lunch"; she approved correctitude in speech. As in return, he had adopted "dinner" for Sunday's midday meal, continuing her English habit of joint, vegetables and pudding.

"Very well, my dear."

He had turned round with his usual gravity of manner, only an eyebrow questioningly raised, before seating himself where she indicated; he probably thought it had to do with her sister's arrival—or did he half guess?

"Hilary, you recall how a year ago—I was coming out of the breakdown—how Father Dennis helped me—and has been helping me since."

"I do, my dear, though I would judge the specialist and the sanatorium helped you at least as much."

"I don't mean to deny it, Hilary. With the crisis—the depression—the time in the sanatorium under Professor Cunningham was of inestimable help and I don't know how I would have come out of that black period if you had not been so understanding and so generous, for I was incapable even of thinking what might help me; I was quite—but never mind that now! Thank God I have come out of it and I trust the stronger so that it need never happen again. And I do thank you, my love, for that and for everything you have been and are to me. Only now I have to ask you—to cast myself on your further understanding and generosity."

Though she paused he said nothing and she resumed,

"No, the Jesuits could not do that for me—all the daily care, the tonics and sleeping-draughts, the rest, the gradual engagement in occupations, when I began to draw again and to embroider... And Professor Cunningham let me talk—about so much that was distressing. Even about Leo... Only there were things you couldn't expect him to understand, that only a priest could, or at least a Catholic: I mean what made my childhood and my family—as it was; how I tried to deal with it, to get away from it, why I wrote the book and then the guilt of that..."

"Yes, I should have stopped you from publishing... I realized you needed to get it off your chest..."

"As I did. But I did not need to guy my father and publish his failings to the world! At the time I was hell-bent on doing just that; I doubt that you could have stopped me. And that I can see it now, that I can talk to you like this, is one of the things Father Dennis has done for me."

"What else has he done for you?"

What else! Even to Hilary she could not speak of the wound left by the suicide of a brother to whom she had been close, the closest of his family; they had grown up together, parted by school, enduring so much… She had been the last to see him alive and he had made her promise secrecy about his great fear—the fear she believed had unhinged him more even than that cruel last letter from his fiancée, though perhaps they were not unconnected: the fear he had gleaned from the R.A.F. doctor, that he was suffering not from pleurisy but from a tuberculosis all too probably contracted in India, and it would mean the giving up of the service he loved, the scholarship he had been awarded to a Cambridge college, his hopes of marriage, of health and ultimately—how ultimately would be unknown—of life itself.

Involuntarily she touched the R.A.F. wings he had given her. Every morning she pinned the badge under her throat as constant reminder of him, and now of hope to be reunited in the hereafter: the hope the Jesuit had given her, purging the anger, beyond even the grief and the guilt the specialist had diagnosed behind her breakdown. To a priest you could reveal what no-one else—not even a doctor—could be told, and still not break confidence; a merciful God had provided for that, setting His seal upon the priest: the so-called Seal of Confession. Leo would have understood that—did understand it where he now was!

"What else?" Her thoughts had flown, so that she seemed to echo Hilary. "So much that has changed my perspective on life. In a sense, of course, I knew it before, about acceptance of one's cross, about sacrifice. But I hadn't applied it to things like depression and—and sin, how we have to keep picking ourselves up and seeking to walk in the light, though not necessarily finding—anyway feeling—much of it, but knowing—having faith that if we do our best with what lies to hand, God will lead us in ways that are His, not ours. So—I did what I by then could to put right the wrong to my father, calling in the unsold copies, begging or buying them back from family and friends, apologising, having him visit here… All that has healed much."

They had both looked involuntarily toward the bookcase, behind a glass pane of which could be discerned the spine of her novel, in white letters on black: "*Daughter to Dagobert*, by Magdalen Lomax." She had been so proud of its acceptance by a publisher, so sure she was embarked on a career as a novelist. That had been when they were living in a flat near to Deedie while this house was being built. She had not expected her father to see the book, having been largely estranged from him even before her registry-office marriage. But news of it had somehow reached him; he had posted to her a copy, having on its title page written, "Honour thy father and thy mother," and signed it "Dagobert." She had tried to laugh it off as a piece of typical religiosity, but with every thought of her precious brainchild, that sentence, in his spiky hand, as it were visibly confronted her. And reminded her it was not the Fourth Commandment alone she had transgressed. There was also the Fifth.

Over ensuing months she had struggled against these thoughts with increasing desperation, as though against weeds that grew relentlessly, entrapping her in murky depths. Except a drowning person had an end to their struggle, but this agony would never abate unless... With horror she began to understand what drove people to suicide: her mother's father, Leo... Then Hilary, aware she was unwell—He had thought it might be a sign of pregnancy—had inquired, and brokenly, amid strangling sobs, she told him one of the sources of her chagrin; the others she must not, or could as yet hardly admit to herself, far less to him. Having inquired what she wished done, he made no problem about paying off the publisher and reimbursing friends or family members for copies they had purchased; only Agnes refused to return hers. Pawa's copy she kept as a reminder of several things.

A penitent letter informing him of what she had done re-established relations between René and this daughter who most resembled him in his interests as well as in a certain penetrative power of intellect that, adequately cultivated in either, might have released genius. But though the pressure was alleviated, the strain had been intense and by now she found herself unable to elude the question of that other Commandment. The burden continued; she slept poorly and found herself attending to her daytime duties, as she later described it, as through a grey veil, all pleasure in their so carefully planned surroundings and routine eroded in what she thought of as just retribution from God who was not mocked.

Through her spontaneous reverie she heard Hilary saying, "Yes, your father has behaved very honourably and it was a pleasure to have him here and to get to know him better, even if he does have some rum ways! Though I realize he is prevented from fully regarding me as a son-in-law."

"I know, Hilary, and I am sorry," she responded mechanically, "You deserved better of us and..."

He noted that "us," but she had tailed off, still remembering. How on a morning of unexpected cold she had gone to light a Primus stove to warm the kitchen and, being no doubt still groggy from her sleeping-pill, had splashed paraffin which ignited, flaring up in her face. With singed hair, eyebrowless, eyes too lost in the swelling and blackening, and in a fair state of shock, she had been wrapped in a blanket by him and driven straight to the Reading Royal Infirmary. Later she would think her subconscious, searching for a way out, might have caused her carelessness with the stove: that this too was the working of Providence, for it spelled the last defeat. So prostrated that she was almost unable to rise from her bed, she was transferred to a private sanatorium near Oxford where, having one day requested a priest, she was visited by Father Dennis, without whose ministrations she believed she would not have recovered: not mentally. Discharged, she took to visiting him periodically.

Hilary, not in the habit of betraying emotion, had concealed any alarm he felt at this turn of events. Unassuming himself, he had been surprised by the admiration of this elegant, sophisticated woman, who had stood out of the crowd, goddess-like; for whereas thin Veronica stooped to diminish her tallness and Freda fretted at hers, Magda's greater height was borne unwaveringly, almost as though with pitying condescension to the lowly. Here seemed to be offered a second chance to him whose life had been blighted by double tragedy, his first wife having become insane after their only son, in a nursing-home for a tonsillectomy, had bled to death unnoticed in his private room. Could tragedy be standing by to mock his hopes again?

With relief he had seen her returning to normality, but returning also to her Church—her family's Church as he had thought of it, not really viewing her as religious, rather as one of the bright young moderns who had left all that behind and who indeed could be expected to require some ballast of faith as life moved on for them, but would hardly envisage anything more weighty than the national creed that sufficed for such as himself. Suddenly the exotic, suspect Church of Rome had moved ineluctably in as the cure for her soul and hope of a life worthy of the name.

Dimly he began to apprehend the implications for himself; and dimly he detected in himself the surprising response that he could face them even with relief, even as medicine for his own soul. He began to feel that in seeking that divorce he had dishonestly calculated on being able to leave the past behind, something one could never do. His first wife had not failed him, had not meant to fail at all; she had been overborne by human weakness confronting a shattering disaster, yet still was and ever would be the mother of their child and all undeserving to be repudiated as no wife of his. And now the past was catching up with him, as with Magdalen. Only poor mad Dorothy, genteelly mewed in Dumfriesshire, had retained innocence.

So he was unsurprised when Magda continued:

"Hilary, you will understand, will you not, that I have told Father Dennis about your other—your divorce."

"Yes."

"And you will realize how he—how the Church views it."

"I think I do, my dear."

"So—I am sorry, Hilary, and I know the Church of England is not as clear-cut about this as is the Catholic Church, but married to you—and as things stand" (He understood she meant with his first wife living.) "In short, I cannot return to my Church, or not in good standing, not as a communicant member, so long as we—that is, unless we can live, as they say, 'as brother and sister.'"

"I know. I was prepared for that. So be it!"

"Hilary! You—you are so—so like your generous self, and I cannot tell you how profoundly grateful I am to you for making this easy for me, as perhaps very few men would do. My own father—but you know about all that... Father Dennis tells me not to think of it—negatively—but rather as the working out of both our—our salvations. Yet I cannot help feeling I have let you down, deceived you..."

"My dear, you have given me much in the way of companionship, and I think you know I do not set great store by—such things. Not even when I was young; our world was very different!"

"I know you were still hoping—we were hoping for a child."

"My dear, it seems we are not meant to have a child, and that I believe we have felt obscurely. At least I can speak for myself, that I have felt unsure of my ability now—perhaps ever—to father a child, to be a father to it, I mean... I have even thought God took Malcolm before I could fail him. And now I am set in my ways... But as a brother I have experience and can perhaps supply something of what you too have lost."

He glanced at the Royal Air-Force wings pinned to her shirt. He could not, they both knew. She remained rarely speechless, he rarely eloquent as he went on:

"Magda, my dear, I do not know whether your Church is right entirely or who is, but this shall be right for us. The human race will go on without children of ours; there will not be lacking those with the will to procreate."

"That is what I think, Hilary. Bodily intercourse, though right, even necessary for most marriages, is not essential to love between a man and a woman of—of refined feeling. Some married saints have…" She tailed off, confused; the point should have been to affirm their non-marriage. She ended,

"But I do love you and want to live out my life with you—'until death us do part.'"

There was a pause, then,

"I am grateful to you, my dear. Will you wish to—that we sleep in separate rooms?"

"I have thought about that, my love" (Consciously she reverted to her habitual appellation for him) "and it is not necessary unless you wish it. We can leave things as they are."

She did not add that she had obtained Father Dennis' approval for this after explaining their existing sleeping arrangements, on their extra-long beds at opposite ends of their long bedroom. The pretext for this had been her bad sleeping habit, but both had understood that the other welcomed it. Leaving that alone encouraged her doubtful sense that after all this in some way was meant to be, that her illness and accident, even her sin, were the crooked ways through which Providence yet guided one. That in entering his life and accepting his home she had not, after all, strayed onto a false path…

Rising, they turned as one to seal their pact with an embrace. Ironic that this should arouse slight bodily sensations transmitted between them and mutually suppressed, as he returned to his desk, she to the kitchen.

II

"'Bye, Arthur!"

"*Good*bye, young fella! Watch out for Jerry!"

"Do we ever do anything else?"

Ron, cheered by the matey repartee which in these times served to bring all close to all—an elderly Ulsterman like the senior clerk, and now senior Warden, Art Bell, to a Jewish young hopeful like himself—left the cellar of the East London municipal building which functioned as Air Raid Precautions, or "A.R.P.," station by virtue of a wireless, a bank of telephones—Why it was called a "bank" Ron had no idea—and a row of pegs from which were suspended a couple of cardboard boxes containing gas-masks and a number of what, in the jargon of the Last War, were known derisorily as "tin hats." His own gas-mask was slung in its box over his overcoat; regulations said it must be carried at all times. Helmets, though, did not need to accompany one off duty; Ron's balding pate was protected from the early-morning airs of London by the felt trilby that he remembered to brush each weekend, just as he polished his shoes and had his collars laundered, signalling middle-class respectability and a break with the generation of his father: Mr Alderman Keller had never discarded that emblem of the followers of Keir Hardie, the working-man's cloth cap.

Trilby wearing could indeed be looked on as a mark of Londoners' determined keeping-up of a morale that would have deserted Ron, and many another, without the stiffness it signified of the communal "upper lip." So relentless the fiery assaults on their city since the first ferocity unleashed a month ago, they had all but grown used to it! He had missed that first night when the docks had blazed and the poor inhabitants of dockland drifted homeless, possessionless, like lost souls through the crazed streets of an eerily flickering, roaring hell: had missed, that was—and thank God!—being on the scene, for surely no-one within fifty miles could have missed it unless deaf and blind! Vron and he had gazed that night on the hectic eastern flush that mimicked the sun's only less fiery decline, and had known that she must leave with the children—the born and the unborn—and take refuge with her sister: fortunate that she had a relative in the country; so many were fleeing London to lodge with strangers or wherever they could find a roof over their heads! His recent qualifications and promotion, from mere clerk to Buildings Inspector, had exempted him from military service—so far, and again thank God—and having seen them off, he had reported for Civil Defence.

He hadn't been obliged to, but thought not to would be bad from someone in his position; besides, it gave him a pleasing sense of *counting*, and the responsibilities involved—mainly to co-ordinate fire and rescue services—carried with them the camaraderie of sharing in an honourable mission seasoned by the thrill of actual danger. He walked with his brisk, bouncing step towards the nearest tube entrance; at six of a late October morning there was just daylight enough in streets where the lamps remained unlit on their posts in the attempt to conceal from "Jerry" the details and configuration of the great metropolis into which it was his daily and nightly mission to sow destruction.

Concrete steps plunged Ron into ever greater gloom until, turning a corner, he was briefly dazzled by the yellowish lighting, at once drab and cheerful—like themselves, he reflected—of the underground that was Londoners' intimate possession and refuge, held unfathomable by the foreign foe. At the barrier a pair of squat, lisle-clad legs in flat, officious shoes caused him briefly to raise his eyes past the uniform skirt and bulging jacket, to wave his season-ticket below the stare, between the lipstick and the peroxided frizz: a real Londoner that, "cheap and cheerful" and even less to be trifled with than her male counterparts now in the Forces. Ron admired the assurance of these women, some of them literally "wearing the trousers," running the trains and buses—well, not quite literally running them, but who knew how far things might go? And of course in factories, turning out armaments as fast as they could to catch up with the Germans, out of all those aluminium pots they had turned in last year on Winnie's appeal: saucepans into Spitfires, ploughshares into swords. Wiseacres like Ben claimed it could not be done, was nothing but a morale-raising stunt, like the ack-ack, as was said. Well, something had worked for these women: perhaps just the prospect of the time of their lives bossing everyone! He rattled on down more echoing stairs, noting the station pretty empty at this hour, bar a few who like himself might have been on A.R.P. or fire-watching duty. No doubt it had been full enough until the prolonged blast on the sirens sounded the All Clear an hour or so ago. As he emerged onto his platform, he noted a few recumbent figures still having their sleep-out under the platform's curving wall; perhaps they had nowhere to go, perhaps were drunk. At least better than in the last War, when people had sheltered under railway arches, and were doing it again, though the Government warned it was unsafe and some had been killed… But neither had all tube-stations proved safe against modern weaponry, especially the land-mines on their parachutes… Ron shivered and, happening to glance at the track, wondered which would be worse, death under one of the endless stream of trains—become the terminus of choice for lives wrecked in London—or to be surprised by that new horror dropping in on you upon silken wings… Or how did either compare with ending it in the Thames—agelong conduit for those bereft of motive for living? Of course, just to jump onto the track would be cleaner than in front of a train and far quicker than drowning: to be electrocuted on that bright rail marching high on its white porcelain sleepers, carrying the power; they said you could stand on it with two feet and be safe, like the sparrows did at stations overground. They had even provided space under the rails so if you fell or were pushed you might lie and be safe even with a train passing over you—so long as you didn't touch that central rail.

His train was arriving: red caterpillar conformed to the curve of walls that resounded to its din. Above its screeching halt a female voice bellowed to "Mahnd the gep pliz." There was choice of vacant seats at this hour, no need to scramble as, obedient to another inarticulate shout, the doors clunked shut and the train jerked into motion. Tired though Ron was, he must not sleep, not until after King's Cross. To keep his eyes from closing he examined the mesh stuck all over the train's windows, except for a small lozenge-shape in the centre of each through which to read the names of stations as the train drew into them. And notices, alternately threatening with a fine those who might find this inadequate and cajoling them with a cartoon man making to remove the mesh and being reproved in a little jingle:

"I trust you'll pardon my correction,
That stuff is there for your protection!"

That was very English; you could bet the Germans didn't have notices like that: just "*Verboten*!" slapped over everything.

He had been made to study German in school, had picked some up quite easily, anyway easier than French, on account of the Yiddish still mixed into the speech of his elders. And he had been to Germany twice with Jess Lewis, and had appreciated the cleanliness and order when compared with the Spain and France they had previously visited. Until they went walking in the Schwarzwald, as was become fashionable with English youth as with Germans of all ages. With some *Jugend* from their hostel, attempts at *Kamaraderei* had gone well enough until, a suspicion clouding it,

"Sind Sie *Juden*?" one pink Teuton had asked.

Ron experienced again the pang of fear and something like shame mixed with anger—at himself, for what was he ashamed of?—as the bolder Jess confirmed their race. Already the Germans were drawing back, themselves seeming smitten with fear as of an undefined evil, physically cowering away without further speech. Jess, ever insouciant, had laughed it off with mimicry of the "Krauts'" appalled stares, but Ron found no poultice for a wound which would fester, exacerbated by events about to unfold, in his unprotected consciousness. For now, his reaction was to rebel: pluck out this mark of Cain that disabled one from putting on an easy British superiority, from ownership of the noble European culture that held out all that was worthy of pursuit, and for which these arrogant Huns substituted their spurious *Kulturkampf*—so he believed they called it. He read enough of H. G. Wells—a complete set of whose works he had built up monthly from an offer in *The Daily Herald*—to decide Wells was

right: Jews had to assimilate, cast off their conditioning to difference—as he had done. Was that why he had not revisited that Robert Street where he had grown up—not even to see how his
childhood surroundings had fared in the firestorm centred so close
to it? With all that had been happening, he hadn't had time; one day
he would.

At King's Cross he descended yet further, to the Northern Line,
deepest—therefore safest—of the city's buried arteries. There the
same routine was enacted with the same sounds, mechanical and
human. You could tell they enjoyed it, these women allowed to play
at being men! And it did liven things up—and things needed it! Last
night had been unusually dull: several alerts but no bombs, so that
one almost missed the excitement; that must all have belonged to the
fighter-pilots, out there preventing the Jerry bombers and their
escorts from getting through.

"God help them!" thought Ron, something of an instinctual
devoutness combining with a shudder at the thought of the death
they faced nightly up there in the skies, imagining the crack, the
blaze, the mad spin out of control, one's burning flesh one's last sensation… He had to ward off the thought of it or it would torment his
nights, even replacing their previous stock torment: the image of
poor Sammy Goldstein, a distant connection of his mother's family,
who had run away from the front in 1916 and been shot as a deserter;
again he struggled not to see the poor Jew stumbling blindly among
the trenches and the roar and flash of cannon and shells, then falling… Or had he been arrested and court-martialled? Ron wasn't sure;
neither was he sure what *he* would have done, caught up in the same
inferno…

But was he not caught up in one now, like most Londoners? And
whatever he was, he was a Londoner born, and London these days
was the front, from where willy-nilly one sustained the raining of
metal from the skies and conflagration on the ground, staying at
one's post to direct the fire-crews to the blazing buildings and the
ambulance crews to the dead and wounded. Was that so very different from the situation of poor Sammy? It still seemed it. As for flying, Ron shuddered just thinking of it and freely acknowledged he
would be incapable of taking to the air, even without that death-
defying challenge, which was for supermen even among the stoical
natives—and you had to admire them, most of them, anyway,
because of course there were spivs and racketeers and blackshirts—
reds too, who thought to make use of so-called National Socialism to
destroy the British State. Well, he too believed in the Classless Soci-

ety, until all this drove all that into the background—though it might seem to have brought that Nirvana closer as people pitched in to help each other regardless. And not just working-class people, who had always supported each other by and large, and Jews in particular, but now the white-collar workers, people like Arthur Bell—Ron still could not realize himself as "white-collar"—were all pitching in, all pulling together, their hackles once raised by the impudent forays into what they had been taught to regard as their unassailable island patrimony: they were rising to it even eagerly, all naturally following their superiors and commanding officers, that caste bred to stand in the breach...

Like Leo, his unknown brother-in-law; his photograph on their bedroom wall suggested just that breeding in the curl of the lip below the bristling of the moustache. The late losses of airmen had wrung from Vron's mother that it was some solace she could not now be confronted with what would have in any case been his likely loss—but she surely knew that was wrong: Leo's senseless death could not compare with dying in your country's and civilization's just cause, as did those chaps, those supermen!

Again the plane span and burned threateningly on his vision and again he turned his thoughts hurriedly away, knowing himself a coward even compared with Leo, who after all had had a kind of courage; he, Ron, could not envisage throwing himself from a window—even though they said the young man had been out of his mind, but then they always did say that! He wondered what Leo would have thought of his sister marrying a Jew. All too likely not much—unless, perhaps, a Rothschild, or the son of some well-found industrialist, like that poor blighter from Dusseldorf Vron's Cousin Teresa had picked up with and was pregnant by when his father got wind of it and ordered him home. Through Magda, who maintained some contact with her aunt's family, they had learned how Teresa had attempted to communicate the birth of the child, a girl, but had failed to reach either son or father...

Yes, if Leo had lived, everything might have been different. Vron might have married that Andy or another of her brother's friends. For "Avron ben Avram," scion—he liked that word—of Jewish immigration to London's East End, it might be better that she was brotherless. But that he acknowledged ungenerous; it had been a terrible tragedy for them all.

His thoughts turned from the phantom Leo to actual warriors. Neither free-lancing nor "subbing" on a political paper being considered work of national importance, Jess expected to be posted to

Greece, which he seemed to look on mainly as an assignment offering scope for future travel-writing. That might be bravado; Jess was a big talker. Nonetheless, Ron could not but perceive something enviable in the lot of those who, if they won through, stood to gain so much that would enrich the lives they staked. Jess dwelt with his Irish wife in a state of perpetual confusion which seemed to suit them both and certainly enabled him to write: something Ron had done little of lately. They already had a girl and a boy, whom Jess would be leaving behind. Eileen seemed to face it all with equanimity; or rather it seemed her way not to face things but to get on in spite of them. Well, for himself some Providence—so Vron would say—seemed to have decreed otherwise, and for that he could be thankful.

Then there was the fastidious Kurt Baumgarten, a refugee from Leipzig whom they had met at the W.E.A. classes. All Kurt's relations had disappeared into the labour camps about which there were such ugly rumours: not that this inhibited Kurt from comparing everything English unfavourably with its counterpart in the Fatherland: a propensity which, in view of everything, had to be tolerated with British restraint and only the mildest remonstrance. Vron had made a point of introducing Kurt to Freda; they were hoping for something there, but if Kurt and he were to become related, it surely must await the end of the War, or at least their young friend's ascertaining of his family's fate. Kurt himself might not escape death—as indeed which of them would?—yet death in battle, in the light of day—even death in a city blitzed by night—was preferable to that nameless, faceless evil said to be thrusting its tentacles throughout subjugated Europe; Ron recoiled from envisaging what horror must be overtaking actual men, women, children: the families of Kurt and of the nameless lover of Teresa Lumley, Vron's wild cousin—who must be very different from the Lumley-Riggs!

Or if not from all of them, certainly from that prude Freda; he was less than sure he should encourage his new friend to pay court to this sister-in-law, with whom he had more than once clashed over the War in Spain, she insisting the Left had committed endless atrocities, whereas all right-minded people knew that the balance of atrocity lay all on the side of El Caudillo's thugs and their brutal suppression of the Spanish people's democratic uprising—just like Hitler's thugs who called themselves National Socialists to deceive fools and license bullies! Freda was in the former category, perversely opinionated and what he believed Freud had called a hysteric, or was it a hypochondriac? Anyway, always indulging her small indispositions! With Agnes, now, he saw eye-to-eye; a pity she made herself so unattractive. *She* would have kept a man using his talents, not allowed them to become mired in the endless claims of housekeeping and baby-care such as had caused first Vron and then him to abandon the W.E.A classes. Agnes was of course a good bit older than Vron—not so much older than himself…

Ron checked his straying thoughts from a disloyal, even unseemly direction. Of course Vron was right and their children would turn out the better—much better than kids growing up in a chaotic household like Jess and Eileen's; he could never stand to live like that. Though they seemed not to notice it: always cheery when you visited them, picking your way past the milk-bottles on the doorstep, the accumulating letters on the mat, the general clutter… And they seemed to agree remarkably well, Eileen being left-wing and easy-going—which was why she was such a slattern. He himself could have wished to share political zeal with his other half, but after all, Vron was pliant in the matter: no died-in-the-wool Tory like Freda and their mother—Magda too, probably, since she moved in those posh circles and was so well off. Vron seemed to be seeing reason about religion too; she seldom went to Church these days, just Christmas and Easter or with her mother if that became inevitable. And she kept herself pretty and well dressed, if a bit primly, finding times to seat herself on the upholstered stool before the triple mirror for what he called, teasing, her "little prinks." No, she was far and away the pick of them: unthinkable to compare her with Eileen or even Agnes, let alone her other sisters: a pretty frightening bunch if truth were told! Vron was the only womanly one among them—in that like the unassuming sister he had grown up with; you could see how they hit it off in spite of such different origins!

Thought of Jane led finally to Ben, square-bashing, as they called it, up in Yorkshire somewhere; he too would be awaiting posting overseas. Their firstborn, Mark, was over a year old and Ron had accepted to look after mother and child in his brother-in-law's absence and now that his own family were stowed in relative safety at Magda's. He supposed he would be up to the role; he seemed to be doing all right with Elaine, who Vron always said was so fond of him, and he did miss her coming running to be picked up when she heard his key in the door around six o'clock.

He groaned slightly, realizing things would never be the same as in the flat in Finsbury. Elaine would grow and heaven knew when they would have a home together again. Of course, it was a relief to be without the rent. Ever since their marriage they had found themselves regularly in arrears, needing at month's end to borrow and repay, and so it went on. This respite was enabling him to catch up; soon he might begin to put a bit by. With all the war-damage, they had been ready enough to pass him as a Buildings Inspector; there were advantages even to War, and life, provided one still had it, should be easier once it was over. And very necessary that would be, with Vron expecting again.

He had managed two visits since he had ordered their furniture—the giant wardrobe, the dressing table with its triple mirror, the lot—into store and seen her and Elaine off on the packed Green Line bus; Ron remembered it drawing out of Victoria coach-station as he blew kisses from among the packed throng and she waved from the window-seat she shared with the child, whose wondering face, pressed pale to the pane, had been his parting glimpse of them. His brother-in-law would meet them with the car, for which, as a lieutenant in the Home Guard, he had a petrol-allowance: funny, a gent like Hilary, with a car, being his brother-in-law! What would his father have thought of that, who from a stateless youth cast on the slums had founded his and his children's rise to respectability on sheer hard work and a dogged integrity: a perplexing model for his younger son and as a child Ron had felt more secure shadowing his London-born mother. She too was now dead—thank God, before all this!—and with his brother alienated by his marriage, Vron's family had to all intents become his, except only for his sister and brother-in-law and the child for whom he was trying to fill Ben's place...

It occurred to Ron that that rum cove, his other brother-in-law, might be feeling something of the same responsibility for Elaine, even though that was harder to imagine. From Vron's letters he gathered Hilary to be among those the onset of War had brought out of a narrowly private life into some more actively satisfying role—in his case as a lieutenant in the Home Guard—but she regularly complained of having to adjust to his pernickety ways and felt her handling of Elaine, in particular, to be under criticism from him and also Magda. Anticipation of this had caused her to stand out against being billeted on them last September, when Ron himself had caught the general panic—or as near panic as the imperial race permitted themselves. Which was just as well, as it had turned out; it had saved them closing down the flat, storing the furniture, only to start up again, then repeat the whole performance a year later...

For this now was the real thing and no mistake, and God alone knew how it would end! God again—who Vron seemed to have convinced herself would not allow evil to triumph—though if she had actually lived this past month of days, and especially nights, as he had, she might be feeling less sure! As it was, and mindful as they both were of stories such as Kurt's, and that Hitler's racial laws applied to half- and even quarter-Jews, Vron had made blonde Freda promise that in the event of an invasion she would take the child—no, children!—and pass them off as her own. Could they suppose the notorious S.S. would be taken in by that tale? Might it not be better to leave them with their mother? Veronica was dark-haired—like her own mother and the Celts in England's population—and grey-eyed, and Elaine's eyes were brown—not as dark as his, though... Would the coming child be fairer or darker? Ron shied away from these troubling musings before they led him to (He searched for the word)—a cliff-fall of despair he had not yet faced! It helped Vron to have some plan to fall back on and he had kept his doubts unspoken. For himself, he preferred to put his trust in the Bens, the Kurts, even the Jesses and all the little people who had evacuated Dunkirk and the heroes now returning—only probably not all of them—from their night's sortie into the skies.

Perplexing whether to be glad or sorry that there would soon be two children—perhaps the hoped-for son?—to save out of the (again Ron groped for a metaphor), the cauldron of this Blitz and what might issue from it. How was it, he asked himself again, that this precious new life, so rashly brought into being, seemed to insist on coming into a world under threat of such tyranny as Kurt had escaped from, alone of his family? How was it each continued to behave as though he—or she, which was rather more likely—and also their children would escape it? Was that why Hope was pictured as a child? Women seemed to insist on life being carried forward regardless—to what? "Cannon-fodder" seemed this century's answer; gas-fodder might be more appropriate to the Europe of his earliest awareness. Then at least the slaughter, vast as it was, had been mainly restricted to the combatants—Here he pictured fleetingly lines composed of Sammy Goldsteins and other ordinary people, like those about him carrying their gas-masks: like himself. Latterly Southampton's citizens too had tasted the Huns' fury—not that they had ceased for a single day to hurl their envious rage against London, that "flower of cities all," of which he, Ron, was proud to have been born a citizen...

Thus was one torn between fear and the insistent drive toward a future that might scarce, if at all, be realized. This it was had prevailed in that lull last winter when they had decided against leaving the flat: believing in Chamberlain, believing in anything that would deny the intimations that came lapping in on the airwaves. Then it had seemed that something of their earliest ardour had returned, half welcomed by him as aspiring to a Laurentian fulfilment reckless of consequences: by her as service to instinct and a future...

And now it was not so much panic as the atavistic scorn for "Johnny Foreigner" surfacing in plain Britons galvanized to a late frenzy of preparedness: strengthening sea-defences, rearing so-called pill-boxes on strategic eminences, arming and drilling volunteers and of course conscripting the young and able-bodied males, happily now—thanks to that insistent life-force—in sufficient supply again after the depredations of a quarter-century ago. Females too were volunteering for the Forces, as well as being drafted into nursing, civil defence and agricultural work to replace the vanished farm-hands and grow the food of which the nation stood in need as its sea-lanes were subjected to blockade. Vron, in unusual excitement, had told of "land-girls" seen around their countryside; one, a relation of her mother's, had visited and impressed with her tanned and blooming mien and even more her wearing of trousers: Vron was not sure she approved of this last, though Magda had beaten the land-girls to it, having adopted a pair of her husband's dungarees, origi-nally for their joint labours in the garden, but now it seemed she was seldom out of them. Vron was wondering whether to try them too, but before Ron could determine whether or not he approved—on the whole he rather thought he did—the discovery that she was pregnant had ended the question for the moment.

At this point in his musings the train arrived at Hampstead and he gave his attention to hustling through the dim-lit and by now crowded passages that led to the lift: fascinating contraption that penned one between steel lattices with a random company of silent strangers. The blackened, cable-lined walls of the shaft slid by almost noiselessly, then with a jolt and a second clashing of steel all were ejected into something approaching daylight and flowed onward—to encounter at the barrier another female filling out a uniform jacket—and, yes, trousers too: another peroxided crop crammed under a peaked hat...

Emerging from the station and walking in the direction of the Heath, he could see loom through the brightening air the weird grey shapes of barrage-balloons apparently adrift over London, in fact tethered by near-invisible cables. It was but a short step along Heath Street to his sister's flat on the first floor of a stately brick-built block: the "rag-trade" had been doing well until Ben's call-up had put it on hold, for what demand there was at the moment was mostly blouses for women in uniform and otherwise "utility" stuff. Old Uncle Joe,

Aunt Lil's husband, was keeping things ticking over, with Jane herself looking in from time to time; it was an easy ride up from Hampstead and she took young Mark; he received more casual handling than his own child; perhaps that was the difference between having a girl and a boy. Vron did so hope this next one would be a boy, and so did he, if only because otherwise there would be a call for another pregnancy and who knew if then… A working man had to draw the line. But a man wanted a son—especially a Jewish man, and one who had married "out." If they had only girls, his relatives would think of it as a judgment, particularly now both brother and sister had produced firstborn males…

That at least had gladdened his mother's last years, especially the birth of one Ashley Keller, named Avram after his deceased grandfather. Abe's widow had departed this world, as had her husband, suddenly in her sleep—a merciful death!—a few months after the arrival in it of her third grandchild, little Mark Grossman, whose voice Ron could hear as he unlocked his sister's front door, having given two rings on the bell to announce himself. Jane's life up here under the Heath was a far remove from her origins in the smoke-laden air that took its toll of the toiling denizens of London's East End. Nonetheless, reflected Ron, their mother's had been, if relatively short, a contented enough life within the close-knit society of neighbours with similar cares and similar joys—children and work supplying most of the cares, children and feasts most of the joys: he remembered with a pang of nostalgia the days of Succoth when the bleak streets simulated harvest with leaf- and fruit-draped arbours within which men—women too, in the interstices of their preparations within doors—put up a good show of taking their religious ease.

Jane came out of the kitchen followed by a toddling Mark. Ron greeted her with the peck on the cheek that was his family's farthest expression of affection, then dutifully swung his nephew high overhead—to which Mark responded gratifyingly with gurgles and cries of "'gain, 'gain!," so Ron repeated the treatment before self-consciously shouldering the boy into the kitchen. Jane had the kettle on the boil and having made tea proceeded to contrive an omelette out of their egg-ration plus some of the new egg-powder sent by Ben's sister in America. Nor was the dish innocent of some ends of bacon, which she had begun to allow in view of the shortages; she had overcome her scruples at this breach of the chief of the laws of *kashrut*, at all which her husband scoffed as a relic of totemism, and nor did Ron care, having abandoned all that even before he married. He only still balked at eating offal.

While they were all three breakfasting, the post dropped through the letterbox—That would be another uniformed woman—bringing Ron an expected letter from Vron. That she was well, she wrote, had been confirmed by the District Midwife but...

The rest of the sentence had Ron ejaculate through a mouthful of egg and toast, "Well, I'll be damned!" Mark sat up amid his playthings and stared doubtfully at his uncle. Jane laid down her own letter and asked, "What's up, Ron?"

"What's up, why... Well, I'm—jiggered! Would you believe it, Jane, she's—we're—they think she's carrying twins!"

His sister's open mouth firmed into a relieved smile. "Well, Ron, *mazeltov!*"—the occasion seeming to call for Hebrew expression. "What else does she say?"

"She's wondered for some time if it might be twins, as she seems extra large and feels so much more movement than last time, so she was feeling sure it must be a boy. Now she's not so sure, says of course it may be two more girls; but it does give us a double chance... Her sister and brother-in-law too were rather taken aback, but they'll be there to get her into Reading by car, because she can have it—them— in hospital; she thinks they're rather relieved about that as otherwise her sister was going to do most of the looking-after at home and she's not used... Well, actually Vron writes that as Magda's now a V.A.D. nurse at the hospital, she can be with her there too; they just have to get her there in time!"

He broke off to peruse the letter further, enabling his sister to ask, "How's she taking it, then?"

"She doesn't exactly say. She's concerned, of course, to have at least one boy, but she also seems—well, quite proud of herself! Women don't seem able to have enough of babies and I suppose now Elaine's no longer one... I've heard this argument with her mother, who says she finds them more interesting as they get older, but Vron says no, she likes 'em little babbies. I think she forgets how difficult she— we—found getting used to Elaine! Well, she'll have babbies enough to satisfy her now, I should hope! And she seems to have it all worked out: she'll stay on at her sister's for a while after she comes out, but then—this is the other piece of news—they think they've found her a house that's been just built before building was stopped. And she's arranged for Elaine to start at the village school after the Christmas break—It's time she did. And the teacher will bring her home, who lives near this new house. That's going to cost us a bit in rent, but no more than our flat in London, and it's a good thing: she wasn't having it easy with just the one child; they expect everything so regular and punctual, he does especially. I get on well enough with him when I'm there, but I shouldn't want to live with it."

Jane, bred to taciturnity in a household where in everyday matters the British-born wife, ruling with matriarchal hand and voice over her Abe and their sons, relegated the daughter to an adjutant role, heard her brother out, then spooned the last egg from Mark's plate into his mouth, which she wiped before lifting him down from his chair to seat himself contentedly among his playthings on the floor. She poured more tea for Ron and herself, and only then, as she cleared their dishes into the sink, observed,

"I suppose you know Bubba Scheindel, my namesake, was a twin?"

"Our Dad's mother? No, I didn't. Does that mean I'm—responsible? Well, I'll darn well need to be responsible now, with three young 'uns! We certainly shan't be able to afford any more!"

He whistled and added,

"I just hope one of 'em will be a boy—now that our brother has one: show he's not the only hope of the Kellers! Otherwise we know what they'll be saying—that it's a judgment on me for marrying out!"

"Does it matter—now that you've done that?"

"It shouldn't, as none of our children can be Jewish—but they're not likely to be—you know, logical! They'll moan that I wouldn't marry Esther with the egg-shop—who's got a boy first off, I hear!"

"Dad and Muttie had that all fixed up with her folks, as I heard!"

"That's right—thought they'd have me properly spliced with a Jewish matriarch, like Issy—or in this case a pair of 'em, the mother-in-law thrown into the bargain! Made to keep kosher and behave myself! But did you know, Janey, they actually woke me up that Sunday morning, to say they'd this wonderful match all arranged and to get up quick and come and meet the Widow Blumbach—that was the name—and her blooming daughter, because the egg-shop is hers already and there'll be more when the old girl snuffs it!"

"I can believe it. What did you say?"

"I said 'Not on your nellie! Go away! I'm trying to sleep!' And I turned over—face to the wall!"

Jane's short laugh acknowledged this version of the story she had heard interspersed with their mother's lamentations at her younger son's waywardness. Ron knew his sister sympathized with him over his marriage—perhaps wouldn't say so, out of loyalty to the community from which they sprang, but he and she, younger son and daughter of the family, had always had an understanding. Now she and Ben didn't even keep Pesach, no more than he did, not since Muttie died.

"Of course, I don't really care what Issy and Belle think, or if we have all girls," he conceded. "The important thing is it goes all right—the birth, I mean. Twins can be ticklish, can't they?"

Really he didn't know whether to be appalled at this turn of fortune or proud of begetting thus generously. The emotions fighting in him left him incoherent and

"Well, I'm jiggered!" he ended.

Jane asked, "What about your furniture?"

Ron reverted to the letter, reading on to the end.

"Seems I'll have to get it out of store and arrange for it to go by rail. And she wonders if you'd like to come with me, after the—the twins are born, and help get the house ready and stay on for as long as you like. There'll be a spare room. It might be a good idea, Jane, for you and Mark as well as for us."

He glanced at the window, through which a single barrage-balloon was visible. His sister hated to leave London and slept nightly under a Morrison shelter with her son; he had joined them when the sirens had gone, though the raids as yet had not threatened Hampstead— thanks, it might be, to those balloons. But if the invasion should come—which God forbid!—he must look to secreting them as well as he might. There were ugly rumours circulating out of European Jewry...

"Okay, Ron." The Americanism suited Jane's laconicity. She added with a grin, "I'll get some knitting going for the journey!"

"How's Ben doing?"

"Fine. Says he's becoming a Royal Engineer and expects a posting before the year's out. I think he quite enjoys it, though he misses Mark here."

"And you?"

"Of course." Her imperious tone made Ron reflect how different his sister from him! She seemed unsurprised by such turns of fortune as kept him wondering at finding himself in the situation of needing to look to the protection of his womenfolk and their young. It was something that happened in books, or in history, not to him, Aaron Keller. Perhaps his sister had absorbed more of the atavistic Israelite fatalism.

She was saying, "Ron, have you heard about Morry?"

"No, what?" He knew young Moishe had left school, otherwise hadn't given a thought to their mother's sister's son.

"He's seventeen in December. Says he's going to volunteer for bomber-crew."

Ron whistled, conveying a mixture of admiration and dismay.

"Is he really as old as that? I think of him as just a kid."

"I know. I think he's being rather—carried away."

"By all the—the heroism, you mean?" Again before his mind's eye that blazing 'plane was spinning out of control, his kid cousin in it, burning... What would be the sense of that? He thought of kind Aunt Lil, of Uncle Joe playing the fiddle in their kitchen—innocent folk if ever there were—and then of Kurt's family and of those blonde prowlers in the Black Forest...

"He says he can't wait to get at the Hun. He's heard the rumours out of Germany, as well as what's been in the news for long enough. Says he has his wind and limb—good eyesight too—for the defence of—of freedom—and his Jewish brothers—and sisters."

A long and halting speech for Jane, but now it was Ron was speechless as he pondered her news, not knowing whether to fear or admire the more, thinking again how he would funk flying even without the addition of enemy fire. Finally he whistled again and said,

"Well, good luck to the kid! But poor old Lil and Joe, eh?"

"That's what I said, but he says they've always got Sally and anyway they're just as likely to get killed in Stoke Newington! And there's something in that!"

Breakfast finished, Ron took himself off to bed.

III

(1941)

Elaine Keller walked beside her friends from next door, trailing the cardboard cube that contained her gas-mask, making the leaves rustle on the tarred path that followed all the way to school the main road through their village of Long Moreton. It was the first of November, still All Saints Day in the national calendar, but though Elaine did not know this, she knew there had been something special about yesterday. To begin with, there had been a holiday from school so the big boys could help get in the last of the root harvest before ploughing, and she had spent the afternoon at Aunt Magda's. After tea she had followed her aunt into what was known as the back kitchen, beyond the coal and coke stores. There the tools were kept and there anything messy took place, like gluing or painting. There, under Aunt Magda's Bench, were the zinc tubs of eggs preserved in waterglass because of The Shortages, and the broad beans that Uncle

Hilary had grown in rows and Mummy had helped Aunt Magda salt away for winter.

Aunt Magda had been carrying a big mangel-wurzel which she set on the high bench; then she chose a pointed knife from a rack on the wall above and proceeded to slice off the top and scoop out the inside, which took some time. Elaine, standing beside her with her eyes just clearing the bench, had taken a piece of mangel-wurzel from the accumulating pile and nibbled it to see what it was like for the cattle who would be fed on it that winter: quite tasty was her verdict, but when she put out her hand to try it again, her aunt said No more, as it was indigestible.

When the great globe was all hollowed out, Aunt Magda used the pointed tip of the knife to carve two holes for eyes and two small ones for nostrils and then a mouth with zig-zag teeth. Elaine had watched in amazement and a bit afraid; the face looked fierce, but then you knew it was really a mangel-wurzel, like Worzel Gummidge on Children's Hour, who had a smiley head and was a friendly scarecrow and not at all frightening, though you didn't always understand what he was up to. She didn't get to hear Children's Hour very often because it might disturb the babies, or else she might be playing or reading and forget about it, and Mummy would forget too if she was busy with the babies, which she usually was and this meant Elaine spent quite a lot of time up at Aunt Magda's house, which she loved, especially roaming the garden and riding her tricycle up and down the long curving driveway. Aunt Magda always remembered Children's Hour and would put the wireless on in The Quarry's sitting-room with its long windows facing onto the lawn. Otherwise she wasn't allowed in there and she was just a bit scared of Aunt Magda, though more of Uncle Hilary, who liked children to be seen and not heard. He was Scottish, from Scotland, where Aunt Magda said they made lanterns like this for the Eve of All Saints—which was strange, because she had thought saints were good, but the lantern-face was frightening!

By then her aunt had fixed the face onto the broom-handle and inside it a night-light like the one Elaine had on her little chest of drawers at night—and that too was a bit worrying, because one night when they were still in London she had awoken to a burning smell and a hissing noise and Mummy and Daddy were in the room and they had poured a jug of water all over the little chest because the night-light had burned down to the wood and was starting a fire and it was lucky they had smelled it before it spread. Afterwards her night-lights stood in a saucer of water so that couldn't happen again, and a man had come from the Insurance and another man came and fitted a little oblong of matching wood into the top of the chest, like the patches Mummy had sewed onto the tablecloth and her frock. Since then she had dreams about fire that were too frightening to tell, like the one of a cat caught in the tree opposite their house, and the tree was on fire. And since then too the German aeroplane had been shot down and burned on top of the hill...

So it was quite scary when Aunt Magda took a box of matches and lit the night-light inside the mangel-wurzel head and they carried it on the broom-handle out into the dark, where the eyes and nostrils and jagged mouth spurted and flamed in the wind, and they walked it along the gravel drive to the garage, then back to the house to show Uncle Hilary, who had seemed quite kind, clapping his hands and saying he'd never seen a finer Hallowe'en lantern, not even in Scotland, and had come with them and the flaring head to the big gate, that was like a field-gate, which they opened and Elaine didn't want them to go out because of the blackout and Mummy had been fined for leaving a light showing, and the village policeman lived next door and reported it, which was not friendly; but Aunt Magda said they could carry it a little way down the hill and you were allowed to have a torch and besides, Uncle Hilary was head of the Home Guard. Elaine had seen a pile of strange metal balls by the back door that Uncle Hilary and the big boys and men who had not gone to the War sometimes took out on the hillside to practise throwing them at the Germans.

"Pick up your gas-mask and put it over your shoulder like Daphne. Look, like this," said the bigger of her companions, and Mary Brogan slipped the string over Elaine's right shoulder and helped her draw her right arm through it.

"It's heavy!"

"It'll be less heavy like that."

Mummy had said it was a mile to the school from their end of the village, where they had their own house now. They had moved into it in time for Christmas, after the twins were born who were now almost one. Daddy had come for Christmas, actually in the back of an army lorry with a lot of soldiers; they had given him a lift from the station, although it was against the law. Aunt Jane had managed to buy a doll in London, even though you hardly could buy toys because of the War, and it was for Christmas and from Daddy and Mummy too. They called the doll Belinda and she had hair and eyes that opened and shut and little white shoes and socks you could really take off and put on. Only last Easter, when Aunt Freda had visited and Mummy had been able to leave the babies for once, they had gone walking in Weston Woods, and Belinda had lost one of her shoes, and they didn't find it though they walked all through the wood again looking for it, and that rather spoiled Belinda.

Mary and Daphne had moved in first, into the other new house next to theirs, which Mr and Mrs Brown had bought and were making it so nice, digging up the front garden and sowing seed that had come up, but nobody must walk on it until next summer; the grass-blades were thin and had to be protected—rather like the babies, who Mummy had spent the past year keeping warm and dry and fed, and weighing them on the grocer's scales every week to make sure they were gaining, because early on Joejoe had lost weight and Mummy had been worried about it and started giving him bottles.

Mr Brown was the village grocer and he was Daphne's father but not Mary's, because Mr Brogan had died and Mrs Brown had married Mr Brown. So Mary and Daphne had different fathers but the same mother, which Elaine hadn't known you could. In the summer Mrs Brown had sat filling her basket chair on the front porch but nowadays she was hardly seen; it seemed she was afraid to go beyond their front gate even in a car, because Aunt Magda had offered to drive Mrs Brown to Church in Reading, because she was a Catholic, as also was Mary, because her Dad had been one—but Mr Brown was not and Elaine wasn't sure about Daphne. But Mrs Brown wouldn't; Elaine thought this might have to do with the War, though everyone else she knew went out.

Daphne was about her own age, but secretly she liked Mary best, who was nearly ten and would soon go away to boarding-school and was going to be a nurse when she grew up, which she seemed quite near to doing, and meantime Mary practised and had them all playing at Nurses with First-Aid boxes; Mrs Brown and Mummy had found the cardboard boxes and they had drawn on the lids big crosses in red crayon, and in them they had bandages made from old sheets which Aunt Magda was tearing up for the troops, who would need a lot of bandages. And they had splints, which were pencils or rulers, though the rulers did not fit in the boxes, and neither did the real splint Elaine had, because her Daddy had fallen over on the steps to the Underground—She could just recall the red trains rushing under a bridge near her Granny's house—and a real nurse had bandaged a real splint onto his wrist and made it better.

Mary had something even more special: a red rubber tube to be an enema like the one the District Nurse used on children when they got worms because they played in the garden and forgot to wash their hands before eating—especially if someone had a bag of sweets from the little shop whose window they were just now passing, crammed with jars of barley-sugars and fondants and bullseyes and so many others it was hard to know which to spend your coupons on when Mummy gave you sixpence for them. They had all had enemas from the district nurse, who showed the mothers how to do them, and there was a game of enemas which they felt was rude and had to be kept from the grownups, but in summer they had played it in the long grass of the two back gardens, which were actually the bottom of the hill, but where it became flat it had been fenced off and their houses had been built on it. On Elaine's side there was a stile that you could climb over to go up the hill to Aunt Magda's and some gypsies had come from beyond the hill and climbed over the stile and walked through their back and front gardens to the road, which had worried Mummy but she said you couldn't stop people because it was a Right of Way. Mr Brown had dug a vegetable bed on his side and made a cucumber-frame and Mrs Brown had sown some seeds beside it and so there had been a lovely splash of nasturtiums last summer when they hid by the cucumber-frame to play at giving each other enemas, and the orange bells of the nasturtiums were like the secret places of their bodies, and a bit like the dangly little tube on each of her baby brothers.

Now, reminded by the gas-mask, she thought to ask,

"Mary, where are the Germans? Why don't we see them?"

"We don't want to see them," came in superior tones from aloft, "Not here we don't, nor anywhere else!"

"My Daddy has seen their aeroplanes in London!"

Having a Daddy in London gave one a bit of importance, at least if one was not an "evacuee" but a niece of Mrs Lomax of The Quarry.

"We shot that plane down over Binfield way," said Daphne, with the air of defending the honour of Berkshire.

"I know. Uncle Hilary and the Home Guard went. They think the pilot jumped out with his parachute, but they didn't find him. I hope he didn't—die."

"I hope he did, as he was a German!" put in Daphne, backing accepted wisdom.

Elaine was silent. She had gone out with her mother and aunt after Uncle Hilary had hastily put on his Home Guard uniform and left. From the mound on which Jellicoe loved to lie, nose on paws and one eye on the road, they could see the streak of dark smoke rising from the hill on the horizon to north-east. She was glad if the pilot had jumped out, otherwise he would have burned with his plane and that was too dreadful… But was it better if he was dead? Was it better Mary's father was dead and so there was Daphne, but otherwise Mary might have had a different sister?

Mary was saying,

"They'd have found him if he was dead—found his body. He'll be a P.O.W. now."

"He might have burned all up in his aeroplane!" That was Daphne again.

Elaine said, "I've seen Italians," realizing that was feeble even as the words left her mouth.

"So have I!" Daphne would never be behind.

"We've *all* seen *them*," said Mary, again pronouncing from on high. "Italians are not as bad as Germans, so we let them get in the crops. They keep the Germans on islands as the sea's too cold for them to swim away."

This was hard to imagine. From a day's outing to Southend before the War, Elaine had a faint memory of the seaside as a lot of boats on something shiny that was mud; she didn't think that was what the real sea was like and felt silenced by superior knowledge. But she treasured her encounter with the Italians huddled in the back of a lorry that had passed them on the road beyond their house when Mummy and she were picking blackberries. They had been singing in such fine, strong voices, like her Daddy's when he sang "Old Kentucky Home" and "The Raggle-Taggle Gypsies-o," only all together: it was like sunshine pouring from their throats. She would have liked to wave to them but something held her back, perhaps the soldier guarding them with his gun. And they had seemed to look at her and Mummy with dark eyes under their caps, and she thought they might have Mummies and little girls who were missing them. "Those are Italians," her mother had said, and that Italians always sang like that.

That had been one of the happy times, which were not often now unless Daddy or someone visited and unless Mummy had more time, who was often cross, what with the babies and Daddy away and the War and the bombs in London, which you knew about because of the evacuees—who you felt sorry for because people pointed them out and they were often thin, pale-faced children with no Mummies or Daddies looking after them and other people didn't want them really; Elaine was glad they were not evacuees and could stay with Aunt Magda and now they had a house of their own—even if not of their very own like Mary and Daphne's, but Daddy paid rent for it. And in other ways it was much nicer here; you could get away into the garden or play with the girls next door, and now there was school.

In London there had been just her, and only the Close to play and ride her tricycle in. And Mummy used to slap her when she was naughty, but here she wasn't so much around Mummy, who was taken up with the babies. In London she had dreaded that "Hold out your hand!" and once she had put her hands behind her back, and then Mummy had become frighteningly fierce, like that tiger "in the forests of the night" that Mummy liked so much that Elaine had even heard her saying it above the sound of her wee-ing, behind the half-closed door of the lavatory. There was another poem about a little lamb who God made, that was not frightening at all, and Mummy liked that too. The tiger would have eaten the little lamb, though.

No, she didn't want to remember the bad things. Here it was safe, away from London and the bombs, only Daddy had to stay in London and only visited them about once a month. Last time he had left to go and hitch a lift back, Elaine had run crying down the road and he had heard and turned and picked her up and carried her back and she felt comforted, but he had to go, so she had shut the door of the sitting-room and stayed in there while she could keep in the smell of him, mixed in with his jacket and cigarettes.

And Mummy could be lovely, especially when she sat each morning in front of her mirrors and put up her hair in puffs; Elaine liked to watch that and then Mummy would let her peer in the mirrors and move them so she could see herself at the back and on both sides, like Mummy did. Once when Daddy had come, Mummy had worn the evening-dress that hung at the back of the big wardrobe, and they had gone with Aunt Magda and Uncle Hilary to a dance for the Home Guard. Elaine liked to crouch down in the dark of the big wardrobe and finger that dress, which came from Granny's Business and was called crêpe-de-chine and had a pattern of leaves over it that you could feel, soft and fuzzy. The lovely hair and dress made Mummy feel faraway like in a story and not like the Mummy who slapped you, which hurt your hand but it hurt more down inside, because you were bad; but then Mummy seemed bad too, though you knew she was good really.

Worst was when Mummy made her stand in the corner, like she said they did in school when she was a little girl. Miss Churchman at the village school sometimes made a child stand out in front of the class, but not with your face to the wall; that hurt a lot inside, longer than the slaps. Once when Auntie Jane had been there Mummy had put her in the corner like that and Mark had run up to take Elaine's hand and pull her away, and Mummy let him; Elaine thought it was because she knew Auntie Jane felt sorry for her.

And Mummy could be nice when she had more time and then Elaine was good, like when they had been for walks on the hill or in Weston Wood and picked bluebells or anemones. That was when the babies must have been growing in Mummy's tummy; she still didn't see how they got out, nor in; she had thought God must have put them there, but when she asked about it, Mummy said a little bit of her and a little bit of Daddy had come together while they were asleep, and Elaine didn't know how that could happen but she felt she shouldn't ask any more.

For a few days last summer they had sat outside and Mummy had read to her from a book of stories she didn't always understand, but it was nice to sit by Mummy and have her read in her faraway voice that made you feel good. Elaine knew, of course, that she was naughty, naughtier than Mummy knew. There was the bedspread. That was still a secret, because no-one had said anything about it. It was when they were in London; she had taken the scissors, which she was not supposed to, from Mummy's dressing-table, and lying hidden behind the big bed had made a long cut up the stripy blue spread that hung down. She didn't know to this day if that cut was still there because she wouldn't dare go into Mummy's bedroom and look; she hadn't been forbidden, but that door was always shut and she thought it would be colder in there even than the bedroom she shared with the twins, where Mummy stood an oil-stove before they went to bed, then took it out so there couldn't be a fire. No-one had said anything about the cut. Perhaps Mummy had sewn it up, but if so she must know. Sometimes Elaine wondered if it had been a dream, her doing that.

And there were the enemas, though she didn't quite know why that was naughty, except it seemed to do with things you couldn't know about like babies, or talk about like messing yourself; and that brought a bad memory, which was of Daddy this time, of him leaning over her cot—she must have been quite a baby—his voice loud, saying "Oh Lord, not again!" and she had felt a bit frightened but secretly pleased with what she had done that lay warm and brown beside her in the cot and he couldn't do anything about it...

They had reached the school, which was as well because her legs were becoming tired with keeping up. After they had hung up their coats and gas-masks, she followed Mary up the steps at the side of the big class-room where her seat was now many rows behind Daphne, who was not far from the bottom, because on their first day they both had been put in front of the stepped classroom, where there was a row of low chairs, not proper desks, and each child had chalk and a little blackboard called a slate, though it was not like the grey, flat slates you sometimes found in the garden. They had been told to copy some big letters painted up on a blackboard and at first she did, but seeing the teacher begin to do joined-up writing with chalk on the bigger board, she had waited for her to come by, then boldly said,

"Please, Miss" (She had heard the teacher so addressed), "I can read it," and Miss Churchman had found that she could and also do joined-up writing, so she moved her up the class to a desk which sloped, with an inkwell in a hole and a pen with a nib for writing properly in an exercise book.

Miss Churchman was known to everyone in the village. She lived in one of the row of pebble-dashed Council Houses Elaine and her friends passed going to and from school, and last winter, when the twins were little babies, Elaine had stayed at her house until Aunt Magda, or sometimes Uncle Hilary, came walking over the hillside to take her back to The Quarry for lunch and drive her to school afterwards. They couldn't do this very often as the Home Guard didn't give them much petrol, but sometimes she could ride in the grocer's van with Mary and Daphne, though Mr Brown didn't have much petrol either and if he couldn't collect them, they either had to walk home and back in the middle of the day or take their lunches in paper bags to eat with the children who came from farms around; but Elaine was shy of them, feeling herself an outsider and different.

By far the best was going to Aunt Magda's, where she could play in the big garden or look at books if it was raining; besides Uncle Remus which Aunt Magda sometimes read from, they had some big ones with pictures, one about a dragon called Dennis who breathed fire but didn't want to hurt anybody, and another about the Pied Piper who stole their children away from people who didn't keep their promises, and one about the Jackdaw of Rheims who stole the Lord Cardinal's ring and was cursed until he brought it back,

"and then the Lord Cardinal called for his book
and off that terrible curse he took..."

and there was a picture of a fat man all in red with a very shiny ring and a big book and some boys in white like angels and a draggled and humble looking jackdaw-bird who had done wrong and now was sorry, and you felt sorry for him, because he was only a bird and couldn't help doing wrong. Granny called *her* "Bird," which was nice and so did Aunt Freda, though she also called her "Pet" which was not so nice, though better than "Petty" which was what Mummy and Daddy used to call her, but they didn't any more: perhaps they saw she hated it, or perhaps the babies were the pettys now.

Aunt Magda, who always called her Elaine, read her those books because they were special ones you were only allowed to look at with a grown-up, but she had some books of her own and though she couldn't remember learning to read, she remembered the first time she showed she could, which was the first time they came to Aunt Magda's and she read to them *Who Killed Cock Robin?* which was also about a poor bird; there was a picture of him dead, with an arrow through him and red drops of blood falling into a dish that the fish held. She didn't understand that either but it nearly made you cry. Everyone had clapped and said how clever she was at only four-and-a-half, and Daddy, who was there, said she was a little more than that, but you could tell he was proud of her. And when they were back in London, in their new flat, he had brought her a copy-book with a proverb written out on each page in joined writing, and lines under for you to copy six times: "A little pot is soon hot" or "A stitch in time saves nine," which Daddy said didn't rhyme really and you could see it didn't. He had sat with her all one Saturday morning and helped her write out every proverb twice and he had some paper from the Office to show her his own very beautiful joined writing, because he was what was called a "first-class penman" and she would be that too, except she wasn't sure about the "man": boys became men and girls became ladies when they grew up; could you be a pen-*lady?* Anyway, she had loved doing all that with Daddy and Mummy had watched too and said she was clever. That was before the twins, when she had more time.

After they moved back to Aunt Magda's and then into the new house and had their furniture again, they got out the copy-book the first time Daddy visited and did every proverb just once more each, because Daddy too had less time now there were the babies, though he had more than Mummy. After that, Daddy said she could do them on her own if she woke up early, instead of disturbing them, and he left the book on the little chest with the patch in it, because she didn't need a night-light any more. But she couldn't do it in the mornings because it was so cold and if she got up she would be scared of meeting Jack Frost, who nipped fingers and toes. At least the red fox-head seemed to have gone away that used to watch her from the top of the corner cupboard and was somehow connected with Miss Audrey's chestnut hunter named Modrin Roo, which they said meant Red Fox: they had tried to lift her onto him once and she had screamed until they brought her down. She never told anyone about the fox-head, though it had been scarier than Jack Frost, who everyone knew about, but when she used to wake up and knew the fox-head was there, she would lie still and hot under the weight of the bedding, not daring to see or be seen. Nowadays she just pulled the blankets up to her nose until Mummy came to tell her to get up and drew back the blackout curtains and you saw that Jack Frost had been and left his wonderful patterns of leaves and ferns on the windowpanes.

Then one morning Mummy told her to come downstairs, where she had just lit the fire as she did every morning, and in front of the fire was a real little lamb, all weak and folded up because it had been born that cold night and Miss Audrey had brought it in. Miss Audrey was a lady farmer, because the men farmers were all fighting, and Aunt Magda and Uncle Hilary knew her and had told her of the farm near their house that she could rent and they'd arranged for her to live with Mummy as a "paying guest," which meant she paid them money to help pay the rent, and so Miss Audrey slept in the spare bedroom and had her breakfast very early and just once Elaine had breakfast with her and soaked her bread in her tea, which made it nice and soft to eat, but Miss Audrey said "Only Germans do that," so she never did it again.

The three writings-out of the proverbs had been enough, which was how she had come to school that first day able to read and to write and when she had learned all the Tables she would go right up to the back of the classroom. Uncle Hilary was useful here; he had taught her her twice-times before she went to school and now he asked her the difficult ones like seven sevens and six eights. And he had taught her to say the alphabet backwards, which was a funny thing they didn't ask you in school. They said she had a good memory because she always remembered Daddy's songs and the poems Mummy had read in their flat before the War, sometimes to her and sometimes to herself; Mummy liked poems about animals and had made up a song about them all going to sleep which she sang when Elaine was not going to sleep and she would pat her back in time to the song and that was comforting and sent you to sleep like the animals in the song. At weekends when Daddy came down, she would lie listening for the nine 'bong's of Big Ben before the News, and then "God Save the King," because if she was awake for that she was allowed to come down and sit on his knee.

Here the school stood up to sing the morning hymn and Elaine realized she had not been listening to the teacher reading from the

Bible and saying the prayer, though she had bowed her head over the desk with the rest.

"All things bright and beautiful,
all creatures great and small…"

She liked that, though the creatures in it didn't seem to be birds or animals, and she liked more the one about the green hill without a city wall and the dear Lord who was crucified; she knew about that because her Granny had the big Crucifix on a wall as you went into her house and Aunt Magda too had a Crucifix on her desk when you were allowed in the drawing-room to listen to Children's Hour. And she knew what a green hill was like because they lived below one, and that didn't have a wall either. She had had a gold chain with a Cross though no Jesus on it; she used to wear it, but one day the chain had broken and fallen off her neck and down the crack between the floorboards, taking the Cross with it, and Mummy had said it would mean taking the floor-board up and they couldn't now—one day, perhaps when Daddy came…

Then she paid attention because they were saying the times-tables and next it would be Arithmetic.

That lunchtime Aunt Magda came for her while Uncle Hilary waited outside with the car, and when the car-door was opened, there on the back seat was her Granny. Elaine fell into Edith's arms and kissed the softly wrinkled cheek and was kissed and hugged as warmly, and sitting beyond Granny was Auntie Freda to be kissed and hugged too, and it was on her knee she sat as they were driven up the hill and in at The Quarry's gate.

There followed a memorable meal of toad-in-the-hole and turnips mashed with real butter and wonderful-smelling nutmeg, which Aunt Magda explained was a little nut you grated and she would show it to Elaine. Before that, Elaine hadn't thought of nutmegs as real nuts, only magical, as in the lines:

"I had a little nut-tree; nothing would it bear
but a silver nutmeg and a golden pear."

Almost magical was the lemonade made from crystals dissolved in her glass and the cider poured frothing out of a jug for the grown-ups. Finally there was what Auntie Freda herself, smiling kindly at Elaine beside her, actually said was a magic dessert, and it did seem it: ice-cream made in the refrigerator and a hot chocolate sauce to put on it. Everyone said it was just like before rationing and they talked a lot. Even Uncle Hilary talked more than usual, about the Home Guard and the War Effort and what the Vicar had said, and Auntie Freda talked about how she had been fire-watching, with buckets of sand and water and something called a stirrup-pump one night when incendiary bombs had fallen right in their street, though not on their house, luckily.

Then Aunt Magda asked about Pawa, who was Elaine's Granddad, though he didn't live with Granny like granddads and grannies usually did, because they didn't get on, and Auntie Freda, who usually didn't get on either, had gone to visit him in the West End because it was Wartime, and she was telling how he had made a bridge from his flat right over to another high building, and then another bridge beyond that, so he could walk over the roofs and see if any fires needed putting out, and he seemed to enjoy doing that. And when Auntie Freda asked him if it was safe for him to be out on the roofs in an air raid, he had said, "Do you suppose I hold my life to be in the hands of some Jerry up there? My life is in the hands of Almighty God!"

Everyone was silent a moment, only Aunt Magda was nodding in a way that told Elaine it was like her Granddad and very splendid: especially, she thought, that bit about "some Jerry up there" which Auntie Freda said in a scornful sort of voice. It made you feel safe from the Germans when you knew there were people like Granddad. Perhaps not from the Gestapo, who were the wickedest Germans, but her Daddy had explained that if the Germans couldn't bomb their way into England, the Gestapo would have to stay in Germany until we could bomb them.

When she had finished every trace of ice-cream she could scrape out with her spoon—and she would have liked to lift her bowl and lick it but knew that would bring disgrace on her—Elaine asked, as she was expected to, "Please can I get up," and Uncle Hilary, making her feel uncomfortable and small, said, "You *can* get up; the question is *may* you! And are you sure you're not going to get *down?*" and he peered under the white tablecloth pretending to check if her feet reached the ground, though he knew they didn't. Everyone laughed at Uncle Hilary's joke, but when her Daddy was there, she had heard him say to Mummy that Uncle Hilary was too fussy and had no business correcting her English, which was very good for a child of her age. He said this in the voice that meant he was annoyed and Mummy said something in her voice that meant she was being helpful and that made Daddy make a snorting noise. Elaine didn't like being laughed at, but Uncle Hilary would be right and she should remember to say it his way.

But before she could get down, Auntie Freda said to wait, and she took from her handbag a book and Elaine read on it "Alice's Adventures in Wonderland," and inside the cover was written, in joined-up writing, "an un-birthday present for dear Elaine from Granny and Auntie Freda"; she liked to be called "Auntie," like Auntie Jane, but Aunt Magda was just "Aunt" and so was Aunt Agnes. Auntie Freda said she would read some of the book to Elaine at bedtime, because they were all going down the hill to have tea and then Mummy would go back to The Quarry for dinner, but Auntie Freda would stay to look after her and the babies, who she hadn't seen since soon after they were born.

That was a happy meal and that afternoon they had Games in the playground and Miss Churchman—whose name was like Churchill and so made you feel safe—chose Elaine as a team-leader and she wore a red band over her chest and chose Mary first for her team and then Daphne so she wouldn't get left to last, and the Red team came first in the long-jump and second in the relay-race, which was pretty good.

That evening Auntie Freda let her sit in a big armchair and hold Joejoe, whose real name was Joshua and who was bigger and quieter than Leo, and she gave him some of his bottle, which she never had before. After the babies were both asleep, zipped up in sleeping-suits at each end of the cot that had once been hers, she sat in her dressing-gown by the fire in the front room and Auntie Freda read the Alice book to her and showed her the pictures, but not for very long because, like Alice, she was soon falling asleep.

Up at The Quarry, with Hilary gone to a meeting at the Vicarage, mother and daughters were seated at the silken-grained dining-table. For dinner Magda had baked two big trout and a dish of scalloped potatoes and on the floor of the oven she had warmed a casserole containing two precious tinsful of peas with mint from the garden. She always said her ability to turn out appetising dishes was an inheritance from her Burgundian forebears, and though this gift seemed to have passed Veronica by, after tea in her own home, she and Edith had made two good-sized apple pies, one to take to The Quarry and one to leave in the larder for Freda's and Elaine's supper, with some left over for next day.

"How has little Elaine taken to her brothers?" Edith inquired.

"It's hard to tell," their mother replied. "She's such a quiet child—quite secretive, I'm afraid! All she wants to do is go to school and read when she comes in."

"Come, Vee," said Magda briskly, "She'll play for hours in the garden here, with only occasional attention. The other day I made a house for her Teddy-bear with the stones for the rockery and she made a dolls' tea-party with raisins and egg-cups full of water. She plays with her friends next door to you, does she not?"

"Yes, and thank goodness!" replied her sister. "I don't know how we'd manage, all squeezed into a London flat; the War has brought that advantage, at least! Though it's hard on Ron—and on us without him! But tell them what Elaine said when I was in the hospital, Mag."

"After the twins were born, when Elaine was here with us, I wasn't sure how much she understood what was happening and I thought I should break it to her gently, so I asked her if she would like a little brother. She was silent a minute and then she said, 'No, but I'd like a little sister.' She may have had Mary in mind, whom she rather worships, you know, and who has a younger sister."

"What did you say?" asked Edith.

"I confess I was somewhat at a loss. I tried to explain that you couldn't choose but that brothers were good to have too, and I broke it to her that she now had two of them!"

"But tell Mumsie what she said then," Veronica urged.

"You know, Veronica," replied her sister, "I regard that as perfectly normal for a child of her age who has just found herself in a situation in which children surely cannot help feeling some unease—even jealousy." Then, turning to their mother,

"I did not attach any great significance to it and perhaps should not have told Veronica, only she pressed me to know what Elaine had said."

"Well, dear, you can tell me, I hope!"

"I am sure I can, Mother. She said, 'Perhaps they will die.'"

"She's not a small child!" interjected Veronica, who would have accepted Agnes' judgment in the matter, but resented what seemed to her Magda's superior manner.

"No, she is of just the age to understand something but not enough," said Edith. "She may well have been remembering what she'd heard about—other babies dying. She asked me about that the last time I was here."

"Soon after they were born!"

"Yes, but as it related to my babies, my John and Renata; she had learned they had died. In any case, Veronica dear, it is quite usual, as Magdalen says, for a child to feel—displaced. When Magdalen herself was born, Biddie, our nursemaid then, found it necessary to divide the twin pram with a rolled blanket to protect her from Agnes' remarkably well-directed kicks!"

"I know, Deedie; but Agnes was one year old. As was I when Freda was born and I always was very fond of her."

"It is true, dear; everyone is different and we all need understanding."

"Elaine has to learn she cannot have all the attention now. Of course, her Daddy spoils her, because he's so proud of her reading and writing. As I am, but we can't spend all our time in books, women especially. I'm making sure she does her bit in the house these days; she can dust and tidy things, which is just as important for life as books are. I'm sure Joshua and Leo will be every bit as clever in time."

There was silence, until Freda observed,

"It seems we can thank God for this Eastern Front the Germans have opened. Now the Bolsheviks can reap the fruits of their godless alliance and we have a breathing-space and" (with a glance at Veronica) "less worry! We should be praying Te Deums for the Führer's megalomania—and General Winter coming to meet him, just like Boney of old, we can hope!"

"Yes, we must pray," came from Veronica, "me especially with these children—and I do, though I hardly find the time. Ron too writes that the papers are saying it could be like with Napoleon. Hitler must be mad, mustn't he?"

"'Whom god wills to destroy he first makes mad!'" The sentence, dropped by Magda, brought silence until Veronica again spoke:

"But surely—God does not will to destroy! Not even the wicked, does He?"

"'God desireth not the death of a sinner, but rather that he turn from his wickedness and live.'" This from Edith, and from Veronica:

"Then how can we believe anyone is in Hell?"

To which her mother:

"I suppose even Hitler and the rest... that they can repent."

"If one has not put oneself beyond the possibility of Grace by wilful, mortal sin!" That was Freda, seemingly recalling the catechism. To her mother she added:

"Deedie dear, you like to say that to understand all is to pardon all! Can we understand even a tyrant and megalomaniac like Hitler?"

"Indeed, my dears, in general I believe it: that if we could understand… Yet in the rare case of sin that is mortal—that kills the soul, that is a choice out of the dispensations of God, so to speak—like the Devil's own choice, and indeed is a choice *of* the Devil—I don't know if I am putting it very clearly but I mean, Who can know what it would take, or if it is even possible for that soul to live again!"

Again silence and it was for their hostess to have the last word. Magda spoke deliberately and at rare length:

"That saying, about god destroying: it's from the pagans, who modelled their gods on men. Nonetheless, it enunciates a truth, for in giving men freedom to reject sin, God allows us in the end to choose. And the choice of destruction—of self as of others—entails the destruction that may show itself as madness. It is in that sense that God makes mad whom He wills to destroy—perhaps better, 'is willing to destroy,' or 'to let be destroyed': and that, we have to understand, is by the permissive, not the absolute will of God: St Thomas makes that distinction. But as I said, the saying is couched in pagan terms. I learned it from a Jesuit who also told me it in Latin, which gives 'god' as 'deus' but with a small 'd': 'Quem deus vult perdere, prius dementat.'"

Again silence, until, as they rose as one to clear the table, their mother again spoke:

"Children, we must not *talk* of praying, but we must pray! I propose we each and all say a Pater-Ave-Gloria each day until this War is over—and let us begin now!"

Edith lifted her hand and all followed, signing themselves with the Cross as she began:

"In the Name of the Father and of the Son and of the Holy Ghost…"

IV

(1945)

The first light of a May dawn had woken her, and filtering through the faded green curtain by her bedhead made the room too seem to be peacefully awakening. At weekends this was the best time, when she could just lie and think and then pull the curtain a little aside so as not to disturb the sleeping twins, and read until her father would come in to "potty" them. That was to prevent wetted beds, which would mean a bath full of soaking sheets and heavy washing for Mummy, who had a lot to put up with these days.

Elaine's eyes followed her thought to Joejoe's bed, on the opposite side of the room, his head away from the window. She had pleaded to be at the window end because of when she woke early and read, which would disturb the twins; but also she felt she needed some space in the cramped room: the door just missed the foot of Leo's bed across its other end; beneath it she could just see the wooden toy-box Granddad had made, long and shallow to fit under and hold the twins' jumble of things—wooden bricks and bats, trains and trucks, balls, plasticine—accumulated in spite of the War. She of course had outgrown such playthings and the heap of dolls which spilled out of their toy cot under the green-painted table beside her bed.

On the table lay the exercise books from her homework begun last evening; it was the most peaceful place when the window gave good light, but through the dark days, and when the fire was lit in the grate on their return from school, she had worked at the big table in the sitting-room. In the table drawer were kept her pen and ruler and crayons, with her stamp-album and a few letters and postcards. When she sat there in front of it, it was almost like Aunt Magda's and Uncle Hilary's desks at The Quarry, which had drawers, not like desks at school which had lids you lifted up, and not like Granny's desk with a flap that came down, which she liked best—and when she was smaller she used to think that if Granny died she might leave Elaine her desk, which was what people did when they died and went to heaven; but that was a wicked thought and she knew now she would just hate Granny to die and would miss her dreadfully and the desk wouldn't be worth that even if Granny did leave it to her, which was very unlikely; almost certainly Auntie Freda would have it who lived with Granny and you certainly couldn't ask either of them...

In front of the drawer was a spindled chair with her clothes over the back for when she got up. Granddad had cut the chair's legs down when she was small, so now it had a book and a cushion on it for her to sit at the table. The only other piece of furniture was the little chest with the patch from the night-light fire; its two drawers held her other clothes and the twins' were kept in the "press" in Mummy and Daddy's room; she thought it was called that because the sheets and things were folded and stacked between its shelves and the twins' things too were put away neatly by Mummy, but her things in the chest were often not neat, though more so since the day she had come home from school to find both drawers tipped out on the bed and Mummy announcing that was what the nuns had done if girls at school didn't keep their things tidy. Elaine thought she wouldn't have minded a nun turning out her drawers the way she minded Mummy doing it, and the way she said it, which sounded like she was getting her own back on the nuns. At school you might have swaggered a bit behind the nun's back and impressed the other children; at home it was just shaming and she felt the twins beginning to gloat.

Nuns did seem more frightening than ordinary teachers. Elaine had had to sit next to one on a bus, who Mummy said was a Sister of Charity and who wore an enormous white headdress with stiff wings like a great bird, which was why it was the only seat left because only a child like her could sit under the wings. The Sisters of Charity had an orphanage for children with no Mummies or Daddies, which was strange, though perhaps they had been killed in the War and you felt sorry for the orphans when you saw them out walking in a "crocodile," holding hands two by two with a nun with a big headdress walking beside, who might be a bit like a crocodile because Mena's brother Jack had said the nuns had whips under those long grey skirts. Elaine wasn't sure if she believed that as it didn't *look* as if there was anything hidden under the skirts, but Mena's family were Catholics and should know about nuns, and anyway it did seem very miserable being an orphan…

Some of the boarding-school tales were horrid, too. There was a piano-teacher nun who used to hold on to your hair and pull it when you played a wrong note, and in the older aunts' time you had to wear a white gown in the bath, which Aunt Magda didn't seem to have minded, but Aunt Agnes would tell it in her most scornful voice. Only if that was the worst thing—and actually Elaine would have rather liked to try it and see how you could get the soap up under—it made her wonder if their convent schools hadn't been rather fun, as some of their stories suggested. Aunt Magda said the Sacred Heart nuns were excellent teachers and she was grateful to them, though she claimed to have been a rather naughty girl at school and idle at her lessons, whereas Aunt Agnes had been good and when cards were handed out at the end of each week, Aunt Agnes always got the blue one, which was Mary's colour and only given for the very best behaviour and marks. Mummy and Freda hadn't been at the Sacred Heart school long but had gone to other, cheaper convents because Granny and Pawa quarrelled and didn't live together and had moved house a lot and Mummy had made a resolution that her children would not have these upsets. Elaine knew she had to be grateful for that.

Now her best friend at Manor Park Primary had been put down for a convent school, after Mrs Nichols—who, surprisingly, was

Catholic—had asked Mena's parents to come to speak with her about it. And though Scholarship girls could not be boarders, it was a real boarding school and even had a Spanish princess. Mena was older than Elaine but they were both in Form Four because after Form Two Elaine had gone up straight into Form Four, and now she would have to stay there another year because the Government didn't let you sit the Scholarship until you were nearly eleven. She would be sorry not to go to school with Mena and had suggested she might be put down for St Bride's next year, but Mummy said Daddy would not stand for a Catholic school, and when she asked him he said everyone ought to go to a government school. Mr Ponsonby, the Headmaster, had suggested to Mummy and Daddy that Elaine could get into Beale College, the school his own daughter, Kitty, was being put down for, who was usually only second in class after Elaine. Beale College was a Girls' Public School and also Grant Maintained, which meant it was partly a government school but it had its own entrance-exam. Mummy had explained it would mean a long bus-ride and then a walk and be bad for Elaine, because she stooped. Elaine felt uncomfortable about the stooping, but quite glad not to have to do an extra exam like Kitty, and when she learned her government grammar school was for girls and had a uniform, it did sound a bit like schools in stories, even though you wouldn't be able to have midnight feasts and moonlit swims and play cricket like boys.

She pushed the curtain aside a bit to look out on the patch of waste land behind the flats where they played and people who didn't have balconies hung their washing. The first-floor flats had the balconies, like Mrs Drake's below, who they called the Horrid Lady because she complained if the twins made a noise, which they often did, Leo especially, and the Drake—which was what Daddy called her—would bang on her ceiling, with a broomstick, they thought.

Mrs Drake's and theirs were the end flats in The Parade, which was what their block was called; she thought it might be because it went in a sort of half circle, like a parade of soldiers wheeling round, but Daddy said it was because the shops at street level with their big glass windows "paraded" things you could buy before the War. Now some of them had boards over their windows, but not the two on each side of their doorway, Darby's the Newsagents, which was also a sweet-shop, and Harris's Bakery, which was the last shop in The Parade and just now you could smell bread baking, which was nice, though it was less nice when you ate it, and Mummy said it wasn't a good bakery. But it was convenient: you only had to run downstairs to buy a loaf, or for a treat there were currant buns and doughnuts and jam-puffs, but these cost as much as fourpence each, so most of the time there were just the rock-cakes Mummy made and stored in a tin on the high dresser shelf, out of reach of the twins unless they climbed up—which naughty Leo did, as Elaine had seen him, and she thought Joejoe must too, though she hadn't seen him.

And what she mustn't think about was her great secret fear, that a fire might start in the bakery below, like the Fire of London that Daddy had told her about when he took her to his office and they saw the Monument; that fire, he said, had started in a bakery. Otherwise she would start worrying whether it was better to be in their top flat, further away from the fire, or in Mrs Drake's flat, which would burn first but had the balcony you could get out onto. She remembered Daddy had told her how firemen rescued people from windows and balconies, and he had said if you knew how, you could jump from a high window and not hurt yourself, or not much; you had to remember to bend your legs or they would be broken. And she had decided she would jump onto Mrs Drake's balcony if there was a fire, and she hoped she would remember to bend her legs in time, but even broken legs would be better than being trapped in a burning room: this at least gave you a plan, which made it a more bearable fear than the red fox-head during the War when she was little—though that had been silly, she now saw. Also, that the balcony might be burning was something you had to not think about and in the end just hope they were very careful in Harris' Bakery.

And she knew what fires were like because of the incendiary bombs that had been dropped on houses in Granny's road when they went round there in that in-between time before they left again because of the Flying Bombs. Thank goodness there were no more incendiary bombs now! She remembered broken windows and charred wood everywhere, and mattresses still smoking in front gardens where the fire-watchers had left them, because you couldn't put out a fire in a mattress with just water and a stirrup-pump, like Auntie Freda had. That already seemed a long time ago. Now there were no more flying bombs either and the Germans had been defeated, just like Mummy had said they would be, because God wouldn't let evil win in the end. And Hitler was dead, at least most people thought he was, and the other Nazis were either dead or in prison and would be hanged. That was very terrible, even if just, and Elaine had been praying for them, even for Hitler, because they could go to Hell, which was even more terrible. She didn't know if you were supposed to pray for them but she thought she should as Jesus had said to love your enemies and pray for people who wished you harm. She had been given a Bible for her ninth birthday and she kept Mrs Nichols' Bible pictures that she gave for good work in it and she had read most of the parts about what Jesus said and did, which were easy even if the words were sometimes strange.

Elaine's gaze turned to the little brass crucifix that stood on the low chest of drawers, or rather on top of the teeny chest of three drawers standing on it, that Uncle Hilary had brought from Japan, before that was our enemy too in The War, and that Aunt Magda had given her; she supposed Uncle Hilary had said she might. In it she kept her coral necklace that was from Granddad and the crucifix on a chain from her godmother Winnie, who lived in Ireland now and had tried to be a nun and she had had a nervous breakdown, which was only what Mummy expected. And Mummy would tell how when Winnie was in the convent she had taken Elaine to visit her and she had wet the parlour carpet, which Mummy thought was a funny story but it made Elaine squirm when she told it.

But the brass crucifix had belonged to Mummy's brother Leo, because when he was a boy he used to play at being a priest and there had been two little brass candlesticks that had got lost. Maureen, a thin child who went to school with Elaine before the flying bombs, had come home with her once and seen it and said, "Oh, let me kiss Jesus!" and had seized it and kissed it many times, to Elaine's surprise as no-one in her family did that. She had felt that Maureen was sad somehow and her mother seemed always cross, and when they got back from Aunt Magda's after the flying bombs she wasn't at school any more. Elaine had gone to call for her in the flats over the shops on the other side of the Circus—which wasn't a circus, any more than the shops were a parade, but a roundabout with grass and weeds in the middle and a brick bomb-shelter and the old air-raid siren on a high pole—and a strange lady had opened the door and said she didn't know about them. Elaine wondered if Maureen might be dead, perhaps from a flying bomb, or perhaps from being so thin and sad. Remembering how she had kissed the crucifix like that made it seem she had been going to die.

Elaine rather wished she hadn't missed the flying bombs, as they hadn't damaged the flats or her school, so it would have been quite safe and rather fun. Once, before they went away to Aunt Magda's, she had been in the school shelters during an air-raid and everyone had sung "Ten Green Bottles" and "Pack up your Troubles." Just once, too, she had stood in the playground turning her head up to look where some boys, who seemed to know everything, were pointing to a puff of whitish smoke against the blue, which they said was a V-2 our guns had exploded. Elaine didn't see well without her glasses and Mummy had said only to wear them for reading and writing, so she wouldn't get too used to them.

About that time the wail of the siren had sounded quite regularly in the evening and Mummy and Daddy would fill the bath with water in case… She would hear it running in the bathroom on the other side of the wall by her bed and then they would be got up and the twins dressed in the siren-suits Mummy had made them on the sewing machine Granddad had put in order from the old Business and which had "Made in Germany" and a pattern of flowers over it. Winston Churchill had invented siren-suits and wore what must be a very big one. The twins' ones were little, of course, and no-one else in her family had one, but she had a woollen dressing-gown to put on over her nightie and the woolly vest she wore under it, and they would all sit beside the bright bar of the electric fire that was set into the bedroom wall and was a luxury after the cold bedrooms in Long Moreton, and Mummy would pour hot water into mugs and stir in a spoonful of sweet condensed milk from a tin and cut up squares of bread to go in it, which was a treat, and usually nothing more happened till the All Clear sounded.

But just once they heard the thudding of guns and Daddy said it was a long way off but they would go to the shelter in case, and before they reached the front door there was a louder thud so that the flat shook, and once outside you saw flashes in the sky and she was scared and dropped Tiny Ted; she had chosen him to take to the shelter and not Teddy, who was her favourite and so worn that Aunt Agnes had made him almost a new face out of a piece of blanket, but she had felt people in the shelter might laugh at a girl as big as her with a Teddy Bear, so she had picked Tiny Ted who she could hide. But as they made for the brick-built shelter behind the flats, she had let him drop. Daddy was lighting the way with his torch, pointing it carefully down because of the blackout.

"I've lost Tiny Ted!" she had exclaimed, but Daddy said they couldn't go back and hurried them on and she had had to be brave. People were crowding into the shelter and she slept on a blanket on a metal bunk. Next morning she looked for Tiny Ted and she found a piece of shrapnel, not a big one like some boys at school had, but a lucky find and she put it carefully into the little drawers with the corals and the medal. Only there was no Tiny Ted, who some other child would have and she hoped they would be good to him. After that she was glad when they went back to Aunt Magda's on the train. Of course, they didn't have their old house and again Mummy was not happy staying with Aunt Magda and Uncle Hilary, who found the twins trying, especially Leo who even Mummy said was a scamp, though she said it in a way that told you she was proud of him really.

They had stayed at The Quarry for eight months and Elaine hadn't gone to school as Mummy said she wouldn't learn anything there now and she would teach her herself, so most afternoons they did lessons at the dining-table. Elaine liked History best, which was about the Angles and Saxons and King Alfred and the Danes, and Mummy made up a rhyme to help her, which began:

"About the year five-hundred A.D.
Came Angles and Saxons from over the sea..."

She didn't like Geography much, though an old Atlas that Uncle Hilary had had at school was quite interesting—more than the tiny globe that was really a pencil-sharpener. Mummy didn't like Arithmetic, but Elaine did finish learning the times-tables, all the way up to twelve, and Uncle Hilary usually couldn't catch her out. And Mummy taught her some words of French and two French songs: *Frère Jacques* and *Alouette*, which they did with actions, like Mummy had with the French nuns at school, only Elaine was a bit doubtful about the nuns, and also the French, when Mummy explained what *"je te plumerai"* meant; it surprised her that Mummy didn't seem to mind a song about a poor little bird having its feathers pulled off, but she sang it in a jolly way, so there must be something about it that grown-ups understood and a child like her didn't.

Before lessons, Elaine had to do Exercises in front of a window: deep-breathing and stretching up and down to touch your toes, and if it wasn't raining there might be garden-exercises afterwards, like walking along a plank held up on bricks, which was to give you good balance, but it made Elaine nervous and she usually came off before the end. She couldn't do cartwheels either, though Daphne, who was smaller and lighter, did them all across Uncle Hilary's lawn, making Elaine hate Exercises even more. And if it was raining, Mummy could make her walk across the room with a book on her head and she had explained it was better than something called a backboard which girls in the past had had to make them stand straight. Mummy had never had that, although she "stooped" from being so tall, which Elaine mustn't. Auntie Freda was a bit taller than Mummy, but it seemed she didn't stoop, which might be because she had done more Exercises. Mummy and Auntie Freda had belonged to something called the Women's League of Health and Beauty, who

The Business made clothes for to do their exercises in. Boys seemed not to need Exercises, and men didn't have Health and Beauty.

So when she had gone back to Manor Park and into Form Two, she had been ahead in some ways but behind in others, especially Arithmetic, which was a worry because she would need to sit "The Scholarship." Daddy had tried to teach her, but that stopped after one terrible day she would like to forget, when she couldn't understand something which he said was quite clear and he was cross and said she wasn't trying—and perhaps she wasn't, and she had been a bit whiney, but then suddenly he was roaring that he'd give her a hiding and she had run away into the bedroom and he after her, and then Mummy came and stopped him and for that she was so grateful, because it had felt as if something unimaginably terrible was going to happen...

Later Mummy had explained that they had such a good Daddy who worked hard for them all, travelling to the East End and back every day, and he wanted to publish his poems but he couldn't, but this man on the Council had read them and Daddy had read his and then the man had said they could have this flat, which lots of people didn't have and had to live with other families. Elaine would have loved to live with her Granny, but she knew she should be grateful: Mummy said Daddy had been so fond of her as a baby, and she knew she had been fond of him and it was because she was a bad child that things were so different these days.

Mummy could be angry too, in another way, not wild but cold. Once Elaine cried so much she couldn't stop, which made Mummy angrier and she ordered her to stop crying and was frighteningly fierce, like that tiger "in the forest of the night." And the sobs kept coming all by themselves, which frightened Elaine even more and perhaps Mummy saw she really couldn't stop that jerking in her middle, because she went away and then it stopped. It still felt unfair that she was the bad child, because she hadn't wanted to be and Joejoe found it easy to be good and Leo didn't care; people seemed to expect him to be naughty.

Perhaps now the War was over things were going to be happy. The other night they had gone to a park with lots of people to have a party because of winning the War. Elaine had never seen anything so wonderful as the coloured lights that were strung in the trees; it was like a fairy-tale, only not like *Snow White* that Daphne's father had taken them to see in Reading, which was a frightening film where the trees in the dark forest had branches like claws to catch at you. Mummy had made cakes to take to the park, but they were plain ones, not like the real fairy-cakes with sugar-icing some Mummies had brought; Elaine had one and it had hundreds-and-thousands scattered on the white icing so that it looked and tasted as if it might have dropped from heaven. And there were jugs of lemonade and a man with an accordion and people danced, even Mummy and Daddy, and she learned to do the "Hokey-Cokey," which made everyone laugh boisterously; they were all so happy the War was over and they had not been bombed, or not most of them. Perhaps those who had, or had people killed in the War, didn't want to dance and had not come...

And although Daddy hadn't been a soldier, his friend Jess Lewis had and so had Uncle Ben and both had sent her presents: Jess Lewis a real seahorse and a piece of sky-blue silk ribbon from Italy, and Uncle Ben, from Africa, a little book made to fit in a soldier's pocket; it was covered in good-smelling leather on which was printed "Shelley" in gold letters, and the poems in it were mysterious and hard to understand, but the one about the "blue Mediterranean" made her see its "crystalline streams" enclosing the strange sea-horse in the ribbon's blue, and almost ache to travel to that land of the singing prisoners and that sky-blue sea.

Then Daddy's Cousin Sally had married Danny, who was an airman and wore his uniform as he stood with Sally in a long white dress and veil under the canopy at their Jewish wedding, and it reminded Elaine that Sally's brother, Cousin Morris, who she had never seen, had been an airman and gone to bomb Germany and never come back. Mummy said Great Aunt Lil still believed he would, but that was because a mother could not bear to lose her son and Morry, as they called him, had been missing for too long for him to be still alive.

That was very sad, especially for Aunt Lil, who probably wouldn't dance the Hokey-Cokey like Mummy and Daddy, which Daddy enjoyed hugely and Mummy did to please him even if she didn't seem to enjoy it as much as he did. And come to think of it, there was someone missing from Mummy's side of the family, who should have married one of her grand cousins who they never met, but Elaine had heard Granny and Mummy saying he had left Teresa to have a baby all by herself and gone to Germany and been caught by the Nazis, and if he had done right by her he would still be alive, and they didn't quite say it, but you felt it was a Judgment.

By now the sun was stealing in behind the green curtains so Elaine stopped just thinking, took her book and glasses from the green-painted table and leaned on her elbow to read. For her birthday, Auntie Freda had given her *At the Back of the North Wind*, which had belonged to her and you couldn't buy books because of the War.

Elaine had read most of it several times, because when she got to the end she looked back at her favourite bits and started reading it over again. It was strange, but not like *What Katy Did*, which she had taken out of the library, and *Little Women*, which Aunt Agnes had given her because there was an extra copy in a library for crippled children where she worked, and she had explained it was about America in a War they had had there long ago to stop black people being slaves. In London they had seen some black American soldiers who didn't seem like slaves as they were laughing and talking loudly and chewing gum, which Americans did. Uncle Remus had been a slave and told his wonderful stories to white children. She wondered if he would have chewed gum...

At the Back of the North Wind was about London, Elaine's own city, which was the greatest in the world, and once when Mummy and Daddy had gone there from Long Moreton, they had come back indignant after some American soldiers in the train—white ones, she thought—were saying New York was bigger, which was all you expected from Americans, who were uncultured and had more money than was good for them, Daddy said—though it seemed it hadn't always been like that, as the girls in *Little Women* liked Shakespeare and were quite poor. Mummy and Daddy said *they* were poor, but she was not as poor as the little boy in this book, who was ill and died, and so did lots of people in London in the old days when there were no trains and buses but only horses, which her Granny remembered. Now there weren't many horses, only the milkman's and the coalman's and once there had been a horse she thought might have been more a nag as it was thin and dirty, not like the milkman's sleek one, and it drew a wagon with a man on it who shouted, "Any old iron! Any old rag, bone and bottles!" At least, that was what Mummy said he shouted, because you couldn't understand him.

When she heard Mummy and Daddy's alarm-clock ring, Elaine knew it was ten to seven and a new week; at half past she must get up and make herself ready for school. She walked there on her own now, except she usually met Mena, who lived the other side of the Circus, near the gasworks. Mena's father had been in the Irish Guards, but now he drove a bus and her mother went out cleaning but was still a lady, because Mummy said Irish women were "natural ladies" and at her convent schools the Irish girls had been expected to behave better than the English—which seemed a bit hard on them. Mrs Casey had black hair and blue eyes that seemed always smiling, like in one of the songs they had sung when the Caseys had a big party with an accordion and crates of something called porter.

They had met Mena the first day Elaine went to Manor Park. Mummy had walked with her and wheeled the twins in the old pram that had been Elaine's and was big enough for both of them to sit up one at each end with their feet down a sort of well in the middle. This led to mischief, especially from Leo, and though they were harnessed to stop them tipping themselves or each other out, they were quite difficult for Mummy to manage and she was watching out for nice-seeming children for Elaine to walk to school with. Mena was look-ing after her own brother and came up to see the twins and Mummy let her push the pram for a bit and when she asked her name, Mena said, "Philomena," and Mummy had said "That's an unusual name!" and Mena said, "Yes, I only know three Philomenas: my Granny, my Auntie and me!," which had amused Mummy, so that she told it to Daddy and to Granny and Aunt Freda when they came.

Through the wall Elaine could hear Daddy peeing; that was the proper word, though most children said doing wee-wee, and both were rude, so in their family they said "doing ah-ah," which seemed to be less rude, perhaps because it was said in a way that told you it was better not to mention it at all, at least for grown-ups, though just once she had heard her grandmother, in a hushed voice, refer to grown-ups "making water."

Now she heard the lavatory flush and Daddy wash his hands, which he was always particular they should do and also brush their teeth well. Then he came in wearing the stripey dressing-gown his friend called Kurt had given him because he had escaped from Ger-many with not very many things and Daddy had helped him, and in Germany he had been rich and the dressing-gown was a good one. Daddy didn't say anything to her but took the enamelled chamber-pot from beside the toy-box under Joejoe's bed and stood the little boy up all sleepy and undid his pyjamas which were getting too small, holding the chamber—which some people called "the poe," but that was vulgar—while nothing happened except Joejoe rubbed his eyes and Elaine knew he wasn't wet today because you could smell it and Daddy would be cross. Then she heard the tinkling sound and when it stopped Daddy pulled up Joejoe's pyjamas and let him fall back onto the bed and to sleep again while he went to Leo and did the same, only Leo shouted something when he was woken up and Daddy said, "Shut up, Leo, and stand up!" and then he said "Dam-nation take it, he's wet!" and Elaine could smell it and felt quietly smug and Daddy let Leo, still all sleepy, drop back onto the wet bed, and went to tell Mummy, sounding cross with himself and her as well as Leo, because they had stopped picking him up late at night as Leo had been dry for so long now. Then he went to shave himself in front of the bathroom mirror and Elaine hoped he wouldn't cut himself, as happened sometimes and would make him crosser.

Her smug feeling was because she had not wet the bed since she was a baby and all babies did that, as well as what in their family they called "yellow," which rude people called "poo." It seemed boys, with those ugly dangly parts, were a lot more trouble than girls. You saw that at school, too; it was almost always boys who got into trouble, and only ever boys who got a ruler across their hands or a black-board-duster across their knuckles, which hurt much worse, though usually they didn't cry and pretended not to mind. But she had come across one little boy in her class crying in the cloakroom after Mr. Ponsonby had caned him, which was the worst punishment, but only for boys; girls were safe. Poor Alex was sucking his hands, which had red cuts across them. She didn't know what he could have done, as he wasn't usually one of the naughty boys, and she didn't know whether to feel sorry for him or superior, but she liked Alex and had stopped at his house on the way back from school to swap stamps, but only once, and once he came home with her. His Mummy and Daddy might have stopped it because they had their own house and didn't want him going to the Council flats. Or it could be because her Daddy was Jewish...

And Elaine remembered a dark evening in Granny's street when she was quite little—It must have been right at the beginning of the War, before they went to Aunt Magda's the first time. She had been playing with some children when one boy asked her, "Are you Jewish or English?"

She hadn't known what he meant, but not to be English could mean being German, and everyone knew what that meant; even her Granny, who was kind to everybody, would put on a frown and say, "I'm that German lady!" which was a sort of game she played when Elaine did something she shouldn't and Granny was too nice to scold her. So she had said, "English, of course!"

Later she had learned that her Daddy was Jewish and he had explained that meant someone who didn't believe in Jesus. That was a shock, that anyone did not believe in "the dear Lord who died to save us all," like it showed on her Crucifix that Maureen had kissed and Granny's big Crucifix on the wall and Aunt Magda's on her desk. They all believed in Jesus and Elaine had thought everyone did.

She had run to her father saying, "But we love you just the same, Daddy" and he had taken her on his lap and Granny and Aunt Freda, who were there, and Mummy were all very pleased at her saying this, as if it was something clever, though she had only wanted him not to feel different from her and all of them. Yet it seemed Jews *were* different and some people didn't like them even in England, though not as badly as in Germany where they had done dreadful things to them, which was why Kurt had escaped to England with his good German dressing-gown and all the rest of his family had been killed by Hitler and the Nazis, and why Cousin Teresa's baby's Daddy had disappeared after he went back to Germany. She knew too that what had happened in Germany had upset her Daddy and made him somehow different, which might be why he and Mummy were so cross, as well as the Shortages and the other things that they said made it so difficult these days. At school, teachers got cross too, but you could see it coming and it was usually with boys, never with her. At home it seemed to be the other way: the twins might be scolded, even shouted at—Leo, anyway—but not slapped or stood in a corner like when she was little. Even when Joejoe took her sweets and hid behind a chair and ate nearly all of them, people laughed and although they said he was a greedy boy, you could tell that a boy like Joejoe was expected to be greedy for sweets.

But now the War was over, now that there had been that party in the Park with everyone happy and friendly, perhaps all that would change. In about a week they were all going to go up to London to see the King drive to St Paul's Cathedral to thank God for the Victory, and they would see Churchill and Monty. Only it wouldn't bring back Kurt's family and Daddy's Cousin Morris and all the rest who had been killed by the Nazis or in the fighting and bombing.

At this point Mummy came in to get Leo up and the sheets and him into the bathroom, and she shut the bathroom door because he was making such a fuss. Then Daddy came in again, dressed in his coat and hat and carrying his attaché-case, which was for the packet of sandwiches Mummy made for his lunch while he drank his two cups of tea with sugar and ate his porridge, or sometimes it was bacon. So Elaine knew it was time to get up and today she stopped reading and he came over and kissed her goodbye, which he didn't always and Elaine didn't always want him to; she would just say "Goodbye" without really coming out of her book. These days kissing could seem a bit silly, except for something special like a present, or someone special like Granny.

Daddy would have a bus-ride to Hammersmith and then a wait before the long train-ride and a walk at the other end. He went to Hammersmith to be sure of getting a seat as it was the end of the line, so for most of the way he would be able to smoke and read the newspaper. It was a surprise to Elaine that there were still going to be newspapers now the War was over; she hadn't thought there'd be anything to put in them.

PART III
Pawa

I

(1948)

VERONICA had opened up her mother's house and laboured with duster, carpet-sweeper, broom, mop, bucket, hunting down grime, swabbing floors, polishing windows and even the spoons and forks in the massy canteen on the sideboard. The dining-room had a door onto the garden and caught the morning sun; she had folded away the table and Ron, with the help of a neighbour, had brought down Freda's bed, on which last night she had slept, only half-undressed, under an eiderdown. Now she had made it up with sheets, blankets and several pillows, and turning back the candlewick bedspread placed in it the hot-water bottle she had been able to buy at Boots the Chemist; it seemed the supply of rubber had been increasing since the War ended.

Yesterday she had bought in boiling beef for their supper; now she was busily making pastry for apple pie and jam tarts, and had an egg custard ready for the bottom of the oven; she thought Pawa might eat that with the leftover strawberry jam. Activity was helping her through the anticipation of seeing him even more emaciated and all of them exhausted by their long train-journey. Unless, of course, a miracle of healing had taken place at Lourdes; this she hardly expected and, knowing that he had advanced cancer—"Poor chap," the Specialist had said to Deedie, "He's full of it!"—nor, she supposed, did he. For him, they as good as knew, this life was coming to an end.

She cleared the kitchen table, boiled an egg for her lunch and after she had eaten sat on, attempting to read that morning's *Telegraph*: paper Ron abominated but Freda took. Everything seemed so peaceful and normal and actually rather pleasant to be in her home of all those years ago—was it thirteen now? So much had happened in that time!—and if truth were told, to have spent just one night without Ron beside her snoring or grinding his teeth in his sleep as he sometimes did; and without his work and the children's school for which to rise and gird herself. All those months of the flying-bombs she had fretted at Magda's, not realizing how unremitting would seem confinement in the flat they were so fortunate to have awaiting them. Hilary's fussiness might be trying but the children had had the run of his garden and Magda would invent for her niece and nephews such pastimes as wartime did not prevent: papier-maché made from newspaper and flour-paste, pots from garden clay to be baked in the range's oven, an orange-box become a dolls'-house, its furniture fashioned from matchboxes, its denizens from rag and ribbon wrapped around pipe-cleaners. For Christmas she had even contrived a Crib with figures modelled from cotton-wool mixed with paste, which hardened and were then painted. Magda had both the skills and the time, but here the children had little space indoors and a dreary patch of land behind the flats for their playground. They bickered and got ill; Elaine had run a fever every month or so that past winter and into the spring; the doctor said her tonsils should be removed, but Edith said she would grow out of it. Veronica too had misgivings about an operation; both had in mind what had happened to Hilary's little boy.

And Elaine did seem better with the summer weather and the holiday Deedie had arranged for them, taking a house on Hayling Island. The August weather had been abominable, but the children had paddled and even swum (The twins vying to emulate their sister who had acquired this skill that last summer at Cliftonville) and for some ten days breathed unlimited volumes of sea air. If only they could get a proper house with a garden like this one, Elaine could have a room of her own; at nearly thirteen she should not be sharing with the twins. Thin though her daughter was and reassuringly like herself, Veronica could not but notice on her the dreaded signs of pubescence...

Of a sudden the taxi at the door, then Pawa being helped in by Ron, who had gone with Agnes to meet them at Victoria. It was clear his lion's strength had all but left her father. Veronica hastened to kiss his grey cheek and the almost as exhausted faces of mother and sister, then went to make tea while they settled Pawa into the room prepared for him.

An hour later the house was quiet as all slept, Freda in the spare bedroom, Veronica intermittently dozing on the sofa, listening for Pawa, but he was sleeping too and at four she rose to make more tea and take it to them. The District Nurse came to check on Pawa and would come again each day until, they said, he should go into hospital to die. As Edith sat reading to her husband, Veronica, preparing the evening meal with Freda, heard the story of their pilgrimage.

Even on the outward journey it had been hard, especially the part from Paris, some of it at night and in unheated trains with their slatted wooden seats, because France was still all unrecovered from war and occupation: it had been hard even for the well in body, let alone those, like Pawa, desperately sick and in pain. But the evidence of the recent sufferings of the French had actually helped to keep up spirits; from so much evil, good had to be made to triumph and everyone had their portion to contribute: "filling up," as their priest-confessors urged in the Apostle Paul's words, "what is wanting in the sufferings of Christ." Pawa had joined in singing the Lourdes Hymn and other favourites and been remarkably cheerful, and though Freda and Deedie didn't have a singing voice between them, they had prayed with the rest and helped make the sick as comfortable as possible.

"I can't tell you, Vee, and I know it will be hard to believe after all the years of bitterness; I just wish you could have seen them in that train, so solicitous for each other, so wanting to be with each other, so—loving: there's no other word for it. Everyone on the pilgrimage assumed they were Darby and Joan coming to the end of long and happy days together!"

Pawa's cancer had not been cured, yet a real miracle, Freda concluded, had taken place in the healing of their parents' marriage. With the return journey, Pawa had become weaker and towards the time of their arrival despondent.

"He was realizing he was not going to get better; he was going to die. Yes, it was hard and we were so thankful to be met by Ron and Ag at Victoria, who I know were shocked to see how ill he was. But only yesterday it must be—I seem to have lost all sense of time, but when we were still in the train, I woke at one point to hear him say, 'You don't think I ever wanted to hurt my beautiful wife, my dearest Edith!'"

Freda's voice was struggling against her tears. Her sister asked, "What did she say?"

"She said, 'Of course not, dear; it was all a mistake—not what either of us wanted!' So soothingly, so—lovingly, both of them! They didn't know I was awake and I didn't say a thing, but if my faith should ever fail, I shall only have to remember what I have seen and heard with my own eyes and ears!"

Exhausted, Freda broke down and wept. They hugged one another and shed tears together.

That evening Magda was due to visit and stay at a friend's flat. Veronica returned home on the bus with a shopping-bag of gifts from the travellers: for Ron a half-bottle of Cointreau, for herself a plaster statue of Our Lady of Lourdes, for each of the children a tiny

coloured rosary in a smoothly rounded "egg" made of the new plas-
tics, though they looked like wood and the egg unscrewed in the
middle. She was unsure about the *objets de piété*, but Elaine, at least,
showed a religious bent, and Joe-Joe too, she thought; they might
have a good influence on the quarrelling. The statue could go in the
children's bedroom. Ron would assuredly be pleased with the
liqueur.

Over the next week she made the journey twice more to her
mother's house, staying overnight to relieve Freda. On the Saturday,
with two daughters at his bedside, Pawa asked forgiveness for any
wrong he had done them.

"You never did me wrong!" said Veronica and stooped to kiss him.
Freda only said,

"Yes, father," but took his hand and raised it to her lips.

"I could not truthfully say he had never done us wrong!" to
Veronica she later exclaimed.

On Sunday Ron joined them. Pawa asked to see the children and
they said, "Next weekend," but it was not to be. That Thursday
Veronica arrived in the mid-morning to learn that her father was
sinking, though in no great pain and the doctor had said there was
no need to move him into hospital. Father O'Shea was just leaving,
having anointed Pawa and given him the Viaticum; he would be
back to say more prayers over him this evening. After that, Pawa had
asked Edith to read him a passage from the Gospel of St John.

Thus when Veronica tapped on the door and looked softly round
it, the words she heard were, "And in the morning early on the Sabbath came Mary Magdalen to the tomb…"

The sun was slanting across the further end of the room and
beyond the garden door marigolds were flowering on the hump of
the old Anderson shelter. Pawa was so quiet, he seemed a giant lulled
to sleep. Edith looked up momentarily but continued reading. Still
softly, Veronica closed the door and went and cleaned and cooked
busily until Freda came back from work early and took tea to their
mother, but their father would not drink again and that evening the
priest was there to read from his book, "Go, Christian soul…" when
Pawa died.

II

On that autumn day of Granddad's funeral, day soggy with wind-
whipped rain on fallen leaves, Elaine, with a firm hand on a wrist of
each, was leading the only slightly subdued twins home from the

Caseys' house, over which the gasworks towered monstrous in the fading light. As they crossed The Circus, nothing had changed in their suburban landscape since they moved into their Council flat in that interlude between Blitz and Flying Bombs. The area had remained unscathed, Harris's Bakery had started no fire, and if any-thing there were even more newspapers—of which some were very vulgar, as Mummy and Daddy said and as Elaine could observe whenever she was sent down to Darby's because they had run out of cigarettes. That summer, too, a fizzy drink called Tizer, beloved by the twins, might be purchased there, and best of all, an ice-cream in a round of paper, and if your pennies would run to it, a wafer-cone they put it on. Sweets were still bought with one's green ration book, after Daddy had given out the pocket money.

This ritual took place after Sunday dinner. The twins, for once almost still and attentive, would hover, looking up at their father until, with something of the air of a conjurer, he would take three sixpenny-pieces from his fob-pocket and holding them up one by one, drop one each into the outstretched hands of Joejoe and Leo and finally Elaine, adding, since her birthday, a brassy threepenny piece. This seemed riches until an inquiry by her form-teacher revealed that no-one else in her class got less than a shilling, and some got half-a-crown, and she wished the teacher had not asked them all so publicly. But when she told them at home, Daddy had said he would put her pocket-money up to a shilling at her next birthday, which was good of him, and Mummy pointed out that no-one else in the class had more than two children in their family—which made Elaine wonder if they would have had only two if the boys had not been twins, but she didn't like to ask about that.

Mena, though, who in addition to two brothers had now a baby sister, received no weekly pocket-money, only sixpences for doing jobs around the house; yet since she had gone to St Bride's she seemed able to hold her own even with the foreign princess. The nuns had found her a white dress and veil to make her First Communion and she had worn the dress to sing in the chapel on their Open Day. To this she had taken Elaine, who had been very impressed, especially at her friend's catching up the ample skirts to curtsy to Reverend Mother and the Chaplain as each of these august persons passed by. It all made Elaine wish she was at a boarding- and best of all a convent-school; still, she was happy at her Girls' Grammar, where Miss For-ster-Davis, the Head, was old-fashioned, which Mummy liked, but some parents complained she should move with the times and allow things like Athletics which Forsey (as they called her, and sometimes

Horsey) thought were not suitable for girls. But they had netball and hockey, with tennis and rounders in the summer term, and gym in a real gym with bars and ropes for climbing, which Elaine quite liked doing, and a "horse" with a springboard in front of it for vaulting, which she did not like, as Miss Crompton, standing beside it, would bark at you to "Spring!" and then haul you over if you needed it—as quite a number of girls besides her did.

Mena's convent seemed to have fewer games and no gym and Elaine would have preferred that. Also she discovered that several girls in her class were there because they had not got in to Beale, which it seemed was a snobby school in a different way from Mena's; there were no princesses but a Government Minister's and even a bishop's daughter went there, and when they played them at netball or hockey and the teams had to cheer each other, because that was sporting, the Beale girls always said "Hurrah, hurrah, hurrah!," while the Grammar girls said "Hooray, hooray, hooray!," and Elaine wished Miss Forster-Davis or Miss Crompton would tell them they must say "Hurrah!" like the Beale girls, as being higher-class. Yet some of the girls at the Grammar seemed to be quite rich, with their own houses and went to Switzerland or France for holidays, and some of them were there because they were Jewish and had escaped from the Nazis, or their parents had. One girl's parents were whispered to be German; Lotte was shy and shrinking and had no friends and was so useless at games that Elaine was relieved to know she herself could never be worst in the class. In fact at some things she was quite good; she could run fast; if they had had Athletics she might have shone at that, but she could speed down the wing at hockey—the left wing, as her sight was too poor the other way.

And Miss Crompton had not sent her for Remedials. Mummy had been pleased to hear they had Remedials and inquired specially about them for backs. Lotte was sent to Remedials, which happened in the gym in lunch breaks and were really for boys who would have to go in the army and must not stoop or have flat feet because of drill and marching. But girls' schools could have them too; hers probably did because Miss Forster-Davis was old-fashioned—which was why they didn't have Athletics.

What they did have was Deportment badges, and Elaine had gained one this term; she had been quite surprised when her name was read out at Hall and she had to go up on the platform to collect her badge, which was just a round green button, and everyone clapped. A Deportment Badge meant you were polite and neat and did not run in the corridors—or not when a teacher was looking—

but also that you carried yourself well—and certainly *did not stoop*! It did all lead her to suspect "stooping" had not been the chief reason for her not being put down for Beale, but that Mummy and Daddy had not wanted her be in a posh school like Beale, with rich girls, where she might "get above herself."

But Mena had not got above herself and didn't seem to mind being at a school with a princess and nor did her parents, who seemed quite proud of her. Arrived back on the bus that day, Elaine had gone as arranged to her friend's house at the end of one of the terraces that also belonged to the Council and had waited for the twins to return there with Mena's brother Jim, nine years old and a whizzo shot with a catapult; he said he had killed a squirrel, and like a squirrel he climbed high into the branches of trees—and once he fell and spent a day in hospital. (They would be shocked but not very surprised when fifteen years on he would die trying to land his plane on an aircraft carrier.) Leo liked to boast that he too could do these things, and while Jim did them he would lounge with his hands in his pockets, muttering things like "Go on, Jim, old man!" and secretly practised similar exploits; so, perhaps, did Joejoe, but if so, he said nothing about it.

Neither of her brothers seemed unduly impressed at Granddad's being dead—not that you would expect it in front of Jim. Elaine, though, was remembering their first seaside holiday after The War, with Auntie Jane and Mark and his new sister, Rachel, because their Daddy had still not been demobbed. They had stayed a whole week in a boarding house in Cliftonville, which was near Margate and Elaine had wished it *was* Margate, because that was a well-known seaside and her patrol-leader at Guides had been there. But Mummy said Margate was vulgar and Cliftonville much nicer.

Certainly it had seemed nothing could be nicer than that seaside, and Elaine, who could only remember the shining mud at Southend—though Mummy said it was not Southend but Leigh-on-Sea—had spent the first few days marvelling at it: the sea so much bigger than one could have imagined, and the sand, and the rocks—where you could climb on them, because further down the beach they were guarded by barbed wire and notices proclaiming Danger of Mines. Then Granddad had come and put up at a house nearby and borrowed a coal-shovel from his landlady and made them a sand-castle so big they could all sit in it; even Rachel was squeezed in, wearing her sun-bonnet, and screamed when Auntie Jane took her away because she began eating the sand.

Then last Spring Granddad had taken Elaine and the twins to the

Science Museum and afterwards they had gone on a ferryboat across the Thames, and come back and gone again without paying any more fares, just because they enjoyed it and Granddad wasn't in a hurry to get anywhere. And another time they had all gone with him to the Zoo and he had read out the notices on the cages as "These animals are Dang-aroos," to rhyme with Kangaroos, though what they really said was "dangerous"; Elaine had thought this quite brilliantly funny. And when, tired after hours of walking all round the Zoo, they left to catch the bus, suddenly Granddad had stepped out into the road and hailed a passing taxi-cab and he took no notice of Mummy and Daddy protesting that it was too expensive, but ushered them all in and paid the fare. She had felt proud of him doing that, stepping out in his shabby coat and his white hair flying up in the wind, because they were tired and money was not important. That fitted with her early picture of him striding over the rooftops of the West End in the air raids...

But that last time she had seen him he had looked ill and sat on the sofa in their sitting-room telling of his visit to a hospital and what he had said to the Specialist, which seemed more important than what the Specialist had said to him, though Elaine didn't understand it, only that it seemed still the same Granddad who had defied "some Jerry up there." Now it turned out he had been defying a more insidious death from within.

Mrs Casey, who was Mena's mother, had given them tea, which she poured from a big metal teapot with a dent in it, and milk and sugar and currant buns from Harris's. So after Elaine had got them home and extracted the key hanging on a string inside the letter-box, and turned it in the Yale lock, and been careful to push it back inside again, the twins went straight to play in their bedroom and she to lie on her bed with a book, and today she chose to read in the quaint old book of Bible stories Granddad had given her, because that was fitting on this solemn day and would have pleased him—or she felt it did and that he would know what she was doing, as he surely was with God even if not quite in heaven...

And today the twins' playing hardly distracted her, for by now a curtain had been hung across her end to give Elaine almost a room of her own, and it was Granddad had put up the rail for it, who was—who had been—so good at Carpentry, and he'd made the shelf over her bed for her books and things she wanted to keep away from the twins. At weekends, when she made her own bed, she had to pull back the curtain so the twins had space and more light to play. During the War they had built their wooden bricks into forts for their lead soldiers, and now they were allowed to play with a wonderful box Granddad had given to Mummy, that was inlaid and it was a chess board on the outside and a backgammon board on the inside, where all the pieces for games were fitted into wooden boxes which Joejoe built into strongholds guarded by the chessmen, because he said there were diamond mines under a particular orange lozenge-shape of the worn patterned carpet. Leo was generally content with a solitaire board Granddad had made out of solid mahogany, with round it a run for marbles which would roll down it as you picked them off the board and disappear through a hole into the hollow below. And Leo would pretend it was a pyramid full of gold and precious stones, with to guard them his carved elephant with the real ivory tusks which Granny had given him as a Christening present, because he was called Leo after their dead uncle who had brought it from India.

Sometimes Leo would say the elephant guarding the treasure was a mummy, which Joejoe didn't like, who was nervous. But Joejoe had Black Pussy, who had belonged to Elaine only she couldn't remember and Mummy said she had never cared for him so he had become Joejoe's. By now Black Pussy was shabby and had a green bead on either side of his head which Mummy had sewed on—but not until Joejoe had stopped sucking the head, which had made the first eyes work loose and also taken off the ears and a good bit of black fur. Nowadays Joejoe said Pussy was the strongest and could work powerful spells to bind Leo's elephant and capture the gold and jewels. So then Leo made up a time-machine that would turn even diamond-mines into sand, because diamonds were only rocks and that's what all rocks would be one day. Mostly, though, they worked together to conquer the world and were as one in the ongoing row with their sister, who complained when they left their toys over her part of the room, and they complained if she tried to clear away their things. Sometimes she just happened to bump into their forts and other buildings, or so she said; they said she did it on purpose, and so it went on.

So these days Elaine preferred to do her homework at the dining table and on this day of Granddad's funeral she was sitting there when Daddy's key turned in the lock and he and Mummy came in. They collapsed into chairs and took out cigarettes and Mummy told Elaine to put on the kettle, because although they had had tea at Granny's house after the funeral, they were needing another cup. And Elaine had gone without protest, because she was grown-up enough now to get the tea and Mummy must be sad her father had died and been buried. And while she was arranging a tray nicely with a fresh tray-cloth and softening and spreading butter and cutting the bread nice and thin as she had learned to do, and waiting for the kettle to boil on the gas, she heard Daddy say, "You have to hand it to the Catholics; they know how to do these things! The sheer poetry of that funeral-service…" It seemed Mummy thought it would have been nicer in an old church with a graveyard, but Granddad had been buried in a big London cemetery, which was not so nice, though Elaine knew that was what he would have wanted as Catholics were buried there since all the old churches that had once been Catholic were Church of England because of the Reformation.

After they had had their tea, Mummy called the twins in because she had something for them, and she took her purse out of her handbag and gave each of them a silver florin and to Elaine a whole half-crown: these coins were all the money that had been in Granddad's overcoat pocket when he died and Granny wanted it given to them. The twins were jubilant at so much wealth and Elaine would have been too, only it struck her as not sad exactly but touching that Granddad had been poor when he died, although he had once been rich, before The Business went bankrupt. So she put the heavy silver coin in a drawer of the little Japanese chest under the brass crucifix. In time she might think of something to spend it on; for now she'd just keep it.

PART IV
Growing Up

I

THEIR third seaside holiday proved different again. Cliftonville had
established the sea as a known entity which Hayling Island by its situation and its marshy breeding grounds for birds enlarged; both
would seem in memory tame by comparison with the Cornish headland where they camped with the Tregarthens, who had a caravan
and lent them a tent big enough for them all to sleep in—even eat in
if a squall should blow up—which, disappointingly, it never did
quite—or only that night Elaine would remember. Mr Tregarthen—
who the grown-ups called Godfrey, which was a new name to Elaine
and connected him to God—was big and remote-seeming, reminding her of the liners they had seen steaming majestically up the
Solent last year, coming from America. He was a Rector and seemed
from a different world from other people they knew, who were usually Jewish or Catholic; though oddly it was through Daddy that
they knew this Church of England family: Doris Tregarthen had
been at the same evening classes for Workers before she married Mr
Tregarthen and Daddy married Mummy.

Doris was small and birdlike, darting around after the Tregarthens' two boys, of whom one was older than the twins and the
other only three and neither of them did what they were told, which
was because their mother believed in Free Expression, which Elaine's
mother did not—and she guessed Mr Tregarthen might not, or not
so much, but he took little notice beyond telling his boys "Be good,
now!"—and of this they in turn took little notice. The younger, the
Kellers considered, was especially naughty: his mother would chase
after him at mealtimes trying to get him to sit at their table beside
the caravan, but soon he would be off again and his mother chasing
after him with a spoonful of food. Mummy said they were both very
spoiled and Daddy agreed that if it was their children they would
either sit at the table or go without; but Elaine and the twins were
warned not to repeat these things in front of the Tregarthens, who
knew they were too poor to have a car and a caravan, or probably
even a tent, and had wanted to share their holiday with them, which
was very kind.

In retrospect it would seem to Elaine as if the sun had always shone on that holiday—and even if it had been at times dimmed by racing clouds, the changing light only added to the magic that made that coast a paradise, with its caves to explore, real cliffs to climb and the breakers running up the broad sands to imprint them with ripples and leave behind shells and clear pools where you found crabs and other creatures hiding among unimagined seaweeds. From the cliff-top the sea could show as blue, Daddy said, as the Mediterranean, and he took her for a memorable walk, that was just her and him, to the next headland. There they met with a barking dog and Daddy was afraid to go on, but Elaine, who knew about dogs because of old Jellicoe and his successor, a Scottie called Toby, and who didn't want their walk to end in panic, made herself walk calmly past and the dog didn't do anything and Daddy followed and she felt quite protective of him, as well as a little superior and happy because he seemed happy out here with her and away from London.

All this beauty and peace had been the setting for that disturbing scene by the light of a storm lantern in the darkened tent on the cliff-top one night when a wind had got up that made the canvas shake and the tent-ropes tug and moan quite thrillingly. The twins were asleep in their ex-army canvas beds, but Elaine lay awake on her creaky metal one, her face turned to the tent wall which undulated in the gloom. Suddenly shadows sprang upon it as a light was sent wheeling round the tent's interior; then, "All asleep!" said the soft voice of Mr Tregarthen and the reeling shadows subsided as the lantern was placed on the table just inside the tent entrance and more than one person seated themselves at it who were in the middle of a conversation. She heard the Rector say, "I would not encourage you to expect quick results, my dear Veronica, but I believe that with time and your example he will be won over."

So her mother was with him and she and Mr Tregarthen, Elaine knew immediately, were talking about her Daddy, who was not there, and Elaine felt that even if there wasn't really anything wrong in that, still her mother would not want it known about. For a moment she was unsure whether to reveal that she was not asleep, but a premonition of the embarrassment this could cause reinforced her curiosity to hear more and she lay still, straining to catch their low-spoken sentences, which, if not lost to her ears, often were to her understanding. Except she understood that the Rector was giving advice and her mother was listening with an occasional murmur of agreement or phrase uttered in a certain tone that Elaine thought of as her "rightness," and which would make her somehow squirm. They were agreeing that her father would be "won over" by her mother's patience, also that Roman Catholicism was not the best sort of Christianity, which was to be found in Mr Tregarthen's Church—and how sad it was that her Granddad had been so wrong about that—and about so much! She hated to hear that—and with Granddad dead...

The conversation had not lasted very long and Elaine guessed had begun on a walk they had been taking and they had come into the tent because the wind was making it hard to talk. Her Daddy and Mrs Tregarthen must be somewhere else, perhaps together and talking too; she knew they were old friends and wondered what if Daddy had married Mrs Tregarthen—Doris—and Mummy Mr Tregarthen: only they wouldn't have known each other, would they? And then she and the twins, and also the Tregarthen boys, would not have been born—or could they have been with some other arrangement by God?

With such disturbing thoughts, after the pair had gone out she lay tense and sleepless, guiltily triumphant in having heard what she was not meant to—as heroic schoolgirls overheard smugglers plotting in caves in stories in the "Girls' Crystal"; their cliff-top setting was suggestive of this. Except Mr Tregarthen and Mummy were not at all like smugglers and the plot was not against coastguards and the Law but against her Daddy—not that it was against him exactly, because though she didn't like him being talked about by Mummy, not even with a Rector, yet she also knew it would be good if he could believe in Jesus and become a Christian; she supposed he would have to be baptized, like the twins had been, and her mind went back to the scene she could remember, because she had been there: the stone font at the back of the dim church with Granny and Aunt Freda and the babies in their pram, and then there had been a surprise when Daddy appeared, though not Mummy. The babies had cried, though Joejoe only a little and it was as well they had done him first or Leo might have set him off. Auntie Freda had held them in turn over the font and the priest said something and poured water quickly on their heads and wiped it with his towel. When it was over he told Daddy that Leo and Joshua were both very good names and Joshua was the same as Jesus, and Daddy said it was his uncle's name. Now again she tried to imagine how it would be if Mr Tregarthen baptized Daddy, who you couldn't hold. Probably he would have to bend his bald head over the font—would it be backwards like the twins, or forwards? Either way, and while she was still perplexing herself over it all, she must have dozed off, because next thing she heard her parents both come in and whisper as they undressed; then they too got into their camp-beds and everything was quiet except for the wind, through which came also the sea-noises. Listening to these she had fallen asleep and when she woke again, the twins' beds were empty and the sun filtering in at the tent door, through which her mother also was entering. Her eyes ached and she felt hot.

"I don't feel well," she said in an ill, whiny voice, and Veronica came and placed a hand on her forehead and, suitably alarmed, rushed off to ask Doris if she had a thermometer. Being ill brought privileges, usually in the shape of staying in bed, piled round with pillows, eiderdowns and hot water bottles, and plied with eucalyptus, Vick, aspirin and Lucozade. You could read, so long as some of these precautions prevailed, for aching eyes could make even reading unpleasant; a couple of times her temperature had soared to a point where voices blared and the wallpaper's patterns danced madly...

Most of these remedies being lacking, Mrs Tregarthen suggested they keep Elaine in bed in the tent that day and bring her temperature down with aspirin; then tomorrow they would take her to their Rectory for the weekend as Godfrey had to prepare his sermon and take the Sunday services. There, if necessary, their doctor could be called. Mummy thought perhaps one should be called out here, but as that was difficult she agreed, and in fact Elaine felt much better after she had had some aspirin and lemonade, and Doris reassured Mummy that she didn't need a hot-water-bottle or more blankets, just a cardigan for sitting up and to be moved nearer the tent door so she could read, and she had a lovely read of *Little Women*, which she had brought with her. Elaine liked Doris, who was practical and unfussy, even if she let her little boys run too wild; but they were quiet enough in the back of the car the next day, while Elaine sat in front with the Rector so she would not give them germs.

That weekend at the Rectory had been wonderful; she had marvelled at a house with so much space. The houses she knew were Granny's in London—three rooms and a bathroom up, two and a kitchen down—and Aunt Magda's, which was much bigger but also "modern," not rambling into room after room like this one. The garden was much bigger at The Quarry, but that didn't matter as the weather had changed for the worse and she had to stay indoors nearly the whole time; Aunt Magda always sent you out to get some exercise and air. On the other hand, there weren't as many books and she didn't find those she saw very interesting, though Mrs Tregarthen gave her a pile of magazines with tips on how to do your hair and look after your complexion and what make-up to use, and she showed her how to begin to crochet with a little hook, which Mummy didn't do, though she had taught her to knit. Best of all, there was a little white piano she was allowed to try; Granny had already started her off on the old piano her mother and aunts had used when they were girls, but this piano was new-looking and neat; she did wish she could do more than play a scale, some finger-exercises and Chopsticks, and had proper lessons, like some girls at her school.

She hadn't gone to the old stone church with the Tregarthen family on Sunday as it would be cold there, but she thought she would have liked to hear Mr Tregarthen preach, who was not called "Father Tregarthen" like "Father Billings," the curate at home, who she knew because she had started Sunday School, after joining first Brownies at the Church nearby and now the Guides; the Guide Captain was Mrs Billings, and most of the girls went to Sunday School and also Church, especially if there was a Church Parade when the Scouts and Guides carried their flags in procession to the altar. Elaine loved all this and Mummy was pleased to have her occupied and out of the flat as much as possible. But one Sunday when Granddad was coming she had warned her not to tell him she had been at Sunday School.

In fact Granddad had not, so far as she knew, asked where they went to Church or even whether they did; Elaine thought he might have guessed all along. And now they wouldn't ever again listen for his voice calling out "Pop-coo!" through the stillness of Sunday as he walked from the station, past the gasworks and cutting straight across the wasteland that was the Circus with its now derelict bomb-shelter. That was his way of letting them know he was arriving, which Mummy said was "eccentric," and it was true that she wouldn't have liked her own Daddy to do it and make people look at him in the street; on the other hand, she always felt safe with Granddad, so big and distinguished-seeming with his flowing white hair and high collar and the watch-chain across his waistcoat; she thought it was because he was eccentric that he didn't seem shabby but a grandfather you were proud to be with. It was strange he should have been such an awful father.

Mummy had said that she and the aunts had had an unhappy family and she had made a resolution that her children would have a good one, so Elaine knew she should be thankful hers was a very good family. Her parents didn't do eccentric things like Granddad and didn't have too many children, which was part of what had been wrong—though that was odd as, if they'd only had three like them, Mummy would not have been born and so neither would Elaine and her brothers: or could they have been born into another family if

Daddy had had one? She didn't think so and she thought Mummy must be glad to have been born and they wouldn't want to be without any of her aunts, so all in all it should be good Granny and Granddad had had all those children: well, perhaps God might have arranged that the ones who died had never been born, but even then there would have been five with Uncle Leo: she didn't know what to think about him, and Mummy hadn't wanted to say much, so she hadn't asked, but he had died mysteriously not long before she herself was born.

Yet her family did seem in some ways odd, not like proper English families she knew, and not like Mena's Irish one, where everything was higgledy-piggledy and yet somehow cosy and warm, and Mrs Casey seemed rarely to be cross and when she was and told them off it was not frightening and soon over. But it was frightening when Daddy was angry—as when she dropped the Parker fountain-pen with the real gold nib he had given her for getting into Grammar-School, and it was because his mother had given him one which he always wore clipped to his breast pocket; her heart had seemed to stop when, in the middle of Prep, her pen had rolled onto the floor and she was sure the nib would be bent. And when she couldn't straighten it, she took it to the teacher, who tried but couldn't either, and who couldn't understand how important it was or save her from Daddy's anticipated rage... Leo didn't seem to care if "the old man," as he called him these days, shouted at him; in fact he seemed sometimes deliberately to provoke it. And people were never very angry with Joejoe, who was the good child...

Though Mummy's way of being angry was worse because it made you feel how she was right and you were wrong, and you could tell Daddy felt this too, because he became sullen and she knew underneath that he felt upset and miserable just as she did when she knew she wasn't good, and she thought it wasn't fair that Joejoe was naturally good and she wasn't, and Leo didn't care. She did care and it made it worse to know that you were a bad child in a good family. At school, though, it seemed easy to earn the praise of the teachers and the only worry was the other girls might call you goody-goody or a swot. She had to risk that or she would get a bad report, which was worse; just once it had happened, when below her string of A's the form-mistress had written that she must not talk in class... And she had not known, as she delivered the report to her parents, it would seem to turn the sky dark with storm. Another time she had opened her report to check it was all good; other girls were doing that and their parents, it seemed, did not mind. But that had brought another storm, even though the comments and the marks this time *were* all good...

With Granny it was somehow easy to be good, which was perhaps why Elaine loved being with her. But if Granny had a special power of goodness, which Elaine thought she must have and it had something to do with her being Catholic, it did seem to leave it as Granddad's fault their family had been an unhappy one. Yet he had been Catholic too, and anyway that seemed an unbearable thought, even wicked about a grandfather who was now dead and she wouldn't see ever again, which seemed even more unthinkable. But then perhaps she would, because she had the feeling he was with God and had always wanted to please Him even if he had not known how—and that might have been his mother's fault, who Aunt Agnes had hated—but then it seemed she had hated Pawa, even though he was her father and that couldn't be right—still, she had gone to bring him from the station, so she might have changed her mind... But if Aunt Agnes was wrong about Pawa, she might be right about Grandma Rigg, whom Mummy too said was "a terror." Then again, if Grandma Rigg could tell *her* story, one might feel sorry for her, and so it might go on, perhaps forever on a sort of chain back to Adam and Eve. All Elaine knew was that Granddad had been kind to her and she had loved him even though she hadn't really seen him much—not nearly enough, what with him not living with Granny and then the War. And he was her godfather, even if not quite a proper one as Mummy had told her they hadn't asked him to be it, but she thought that he would want to look after her from heaven and God, who knew everything, would let him be somehow not far away—and in heaven everyone would understand who had been right and who wrong, and who had excuses and who hadn't meant it.

II

(1950)

They were assembled in the sitting room: so they called it, treading carefully between "parlour," which Mummy and Daddy said was old-fashioned at best, and "lounge," which was American except for hotels and liners, which were only for rich people.

Christmas dinner had been enjoyed and Christmas washing-up, performed by many hands and in the exceptional effort at goodwill proper to the feast, seemed less than usually onerous; nor had the festive spirit been tested by slippages and resulting breakages to spark Ron's curse and the prolonged moroseness which his children understood as aimed at warding off petty expenses; his sons already treated such exhibitions with contempt, by Joejoe barely concealed, while Leo might sketch a pantomime mockery behind their parent's back. Only Ron's daughter would shrink in dread, while silently reading collusion in her mother's ostensibly mild deprecations of their father's fury. Elaine had resolved that in *her* house such accidents would be accepted matter-of-factly, as they were by her grandmother and aunts, and even in Mena's family, which was poorer than theirs.

If, that was, she had a house; her views on her future had begun to envisage a husband of similarly bookish interests with whom she would share the smallest practicable space and a total insouciance about the maintaining of it. She of course was pleased they now had a house of their own, like almost everyone she knew, but that already entailed unpredictable crises as her impractical father set himself to carry out repairs or refurbishments in the effort not to have to pay someone else—and whether or not it ended in that, this could cast a blight over days and even weeks together.

These days Ron observed with clearly mixed feelings her successes at school, her absorption in reading and intellectual subjects, her aversion from domesticity. His half-jesting remarks on the theme of "bluestockings" would conclude with,

"They all end up at the kitchen sink!"

That stung, and that it was not just a joke rendered her secretly rebellious and the more determined to avoid a fate of which she was reminded by the tasks of every day.

Christmas Day was not every day and, as further insurance against breaches of the peace, Ron, having wiped round the sink and bowl and poured more boiling water through soda crystals down the drain to cut through lingering goose-fat, remained in the kitchen putting away the stacks of crockery, not unwilling to escape the bonhomie of his wife's assembled family. Elaine for her part accepted with tolerable grace to do her share of drying and forbore to irritate him by scrutinizing each item for a carelessness warranting its return to the bowl.

Nor had she muttered at the exemption from washing-up of the twins, playing with their newly opened presents on the dulled and threadbare carpet that had been the elder Mrs Keller's gift of long ago. Elaine already harboured criticism, as yet unspoken, of their mother's claim to treat sons and daughter impartially in the matter of house chores; her brothers' share, she observed, tended to a more congenial doing of errands on bikes that was seldom required of her although she now owned a sturdy Raleigh, bought second-hand out of her Post Office Savings, on which she rode to school so long as weather permitted. By the twins' age, had she not been long employed on the round of dusting and carpet-sweeping, not to speak of the annual "spring-cleaning" that life in the coal-fired suburbs entailed? As for the washing-up, that was endless—and contributed to by the twins' frequent between-meals snacks and their drinks glasses left around anywhere. She concluded they "got away with it" because they were boys rather than because they were some five years her juniors. That "kitchen sink" threatened to be inescapable.

Moreover, it being the twins' penultimate year in Primary School, they were to be "put down" for the prestigious Drapers College; their sister noted that no qualms were raised against the journey—two buses there and two buses back, with Saturday mornings to boot. Joejoe had excellent reports and Mr Ponsonby predicted what Mummy had always thought: that he would outstrip his sister. His Headmaster had a lesser opinion of the indolent Leo, and gave him corporal reason to return the sentiment. His father too grumbled, but threatened strictures were seldom applied or not for long; Veronica believed the insouciant one would be stimulated to emulate Joejoe's successes, and it was what their mother thought that would count in the end.

But for Christmas Day all rancorous thoughts were dissipated in a gratifying show of family unity and even warmth, helped and symbolized by the blazing coal fire on either side of which Aunts Agnes and Freda sat, respectively slumped and stretched in the box-shaped armchairs, heavy and sleepy from goose and pudding: Freda too from the pre-prandial sherry and post-prandial ginger-wine set out on the inlaid chest, together with the bottle of Cointreau Aunt Magda had brought from France. Aunt Agnes did not drink—only endless cups of tea interspersed with endless "cigs"; so when the aproned figure of their hostess loomed in the doorway, she was alert to utter a "Do sit down a mo., Vee!"—which Veronica did, folding her long frame into the depths of the old sofa. The cigs went round and they all three lit up.

The twins were downing their third and fourth glasses of orange-squash, while Elaine—it having been conceded she was no longer a child—had sampled the Cointreau and found it good. When Granny further decreed her a glass of ginger wine, Veronica protested, but too late. The twins clamoured for some too; this was denied, but Aunt Freda allowed them each one sip from her sherry glass, as had been allowed when *she* was their age—and deftly twisted the glass away as each twin attempted to drink deeper.

Thus warmed inwardly, Elaine sat close to the fire on one of the seats upholstered in faded red velour at each corner of the copper-plated fender: this old-fashioned settle had come with the house, only Mummy was waiting till they could do up the room and then it would go, which was a pity, for a similar settle at Mena's had left Elaine feeling that proper families had one. Her immediate interests, though, were more personal. The real nylons she was wearing were from Auntie Jane, who although Jewish gave non-Christmas pre-sents, but they were as prized as anything she had received from under the tree, as making the knees she was hugging appear quite satisfactorily un-knobbly. The knees emerged from a bright red dress that had been passed on from a family acquaintance because nylon had made machine-knit rayon quite old-fashioned. It was already skimpy on her, so that it was less on account of the season than from self-consciousness about her chest's now irrepressible twin peaks that she wore her school cardigan slung over her shoulders with its sleeves hanging down in front. Last Spring Miss Crompton—all tautness and tan from winter sports in Switzerland—must have been observ-ing her dash in and out of the obligatory cold shower, for she had levelled an accusatory finger and pronounced:

"You should be wearing a brassière!"

Elaine had grabbed her towel to her, shamefast at being thus sin-gled out, then by the thought of having to break it to her mother, who might dismiss it as ridiculous or an unnecessary outlay. To her surprise, two "bras" had appeared on her bed, still a little roomy and she was in some doubt how she was expected to wear them; she recalled as a child observing her mother put hers on over her vest, though that was not what girls at school did. Over the months they had become tighter and an aid, she hoped, to shrinking the unwel-come flesh from notice—especially by her brothers.

From contemplating the nylons, Elaine's eyes strayed to her wrist and the watch that had been Uncle Hilary's but was small for a man's watch and Daddy had said it was a good one and she must be careful not to over-wind it. She felt she should temper her satisfaction in this further token of adulthood: not that Aunt Magda—most gener-ous of aunts and from whom she had had that day a rarely-before-seen ten-pound-note—would want her to be anything but pleased with the watch. More than a year had passed since Uncle Hilary had suffered a fatal heart attack while out on the golf-course and for long Aunt Magda had been inconsolable, even distraught, as Elaine had gleaned from the remarks of her elders and the forays they made by turns to stay with the bereaved one in the country until she could establish herself in town. From confidences murmured between her mother and grandmother, she had gleaned something of her aunt's marital arrangements.

Nor did Aunt Magda seem widow-like today, with her legs stretched before the fire in stiff olive-green slacks, her torso bolt upright in a man's Jaeger cardigan, orange over a red-and-blue chequered shirt: she loved colour, and being tall and long-limbed, often settled for men's clothes: good-quality ones in which she carried her height proudly. Because of that height she had had Joejoe bring in for her an upright chair from the dining room—restored from being the twins' bedroom to its original purpose just for Christmas: the twins had yesterday helped Ron carry in chairs and dining table, having first removed Leo's bed into the room over it, normally let out to help pay the mortgage. The current lodger, Mrs Primrose, was staying with relatives for Christmas and didn't mind them using her room in return for some adjustment to the rent.

This lady—Stella as she asked Mummy to call her—was becoming an object of interest to Elaine, not least because she was recently divorced, which Mummy seemed quite to sympathize with—to her daughter's surprise, who had understood Divorce to be something unspeakable; had it not prevented Mrs Simpson from becoming Queen, who was an American—and one of the many things wrong with Americans was Divorce! But it seemed Mrs Primrose—who perhaps should now be just Stella—had been married in a registry office and not in a church, and that made divorce more all right, because it was just legal—even though in registry offices it was written up that by law marriage was for life. Elaine knew this because she had asked about her parents' marriage, which had been first in a registry office and after in a Catholic church—which made it somehow realer and was to please Granddad: Daddy had said both were for life, but it seemed Granddad thought the church made it more so.

That Christmas had threatened more than the usual strains: not that it was the first time Veronica, leaving the goose in the oven with Ron instructed as to the basting of it, had marshalled her brood to Mattins at the nearby Chapel-of-Ease presided over by Father Billings, these days a regular visitor to their home. But that it was the first such Christmas since she had become a Communicant Member of the Church of England did seem to make her extra solicitous that Deedie should make up for loss of sleep through attending Midnight Mass and the fatigue of the drive over in what Magda called the "forenoon": Elaine particularly noted the word, deriving from Scottish Uncle Hilary.

She further noted that Midnight Mass at a Benedictine monastery sounded romantic and all unlike Mattins, a main purpose of which might seem the displaying of ingenious headwear by the female component. Not that that was without its appeal this year, when her mother and she had equipped themselves from C&A's July sale. What made Elaine (in the expression current among her friends) "curl up inside," was hearing, high above her red velveteen coif, Mummy's well-bred tones, from under an aquamarine toque and clear of the subdued mutter of all around, seem rather to inform God than to acknowledge that "There is no health in us." She recalled Daddy, after Pawa's funeral, saying it was the Catholics who knew how to do these things, and resolved next year to be taken to Midnight Mass. Mummy ought not to mind that; had she not more than once told them Granny had made no objection to her "following her conscience" when she joined the Church of England?

Edith had been ruminating on the selfsame event. Veronica's very public action was regarded in the canons, and from the earliest times of the Church, as apostasy and entraining automatic excommunication. Her elder children's vagaries had already obliged her to acknowledge responsibility for the deficiencies of their upbringing: less in their Catholic instruction—That, she could appreciate, had been over-rigidly applied, particularly by their father—than in the integrity of their home life. She had consulted her Confessor and Freda, as well as her own heart and Conscience, and all were in agreement: the best recourse was prayer and such exemplary love of the strayed sheep as should one day draw it back to the fold.

And Veronica had been agreeably surprised, and also relieved, by their lack of remonstrance. She too had gone over matters of Conscience with the Vicar, to whose better experience Father Billings had referred this uncommon case, and stated her objections to the Church of Rome to be twofold: Contraception, which she was obliged to practise, and Hell, in which she could not believe. The Vicar had informed her that the Church of England did indeed believe in both those entities; but that if she found herself unable to accept the latter teaching, it need not present an obstacle to her joining. Her daughter could recall the assemblage of family ostensibly celebrating her own Confirmation, which seemed to have become secondary to the drama of Veronica's Reception: how her mother had focussed on Hell as the more presentable of her objections to Roman doctrine; whereupon Agnes, in that voice she reserved for Religion, had said the nuns at school taught that you need not believe anyone was in Hell except Judas.

That had set off a Ron made doubly sore on religious topics, for while he strove not to see as defection that brave leap he himself had made to cast off his Jewish identity, the death-camps were working to instil into any but the most committed Jewish souls poisons subtler than those that had exterminated Jewish bodies. The very name Judas meant "Jew" and showed the New Testament to be anti-semitic. From there her father had swept on to Hitler as Hell's choicest candidate. Elaine, both shielded and shying away from the worst revelations, yet had learned enough to dim that zeal with which she had prayed for the Führer's soul; and moreover had been minded to make Judas the hero of a verse drama along the lines of *Samson Agonistes*, which they were reading at school.

Probably Father Billings' presence, as well as that of Aunt Agnes, whom Ron could count on for support, had saved that particular occasion from being swamped in bitter argument as Veronica, seconded by the good curate, oscillated between making the Iscariot object of a tolerant charity and praising that other and sainted apostle who—it might seem providentially—shared the traitor's name, though more usually known as Jude. Elaine knew better than to join in, having once before, in virtue of the new responsibilities to which Father Billings had been pointing, tried protesting that the *good* people in the New Testament were Jews too, and been on that occasion seconded by her mother; this had reduced Ron to fumings against Christians in general. She had fled upstairs to sob on her bed in that slip of a room that was hers and that thankfully she shared with no one: the advantage in not having a sister, even though she sometimes wished she had one and thought Mummy lucky, having three...

Some of all this had come back to her at Mattins that morning in the interstices between the carols which livened the familiar service and in which she joined with a will. She should not, of course, harbour mean thoughts about that day of her Confirmation, when Mummy, standing out before the congregation and a mitred bishop to be formally questioned on her renunciation of the Church of Rome, had become the centre of attention; "You could have heard a pin drop!" the new convert had remarked complacently when they assembled afterwards for the celebration, with the twins scoffing cake and lemonade and casting longing looks on the Sauternes and their father setting out to tread warily between approval of his wife's spiritual relocation and aloofness from the quarrels of Christians.

Granny and Auntie Freda, of course, had not been there, nor for that matter Aunt Magda—you couldn't invite Roman Catholics to an occasion they were bound to deplore—but Aunt Agnes, sympathetic to a slap in the face to "Rome," had joined in buying Elaine a plain silver cross and chain—as well as being useful in the church to keep an eye on Leo, prevailed on to wear his school knickerbockers and blazer by a mixture of threats and cajoling. In compensation, Joejoe had rejoiced his mother's heart in a surplice, carrying a candle to light the Bishop's Procession. Veronica had been so buoyed up as to confide in her daughter her hopes of Agnes joining the Church of England as well. Somehow Elaine couldn't see it happening.

When Father Billings embarked on his Christmas sermon, Elaine made an effort to attend which soon flagged: talk of Peace, Goodwill and Christian Charity made you feel hopeful, but somehow things never were like that for long—and all too often that seemed to be her fault. Seemed—for a seed of scepticism had perhaps struck root on a day remembered for one of their more spectacular rows: what about went un-remembered, memory seeming ever to expunge such painful content. Yet memory was retentive enough of a text her mother had early impressed on her: "Let not the sun go down upon your wrath"; Elaine had scarcely applied it to herself until Confirmation classes stressed it was the right and Christian thing to apologize when you did wrong. So late that midsummer evening, she had screwed up resolution to put the salutary teaching into practice, had crept to her parents' bedroom door, tapped, entered—but it was as if her sun had already gone down. Her fumbling "I came to say I'm sorry," had been met from her mother's impregnable height of righteousness with a furious "I should think so too!" which sent the daughter creeping back, "like a whipped cur to its kennel," as she put it to herself. By the next day Veronica would appear to have forgotten—perchance forgiven; even repented her. No more was said, but the soil had been harrowed, the seed struck root.

Her father had said nothing. Nor had he on a subsequent occasion—again she had forgotten the circumstances, except it had directly involved him—when as usual she had fled to her room, her refuge; but becoming, through her weeping, aware of sounds below, had got softly off her bed and tip-toed to the head of the stairs, to hear his voice demanding: What had he done to be treated so by his own child? And crying—her father actually crying! That had been unbearable; she had passed swiftly down the stairs and into the kitchen, to fling her arms round his form huddled at the table, her mother protective beside him... Again silence! She had withdrawn awkwardly, silenced also, and after that it seemed as though some barrier had come down that could not be crossed.

Church at least displayed ordered contrast to upheavals at home;

this too she could reflect upon that morning as they rose to recite the Nicene Creed in the modest wartime "chapel-of-ease," complete with tabernacle and liturgically correct numbers of candles on its dressed altar, red oil-lamp suspended before: they had learned the signification of all these in Confirmation Class. Veronica said, it seemed by way of congratulation, that her own entry on that way to which her daughter recalled Mr. Tregarthen pointing her, had originated in Elaine's going along with friends to Sunday School, so introducing her mother to Father Billings' enactment of Cranmer's liturgies in that High style intended to manifest the Church of England's oneness with that Rome whose less congenial doctrines it enabled one to eschew.

But was that right? "Rome," Elaine was discovering—as viewed by Aunt Agnes in particular, but it seemed by non-Catholics generally—aroused something like the odium more recently attaching to "the Germans": yet to Elaine's ears was tinged with the tenderness of her bond with her grandmother—mingling mysteriously with a day remembered from Primary School, when they were learning about those Ancient Romans who actually spoke Latin, and the teacher, with unwonted verve in voice and expression, announced: "On this day our soldiers are marching to liberate Rome!" She had begun to absorb the Romans' lapidary language wherever she met it and now was officially learning it at school; most of the class disliked Latin, but she had loved it ever since Granny first took her to Mass, and the two or three times she had been with her since she had found she could understand quite a lot.

Meanwhile Grammar School was widening her horizons in other ways that disturbed. Her classmates could appear so much more knowing about grown-up life; their parents must talk about such things more than hers ever did. Just recently she had found herself in a gaggle comparing notes on their families and one girl had voiced the opinion she was lucky to have "such a *young* mother!" Elaine hadn't thought of her mother as younger than other girls' mothers; it had never seemed like that, yet all agreed that having a mother still in her thirties would make you like sisters. Only it didn't—even though at about this time a visiting colleague of Ron's had declared that Veronica and Elaine, standing side by side, could be taken for sisters. That had hugely delighted them all: Ron as possessor of a superior wife, Veronica for the compliment on her youthful appearance, their daughter the testimony to her budding adulthood. Ron on occasion was known to tease his wife about her "admirers"—and while Veronica would deprecate the term, the tease would have them both in rarely good humour.

Not so another tease, ventured in imitation of another school-mate—and Elaine squirmed inwardly, recalling a chilly November day and the two of them standing at the bus stop. Gesturing at the pimples the cold had started in the gap between Veronica's glove and coat-sleeve, she had put on the chummy voice that mimicked her friend's utterance:

"Oh, Mummy, you're all *goosy!*"

Whether it was the calling attention to her quailing flesh in front of four or five persons in the bus-queue; whether the egalitarian presumption of her daughter's tone and words—doubtless too because the cold and the wait were trying her mother's patience—again that cold fury: somehow Elaine associated it with the carbon-dioxide ice her father had shown her in his Council's laboratory, where they tested ice-creams from street-barrows. That would cling and burn if you touched it; such now the smart of Veronica's accustomed formula:

"How dare you!".

Mother-daughter intimacy would not be attempted again.

In some ways, though, Mummy *was* treating her as more grown-up these days and the foray to the West End Sales that had yielded the hats deployed at Church that morning made a shared interest in Churchgoing surer than the Catechism. As for the Church of England, Elaine had provisionally concluded that a Universe without God made no sense; that was the Church on offer and she had taken to its Sunday School and Confirmation Class, earning the praises of Miss Penny, its good spinster teacher, and of Father Billings.

For Confirmation her mother had made her a white frock out of some table-damask that had been on sale. No one else had a white frock, but it was a bit like Mena had had at her convent—barring the veil, which Elaine would have liked, but it seemed you couldn't have in the Church of England. Veronica, perceiving in her daughter a kindred pleasure in her appearance, had set herself to follow in her own mother's path, and not having the resources of The Business, laboured with the old Singer machine that Granddad had done up for her, cutting, stitching, trying on and adjusting in some instinct to re-fashion an umbilical line she sensed had slipped over the past dozen years and more. Elaine was pleased by the dresses and the interest in her appearance, but on any other plane the gulf between them continued to widen, with Elaine impelled towards flight from the nest, yet hesitant and fearful as the fledgling bird. Criticism, conscious though unspoken, coalesced around her embarrassed consciousness of a "holy" air that hung about the State Church and was all unlike the atmosphere of silent devotion surrounding the mystery of that rare "Roman" ritual that fed, and fed on, her new-found delight in the Latin language. And the umbilical line subsisted still in the row of Murray translations in the glass-fronted bookcase: tokens of an unlikely-seeming romantic past to which that mother had alluded briefly and mysteriously. The daughter sampled them, found them indeed mysterious and, though all unlike the majesty of Latin in either its Church or school guise, somehow, she knew, related to that alluring ancient world that lay behind the Church— more especially the Church of Rome—and behind their present. If only she could learn Greek! But Greek was not taught at the Grammar School.

To the glass-fronted bookcase Elaine now paid regular quiet visits. On its lowest shelf two heavy volumes stood since purchased long ago by Ron via the *Daily Herald*: The Collected Works of Shakespeare and The Collected Plays of Bernard Shaw; Ron seemed to admire them equally and would speak reverentially of *Saint Joan* as the Irishman's greatest play. Though he accorded due veneration to Shakespeare, it was becoming clear to Elaine that her father had little acquaintance with his works.

Her mother clearly had more and so The Bard seconded the Greek playwrights as links still holding in that fracturing chain. The turning of the key protruding from the glass-paned doors and their opening heralded disclosures with the faint must of printed pages and dusty cloth covers. Elaine would tip down one or the other massy tome to bear off to her room, where she would read "at" both, gradually and impartially. On a higher shelf was marshalled a neat row of D. H. Lawrence in matching red covers; Ron had acquired them through the same Socialist book club. These she would open standing, then hurriedly replace, feeling they would be disapproved.

On the highest shelves were more exotic evidences of her father's self-education. She began to take furtive snatches at Huxley, Voltaire, Renan...

III

Veronica's abiding unease about her daughter had latterly focussed on Elaine's evident interest in Mrs Primrose, the lodger. Stella Primrose had a past—so Veronica instinctively phrased it to herself—as a minor actress and hoped to resume this career once her current divorce-arrangements were settled; meanwhile she was working for

Marks and Spencer's: (such good employers and were paying the lawyers' fees for her divorce from Mr Primrose.) A good-hearted woman, she soon felt for the awkwardly budding daughter of a rather forbidding, strait-laced mother, as she considered her land-lady. Evidence of this kindly interest was even now hung about Elaine's neck in the form of a chromed chain with pendant set with paste that sparkled from between the shy little peaks under the red rayon dress: it was her favourite among some few pieces of "cos-tume" jewellery she had acquired and that were set out on beds of black felt on the drawers of the miniature Japanese chest.

Her mother, she knew, regarded it as "cheap"—not in monetary terms; Veronica had learned in The Business to judge the quality of paste: rather as a sham, as counterfeiting diamonds and genuine sil-ver. Combined with the fact that she had heard her father refer in jest to their lodger as "The Primrose Path"—eliciting frown and tongue-click from Veronica—its ostentatious allure somehow con-veyed that other things might not be as they appeared; that perhaps its donor's divorce would not make way for a true marriage; that per-haps Father Billings' "spiky" (Freda had used that word) posturings were not of the True Church...

In a rare moment of near-repose Veronica's regard was indeed caught by this "cheap" item reflecting in flashes the light of the fire: ostentatious, in another word, "vulgar." The child's taste required moulding; there was a streak in her that her mother supposed derived from Ron, albeit she thought to have tamed it in him: anyway from his mother, whom her daughter-in-law guessed to have been "a bit wild"; there had been that sleight-of-hand with the engagement ring and Grandma—as Ron's mother had been known—had, in the few years Veronica remembered her, used dye to refresh the native russet of her hair. Behind Grandma lurked the memory of Veronica's own quest for a husband, with its abiding sense that she had "let herself down," and the unscripted entry of this daughter whose path was to redeem past waywardness...

Yet so far, Veronica assured herself, so good. Elaine's interest in the theatre might have been stimulated by Stella but had been happily steered into the higher end of dramatic production by the extraordin-ary purchase of three "pit" tickets for a matinee of *Twelfth Night* on her birthday. They were still in that flat when it had been suggested by Elaine's running one of her "temperatures" and the calling in of Doctor Aldridge, an eccentric, Eton-cropped lady in whom Veronica reposed great faith. Finding her patient propped up in bed, and propped against her knees a heavy volume, the doctor had bent to take a look and exclaimed, "Great Scot! She's reading Shakespeare!" Having prescribed the usual aspirin and fluids, Dr Aldridge—as Veronica would recount to an impressed Ron—had lingered in the flat's narrow hallway to urge the importance of encouraging such precocity.

The good doctor's admonition, combined with her patient's entreaties, resulted in a detour by Ron into the West End to obtain those "pit" tickets. *Twelfth Night*, a favourite, was pronounced by Veronica to be suitable—the more so as compared with the other possibility, *King Lear*. That play's being ruled out had prompted Elaine to remember what a precocious school friend, who read James Agate in the *Observer*, affirmed to be the greatest of the Tragedies: contradicting Veronica's emphatic pronouncement that it was inferior not only to *Hamlet*, but also to *Macbeth*, which was "sensational"; but striking to her daughter was the half-choked voice in which she declared,

"I cannot *bear King Lear.*"

A strained expression had come over her face as she went on:

"...utterly unbelievable... unnatural! No daughter could treat a father as those two...!"

Elaine, being unequipped to have an opinion, could only acquiesce, but struck by her mother's demeanour lost little time in acquainting herself with King Lear, and after, or indeed as she read, it occurred to her that Granddad—old and white-haired as she remembered him, bestriding the wasteland of The Circus, calling out "eccentrically" to herald his arrival—might be King Lear...

Twelfth Night had been a gala occasion, and to this bounty her parents added the gift of her first handbag, in a grey imitation suede, and in it she carried, besides her glasses, one of the four embroidered handkerchiefs that were Aunt Jane's gift, sprinkled with lavender water from Aunt Freda; truly, she felt with satisfaction, she was becoming grown-up! The performance itself, if unmemorable in the annals of such, had opened a vista of gaiety and meaning that would colour Elaine's understanding of much now sensed as lying beyond this merry-mysterious glimpse of a bygone English and wider world.

Blending with all this promise—and in despite of the dragon of War rearing its head in the Far East—the year now ending had been the first "Peacetime" Roman Jubilee, and numbered Edith and Freda among pilgrims flocking by land, sea and now—as in their case—air, to Rome, to hear Pope Pius proclaim the Dogma of the Assumption in the great Piazza—so the *inglesi* learned to call it—before St Peter's Basilica. Great too had been the excitement of their return, no-one in the family having been so far since before the War, and no-one ever in an aeroplane; undoubtedly it would be again the topic this evening, once the twins' zeal to play "Sardines" and "Murder" in the unaccustomed space of the new house had been indulged.

Elaine had inquired what the Assumption might mean, to be confounded by the answer. That Jesus' mother had spoken with the Archangel, as was shown in the framed copy of a picture by the Italian painter Leonardo that Granny brought her from this pilgrimage, that was familiar enough from the Bible and from school Nativity plays. But that she had gone in her body to heaven—like Jesus himself, Who was God...? How could that be believed?

Her mother's reply was non-committal: some believed it, others did not; the problem, as ever, was with "Rome" being dogmatic. Her father was in no doubt; it was obvious nonsense and just one of those things priests and suchlike got credulous people to believe. Indeed, it was not so difficult to believe that Pope Pius believed it—an Italian whose very name sounded Roman hypocrisy in English ears—as that all those pilgrims, including her Granny and Auntie Freda—presumably Aunt Magda too—should believe something so novel and certainly not mentioned in Confirmation class. Elaine was incredulous at the numbers of credulous people there appeared to be, and it seemed not just people from countries steeped in Catholic superstition, but Americans and Australians, Irish—well, of course Irish—but also English like her Granny and Aunt: all come to hear the Pope assert this astounding thing which she herself could never believe. And since Catholics had to believe what the Pope "defined" in this way, as Freda tried to explain, Elaine concluded with some regret that she never could be a Catholic. She imagined her grandmother from her deathbed adjuring her to embrace her own Faith, and herself obliged to say she could not... She did hope that was not how it would be.

This, the first Christmas to be celebrated in conscientious Christian dissent, with compensating show of amity, saw Edith dispose herself on her daughter's marriage-bed, its veneered headboard still matching the giant wardrobe, the "press," the dressing-table with its triple mirror. The blue-striped coverlet was long gone, replaced by a green one that matched the curtains in the bay window. This Veronica turned back and was solicitous in removing Edith's shoes, drawing the eiderdown over her and supplying a hot-water bottle, together with spectacles, Missal and a glass of the ginger-wine. Mistress at last of her own house, she had added reason to be grateful to her mother, who as she surveyed the room from out the glow of a piety aided by a good digestion—and a modicum of alcohol—was exclaiming, not for the first time,

"I can't tell you how thankful I am we managed to get this for you!"

"Nor I how thankful I am—we are—to be out of that flat!" "And," her daughter added, "It's you we have to thank for it, you clever Deedie!"

"We must thank Providence, dear; I merely saw how it could be contrived out of—circumstances. I was becoming quite concerned that dear Elaine, at her age, was sharing a bedroom with her brothers. Your need was as good as most and I felt justified in my bit of scheming."

Edith had persuaded relatives still legally debarred from selling a house requisitioned early in the War, to make it over to the Kellers' occupancy in return for a sum to enable Veronica and Ron to put a down-payment on a house of their own. Providence, as they were pleased to agree, had favoured their finding this one going cheap because fallen into disrepair and being on leasehold—and Ron believed (presciently as would turn out) that the Labour government would abolish this barrier to progressive property-ownership. On the dilapidations they were slowly working, he fretfully, she determinedly.

Veronica settled her mother, spectacles on, Missal in hand, within the bedside lamp's circle of yellow light fast superseding the greyness filtering through the nets that shrouded the bay window. Then she descended to rejoin this first Christmas in their first "real" family home.

"We want to play 'Sardines!'" Leo clamoured as soon as she appeared.

"Later. After tea."

"But that's *too* late!" came back, between a wail and a bellow, from her son.

"Perhaps after a *cup* of tea, Vee," put in Freda, with a smile of tolerance in the direction of this unrulier of her godsons, and withal her slightly irritating air of privileged empathy with the young, now certified by a hard-won Social Science Diploma qualifying her to launch on a late-discovered vocation as their champion.

"Yes, we shall hardly be wanting cake or anything to eat for some time," put in Agnes, "But I could do with some tea right away, and I'll happily go and make it for whoever will join me."

Sitting with their teacups, the four sisters were soon launched into reminiscences of their schooldays, to which Elaine listened enthralled, especially to the elder aunts' account of Mother Lawless of the Sacred Heart, whose character as much as her name invited mythologising: in fact it was Freda, who could scarcely have known the good Mother, who elaborated some of the best stories about her, while Agnes, who well remembered her, interjected little sallies in tones conveying she regarded the whole set-up as at best ridiculous. Magda's contributions were almost asides, but shrewdly humorous and tending to counter Agnes' acerbity; Elaine noted it as the greater "sophistication" of this aunt, to whom she was increasingly drawn since she had let go of vying with the twins for Auntie Freda's favour. Of course she liked Aunt Agnes too, who in her own way was generous with gifts, mainly of books; even in wartime she had contrived to obtain classics like *Ivanhoe* and an illustrated *Robinson Crusoe*. Yet Elaine, obscurely feeling herself object of a campaign, was made especially uncomfortable by the outspoken hostility to Granddad that was ever liable to erupt in the stream of this aunt's loquacity.

Aunt Magda, once sufficiently recovered from the shock of Uncle Hilary's death, had taken a flat in St John's Wood with a woman friend who inspired some awe as the War had enabled her to rise high in the Civil Service. Thither Elaine had been making her way by bus on Saturdays to sit for her portrait in oils in the spacious north-lit room—studio by day, by night bedroom—shared by her aunt with her friendly Collie bitch, Toby's successor. This, unknown to either of them, was a scheme devised by Edith for the good of both; the family had feared the loss of Hilary sending Magda into another breakdown, while at the same time Edith felt anxious about Elaine, seeing her thin, nervously insomniac and at unhappy odds with her parents.

The portrait painting furthering this new bond, Aunt Magda had that past summer invited her niece to accompany her on a trip in the smart little Hillman with which she had replaced the old Morris. North Wales had been a revelation. Some girls at school had been skiing in the Alps, making Elaine long to see the unearthly majesty of mountains—and even in this lesser wildness of valley and stream, they had fullest impact upon her. Wales was next best to that magic destination "Abroad"—a dream to be fulfilled in the form of a school trip to Paris in the Easter holidays using all the savings from her pocket-money, regularly handed over the post-office counter at the back of Darby's the Newsagents when they had lived above it. Combining with contributions culminating in Aunt Magda's unbelievable ten-pounds, they would turn dream into reality!

Thus, while Uncle Hilary's death was sad, it was not as sad as Granddad's, and had made for some promise of richness in her life;

even Uncle Hilary's wrist-watch—not the big gold one he had won
playing golf, but the smaller steel one—had delivered her from being
the last girl in her class without one. At the same time she had begun
to sense Aunt Magda's attitude to Religion as different from the piety
of her grandmother and sentimentality of Auntie Freda. Aunt
Magda appeared more matter-of-fact—or was it more "worldly"? Yet
despite what seemed enviable affluence—Could it even be because
of it?—from another point of view she appeared less worldly than
they; the thought had occurred to Elaine as she watched her aunt at
her painting, that it was her artist's eye, as she began to give it scope
in the months following Uncle Hilary's death, that helped her
appraise *things as they were*.

Veronica, having contributed little to the "Mother Lawless" rigma-
role, and reminded by stirrings above, went to arrange a fresh tea tray
and carry it to her mother, whom she found in the familiar occupation of bandaging a varicose leg preparatory to getting up. Edith
some two years previously had entered her sixties as author of that
historical romance begun long since, having spent the War in rewrit-
ing, with Vee and Freda to type it out: happy to contribute that skill
for which their mother had provided, happy too to play the critic;
many a teatime discussion had relieved days passed by the one in her
cramped flat and its circumference of shops affording the near-daily
walk, heavy basket on arm, by the other more glamorously in the
London office of the American steel firm which employed her as
Manageress. The book was dedicated to them and its appearance in
print, with a fine Renaissance portrait on its dust jacket, had occasioned considerable jubilation; also produced sundry newspaper
paragraphs under "Grandmother publishes first novel" headings.
Now the authoress had completed a sequel and despatched it to the
agent.

Between sips of tea, she said: "I have some news, dear. Winifreda
has secured a training position with a Borough Council in the New-
castle area, conditional on completing her Diploma, so starting next
summer. I have concluded that might be the moment to sell up and
prepare to move to wherever her next posting may be: we hope in or
near London, once she has the required year's experience behind her.
And I wondered whether in the meantime I might rent your room
here. That is, if Ron is agreeable."

"Oh Mumsie, it would be such a relief to have you here instead of
some lodger! I believe Stella will remarry soon—and I'm sure Ron
would be agreeable to something so helpful to us all! Only I'm afraid
we should have to charge you rent."

"Of course, child, that goes without saying. These days I can well afford it and it will buy me not just a room but a room in your household. I should be lonely without Freda—though I know that her company is—alas!—more than I had a right to expect."

They were silent, thinking of Freda's advancing thirties and failure to attract a husband. Veronica's plan regarding Kurt Baumgarten had come to no more than a couple of theatre outings, after which he had faded from their acquaintance: they believed emigrated to America. Ron's opinion, deprecated by his wife, was that her sister would have choked a chap off with her stifling propriety. Veronica's preferred explanation was that Kurt had balked at making a gentile marriage that in the infernal light from Belsen and Birkenau must appear so much more treasonable to his people than had her and Ron's rash elopement. This last elaboration had the advantage of addressing a troubled consciousness she sensed lurking below her husband's humdrum level of daily living. Irritated by Leo's disobedience or Elaine's pertness he was liable to announce, in tones that mingled jest and menace, "My people always said, 'They'll turn against you in the end, Aaron!'"

This, at least in part, it was made Veronica grasp at the prospect of her mother's presence in the household, as Edith intuited, and it combined with her solicitude about her granddaughter at a delicate stage of her growth. Whether or not Ron would be altogether "agreeable" to the prospect of his mother-in-law's presence, it was settled that he should consent.

"How are things going with dear Elaine?" Edith next asked,

"It depends. She can be very wayward. Only last week, at the school's Christmas concert, she'd gone ahead of us and was on stage, in the front row of the choir, before I realized she'd gone and put on my lipstick! *Such* a guy as she'd made of herself: I mean, so *cheap*! In the interval I collared her and sent her to wash it off, but as I said to her, I dread to think what Miss Forster-Davis must think—as if we allowed that kind of thing!"

"The Headmistress is probably too experienced with girls of that age not to realize… And I dare say other girls…"

"Of course, that's what Elaine said, but we really can't have her looking so—*common*!"

"Well, I never have used makeup myself. I remember being quite shocked at seeing poor Queen Alexandra at the theatre, all rouged and powdered! But then Magdalen started to use it—injudiciously, I always thought. I don't think Agnes ever—but you and Winifreda did in time, and by now just about all the young things—*and* the not so young: Magdalen still puts on lipstick if she goes out! It was the War and those American soldiers bringing it with them—with the films, you know: not that I ever see them. But I meant, how are things with dear Elaine's—development?"

"Oh that! No better, I'm afraid. Her periods still haven't started. It's a worry. I was late starting myself, I know, but not as late as this is getting, and I had thought Jewish women… Of course, we don't know which side she inherits from, and it's not that I wanted her developing early—God forbid!—or that I would wish it on her—the Curse!"

Having discharged the vulgarism with vehemence and something like a shudder, Veronica glanced down to see how it was received, automatically taking a cigarette from the packet of Weights her mother proffered from the bedside table.

"You've consulted Doctor Aldridge, of course."

"Yes, back in the summer, before school started. She examined her and said she had all the—the parts, you know, in place. But still nothing has happened… You know, I almost have the feeling she doesn't *want* it to, that she's holding it off somehow. Do you think that's possible?"

"I don't know, dear," said her mother, whose opinion was that these deep waters should remain undisturbed. "I'm sure it will all put itself right. We must hope she will grow a little less thin and sleep better."

"With her working so hard for her exams, that's not likely. We've had to have sleeping-tablets: phenobarbitone, she's sometimes in such a state! I had hoped Freda's masseuse would have some wisdom to offer; we were prepared to pay for it. But when I took Elaine to her, all the way up to the West End, she just clammed up. I think she was frightened; the woman is Oriental, you know—I think she may be a refugee from this new War it seems we're into—and thank God at least it's as far away as possible!—plus she's albino or something, so—but I know Freda has great faith in her. And she was quite sympathetic—I think she saw how things were. She said it was best for now to let things take their course."

"Perhaps that *was* wisdom."

"Perhaps. Naturally I want to do the best by the child. It's not as though they were left to discover it all for themselves these days! Before she went to the Grammar, Miss Forster-Davies talked to the new parents, and she particularly asked that the girls be told about—about menstruation—before they noticed things, from the older girls, you know. So I had to tell her."

"What was her reaction?"

"Not much. She said she'd heard something from a girl at school with an elder sister. Which is how I learned myself, from Agnes."

"But you can be sure I had told Agnes in good time, and would have told you myself if she had not first."

Feeling Edith sensitive to a touch of reproach, her daughter replied, more generously than frankly,

"I know you would, Mumsie. But my friend Winnie's mother didn't and she was terrified when things started; she thought she must have been injured somehow."

Edith resolved to look for an opportunity for a tactful word or two with her granddaughter. Freda had told her how, a year or so previously, she had been on hand at bedtime to comfort the child, who had thrown herself in her lap sobbing, because of something she had seen in a newspaper, about a woman who "became a man"; she had seemingly become obsessed with the idea that this could happen to herself, but had not confided her terror to her mother. More recently the child had complained of what appeared to be a spasm in throat or larynx, which she said "made a noise" when she most needed to be silent; she had forced herself to this confidence because sure her schoolmates must notice. On a word to a mystified Veronica, it was reported to Doctor Aldridge and subsequently examined by a throat-specialist, who found nothing amiss—so Veronica assured her mother, but Edith remained observant. Clearly there was *something* amiss, which if not physical might be "nervous"; she had mentioned it to Magda, who said it was a tic and some "syndrome": Edith didn't remember its name and was anyway sceptical about syndromes. But Magda had gone on to vent a rare anger at her parents' treatment of Elaine, which she termed "abominable": the word had struck the mother of this usually reticent daughter and she had felt proper to deprecate it, but Magda had persisted: How fortunate they, to be blessed with the only girl-child of the new generation, indeed with the children on whom rested the hope of their family! Edith knew that "hope" referred to Pawa's family, but protested that Ron's sister and also brother had each a son and a daughter. Magda had remained emphatic:

"Mother, *they* are not hoping as we must! Ron's brother has cast him off and his sister—kind soul, I know, but Jews—who knows what their hopes—her hopes are! I notice she and her husband treat *their* daughter mildly, affectionately, and surely in the spirit of the Old Testament: is not written in Isaiah; we hear it read at Christmas, or is it Epiphany? 'Your daughters carried tenderly...'?"

Edith had dropped remonstrating, but been made uneasy. Magda had herself suffered what they called a "breakdown." She had been helped by a Jesuit, who was a psychologist but not like the one who had brought about Agnes' near-severance from them and reinforced her surely excessive detestation of poor René! Who, if they had had psychologists in his day—if one could imagine his parents, or him, consulting one... But no, imagination boggled! Their and their parents' generations had borne their burdens of sin—that Original Sin and its Effects: had struggled on with it to their graves! As must succeeding generations—and yet...

Edith recalled the solemn Act of Forgiveness of her erratic and dogmatic husband, made and repeated "as she herself hoped to be forgiven" that part her own pride and contentiousness had played. And yet! A something in this notion of Psychology might seem to make forgiveness easier, helping one understand—not all, but indicating all might ultimately be understandable—nay, be understood! She would not confide any of this to Winifreda, who would blame Ron rather than the sister to whom she remained close. And Psychology apart, one should make allowances for Ron, surely unfortunate in respect of the "invincible ignorance" that was the charitable explanation of his continuing aversion from their Faith! As ever, it might be all too easy for those who professed that Faith to "have the greater sin..."

Distantly reverberated in memory that conversation with Veronica after Elaine's birth. She had inquired into the House of Atreus and owned to seeing some relevance: as if even the pagans had insight into this entail passed from generation to generation. Allowances had best be made before each life was weighed in the balance; safer to her soul to conclude these uneasy ruminations with that utterance of French wisdom she had made use of for her novel:

Tout comprendre est tout pardonner. To understand all is to pardon all!

PART V

Idyll

(1959)

I

IT WAS SOON after Lent Term began, in the doldrums of the calendar, that Ian Roody sat at the window of his room, gleaning such remains of light as the narrow street and the flank of medieval gatehouse beyond allowed to fall upon his desk. As a College Scholar in his last undergraduate year, he had had his pick of rooms and had he been wealthier might have commandeered one of the spacious suites giving onto the Great Court—though those were vulnerable to noise and occasional invasion from late party-goers. This room had been a compromise between his means and a last opportunity to indulge a bent for the medieval unsatisfied by two years in the Victorian Gothic Court behind its Victorian Decorated archway on the other side of Trinity Street. And his First obtained, the College had allowed him to continue in it for this further year of preparation for the Colonial Service.

Looking out he could reflect that he had virtually grown up a Medievalist, almost literally in the shadow of Ely Cathedral, exchanged for a Cambridge whose oldest stones rested in a European past on which England had turned her back when she sent her pioneers and buccaneers forth to make them a New World. Though even before that, the seed of modernity had been sown by Cranmer and the Arch-Reformers gathered around St Edward's Church in that small precinct left behind when Henry V's pious son had his grandiose Parade driven willy-nilly through the old town, the better to set off the glories-to-be of his King's Chapel. Cambridge would witness the burning of Prior Barnes, of Luther's Order and persuasion, under a later Henry's invocation of the law against heresy; then the kindling by his daughter of Smithfield fires and that pyre in Oxford which the same Cranmer prophesied should never go out; and indeed the stakes had but re-formed into the gallows-tree from which, through succeeding reigns of Tudor and Stuart, the inward and privy parts of priests and their disciples would be cast into the cauldron before their agonizing eyes…

But of late had come a *revenant*, a Benedictine monk released from his cloister to teach in the Cambridge of Latimer and Ridley and draw children of Enlightenment and *Sturm und Drang* to contemplation of the common European heritage. Already too the Order of Savonarola and of Torquemada had returned to the city where, four centuries earlier, the Puritan founders of the state of Massachusetts had built Emmanuel College—since disrespectfully known as Emma—over the ruins of their friary. Now their white-robed brethren had taken to descending each year from Oxford to preach their scientifically adjusted doctrine in the Mill Lane Lecture rooms to nurselings of Darwin and Rutherford. Curiosity had impelled Ian, with many another, to attend.

The colleges' religious past on the eve of the Reformation had fascinated him after he was admitted to that Trinity founded as monument to the Eighth Henry's Renaissance magnificence upon the closure of two existing houses of study. By contrast, Bishop Alcock of Ian's own Ely had not awaited the king's self-serving zeal, but on the decayed St Radegund's nunnery had founded that college on which, all unmedievally, he bestowed the Holy Name of Jesus. And it was in that nunnery's heart, that panelled room by tradition the sanctum of its Prioress, that at a lecture Ian first met Elaine.

It seemed she had been drawn by an old love of Latin, surfacing through the unsatisfying English thesis on which she had embarked —rather as he had been drawn away from the tedium of more contemporary studies by his resurgent love of the medieval. She had entered just as the distinguished Latinist was about to begin his lecture, had seated herself at the long table in the vacant chair beside Ian, placing a bag by her feet from which she took out a pair of glasses in a case and put them on, and a fountain-pen which she unscrewed, then found had run dry. She was stretching down to rummage in the bag when Ian silently proffered one of the small collection of Biros he carried in the breast-pocket of his Harris tweed jacket. It was accepted, and turning to receive her smile of thanks he was struck by the curve of her lips and the dark sheen of the hair dropping heavily to curl inward on her shoulders. Both fell to taking notes of the lecture—Ian, who seldom made notes, to counter the snare to his senses at his side. By the session's end he had made up his mind, and when she put away her glasses and made to return his Biro, he said, "Keep it if it's useful to you; I've three more here" (indicating his pocket). "I only use a fountain pen for exams, to make my scrawl more legible. Biro's good enough when only I have to read it!"

"That's sensible really," she had acknowledged; "I'm just—well, superstitious about my pen. My father gave it to me; I think it was symbolic to him—of education, which he would have liked to have had more of and I am lucky to be having."

Her candour surprised him and as he looked round the dim, already emptying room, banished any remaining indecision.

"Do you know anyone here?" he asked.

"No."

"Nor do I. You know, I'd like to discuss what we've been hearing. Would you have coffee with me? I sometimes drop in at the Dorothy on my way back to College."

The readiness with which she accepted reassured him she returned his interest. As they walked he told her his mother had once worked as a waitress at this same Dorothy Café, before becoming a teacher in King's Lynn where she met his father, come down from Glasgow to be articled.

"Mum's from Ely and always wanted to live there. My father was able to join the law-firm there about the time I was born. Now he's a Senior Partner. Have you been to Ely?"

She had not and he checked his impulse to offer to show it to her, telling himself it was absurd; they had only just met and already he was wishing never to lose sight of her. Instead he told her of the Cathedral that had moulded his interest in the Middle Ages and monasticism, and of Queen Etheldreda, foundress of a double monastery, for both men and women, on the remote Isle in the fens: a true Englishwoman, determined and self-determining...

"Like Hilda of Whitby." She had known about her.

"Yes, another splendid Saxon woman, like Audrey—that's how Etheldreda became known; I suppose the Medievals couldn't cope with all those syllables! Your name, too, is medieval for Helen—very English!"

Helen of Troy, Elaine, Lily Maid of the Isle of Astolat; Isle of Ely, Etheldreda, Audrey, Elaine... Associations were circling wildly in his head as she rejoined,

"Yes. I sometimes wonder if that's not why my parents chose it— subconsciously, perhaps. Because in fact I'm—not pure English!"

They had reached the Dorothy and he settled himself at a table opposite her. The eyes that the glasses had screened, observed from behind his own glasses, seemed less dark than sun-flecked and were overarched by brows almost black, though her hair was glossy brown... His own hair stuck up, flaxen wire inherited from his mother, who said it proved them descended of Jutes. Ian had grown sceptical of the etymology from jute, but in him there operated a predilection for otherness prepared by the grafting of Saxon and Norseman on Celt.

Again he jerked wandering fancy back to her concluding words.

"What are you, then? Irish? No, let me guess again: French!"

Behind his glasses the eyes set deep under a prominent brow were blue. Elaine sighed a little diffidently; her half-English—not even quite that—half-Jewish mix had stood in the way of friendships before, and that not only with men, nor only with gentiles. A Jewish girl had been her first friend at the Grammar, only to be weaned away at puberty with its reminder, to families if not to children, of their role in rebuilding the Chosen Nation of which they were, too literally, the survivors.

One brief friendship at Cambridge had been with a Jew. They had met sporadically for a term and he, in contrast with others over-anxious to assume familiarity, had gone only so far as to put a tentative arm round her shoulders as they sat in a London theatre the following vacation. And that had been that; perhaps the impulse itself or his family might had warned him too of unfaithfulness to his Israelite birth and vocation; perhaps someone more eligible or more attractive had crossed his path—or been placed in it. Though she had liked Simon, she made no attempt to recover him. Saddest of all, about that time her cousin Mark, now a freshman reading Law at Oxford, had gone off to Jerusalem in search of roots his parents had left untapped and she was aware that, while their families continued to visit, her childhood playmate held himself aloof.

"I am a little French," she answered, "On one side, that is. The other side—my father—is Jewish."

"Ah—who gave you the fountain-pen! Is he—living?"

"Yes."

"He must be proud of you."

"In a way, yes."

"My best friend in College is Jewish. A good bloke: we met through the Rambling Club. We hill-walk in the vacations, from my uncle's in Stirling. Will's been filling in the background to Medieval thought for me; he's a real German Classicist. I sometimes wish I'd done Classics. It was a toss-up. I did A-level Greek with Latin and History. Most Historians did Latin and English, but I decided you could read English yourself."

"It's not quite that simple, or I wouldn't have been at the lecture this morning. I did read English, though now I'm working on a thesis—supposed to be, but..." (She grimaced.) "I did Latin A-level too. I wish I could have done Greek, but we didn't have it at school. At the school I could have gone to—Do you know Kitty Ponsonby, a Classic in my year? She's a good friend now but in Primary School we were always rivals for top of the class. Her father was the Head-master and…"

She broke off, ashamed to be airing this old grievance about her schooling to someone she scarcely knew. After all, she had got to Cambridge, and even if her road there had been rendered less smooth than Kitty's, it was she who had ended up with the First and the Research scholarship.

"I think I've come across the name. Her father must be pleased you both did so well!"

"Maybe. I think Kitty hardly sees him now. Her parents divorced. I think he could be a bit of a brute; I know my brother Leo came up against him."

"And did you?"

"No; he thought well of me—because I was a 'swot,' I suppose. That's what my father called it—and Leo, of course: 'swotting'—and at my next school I had to be one even more, while Kitty… But I don't know why I'm telling you all this. It's 'water under the bridge'! I'd have liked to do Greek, though; I used to read the Greek plays my mother had—in translation, of course. And they stood me in good stead for the Tragedy paper in Finals. I was brought up to be inter-ested in Greece; my mother had known a Greek before the War, and I managed to trace him when we went there."

"You've been to Greece?"

"Yes, the summer before last, with Kitty and some other girls."

"Will and I went last summer."

"Will—your Jewish friend?"

"Yes, Wilhelm, born in Dresden not long before they had to get out. Most of his father's family ended up in Auschwitz… But tell me about tracing your Greek."

"It wasn't very difficult; he was in the Athens telephone directory. He was very surprised to hear from me and he told me his history."

"Which was?"

She was remembering. Sitting in the shade of a pine-plantation, outside Athens, where Panayiotis Andropoulos had recently suc-ceeded in reclaiming his piece of land between those bare hills with the legendary names: Parnes and Pentele.

"He'd been a liaison officer with Churchill but after the War the right-wing government imprisoned him on an island. I found him even more fascinating than—than the Parthenon and all that! In fact he had very little time for antiquities: said he would show me the real Greece."

"And did he?"

"Up to a point; listening to bouzouki in the Plaka—there wasn't time for much. But I should like to go back. My mother wants to go too; there was some romance between her and Andy, as she calls him. I think that's why, at the end of the War, she took up collecting clothing for Oxfam, to help in the terrible state Greece was in."

"Your family sounds more interesting than mine!"

That her hybrid birth intrigued him had the effect of further loosening some sluices behind which welled feelings: about her father, how disappointed in his ambitions, how scarred with the sufferings of the people he half accused himself of having betrayed—how irritable become! Proud of her, yes, but with mention of that symbolic pen a recent wound had been touched.

"I could have sent you out to work as I had to and not gone on supporting you," Ron had told her—too dumbfounded to protest she had cost him little since she left school, or ask whether he would have wished her to leave at sixteen and become an office-girl or a secretary as her mother had… She felt an urge to confide something of all this, but they had only just met; it would be disloyal…

"I suppose so," lamely she concluded. "Sometimes I wish they were more ordinary. They mean well, I know…"

"But?" He had seen tears brighten those eyes before being blinked back.

"But my father is weak and my mother, in a way, too strong. She overbears him by sheer force of—of being right! I don't know why I'm telling you all this," she ended tritely, "I don't usually talk about it—not ever, really. I'm not even sure I'm seeing it right: that it isn't just how I feel and wrong… Tell me about your people."

"There's not much to tell. My father's a 'son of the manse,' if you know what that is: his father was a minister in Perthshire and had six boys, so they were pretty hard up; apart from schooling—pretty oppressive in Scotland!—Dad was self-educated, and it's all left its mark, but it has its good side, as the old man believes in education and has given me the best he could. And he doesn't believe in large families—only perhaps somewhat larger than my mother did! Anyway, the result is I'm an only child. She's English, very! She was a primary-school teacher but Dad doesn't like his wife to work so she just keeps house, which I don't think makes her happy."

He had wheeled her bike for her as far as Trinity Great Gate, where he pointed out his window high above, and asked,

"Will you come to tea tomorrow? We can talk some more."

She had demurred at that, still struggling with her desire to unburden, to be understood—but why should this offspring of Scottish Presbyterianism understand what had never been said explicitly even to her grandmother?

"I've books ordered at the Library that can't be taken out. I shall need to work there."

"Sunday, then," he persisted, and as though reluctantly, she agreed.

II

That was how he found she had gone early to Mass in the great Gothic Revival church reared, in the teeth of no-popery, on the then edge of town, to become the landmark known popularly as "The Catholic." Having in his 'teens articulated his disdain for the anti-intellectualism of his Protestant background, Ian was not indisposed to set aside received British prejudice towards Catholicism. Now her face, opaquely tinted about eyes suggestive of far-seeing beneath those symmetrically drawn brows, had taken on for him an iconic quality. He seemed as if attached irrevocably to this being so suddenly materialized, and who beckoned him out of what was becoming a defensive, cynically harnessed view of life. They had spent some half dozen hours in each other's company when, playing her one of his favourite records on his gramophone—purchased with the Queen's Shillings saved up from National Service—he found himself kneeling before her seated figure, his arms shaking as they stole round her waist, his head falling into her lap. So they remained, she passing cool fingers through his hair's hempen springiness until the last cadence of Mozart's horn-concertos blended into their silence.

By next day his mental habits were remonstrating that he had seen no rational grounds for Christian faith as school and parents had presented it; furthermore, as was notorious, its Catholic form set several obstacles in the path that, willy-nilly, presented itself as supremely desirable, even inevitable.

As it happened, his preferred subject of study yielded an unusual ratio of Catholics among its students, with two of whom he was on terms that had taken him to the Chaplaincy, or rather to its bar, where intellectual life coalesced around the presiding figure of Monsignor—known familiarly as "Mugger"—Hervé: notorious to the wider University for his banning of women from his cure.

It was thus natural enough that Ian should tax one of these companions with claims deriving from sixpenny pamphlets of the Catholic Truth Society he had picked up and examined in her room, and which Elaine purchased from the rack in the porch of the great spired edifice, on her way to and from ever less determined grapplings with her thesis.

"Pre-digested pablum, my dear Ian!" pronounced Brendan McNally, "Hardly food for a mind researching—what did you say she is engaged upon? The evolution of Romance...! My dear fellow—*really?*"

Ian ventured to tell Elaine of his friend's response—suitably rephrased—while the tea was drawing and she kneeling before the gas-fire in his room to toast crumpets on what had become their almost daily rendezvous there. To his relief, she seemed not affronted at his mentioning her to his Catholic friend, concentrating rather on the imputation of anti-intellectualism.

"I've tried to read Aquinas," she protested, "but he's more than I can take on at present, feeble though that may sound to your Brendan! Augustine, now—I became a bit bogged down in the *Confessions*, too; the early parts are easy but it gets pretty dense. It was the opening—Do you know it? 'Thou hast made us for thyself and our hearts are restless until they rest in thee'..."

"Yes..." he had said, but she had trailed off, reliving a dark evening of her second term: Kitty and she cycling side by side, returning from a gathering at the Anglican Friars' on Bene't Street, to whom Father Billings had directed her; she could almost feel the gowns that conveniently protected their clothing from rain and bike-oil, flapping about them in the winter wind on which those words sounded, spoken unforgettably by her friend—now teaching in London, awaiting her marriage to a friend met that very evening, now ordained... Kitty had stuck with her High Anglicanism, and had done better in the marriage stakes than herself, though less well in Tripos, as no doubt preoccupied with courtship: there was truth in the witticism that the degree "undergraduettes" most aspired to was their "MRS"!

"Yes, I remember it," she realized he had said. Pushing away envy of what seemed Kitty's easier, more secure ride through life, she ended lamely,

"You've read them, then, the *Confessions?*"

"Yes."

"You seem to have read most things!"

"Well—as much as I can—and that seems worth reading."

With deliberate callousness he added,

"I've read Bertrand Russell on Aquinas and Augustine. Have you?"

"As it happens, yes!"

Again he persisted, telling himself he was cruel to be kind,

"Don't you think he sums them up pretty convincingly?"

"I don't know," came after moments, in a low voice, "I hope not, but I can't really judge."

"But surely, if you can't answer him…"

"Not directly, or not yet. I'm not a philosopher."

"Oh, come on! If you can read Russell—and didn't you do a Philosophy paper for Finals?—and get a First!"

"Probably not for that. It was an option in Part Two: 'English Moralists'—which included Aquinas, also Augustine as well as Plato and Aristotle—even St Paul! I chose the last three, as well as some of the really English ones: Hobbes, Locke and so on. That's how I came to read Russell's book. No, I can't answer him; I just see things as he—does not."

His reading had acquainted him with most of the authors she listed and, his argumentative side to the fore, he continued, making himself be cruel.

"That's not going to do, is it?"

"Why not?"

"Isn't it pretty obvious? The Catholic Church is all very fine as a historical entity, as mediator of Classical and European culture—art, music, all that. But as a creed for the twentieth century—well, certain things are notorious enough!"

"Such as?"

"Divorce. Birth-control."

"Its views on those are challenging, yes, but to me they seem right. Besides, the Church—and the Christian—is meant to be a 'sign of contradiction.'"

"But surely as a woman—and I take it an emancipated one…"

"Why? Do *you* approve of divorce—and birth-control? Artificial, I mean, because, you know, the Church does teach…"

She broke off, leaving him struggling with his feelings. If she was not "emancipated" in the ordinary understanding of that label, it seemed she was less coy about such topics than some women he had met, and he liked that; plain speaking was to be taken seriously.

"I don't know," he replied, "I suppose I do."

"Isn't that what Plato calls an unexamined assumption, a belief that is not knowledge?"

"Plato speaks of 'right belief,' as I recall!"

"And also of sophistry! I presume anyway your Catholic friend doesn't approve of divorce and so on?"

"Probably not. We've not discussed it, but Brendan's not dogmatic about his Catholicism."

"The worse for him!" exclaimed Elaine with what seemed unintended violence. As if in mitigation, she turned to other topics, which they pursued self-consciously until, and without the half looked-for embrace, he parted from her more reluctantly than ever, aware of the cold wash of uncertainty invading that ardour which had surprised him—as it surely had her?—by the simplicity of its appearing.

Perplexed and also resentful at this check, Ian made himself set his feelings aside under the pretext of working for his qualifying examinations. For over a week he made no attempt to communicate with Elaine, though hoping for a chance encounter or that she would write or even come to him—least of all expectable; yet all that time he refrained from "sporting the oak" and would start up expectantly whenever a knock came at the door.

III

Thus was it that, his pen having fallen from his hand onto the page of notes he had been making, Ian was looking unseeing at the buildings on the opposite side of Trinity Street, when an unaccustomed gentle rap made him start up, expectant it would be the very she of his thoughts. But to his eager "Come in!" it was Brendan who made his soft, Irish entry and, his expression shifting between gravity and amusement, began,

"Excuse the intrusion, my dear fellow, but an *unprecedented* event has just overtaken me: Monsignor Hervé, at my door *in person*, purple sash, gaiters and all, looking his most positively *bishop*like: something Mother Church never could risk; he's far too exotic for this dismal age! Well and over a glass of Sauternes—French wine is of course all one would presume to offer him—he first swore me to confidentiality and then broached a most delicate matter, my dear fellow, in order to seek my *advice*, you know. And my *advice* was that he should allow me to speak to you, which he was terribly reluctant to do unless I could assure him you would not regard it as a breach of—of *trust*, you know, and so, my dear fellow, may I hope that you will *not mind*—will not consider me, far less the good Monsignor, as meddling in any way? Otherwise, I do assure you, it shall end here!"

The assurance sought being readily granted by an astonished Ian, alert this might at last prove news of Elaine, Brendan continued,

"It concerns a certain young lady, my dear fellow, in whom as I understand you have—an *interest*. Or have had, in which case you have only to *indicate*, I do assure you, and your feelings—and hers, which is even more *à propos*—shall be spared! May I suppose you know to whom I refer?"

"You may. Go on!"

"I am relieved to hear you say so, dear boy, for the young lady, it seems, broke in upon the good Mugger in a considerable distress! She had already crossed his path and confided her wish to become a Roman—one of us—and her chagrin was that this appeared to have come between her and you! 'Must I be sacrificed for the Faith before even I profess it?' was, it seems, the tenor of her agonized appeal, and it melted the monsignorial heart! Having identified you as a friend of mine, he only paused to put on his shovel hat—oh and I suppose the sash and gaiters, and I don't doubt he dropped in to the chapel, to pray for guidance, you know—before beating a path to my door. I offered to lead him to yours, but he was most anxious to be no more than the *means* of grace, you know, the *instrument* of Providence; I hardly like to call him the *éminence grise*, though I think the role would suit him perfectly, don't you? Rome is surely the only *other* place where one can imagine his gifts being appreciated!"

Brendan, throwing a histrionic talent into disarming his friend, was carefully watching his expression change from surprise to embarrassment to relief.

"Sit down!" was all Ian said and producing a bottle of South African sherry, filled two glasses. These were imbibed in silence until, abruptly, he asked,

"What should I do, do you think?"

"My dear fellow, it scarcely becomes me—*not* a ladies' man—to advise what you *should* do. May I merely suggest that what you *could* do is see the Mugger yourself, with or without the young lady in question—you would be judge of that."

"I thought he didn't deal with women!"

"*Undergraduate* women, dear boy, who in his estimation are liable if admitted to the chaplaincy to interfere with a stage in *masculine* development proper to the discernment of vocations, to looking before one leap... Your—friend, a *post*-graduate I understand, may be deemed sufficiently mature... *Not* that she was bold to avail herself of the privilege; I gather she had recourse to one of the parish priests, but encountered the Mugger while praying in the chapel and so came to confide in him."

"I see. Look, I'd better see her myself and find out if she wants—us—to go. I—I'll let you know, shall I?"

"No need, dear boy, though of course I am willing again to be emissary... But the Mugger is very approachable—more so than may appear, you know!"

"Yes, well, I'll see... By the way, Brendan, do you—I mean, I suppose as a Catholic you go for your Church's line on marriage. You know, no divorce, no contraception...?"

Brendan regarded him as though in surprise, then made a deprecatory motion with his hands.

"My dear Ian, really, I hardly know what to say; not my line at all! Of course, we heard all about it at school and as something of a logician I'd say it all hangs together—if you grant the premises, you know! The authority of the Magisterium, marriage a Sacrament and so on—all quite *inspirational* to contemplate, would you not say? Speaking personally, I'm disposed to leave it at that; I'd doubt my poor power to work it out in practical terms, notwithstanding all the grace of the Sacraments! My parents couldn't; my poor dear mother looked on marriage as a cross to be religiously borne. Of course, my father—God rest his soul!—an Irishman with all the nation's weaknesses... It takes an Irishwoman to control them and my poor mother was English—*is*, I mean... Sorry—becoming disgracefully personal! Are those sorts of things *your* problem, may I ask?"

"They could be, I suppose."

"Then I'd ask the Monsignor rather than me."

"How can he know—in practical terms, as you put it?"

"Dear boy, it's his job! A priest, you know, gets to hear a lot, in Confession and so on. Admittedly the Mugger doesn't have to do primarily with married folk, but there are some—graduates and dons attached to the chaplaincy and others to whom his style of cleric–alism appeals. Of course, you could try a parish priest and be sure you had someone who knew all about the—shall we call it the messier side of polite living? But I'd give the Mugger a try. And you'll reassure the damsel, won't you?"

"Really, Brendan... But I'll at least find out if she wants to come along."

IV

With this in view Ian, half reluctant and wondering at himself, made his way early next day to the flat Elaine shared with two Newnham Science graduates who he calculated were sure by then to be in their labs. Miss Browne, the landlady, gave him an appraising look but let him into the hallway while she called Miss Keller.

Elaine came running down the stairs, taking off an apron to reveal slacks and a polo-necked sweater she had knitted which showed off her tall, slim figure. He had had time to notice on Miss Browne's wall a religious picture: the Saviour, haloed, pointing to his heart on fire. Indeed on their first visit this icon had intimated to the three young women that their landlady was a staunch Romanist—and as she soon revealed, a convert from the Church of England. The two scientists, one Methodist, one Low Church, had pragmatically overlooked this portent in view of the unusually good value of the accommodation, but Elaine had noted it as not the first of such coincidences: signposts, as she was beginning to see them, along her way.

On seeing Ian, her face momentarily showed confusion; then she invited him up and he sat in the small kitchen while she made coffee, aware of her presence exercising upon him an allure more potent than others who had aroused in him passing interest or desire. His acquaintance with women was limited, nor was he given to psychologizing, inclining to view relationships straightforwardly; some would have said simplistically. The love of a lifetime issued in marriage—if destiny was kind: for he hardly dared hope for what would seem a prospect of unending bliss. Yesterday had brought home to him that he had not thought about marriage, what it was or should or might be. The marriage from which he himself issued, if less crossed than Brendan's parents', yet did not seem a helpful exemplar; they had remained in a dependency he could not imagine being broken, but neither seemed to be made positively happy by the other. How had he come to intuit that there might be more to it than that? He was eager to discover her view, her experience.

But as they sat over the coffee cups, with growing chagrin he began to suspect that his own spell was diminished, or some force more potent was overriding it. He looked for an opening but none offered. Eventually he followed his own more impetuous instinct.

"I came," he said, "because my friend Brendan—you must meet him, a fascinating character and a good bloke really, if... He heard from Monsignor Hervé that you were in some—anxiety, following our last talk."

She acknowledged this with a slight nod of her head and monosyllabic assent, almost as though she had thought better of things. There was silence until Ian, afraid to venture further, suggested,

"Let's take a walk on the Fen and then have something at the 'Anchor'."

She cleared up the kitchen and disappeared, to return coated and scarfed, her nose, naturally snub and shiny, matt with powder, her reddened lips startling him. More than once he had envisaged the blissful kissing of those lips but set aside his desire, telling himself to wait upon the time for it. Lipstick had become the norm, but if she used it he had not noticed before and thought it could have done little to enhance her natural colouring.

It was a blustery day of early April; the river ran turbid and fast for a fenland waterway. As they walked and she became more communicative, he steered the conversation to their families; he noted hers did not sound specially happy either. She thought it a result of their "mixed" marriage that her mother had abandoned Catholicism—and he guessed the nature of the "difficulties" to which she alluded.

Behind that lay another and markedly *un*happy marriage that evidently was of great significance to her; she spoke of her grandparents with warmth, despite their errors and frailties. The state of society at large had been to blame and in particular the condition of what she called The Church in England: after centuries of persecution scarce out of the ghetto and—in a metaphor taken from Aunt Magda—enclosed in its own hothouse atmosphere. Ian's historian's sense enabled him to enter into her account of the Faith that had caused her grandparents to endure in their crossed marriage, fashioned by the events of centuries, French as well as English, never questioning its "validity," not even considering divorce, until the approach of the death that, in accordance with their vow, should seal their long apartness had brought reconciliation.

Elaine dwelt too on the English historical romance as she had received it from her grandmother: the missionaries who courted martyrdom; the network of great houses whose Catholic lords were feudal protectors of their tenants; the safe-houses managed by such determined, truly "emancipated," women as Margaret Clitherow and Anne Line; the life-in-death dependency in which all hierarchy broke down except the one precious distinction between priest and layman; the paradoxical enfranchisement produced by the very confinement in which, from virtual house-arrest or actual prisons such as the hell-hole at nearby Wisbech, they struggled to keep the Faith alive. And though she told it like a romance, the story had a reluctant fascination for egalitarian Ian and he was all but silent, waiting until her impulsive narrative ran out. Then thinking to inject a dash of cold realism, he observed,

"It was the Puritans triumphed hereabouts. This is Cromwell country! Did you know Cromwell was Member of Parliament for Cambridge? His house is in Ely, near my school."

"I had heard of that... Not of the house. I've never felt much sympathy, though of course Milton... They say the English are still divided between Cavaliers and Roundheads."

"I'm for the Roundheads!"

"I'm not! The Cavaliers were Catholic, or at least would have liked to be, many of them. And the poor king, who should have been one: look what the Church of England did for him! My mother claims he's a C-of-E martyr."

"Your mother's C-of-E?"

"Yes, though she wouldn't call it that; she'd say Anglican. Or Anglo-Catholic. She likes to think she's still a Catholic, because she was brought up one. A Roman Catholic I mean—though my Aunt Freda and my grandmother say that's only correct for Catholics of the Roman Rite as there are other churches in the Roman communion..."

"I know. Uniates, Maronites..."

"You seem to know a lot—more than me, anyway."

"I was well taught—lucky I suppose, that I went to the best school around these blighted parts! Calvinism, you know, got its grip on England only less than in my father's Scotland, and not least around here."

There was a pause until he resumed,

"I've always been struck that in English History at school we passed straight from the Wars of the Roses to Cromwell—as if the Reformation was too controversial to deal with!"

"So did we—to the French Revolution, or that's all I seem to remember. My grandmother filled in the gap for me. She came to live with us when I was doing G.C.E.s and she used to help me with all my subjects—even atomic tables and things she'd never done: she found everything interesting—even treaties and Factory Acts, which English History mostly was; but it was European History would lead her on. Except the Reform Bill and Women's Suffrage: she cared a lot about them. Then English: Shakespeare and Milton especially; she would put them into the context of the Reformation and I felt I understood them better for that."

"I take it she's behind you wanting to go back to all that—tradition," he ventured.

"Yes and no. I used to think I couldn't even for her; it seemed so— bizarre... And it's not that I would have wanted to live in that past, heaven knows! At best to be banished to a foreign convent, at worst to be martyred—or I suppose I should say at best, if 'The blood of the martyrs is the seed of the Church.' That was the rallying-cry of

Robert Southwell, who might have been a poet almost as great as Shakespeare—It seems they were distantly related—but Shakespeare married and Southwell became a Jesuit—and a martyr."

"I don't believe that saying is original to Southwell. It dates back to one of the Church Fathers, as I recall."

"Yes? What a lot of things you know! There were martyrs in those days, of course, and right from the beginning. But Southwell said it —quoted it, if you like—when so many were—were apostatising out of fear of being beggared by fines and imprisoned, if not worse. Priests like him were tortured and butchered—some lay people too— though all we normally hear about is persecution by Catholics!"

"Still, all that is pretty ancient history now, and…"

"Not to my grandmother it isn't, though she may not be your kind of historian. Nor to my Aunt Freda, who even quite recently suffered—not persecution exactly, but discrimination certainly!"

She paused. Ian had heard the scorn in her voice border on passion and said, again mildly,

"How is that?"

"It was not long after the War. She applied for a post as Personal Secretary to a well-known publisher and was interviewed by him. He was going to engage her when he said, by the way there was a last matter to clear up; she wasn't Catholic, was she? He never could employ a Roman Catholic!"

"And then?"

"She told him she was one and walked out. Actually she wasn't very practising in those days. I think this helped to bring her back. Now she's positively devout."

"And you?"

"I have to expect it too—probably not the obvious kind of martyrdom, but…"

Mindful of Brendan's account of her outburst to Monsignor Hervé, he interjected,

"Is that what makes you *want* to be a Catholic?"

"I *am* a Catholic—by my baptism."

"But not by your upbringing."

"In part, yes. Some of my earliest memories are of things… a medal I had—a little gold medal on a chain, that slipped down a crack in the floorboards—I suppose it was in one of our flats—For all I know, it's still there!"

"They didn't take up the floorboard?"

"I presume not or I might have it still. Perhaps they didn't realize, or…"

"Perhaps they didn't care?"

She said nothing so he added,

"What else do you remember?"

"Oh—the holy water stoup in the hallway of my grandmother's house: I thought it was the Holy Ghost—which shows how young I was! Receiving the ashes one Ash Wednesday... Now I want to enter into my birthright, from which I have been kept by—ignorance."

"Then what has happened now?"

"You may well ask, because it's not long since I had decided I could not believe, and not just in dogmas like the Assumption. And I tried with the Church of England, really tried. It always seemed that whatever faith I had—in something ultimate, even if I didn't know whether to call it God—that this had little to do with going to church, even though I liked some things about that: the hymns we sang at school, the rituals, the music, in Cambridge especially, the old churches—but they had once been Catholic. When my grandmother visited, we went into King's College Chapel, and there, right up in front of the altar, she wanted us to say a prayer—about me, and things I'd been telling her. I was surprised, but she said, 'Mass was once said here.' That meant so much to her, and for me it gave a new meaning to the place: so famous for its architecture, its glass, its choir—but the original point had been lost."

"You don't say what had happened..."

"What happened? Well—the prayer she wanted us to say was about someone I met. Here. The year before last."

"A man?" he asked as she seemed reluctant to continue.

"Yes, a research-student, like I am now. An Australian. And a Catholic."

"And he...?"

"He wanted me to marry him—or thought he did. Later he realized—we both realized it wouldn't do. That was the answer to my grandmother's prayer. I think she suspected then it wouldn't work—even though it was tempting for her to think this was God's way of bringing me to the Faith."

"Perhaps her bad experience of marriage had something to do with that!"

"Yes, I think so. But you see, because she put the truth of things and my happiness first—She saw that though I liked him, I didn't love him; it was a bit like her own story, only she had really needed to marry—needed security, in those days—and I had so much and was just wanting to seem successful in this too... She didn't want me making a bad mistake as she had done—and I'd have been more wrong than her if I had… Anyway, Jim—he got me to take instruction that Long Vac. from the Jesuits in London, at Farm Street. That appealed to me, because of Southwell and Campion and the other martyrs."

"And those Jesuits convinced you?"

"One of them, yes. By then it wasn't difficult and gradually I saw… I remember I was on the top of a bus, going home; the sun was setting and suddenly, somehow, I just *saw*—like suddenly seeing the sunset, even in smog-bound London, that usually I would take for granted, or just think how fine it was!"

"Just that?"

"No, there were other things, other experiences, but that seemed the turning-point—my conversion, if you like. I suppose it was something the Jesuit brought home to me and that seemed to connect—perhaps to the sun in Plato's *Republic.* Or the 'woman clothed with the sun' in the Apocalypse. Or both. And then other people: wherever I went, they seemed to emerge, as if—as if I wasn't to get away even if I tried. And I did try—up to a point—to set it aside."

"And this man? Did you set *him* aside?"

He had felt jealousy kindle dangerously in his breast.

"Yes. I came to see that he was not—not for me. Or not to marry, only to bring me to face up… In that way he did seem to be sent, which made it hard. He probably doesn't realize what he did for me; he finished his degree and he's gone back to Australia. That was one thing: doubting I could live so far away… But I could have if it would have worked. He saw that it wouldn't when I got a First and was offered this scholarship. He didn't envisage a career-woman for his wife. Not that I… I hate housework! I don't want to do that all my life, as my mother has, though I think I'd like a family if… But I don't know…"

She tailed off again. Deliberately he took her slim hand, which felt as if it acquiesced half willingly. He said,

"Last time I saw you we—didn't agree about some things to do with that—with families. It upset me a bit, but I've thought about it some more."

"And?"

"And I think you could be right—at least in theory. It's a fine ideal. Only most don't seem able to live up to it."

"Perhaps they don't want to, or not enough—or not both of them!"

"Perhaps. Shall we leave it at that for now?"

"Of course."

In the detached monosyllables he understood, "What is it to me what you decide?" Unable quite to leave it, he went on,

"Because I thought I could look into it a bit more. I don't have much time now, with my exam coming up, but Brendan suggested I could talk to the chaplain."

She was silent. Reaching the end of Coe Fen, they turned to walk back. As if with the change of direction, she changed the subject, asking him about his work. His matter-of-fact reply drew the comment,

"You don't seem particularly bothered by exams. I suppose with your record you feel very confident."

He was not sure if she intended irony and laughed deprecatingly.

"I do seem to have got the measure of examiners. It's less how much you know than how you make use of it. There's little point to cramming—quite the opposite; what you need is a clear head. I make time for relaxation. Perhaps next term you'd like to come punting with me? I'm part owner of an old punt; we call it 'Cap'n Fred.'"

"It sounds enticing."

Again that disconcerting detachment, no trace of the strength of feeling Brendan had conveyed. He went on,

"I suppose you'll just work away here during the Vacation?"

"Yes, I suppose so. I would go home for Easter but—it may be better to avoid that just now. Christmas was difficult enough; my mother could see the way I was going…"

"What does she say?"

"She *says* that as *her* mother allowed *her* to become Anglican, she allows *me* to become Catholic."

"Does she have to allow you? After all, you're of age!"

"I know; it's as though I was still a child. But that's how I feel still, if I don't fall into line. She makes us feel guilty—me anyway, and my father, not so much my brothers—by sheer force of believing in her own rightness!"

"I suppose she feels in this case you're criticising her."

"Yes."

"Are you?"

"I suppose I am, by implication. And objectively speaking—that's what theologians call it, meaning only God can judge, because a person may just not understand enough, or can be misled: objectively speaking, she made the wrong choice. I think it's had a bad effect on my father. He respected the Church and would more likely have been impressed if she'd stuck with its teachings. He can never become Anglican, even if he too, or a part of him, might like the—the Englishness."

"Do you think he would have become Catholic?"

"He might have, once anyway. Granny thinks so because long ago, when he was ill, he wanted a priest. I don't know. Since then there's been the War and the Nazis and if that wasn't enough, stories out of Poland… That's where his father came from, who must have known things about the Church—one hopes not all bad things; certainly he wasn't very Jewish, not practising… Anyway, it's all made my father bitter; I think he feels guilty…"

"What do you think it would take to make *you* feel grown up—independent of them, I mean?"

"I don't know. Perhaps to earn my living. With the scholarship I'm independent financially, and I need to be, because my brothers are still at school. Joejoe—Joe I should call him; he's Joshua but he doesn't like his name—he, I suspect, is thinking of becoming an Anglican minister—I think he wouldn't say 'priest.' Or so he and my mother give me to understand by various hints, plus he's taking R.K. in Sixth Form, which is unusual combined with Chemistry and Physics."

"And your other brother?"

"Leo says nothing; he's very loyal to Joejoe—to Joe—so he wouldn't say anything to me, but that's certainly not *his* line. He's said he'd like to be a lawyer, except it costs so much, plus he'd have to work a lot harder than suits him."

"And you…?"

"So I'm still dependent, still a student. Even though I'm soon twenty-three and we're sharing the flat here, my parents' house is still my home. And the trouble is, I still want to go back, even though there are always problems. I suppose I feel things are unfinished for me there."

"It might be better if you could make the break."

"I expect it would, really, but heaven knows how long this thesis will take me. I don't get much help from the Professor; I have to ask to see him even once a term. I'm stuck in the Library trying to gather notes, but my topic seems to be drying up on me. I'm wondering whether to give the whole thing up."

"Why? It's surely a good opportunity."

"For what, though?"

"Perhaps for becoming a University Lecturer? Not that you need a doctorate for that; it's a German idea."

He was feeling repulsion at the thought of this girl, so rarely alive, becoming like Cambridge women dons as he knew them: desiccated old maids! He asked,

"What else could you do?"

"I don't know. School-teaching or…"

"Or marriage?" he wanted to suggest but checked himself. Her presence had restored his conviction that this was the girl he wanted to share his life with, come what might of her religious notions, which actually suited her somehow, seemed of a piece… But the moment was premature; he was all the time sensing her diffidence. Instead he asked,

"Would you like that? What would you *like* to do?"

"School-teaching? I don't know that I'd *dis*like it. It would be giving back what I've received and am grateful for, and the holidays would enable one to do other things."

"Such as what?"

"Write, perhaps; writing's something I've always felt drawn to. My father started out as a writer, but he got bogged down, what with me being born before they were—ready, and then the twins… And my grandmother wrote novels but couldn't finish them with all the children she had…"

"Too many?"

"It must have seemed like it, though it's hard to say, isn't it, that anyone should not have been born! And times have changed. One of the Pope's Encyclicals I've been reading says parents should be prudent in the number of children they have. Anyway, she did both in the end: had a family—and a lot of suffering with it, poor Granny!—*and* wrote books. *And* remained a faithful Catholic. She goes to meetings of Catholic authors; she's met Graham Greene and Evelyn Waugh. And she's still writing. Writing's on both sides, you see."

"Have you started to write?"

"Not much. Some poetry. I'm supposed to write a thesis, of course! Not that I believe I'll get to the writing of it, but for nearly two years it's been taking up my time and energy."

"If you hate it, perhaps you *should* give it up. Get ahead with whatever you *want* to write, before *you* have—ties."

They were approaching the Mill Bridge, on which a knot of undergraduates had gathered with beer-mugs; it was by now lunchtime and a fine day. The sluices were open and she stopped walking deliberately so their noise would prevent her words being overheard. Turning to face him, she said,

"I'm wondering if I shouldn't become a nun."

A nun! So that was it, and worse even than a lady don! The sound of the sluices seemed suspended for some moments, then

"Why on earth!" burst from him.

"Why not? If I'm serious about being a Catholic. And I have to find something worth doing with my life!"

"Then why throw it away in some god-forsaken convent!"

That was not going to help, he realized as soon as he had said it, giving in to the rush of his anger. She laughed drily, angry too.

"That's not the way convents see themselves—rather the contrary, I believe."

"Oh look, don't take me seriously... Just an expression. I mean, what good would you be doing by becoming a nun? What do nuns do anyway?"

"If you don't know that, I really don't see how you can have an opinion. The chief thing nuns do is pray."

"Not all the time!"

"Why not? They go to Mass—that is a prayer—and you can pray while you read, keep house, teach, even write..."

"But you can do those things anyway."

"One needs a framework, a base even. At least, I'm no good at doing things in isolation; that's being shown with the thesis. And I certainly can't do them at home, the way things are."

"But how do you know you could put up with other people—not just in school- or office-hours, but all the time: people you haven't chosen to live with, and who don't feel obliged to—to do things for you as your family does...?"

"But they do. A religious community is supposed to *be* a family—only spiritual. Come to that, it's more chosen than families. Besides, if *God* had chosen them—and me..."

"It's a very big 'if'!"

"*If* God had chosen us to live together, that would be like His challenge, and the—the pain of it—I mean incidental to it—would be the sacrifice—in fact the prayer... Look, what everything seems to come down to in the end is, Is life just meant to be pleasurable? Or often painful—as it is to so many people!"

He had to admit her rightness, up to a point. So many, inevitably it seemed, did lead suffering lives. That was the motive—the good motive—behind his deciding to work in Africa, in a secure position of course, but others had chosen lives of suffering: missionaries and suchlike. For a good purpose, though—as they at least saw it. He said,

"How do you find the answer to this 'if'?"

"That's what I'm wondering; it's all rather new to me. Just by trying, perhaps. My mother's best friend at school entered the Carmelites but came out—before she was professed, that is. My aunt says she did it because my mother and her other friends were marrying and she thought she would be a Bride of Christ—but Auntie Freda never married herself, so… Anyway, she found she couldn't stand it, so she knew… But she remained a Catholic."

"What couldn't she stand?"

Elaine laughed, half abashed.

"Mother said she found the other nuns—disillusioning. Some of them, anyway. The last straw was when two of them had a fight, over cleaning the silver or something! She had a nervous breakdown after she came out. That's the awful part. If you have a vocation but can't live up to it, or anyway don't…"

"It sounds as though she was not the only one not living up to it! Better, surely, to come out than to scratch eyes out in frustration! And you'd risk going through that?"

"I'd certainly rather not."

"Then isn't that your answer?"

She said nothing and they walked the remainder of the way to the bridge and stood surveying the pub and its newly opened coffee bar beside the landing-stage.

"What shall it be?"

"A sandwich and a half of cider for me, please. I've had two coffees already today and it doesn't help my sleeping."

"Do you sleep badly?"

"I always have, even as a baby, I'm told. Exam-times were terrible: I had to have pills—and Benzedrine to wake me up."

"Like fighter-pilots!"

"Yes, and for Finals I slept in the college infirmary, so the nurse could keep an eye on me. I suppose they thought I might be suicidal."

"Have you been?"

"Not really, though oddly—before I went up, there was a girl at Oxford who killed herself; it was in the papers and my mother made a point of asking me, if I ever thought of doing that, to think how my grandmother would feel. In fact she said something like, 'Never mind thinking of *us*!' which I felt quite hurtful—as if I couldn't be expected to think of them."

Ian said nothing, not knowing about mothers and daughters, though privately inclined to dislike Mrs Keller.

It was warm in the bar. They sat on stools eating ham sandwiches, he sipping his pint of bitter, she her cider, almost in silence, preoccupied with their thoughts. Finally he asked,

"So what about next term? Perhaps you'll not be—interested in punting? Or not with me!" After all, he was telling himself, still angry, if a girl was thinking of becoming a nun, she shouldn't give a bloke the wrong impression. But it seemed she had no such scruples when, almost as if surprised, she replied,

"Oh no! I see what you mean, but even if—I mean, they like people to have had—other experiences: not to be recluses or misfits or anything."

"But—that's not fair!"

She laughed, he thought mirthlessly.

"Yes it is—if all we want is God's will!"

"But I—don't believe that!"

"Well, you can trust, can't you—in something: in goodness, or reason, perhaps; it all hangs together."

"Things—people—are too often unreasonable—which is how that seems to me."

"Well, in any case, I hope to have found out by then—or at least to have some light on what I ought to do."

"How do you think you'll get that?"

"I suppose I might start by putting it to Monsignor Hervé."

"And I suppose I might go along with you, since there are one or two questions I could ask him myself."

"I think not. It might send the wrong signal."

"Or the right one!"

That took her aback and he was for pressing home—whatever that would mean. After all, it *was* so unfair, sitting in the public bar and wanting to take her in his arms and cry out quite simply, "You're the girl I love; don't leave me!"—force her to acknowledge him. But force things was what he must not do, not now. With an effort he said, mildly he hoped:

"I mean how we get on together might seem not irrelevant!"

She considered before replying,

"Well, not just yet. You speak to him if you like, of course; that's not my business."

"Except it all arose out of meeting you!"

"It has to arise somehow, if one is honest. Like it did for me. Anyway, I'll speak to him and then we'll see."

That "like it did for me" fell like a slap with something impersonal, like a wet towel. But it had to be left at that. Soon would be the Easter break, then his positively last term here, culminating, he hoped, in a posting. Time in which to bring her, he also had to hope, to a decision which must not be for a nun's life: ridiculous, a girl like her!

Though she was right; he knew little of "religious" life—even though he suspected she knew little more. That *revenant* Benedictine had caused him to immerse himself in Bernard of Clairvaux and his

Cistercian Order: all very admirable it had seemed: essential, indeed, to the formation and transmission of European culture. Fine: that was for men! But for women? Nunneries too, perhaps, had been all very well in that past, for women for whom otherwise a marriage would be arranged; who were without other choice; for whom childbirth was the unknown peril. But for today's woman, for Elaine, selected by her college for graduate studies, who admitted she had no relish for a life of domesticity: was not a nunnery even more confining than a home —at all events, the sort of home that was all he wanted, in which one would be free from pettiness, free to pursue things one valued, intellectual things especially? St Benedict, he recalled, had laid down for his monks a vow of "stability," of staying put in one's monastery. Presumably nuns were the same, or rather—worse—were "enclosed": even more unthinkable for someone like Elaine!

Then chastity. Did not women, even one's mother and grandmother and ancestresses generally—who didn't seem to have found sex all it was nowadays cried up to be—at least go along with it for the sake of—of what? Being mothers? Or for a man's protection? Not that "going along with it" was what he envisaged for his own marriage— which ineluctably was taking on the lineaments of Elaine and himself caught up in a vortex of delights… He must stop his imagination straying along those lines; there might be something in what she said: about God's will, or anyway about trusting in goodness and reason.

Here he recalled the troubadours, singers of a love never to be consummated; its exponent, "Andreas the Chaplain," it struck Ian quixotically, might have been a sort of Monsignor Hervé. History suggested clerics in those days not uncommonly permitted themselves trials of human passions the good Monsignor might have sublimated into his own brand of exoticism. Ian did not see himself as Galahad to her Guinevere—even less Tristan to her Iseult—but something of that ideal of selfless devotion should suffice for now as he prepared himself to earn a living. Consciously he had discarded the "bourgeois ethic" of his parents, yet if marriage was to be his hope, he must be in a situation to offer something better than "semi-detached" domesticity, surely hateful to her as to him…

V

It was inevitable Ian should communicate something of his anxieties to Brendan when that youth discreetly probed the course of his friend's interesting affair of the heart.

"She's wondering about being a nun!" the unhappy swain blurted out, and wished he had not when Brendan broke into the nearest thing to frank laughter one could imagine his fastidiousness permitting.

"*Really*, my dear Ian? But that is *just* what one would expect! Converts take themselves so seriously, women especially; it's the *masochism* of the idea that makes it so alluring!"

...He remembered her, "The question is, is life meant to be pleasurable?," but said,

"That's all very well, but suppose she does decide on it? What happens to me—or to her? She's thinking of putting it to your chaplain."

"Oh good! The Mugger will make short work of it; he'll say what I've just said—about converts, that is, not masochism: indelicate with one of 'the sex,' as he would put it! No, you can safely leave it to him."

"But can I? I suppose converts do sometimes become nuns?"

"True, dear boy, they do. I wonder—Will she tell the Mugger about you?"

"I don't know. I offered to go along with her, but she didn't want it."

"No. She wouldn't. She would think that would be to suggest his answer. And it is a factor he should know—if, that is, you are sure in your own mind. I mean, are you wanting to *marry* her?"

"I think all this is showing me that I am!"

Brendan turned on his companion an amused glance from under habitually drooped eyelids before remarking,

"I see! Because previously.... Well, as the Mugger will doubtless point out, the ways of Grace are wondrous. Leave it with me, dear boy!"

"I don't know that..."

"You don't need to know. You know me and that I am, I trust, always discreet."

"It's true, she did say it was my business if I wanted to see the—the padre, only apart from her."

"Precisely; it is as she herself says, and if I put in a helpful word for you: *verb. sap.* you know: the merest word in the right place... After all, the Mugger himself entrusted this to me and would no doubt agree that Providence, in the execution of Its designs, may use the unworthiest tools! With that your *demoiselle* too must agree, and so I beg you, dear boy, make yourself easy; it will all come right!"

Though still somewhat *un*easy, Ian could only acquiesce.

VI

Brendan McNally had procured himself a fourth undergraduate year on the pretext of defective grounding in Greek dialects, though actually out of unpreparedness to quit that *mélange* of the sybaritic with the monastic which was how he saw the Cambridge collegiate life to which he intended, if humanly possible, to commit his future. Brendan's conviction of his own suitability to that life, and to no other, was not unfounded. From origins in Greater Manchester he had attained to a scholarship in Classics at Trinity via Jesuit schooling. The "J"s, though they had not actually beaten the Latin and Greek into him, had surely spurred his native quickness of wit by the exemplary beating of less apt or less compliant pupils; Brendan himself was at pains to avoid confronting physical violence, which retained a horrible fascination ever since perpetrated upon him as a small boy by a father feared even when sober: an outrage he had ever sought to efface from memory.

Schoolmasters and father thus coalesced to yield negative feelings about the religion of his tribe and its paternalist deity. But the mother from whom he derived his refined susceptibilities had also passed on to him, as to the several siblings who followed, a contrary inclination, to her Faith if not her long-suffering: characteristics she derived from obstinately recusant Lancashire forebears.

Brendan's and Ian's friendship dated from their arrival at Trinity, when their Scholars' privilege had them rooming on opposite sides of the same grim stairwell, instead of in "digs" like the Commoners. They had assisted each other through such necessities as finding that other stairwell at the foot of which was located the nearest bathroom and alternatives to the commissariat provided beneath the ornate Tudor bosses of the great dining hall. Both found this inadequate, Ian in point of quantity, Brendan of quality, and they were at one over a prevalence of prunes and the marked inferiority of dishes placed before undergraduates to those borne to the Fellows seated beneath Holbein's life size portrait of their royal Founder.

Tudor too, albeit more modestly, was a different structure to which Brendan introduced his new friend: the house in the centre of Cambridge where Monsignor Hervé had established the Catholic Chaplaincy. Wealth inherited from his part-French family's wine-business had enabled Maurice Hervé to be ordained "on his own recognizances," and so to retain independence in the disposing of it. To such a man a bar was of lesser importance only than Chapel and Library—and he rather rejoiced than otherwise that this third amen-ity was his foundation's chief block of stumbling to earnest adherents of the Cambridge Inter-Collegiate Christian Union, already wary at this confident intrusion of "Rome." Better that the bar offend them, he was wont in the conviviality of that precinct to observe, than that more traditional stumbling-block: the Tabernacle, House of the Housel!

Nor did the Monsignor overlook the pastoral value of fodder for hungry sheep, including guests not of his fold; he had been young himself, albeit under a sterner star, and though he would scarce have soiled his consecrated hands with cold cuts and pickles, was happy for his assistant and their "daily" to make provision for a luncheon following midday Mass. On such holy days as fell in term-time—Candlemas, Lady Day, the Ascension—multiple cheeses, cocktail sausages, syllabubs and meringues witnessed to Mother Church's joy in the Lord of Creation and the inventiveness of His crowning work. Contrariwise, Fridays in Lent put forth nothing but bread and "mousetrap" cheese.

Of such "fasting and abstinence" rules as remained in force, Brendan took a relaxed view, reflecting a childhood during which his mother, when not excused because pregnant or lactating, often was excused on health grounds checked with the parish priest, while his father compensated for limitation of solid intake by enlargement of liquid, thereby turning Lent into a period of added trial for his family. Until, that is, cancer carried him off while Brendan was facing the prospect of military service: a moment premature for the deceased but opportune to secure his gifted oldest son's subsequent passage to Cambridge rather than into gainful employment. Librarianship had been fixed on for him: compromise stitched up by his mother's intercession backed by the authority of the reverend headmaster, anxious the precocious boy should at least stay into Sixth Form. Thus Brendan had been positioned to take full advantage of the paternal bar to University being so providentially removed.

A compromise he had himself reached with Lent was to go easy on fasting but attend both Friday and Saturday midday Mass. The house chapel being small, the more frequented Masses took place in the Library, which also housed the bar and, for these occasions, at the back of the room the table on which was set out a collation still modest but more varied on Saturday than that of the previous day. Between these two sources of refreshment was wont to linger a self-selecting group of serious minded undergraduates. Who, as Brendan joined them on the final Saturday of term, were already deep into a topic perennial in that place and company. Thus the first words

Brendan heard emanated from the short, vivacious figure of Robert Froude, from a famous convert family and Trinity's other Catholic Classic, though of the year's intake after Brendan and Ian.

"It's the fault of the Statutes, admitting ten men to every one woman: condemning the women to a world in which they must compete using men's weapons or else… Brendan, hullo-o-o!"

"Greetings, Robert; greetings all!" from Brendan and

"Greetings, Monsignor!" came from various working lips as the chaplain joined them, having completed his post-Mass devotions.

"Robert is prophesying the end of the University—if not of the Universe as we know it, Monsignor," said another voice from the knot; "Equal numbers of women to be admitted—here too! Not, he concedes, so long as you are in charge!"

"No, indeed: over my dead body that would have to be! You young men have already distractions enough. When I was young…"

Seeing their smiles, he broke off, genially rubbing his hands. "Well, well: things were far from perfect, I own, and ever will be, but it was possible, if one was so minded, to concentrate on one's studies with fewer attentions from the weaker vessel!"

He smiled benignly as a suppressed onset of laughter testified to incredulity that the Mugger would ever have received—let alone countenanced—such attentions.

"The Ivory Tower!" murmured Brendan provocatively.

"But, Monsignor," came in expostulation from the ebullient Robert, "Your Ideal Cambridge, it's like the Platonic model—'laid up in heaven'—and unobtainable on earth! The admission of women to Higher Education has to make a difference, and if you hold that women should not have been admitted…"

"My dear Robert!" the chaplain imperturbably interrupted, "Far be it from me to deny the cultivation of their minds to that half of the human race through whom the Almighty in His Wisdom has seen fit to bring us into the world…"

"Come, come, Monsignor!" murmured Brendan, while Robert all but spluttered,

"You could as well say we men bring women into the world—well, almost. Anyway, I fail to see…"

The Mugger laid a deprecating hand on his arm.

"Steady, my dear Robert: less heat will enable more light. Not to wish all talents developed to the full would be to deny the Gospel. But intellect is not the whole of mind, indeed is the least feminine of the mind's powers—as I believe the Psychologist Jung has postulated—and it is to the cultivation of intellect that the University is properly dedicated. Therefore the University properly is for men: certainly our older Universities where in the past every student was a clerk, every fellow of a college in Holy Orders..."

It was Robert's turn to interrupt:

"Church of England Orders! And yes, a century or more ago it was still like that, and we hear less of intellectual brilliance than of port-bibbing and of—ah—'women of easy virtue'!"

"My dear Robert, I refer, of course, to the Catholic Middle Ages."

"Then, I grant you, the port was in smaller supply; but we hear of much roistering and wenching, do we not, Monsignor? Isn't it healthier that today's undergraduates—considerably older than they were—should be able to associate with women capable of understanding what we are talking about? It surely makes for happier marriages."

"Soul-mates and helpmeets," murmured Brendan.

"It may be so and certainly women should be so educated as to correspond to those situations in life to which God pleases to call them. Only the presence of young ladies in this University tends to concentrate the minds of you young men on *marriage*, at a time when you should rather be considering—ah—whether you have that vocation or it may be another. Therefore, while the care of the female soul is also, of course, of utmost importance, I do not regard it as my responsibility and it has accordingly been otherwise provided for. I feel bound to maintain, to the extent of my small powers, that monastic tradition that made Cambridge what it is. I could never"—Here Monsignor Hervé's eyes travelled fondly round the room, book-lined between bar and table—"*never* permit our little society here to take on the character of—of a cocktail-party!"

There was a slight titter, but the vehemence of this sally suggested finality and the Monsignor turned his attention elsewhere. The little group dispersed, with Robert and some others soon leaving, but Brendan lingered until he was alone with the chaplain.

"Monsignor, may I have a word with you?"

"As many as you like, my dear Brendan; I trust I am always at your disposal. Let us sit down. Now, what can I do for you?"

"It's rather for the friend of whom I told you: Ian Roody, an Historian, Monsignor, and particularly interested in the Medieval Orders. Not a Catholic, in fact not a believer: very serious half-Scot, left-leaning..."

"I seem to recall your bringing him here, though we hardly spoke."

"No; he finds this place curious—and curiously congenial. Of course, he has all the usual deep-seated prejudices."

"That can change, more especially in the youthful idealist who suddenly perceives, through the wool that has been pulled over his eyes… Take Douglas Hyde…"

"*Such* an unfortunate name, don't you think, Monsignor! I mean, in Stevenson's *muthos*, Hyde is the evil face of Jekyll, is he not? Now poor Ian—twice as intelligent as most around here, and correspondingly, as I indicated, intense—could be a suicide risk, I'd say, without meaning to imply there is immediate danger—having—ah—fallen in love, Monsignor, with the young woman you have met, who wishes, I understand, to be received…"

He hesitated, aware he was venturing on ground of professional delicacy.

"I know the young lady to whom you refer."

The hint of distance in the chaplain's tone warned Brendan to forebear a plunge into others' confidences.

"Far be it from me, Monsignor, to probe private matters! I merely think you should know that I was auguring a—a match for Ian that could be the saving of him. She if anyone might be up to him intellectually, while attractive in other ways: not, you will agree, the blue-stocking type!"

"Indeed, her Catholic leanings—in the face of, I believe, some personal difficulties—argue well for her in respect of both mind and heart: or rather mind and heart would appear disposed to follow the promptings of Grace."

"And only Grace itself can so dispose them, is that not the case, Monsignor?"

"That indeed is Catholic teaching, and for present purposes I trust we may leave aside the question of how far Grace involves an assent of the will in any sense meritorious."

"For present purposes, certainly, though I find it a fascinating area of speculation."

"Fascinating indeed, and dangerous, like most 'fascinations': the word, you will be aware, denotes the evil eye! It is on just such speculations that the Reformation turned, so far as it was doctrinally based. But let us return to these young people and in what way you consider I might assist them."

"Yes, Monsignor. Ian is very—smitten, you know, and although her becoming a Catholic at first gave him pause, he was, I believe, on the way to being reconciled to it. But now, it seems, she is talking of—of a life in Religion! That cannot but be puzzling and distressing to him. He is expecting soon to leave for a Commonwealth posting, so cannot afford to be in doubt; besides, as I indicated, I believe he could be—adversely affected by such a decision on her part."

"I see. It is a not uncommon response in serious-minded converts."

"That is what I have told him. I should add that he did not ask me to intervene with you; I took the initiative—though of course you had already involved me—in the hope you might dissuade her..."

"That must depend upon whether I consider she may have a true vocation, and further must await her confiding in me herself."

"I believe she will shortly do so. That is why I wanted to alert you to Ian's situation."

"Which, I agree, is not immaterial, at least when I can discover how she herself is disposed. I cannot, you understand, say more, but what you have told me will be of assistance in arriving at the best—the Providential—decision for all concerned. And now that we have considered the possible future of these two, Brendan, it is opportune that I raise the matter of your own."

Brendan stirred in his chair and performed a little wave of both hands accompanied by a deprecating murmur. The chaplain persisted,

"You, I take it, have at present no matrimonial intentions—*you* are not 'in love'?"

"Alas, no, Monsignor!"

His interrogator glanced up sharply, as though to pierce the elusiveness of tone and manner.

"And have I rightly inferred that you are not much inclined to the state?"

"Are we poor males not *all* so inclined by nature, Monsignor?"

"By nature, undoubtedly; yet to some is given the gift to be 'as eunuchs for the sake of the Kingdom'."

"But to most, permission 'to marry rather than burn'?"

"It may be so, my dear Brendan; St Paul may seem to suggest that, albeit in his times... Again, speculation is little to our purpose; we cannot judge but must attempt to discern, and on me has been laid the charge of helping each youth in my cure to do just that. Which is why I address myself to you now, having long hesitated while I observed... In short, I urge you to give serious thought, and, of course, prayer, to whether you do not have the vocation..."

"I think not, Father."

"Not too hasty, I beg! Far be it from me to incite you, or anyone, against your maturer judgment. There are many types of vocation, many mansions in our Father's house. I rather imagined the monastic as suiting your gifts and temperament. But I only ask that you consider well. Place it before Our Lord on the altar and before His blessed Mother, remembering how much may turn on it."

"My salvation, you imply?"

"Conceivably, yes: conceivably in the end even your salvation! However, I would not over-dramatize. We are all bidden to walk warily and enter in at the strait gate; yet Our Lord's mercy—thanks be to Him!—is greater than to hold us accountable for errors in the ways in which we choose to serve Him—that is, speaking *humaniter,* for His ways are beyond ours and He will lead us gently in them if only we endeavour so to dispose ourselves. No, I was thinking rather of your happiness, of the best use of your talents. These are the usual tokens of His way for us."

"I don't believe a monastery would make me happy, Monsignor. Indeed, it might pander to my weaknesses—be a temptation, you know… But I will bear what you say in mind."

"And, I urge you again, dear boy, in *prayer!* Think well on it. You may be assured I shall be praying with you, and I shall not raise the matter again unless you do."

Irritatingly perturbed beneath his satisfaction at having set Ian's business in motion, Brendan took his leave.

VII

In fact Elaine spoke no more of nunneries and though Ian dared not inquire about a meeting with the chaplain, she seemed not averse to seeing him every few days. He sent her a Valentine card—deliberately a day ahead, hoping for a reply in kind. Which arrived promptly in the form of a medieval poem; she had not been unprepared, he reflected, reading the successive lines of French, English and Latin, then re-reading the third stanza:

"Mon très duce et très amé,
night and day for love of thee
suspiro.
Soyez permanent et léal,
love me so that I it feel,
requiro."

Ingenious—and she must intend it, but how much? Embedded in the courtly sentiments that might pass muster with Andreas the Chaplain's overt prescriptions was that hardly ambiguous "so that I it feel." So too might the author have wished to hide behind his poem's conventions. "His"? The first line showed it addressed to a man ("*mon*" and "*amé*"); was it written by a woman? Or she had adjusted it to send to him? Or? Uneasily he thought of his friend Brendan, surely what was known politely as "epicene." He must check the poem out...

That apart, selfless devotion, Ian told himself, was all very well as an ideal; in practice, one needed to behold its object: even the troubadour would cleave to images of his Lady. Thus it came about that hardly would he be in *his* "lady"'s presence than courtly distance shrank as hands touched, then one day lips, until he muttered "Love me so that I it feel!" behind clenched teeth as he drew her to him and fell to kissing her neck and the shoulders beneath the easy-fitting knitted jumper, and felt her succumb with what seemed token reluctance.

As the embrace became expected, she began to return it with passion; they would sink on sofa or floor, hands and lips exploring up to the point where both drew back at the frail barrier of their virginity: his, having survived two years of military service, saved up out of an implicit faith in a love he hoped now to have found; hers attempted, not yielded—she was unsure why but connected it vaguely to her background in a faith which under present temptation rose up to confront her with past and present compromises in desire and act. "Brinkmanship," as he referred to it, began to prey on the nerves of both, driving him towards consummation, in her vying hectically with notions of religious consecration and a bid for his mind and soul. Her arguments would encounter his dogged critique, then, out of compunction if not conviction, he might yield; still the embrace that crowned their colliding inflamed even as it quieted, until mental and physical joustings appeared inseparable and ineluctable. Between times their clashes would be carried on in notes that encrypted agonies of mind and sense.

One such evening after he left the flat, she followed, cycling through darkening streets to find his door open but him not returned. She sat awhile leafing through a copy of *Don Camillo* in Italian, a language she was attempting to master. Then, as he did not come, she found pen and paper on his desk and began to write— purblindly, realizing she still scarce knew him and must choose the words she judged would hold him to her, yet gain an apartness in which to know her own mind, threatened by opposing impulses:

"Sweet heart, I've been very 'pensive' since you went. Restless too, evidently, since I've come here to leave you 'a woman's last word' tonight. For tomorrow we must have finished with talking and be living our resolves, I think.

Don't think I underestimate the problem, Ian mine!" (She hesitated over that, but concluded his infatuation would excuse any mawkishness.) "What I've been trying to get at is that it should be one of the glories of love to enable one (or rather two!) to overcome all difficulties by a perfected strength. And this difficulty is thrown up, not simply by life but by living *well* and loving *truly*. We know a true love makes sacrifices where necessary, and is something better than a love that simply goes on to its own satisfaction. We're resolved to do the right thing, let's also resolve to do it in the right spirit— then I am sure we shall find it rather a fine achievement and this will make us happy. And we'll have done it *together*: become one in spirit if not in flesh. You said you'd try and I know it's harder for you than for me. But don't think it's entirely easy for me either. I do love you and when I am with you I feel the urge constantly to express that love. If I restrain myself, I too feel that I am not expressing what I feel." (This, she recognized, was not strictly true; she was unsure of her feelings and also held back by fear—of what? Of so-called "consequences"?) "But if I know that we are *both*, in mutual agreement, restraining ourselves, then I mind less because I know you understand. And you must know that I understand and do not think your love any less for not being expressed, but even more because of the effort it costs you, and which you make out of love."

That should do it, she thought and finished, "Let us trust each other's understanding and love, and make this a victory, not a mere succumbing to the inevitable. Darling, you'll try—of course one can't do more—for my sake, won't you? Because I know it's the right thing, and you know it too. My love, dear Ian, my truest love, Your Elaine."

She sat a while gazing at the inner door which gave access to his bedroom, which she had never entered, then on an impulse opened it. She found the bed unmade, vulnerable somehow… She hesitated, then proceeded to straighten it, expertly tucking in the corners as she had learned as a Girl Guide. Returning to the desk she added, below her signature:

"There, I've made your bed for you and I think that will please you, which pleases me."

She placed the paper on the coverlet, above his pillow, closed the bedroom door and retreated, tiptoeing down the staircase and flitting along the shadow of the wall to the Great Gate, afraid she might meet him; then pedalled swiftly away, the long graduate's gown billowing back in the March wind.

VIII

Full Term ended, then Long Term and Ian, in the 'Varsity jargon into which even he had fallen, "went down." He heard from Elaine that she had met with the chaplain. The Mugger had been sceptical about "the nun-nonsense," as Ian was characterising it to himself; it was best, Monsignor Hervé opined, to take one thing at a time. He was arranging for her to receive instruction from a Dominican Father over the vacation: this, he emphasised, was to be regarded as adventure, not foregone conclusion. Somewhat relieved, but with feelings sharpened as by fear of an unforeseen rival, "Galahad"— as Ian now ironically cast himself—hastened to embark on a correspondence to keep himself well before her mind.

"My sweet Elaine" (he wrote after several tries at an opening),

"I've just arrived home and am already missing you—the excuse (if you want one) for writing this. Excitement so far has been a visit to my father's old office to be shown off to the head of the firm. I think the old man still hopes I might be persuaded to follow in his footsteps and be articled, but I'd do anything to avoid that dead world of offices (with homes to correspond) throughout the land. I'm hopeful you'll agree with me—and that the Colonial Service will come up with something more stimulating.

What have you been doing? Have you heard from the sanctuary of Thomism yet? Tell me when you plan to leave Cambridge. If not for a while, I'll come and visit you, if you'll let me and if I can find somewhere to stay.

Write to me soon, darling Elaine, and love me. I love you. I know it's been cruel sometimes this past term. But I'll do better, dearest. Don't let anything worry you, but rest and be happy. I love you. Don't let's waste our chance of happiness! Ian."

"My dearest Ian" (self-consciously she wrote back),

"Although I said to wait before writing, I was very happy that you didn't and that your letter was so full of love. It seems a long time since we were talking in your room. I enjoyed that, even—perhaps especially?!—your getting cross with me.

What have I been doing? Apart from continuing to drive myself through my Victorian Romantics, I've been reading Freya Stark's *Valley of the Assassins* to try to get a feel of your exotic leanings and Othello-like tales of the anthropophagi! You've been broadening my outlook and now Miss Stark is carrying on the good work. What a splendid desert-loving Englishwoman!

I also heard a talk on G.E. Moore, who as I understand it regarded 'goodness' as a quality undefinable in other terms (such as happiness or utility). Sounds incredibly naive for a 20th-century mind, doesn't it?

Which only increases my interest in what you call the 'sanctuary of Thomism' so disrespectfully—for I suppose if Thomas is a saint he's entitled to a sanctuary! Anyway, I propose to enter the holy of holies on Sunday morning. In case I never emerge, I enclose the letter I received from the relevant friar. It seems quite reassuring, and you can't suspect 'jesuitry,' as Dominicans and Jesuits are old rivals!

Pause while I array myself for dinner, to which Ann and Elizabeth have invited a science don (female). Being currently in revolt against the complexities of femininity, I am denying myself all trinkets and make-up—perhaps a result of reading about the nomads, or the aura of the brethren of Savonarola, but please note that I waited until you had gone before passing this sumptuary law. In particular I never much like lipstick, and you'll admit it has practical disadvantages! Behind this dislike may lie the first time I put it on. There was a great to-do from my mother: I'd let myself and my parents down, looked 'common,' and what must the Headmistress have thought! But now, you see, after a few years of being grown-up enough to use it, I'm becoming more of Mummy's opinion—not that *she's* given it up!

Sorry to go on about something so frivolous, but it's probably more my level than St Thomas Aquinas. Besides, I want to know what you think. Actually, St Thomas may not be irrelevant; in a novel I read about him, he tells his sister it's all right for her to wear make-up if it's to please her husband!

Finally, darling, you have been more understanding and patient than I had any right to expect. All this is a finer thing than I'd imagined love to be and if I haven't responded to it as I might, I can say with you, 'I'll do better, dearest.' With God's grace we'll both do better. Yes, I'll rest, and of course I'd love you to come, but I don't think you could stay here overnight. And how long I'm in Cambridge will partly depend on Sunday's meeting with Father Digby (the Dominican). So I'll let you know.

My love, Elaine"

"My dear Elaine,
I hope you didn't really expect that I would wait long before writing—because I couldn't. I'm feeling that longing to be with you

that's been with me almost incessantly for some time and my only outlet for it at the moment is in writing to you and hearing from you—unless you give me clearance to come (sorry, army phrase!). I've never felt so utterly out of place at home. My parents seem given over to trivialities and my world is remote and almost meaningless to them. The words and phrases they give me are exactly the same as when I last saw them. Everything has stood still; it's a dead world and I'm dying—until I can hold you in my arms again.

Right now I'm being ordered out to do some shopping so afraid only time for a note on 'sumptuary laws,' etc. Look as bright and beautiful as possible; I love it, and I'm sure one's happiness is reflected in dress (women's anyway!). Lipstick too, especially as you had to suffer for it!

Write at once, please, darling. I'm at your mercy. Until I hear, I'm kissing you goodbye. Ian"

"My very dear Ian,

This is much more like it! I think you'll like, or anyway respect Father Digby. He's a very different proposition from Monsignor Hervé—very English, with a straightforward air of *healthy* sanctity— very different from 'muscular Christianity,' though, and quite medi-aeval, I should think, with a sort of reserve and inner strength cou-pled with humanity—Sorry, can't describe it better. I was shown into the Library, a large, shabby, book-lined room with some easy chairs, and I waited in some apprehension, when all of a sudden I was aware he had appeared—materialized, almost—and was standing near the door looking at me, quite tall and a bit gaunt, with his hands folded under his scapular. (That's the long garment hanging down back and front—as you'll know, it's from the Latin for 'shoulder'). Decidedly mediaeval in appearance, but he proved quite gentle, though of a fas-tidiously critical intellect, which should appeal to you! We talked about Thomism and I told him of your doubts. His reply, more or less, was that Thomism is not a rigid system, as is sometimes sup-posed. It is useful to the Church primarily for its teaching value and its comprehensiveness, and starts, naturally, with such basic tenets of Catholicism as the existence of God and the value of human reason, but it is a tool fashioned for the convenience of a faith twelve centu-ries old at the time, so clearly Catholicism itself cannot 'depend' on Thomism. I told him I'd only studied a few of Thomas' hymns—He asked me whether I thought the 'Adoro te' was genuine!—but that you had read more about him. I even think I've made him a little apprehensive of you, so you'd better live up to it.

The most delightful thing was that after this academic encounter, he suddenly looked very apologetic and said he'd promised to peel the potatoes for the housekeeper, who'd cut her thumb. Of course I offered to do them and we went off to continue our conversation over the sink, but it turned out the housekeeper had decided to do them *en robe de chambre* (in their jackets to you!). I felt there was something answering to my own notions in this compatibility of the Angelic Doctor with the earthiest of roots! I'm to go again tomorrow, and it's all adding to my inclination to stay here as long as possible— perhaps even for Easter, but I'm still weighing it up. For now I'm living in the present, as Mgr Hervé advised, and life does seem cheerful and good. You're a great part of that present. I think of you a lot and know you think of me at the same time. My love, Darling! Elaine

PS. Have just re-read your dear letter, and do hope you're not lapsing into gloom. Do, dear Ian, make an effort with your family. I know how hard it is sometimes to feel one has any point of contact but one has, and the very fact you have so much more than them— wider horizons, a sharper appreciation of values—means you have a duty to be your best self for them. Once when I too was inveighing against bourgeois shallowness, my Aunt Freda pointed out that humdrum lives which seem to revolve around the 'telly,' the pools, the state of the back lawn, Mrs Jones' new washing-machine, etc. are yet, deep down, motivated by love—and you'll agree that it's not a 'dead world' where there is any love. Of course, it's not always so— but then the loveless may have all the more need of our sympathy! So let's try to spill a little of our great charge of love over onto our families. 'Physician, heal thyself,' you may well say! I'm beginning to realize I need to go home resolved to do just that, and I know I shan't find it easy! What a long letter—and excuse sermon!

Love—joy—peace (and it needs an effort not to let them slip away) from Elaine"

"Elaine darling,

Your letters can never be too long for me.

I'm glad you gave Digby a better account of my abilities than they're worth. I'm hoping he'll pull out the stops and not 'talk down.' I'd prefer to have to think hard to understand than to despise him for being despised by him—if you see what I mean!

Regarding this, yesterday I was at dinner with a master at school who taught me Latin and some Greek. The conversation got round to what people were thinking in Cambridge these days, so as a try-out, I mentioned that the Thomistic outlook was being noticed again—even if not agreed with. He was aghast—'What, has that raised its ugly head again?' He is an Oxford man, accepts the logical positivist position that statements both that there is a God and there is not a God are meaningless. Then he looked at me piercingly and said, obviously saddened, 'What do you think it is, Ian, a failure of nerve? It's a sign of a dead civilization when that kind of archaising takes place.' I didn't say anything at the time, partly because this corresponded only too well with my own thoughts and their bitter results. Oh Elaine, your Dominican will surely see the Devil in me impeding your spiritual progress! Are you sure you still want to listen to him in my company? Elaine darling, last term was the best and worst few weeks of my life, but I think I helped you to a saner, more confident outlook on things. But it seemed as though the only way of helping you was to give up all my own steadily built up props. I don't want you to give up any strength *you* have gained for me; that would undo the work I hope I have done. I don't want you to try and see my position too clearly, for the end of that position is death.

Preacher, save thyself, is what I'll say! You gave me a good sermon at the end of your last, darling, too good indeed: I can truthfully say that your vision of goodness made me writhe in agony for my own insufficiency.

I've not 'lapsed into gloom.' My dreams goad me on—and the thought of you is the strongest and noblest of them. But for all my love of you, and I think it is real love, I am still the only captain of my soul—drunk though the captain may be on half-truths, lies, folly, pride, wilfulness, weakness…

And your vision of love blinds you to this humdrum suburban world. Alas, alas, there's not much love out there—don't delude yourself. You'll become unable to see the genuine article, if you equate it to clinging, habituated coexistence!

This is a frightfully negative letter compared with the last, and I feel a little ashamed at disturbing the beatitude shown in yours. As for your 'sermon'—well, I can at least tell you that my parents are obviously delighted to see me being so generally happy and successful—as they see it. The distressing part is that in having to put on a superficial 'happy to be home' outlook—just as you wish—I have to bottle myself up. But for you I do it, darling Elaine,
with my love. Ian"

Saturday 29th March
"Ian, if you were anywhere near I'd have rushed round to you today and told you that I'm finding things as distressing as you, and

when it comes to the point I can't put my preaching into practice. I've failed conspicuously this morning, because I'm in such an edgy state that the slightest thing touches me off, and my already effervescent family can't be expected to understand that. Result: I got in a temper with my mother over the slightest thing, and it was really because I'd been hoping there'd be a letter from you and knowing that I'd have to wait until Monday, and anxious because I fear I fail to be of any help to you. If only you were here to hold me tight and say, 'Don't, Elaine, don't!' I should be able to relax. As it is, hour after hour goes by and I can't be still. I need you, Ian. I have to confess—because I was proud and you've undone that—that I feel a need for you that overrides everything at the moment. Have more pity than I have had and write to me whatever you can that comes from your heart. Because I'm broken, Ian. I'll not try to fly high any longer, because then something like this morning happens and shows me what a worm I am. Very well, I'm going to be content to be so contemptible and weak and beg for your love to help me grow stronger by degrees.

Give me love, Ian; it seems only your love can give me rest, and until I can rest I can't be all I want to be for you. I'm begging you because I'm broken. I shouldn't have written this otherwise. Tell me what to do—in everything, little and big. Ian, do you realise from this letter how I love you? If you do, and if you feel as I do, you will have the calm and strength and security I want you to have for us both.

No, this is not an 'April fool,' or rather it is, because it's the broken down, basically foolish me. Don't let me forget it!

Elaine"

Wednesday, 2nd April
"Dearest Ian,

I am so happy again since your phone-call and *overjoyed* that you will be coming on Easter Monday before going on to Wales. Not many days now! I have been keeping myself on an even keel—more or less—by following Holy Week. This morning I went to early Mass with Granny and Aunt Freda and we made the 'Stations' afterwards, which was Aunt Freda's 'penance'—and I only wish I had been able to go to Confession as they did; then I feel I'd be treading on air, I'd be so light-hearted! Last Sunday—Palm Sunday, in case you forgot!—I was at the English Martyrs Church in Cambridge and received my blessed palm and stood through the long Passion narrative, which was beautifully read by the priest and two other men, and in English, but I also found I could follow the Latin liturgy quite well.

That afternoon was my last meeting, for now, with Father Digby.

We talked about Grace, because I asked him if we could know we are saved, and he said No, which is discouraging, except he went on to say we couldn't really *know* anything this side heaven. He says it's a philosophical point, so I'm extra keen to have your comment! It seems we just have to trust—in our senses, but also in God, who he said is the Foundation.

My parents must realize the way I am going but they haven't said much. It somehow makes *me* realize I must be especially devoted to them, so they don't feel I'm being snatched by something alien. Not that it ought to be 'alien' to my mother, who was brought up in it—except that she's discarded it, or rather she's persuaded herself the Church of England is the same. And my father may not really care—in fact deep down he may sympathize. I think you will get on well with him, both being left-wing!

But remember, though you are plotting to escape *your* aunts, it may be a case of 'out of the frying pan…,' as you'll have to reckon with some of my collection, namely Aunts Magda and, in particular, Freda, since it is at her and my Granny's house, in the next road to us, that you will be spending the night. They moved there to be near Mummy and it's lovely for her to have them so near and also for me—less perhaps for my father!—and very convenient, since one of our bedrooms continues to be let. You need to know about Freda. She was my favourite when I was younger, as she is quite a dear with children, but she's less intellectual than Magda and, I warn you, much more openly devout. Magda keeps her distance from my 'conversion,' out of tact towards my mother, but Freda hardly conceals her enthusiasm. The latest thing is, she has introduced me to a nun, a Benedictine who she has worked with and who together with some others are experimenting with living 'in the world'—out of their Abbey, that is. They live in an ordinary house in Essex and don't wear habits except for Office in their chapel, but work at ordinary jobs; another is a teacher and one a secretary and all but the Superior are converts. And they have invited me to spend Saturday with them on a sort of Retreat. That should be very interesting and the best preparation for a holy Easter, please God culminating in the joy of seeing you! I shall be going with Granny and Freda to the Vigil Mass at the monastery near here. I went at Christmas and found it very beautiful.

I further warn you, dear Ian, that you have to behave yourself impeccably to win favour with both these aunts—though I'd say Freda is the stickler for 'form' and Magda more for 'content'! For example, Aunt Freda made a great fuss after I once introduced her *to* a friend, instead of the other way round, so I have to remember to say, 'Auntie Freda, this is Ian' and not, NOT—to you—'This is my Auntie Freda.' Magda at most might say later, 'Elaine, dear, I think you ought to know…'—in other words, might want to save me from a social blunder, but Freda will feel slighted!

Sorry about all this, but it's best to be warned. My parents aren't sticklers for that sort of thing—certainly not my father—but in general they are decorously old-fashioned, so we must be discreet: no fervent embraces—though in any case, I'm not sure it's right at present. Don't be angry at me for saying this; remember I can't be happy if I'm in doubt and I don't want to upset what promises to be a beautiful Easter, crowned by your visit.

You see, since Mass I am happy and calm again, though I hardly dare hope it will continue. The line between happiness and unhappiness seems so thin! I feel that, like the psalmist, I have been walking in the valley of the shadow for much of last term. But now, in my better moments, I can see life opening out before me, an unknown country, beautiful and savage by turns. But the 'rod and staff' *have* guided me, and looking back the way behind seems as mysteriously splendid as the way before. Then I know that so long as I trust I shall be led and need 'fear no evil.' My trust is imperfect still and I shall probably go through more dark patches, but I hope to remember that I shall be brought out of them.

I have to write all this because it is uppermost in my heart and because I want to give you some of my present serenity, after my last. But you seemed happy when you phoned and that helped me. Now I want to help you. You spoke of next term and yes, I'm looking forward to it, but we must take our love calmly and not get run away with as before, or we'll be disappointed. For now, be happy, dear Ian, until next week you see,
    Your Elaine"

Wed. 3rd April
"My darling Elaine,
After my second telephone call, I picked up a book and tried to read it, but it's impossible at the moment—I must write to you. As I can't see you and touch you, all I can do is write. Elaine, I can't live without you—can't do anything without you. You are my world, my everything.

Elaine—I too have no pride left. I'll give you everything—but please don't be too hard on me now that I'm absolutely at your mercy. I need you now as I've never needed anything, not food, sleep, friends, family, anything. Don't be angry with me for this and don't become proud now that I've flung myself absolutely on your mercy. My body aches and my mind whirls. My hand is trembling as I write. Elaine, love me. I love you.

I hope this reaches you tomorrow, when I'll write again. When the post came this morning without a word from you, I nearly went mad with the thought that I'm to go walking—which I love—for a whole week in Wales without reading your voice! I suppose—I hardly dare hope—You wouldn't come walking with me—that is, with the group, would you? I wish we'd planned it before; it would be so wonderful to be together in 'mysteriously splendid' scenery (your phrase!). And now I must stop to catch the early post and give you the best chance of saying Yes. Do, dearest Elaine! And in any case, my love, be happy. Always remember I love you more than I can ever put in words (or even in kisses). I love you with everything that is me. I'm yours, darling, Ian"

Thur. 4th April
"My dearest Elaine,
Though you hadn't received my last when you wrote, I gathered from the general tone of your letter that you'd detected my 'jumpy'-ness in my two phone-calls. Don't be too hard on it; I'm making an effort to be calm and secure. I will however state in my own defence that your judgments should be just a little tempered with mercy by the realization that I haven't your 'rock of St Peter' on which to build myself up. Still, that's up to you. I will only say that my ideal is not now the Stoic's calm strength but gentleness. I know that this last is my only hope of salvation from stubbornness of will and pride. It would be quite easy for me, I believe, to indulge in displays of strength of will but I have an idea that I have seen something better though much more difficult to attain. Please be patient while I try.

Elaine, my sweet, what I will write now may seem very evil but I feel it deeply. Your visit to those nuns and your enthusiasm about it frighten as nothing else can, that you will want to join them, as you had in mind last term. Oh, forgive me, forgive me, Elaine. It may be you would make a good nun, but I'm in agony at the thought. I know I'm selfish and that I ought never to stand in the way of any-thing you want, but I'm simply not as good as that. Your letter made me realize again that the fear of losing you to the religious life was all that stood between me and the path to the beginning of real happi-ness. You see, what I make of my life depends on you and until I know what you will do, I cannot move. If you really want me, we can begin to move forward; if not, it's 'Vae victis' for me. You wrote that we must take our love calmly next term. Yes indeed, darling, but I'm calm enough now. I know what I want and next term you'll know too (if you don't already).

At this point your telephone call rouses me and I now feel so happy that you are thinking of coming, that I'm even more ashamed of what I have written, but in honesty don't dare retract. This may be just plain stubbornness again, but I know you won't mind too much. Because if you come, I shall hope nothing can come between us! Please take my meaning, dearest Elaine.

And by the way, I think you should know—if you don't already—there is someone who would have liked to come between us and who will be on this trip. I just wanted to state again that all the enthusiasm has been on her part and not mine.

Just to prove that I am trying to enter into your world, I managed to read a little more of *Mediaeval Thought* yesterday. Avicenna and Averroes, Essence and Existence... Lord, what fools we mortals be! By the time I see you, I'll be able to tell you how many angels can stand on the head of a pin! Faith and Reason, Handmaid of Theology—it's all rolling round in my mind at the moment, with Everyman his own Pope and Joyce's 'Long live the Holy Father, Holy Joe, Holy Moses, the Holy Alliance...'

This must stop! Since your phone-call I'm a little light-headed, as you can tell! Because I'm happy in feeling more sure of your love. Love me, Elaine, and I will love you for ever. Never fear. Goodbye, my sweet, with all my life and love,

Ian"

Good Friday

"My precious Ian,

I'm writing at once to make sure of this reaching you before you come and to tell you I've definitely decided for Wales. Fortunately Leo has some walking boots that fit me, and I've been sedulously a-dubbining 'em! But this is to answer quite straightforwardly all you said in yours—so you must forgive what might seem like another outburst of sermonizing.

So far as I know, I haven't a 'religious' vocation and I doubt that tomorrow's 'retreat' will change that. It's just preparation for Easter. As you know, the idea did hit me about the middle of last term—and *terrified* me; that's when paralysis set in—physical even; certainly moral. The idea, though not explicit, was there, that God was a tyrant who had death and judgment in store for us and could demand that I throw away all the good things he apparently offered me in life, and submit myself at once to death, which made all the values of this life as I thought—art, human love etc—null and void. Am I not being honest with you? Do you see how this explains much of my behaviour last term? At the time I could do nothing but, when I woke in the nights in terror, only say, 'Very well, God: if this is what you will demand of me, I shall have no course but to submit, and therefore I shall submit; only give me strength and show me plainly what you do want.' This might seem addressed to a tyrant, not a Father. But it was a prayer of sorts and it has been answered. I was brought through the valley, as I've said before, and the experience has been valuable to me; it has given me a first-hand illustration of one more doctrine I would have laughed at a year or so ago—belief in a force of evil as wily as a serpent whispering to me: God is a tyrant and a deceiver. It's the very sort of thing anyone ought to expect who approaches Catholicism—only until they've got hold of the Catholic viewpoint, they're likely not to realize this and so to be vulnerable. Talking to Father Digby, even though not explicitly, has given me a better sense of these things, I think.

And there were other assaults connected with this: worrying about the future, about my thesis, thinking all the time of myself—assuming that that highest form of spiritual life ought to be the one I was cut out for, that I could be a saint from the word Go—a beautiful illustration of Pride!

But you see, one *isn't* tried beyond one's strength. I knew this in theory then, and in fact it was Monsignor Hervé, realizing that in some obscure way I was frightened of Catholicism coming between you and me, who early on said nothing was demanded of us out of fear, only out of love, and that no true human love could possibly be in conflict with divine love. So the very fact that I was afraid of the religious vocation would show that it couldn't be of God. I told my grandmother some of this recently and that's what she said immediately. Also, what I knew to be true, that this is a very rare vocation and in defect of a very real awareness of a call to it, one should assume that, provided one did nothing actually sinful, one's present walk of life was in accordance with God's will, and if one felt dissatisfied with it—as you know I do with mine—one could pray quite simply that, if it was wrong, one should be led into doing what was right, and meanwhile one should carry on. At first I couldn't do this, which I recognize shows a lack of trust in God, but now I feel that I am recovering something of the trust and peace of a child and that this is right.

My Granny told me it was through her that my godmother—my

mother's school-friend—got the introduction to the convent that turned out so badly for her—and she regards that as a caution.

Anyway, it's absurd to be dreaming (let alone having nightmares) about such a thing when I'm not even *in* the Church—not on the pipeline of grace, as it were! And meanwhile you and I know that we love one another and there is already such a bond between us that you can write to me as you just have and I unfold my most intimate thoughts as I am doing now, and have no fear of misunderstanding or repulsion. Neither of us planned to bring this about, far less committed any offence in so doing—it happened, and I am content to assume it is a good thing sent by God. The Catholic aim is perfect fulfilment—Monsignor H. said this and it seems to us that we shall be greatly helped to such fulfilment through each other. If this is not so, we can trust to be shown it is not the way of fulfilment, of true happiness, either for you or for me. But if it is so—as we are agreed it seems to be—much good will come of it for us both separately and jointly.

So you see, dear Ian, it's ALL RIGHT and you can learn from my mistake and not let a (hypothetical) devil make *you* afraid. All we have to do is wait to see our love confirmed and growing from strength to strength. This is why we need calm, and I was not 'hard on' your agitation, darling, just vexed that my love must have seemed wavering or you would not have been agitated. Really I am such an unstable sort of person sometimes, and especially recently! But I'm endeavouring to clamber onto that rock.

I shall post this on my way to the Good Friday service. See you on Monday, darling Ian, and for a WHOLE WEEK afterwards! The girl you mention is nothing to me if she is nothing to you. She sounds rather pathetic if, as you told me, she actually threatened suicide when she heard about me! Flattering perhaps, but in any case threats of that kind are seldom carried out. People who want to do it usually don't give warning, I believe.

So, till Monday be happy, as I am. Yes, Happy Easter! Love, Your Elaine"

IX

Despite her epistolary bold front, Elaine found herself still walking in the valley of the shadow and would look back on their week in Wales as a paradigm of life after as well as before: above each valley the "tops," fitfully sunlit, and this time not merely to be admired but scaled. Inexperience and lack of preparation made this the more challenging, and her brother's boots, which Ian assured her were the better for having been broken in, yet had not been broken in by her. From the first day's ascent, she found herself lagging behind not just the foremost group, which would normally include Ian by right of physique, but even the three girls who out of the five of them habitually brought up the rear.

The fourth, a student nurse, forged ahead with the best of them: "like a tank," Elaine put it to herself, noticing that as Ian periodically fell back to encourage herself, Sylvia too slackened her pace, falling back so as to await his catching up. This must be the girl of his letter's allusion; she looked far from any suicidal intention and Elaine was already half remorseful at her letter's comment, which Ian might judge unfeeling. It further occurred to her he might have persuaded her to come as protection from Sylvia's attentions—and perversely to the ongoing turbulence of her emotions was added the stirrings of a jealousy she struggled against. Sylvia was sturdily fleshed out, appearing strappingly healthy where Elaine felt herself to be thin and shrinking. Might he be having regrets, seeing how little adapted was her slim build to this favourite of his few recreations? She had been nervous, too, of the communal sleeping in youth-hostel bunks, fearing her insomnia and the effects of daytime strain and exhaustion. The first night, as precaution against the excitement of the journey and the stimulus of his presence, she took a sleeping pill. The second, after a not unduly taxing climb and ridge-walk and encouraged by Ian's approbation, she felt unusually relaxed and in hope to sleep soundly, settled herself to read until lights-out, after which she would say her night prayers. Her presumed rival had taken the bunk opposite; could that be deliberate? Moreover, Sylvia produced no pyjamas from her rucksack but stripping bare, inserted her rounded proportions unclothed into the regulation sheeting bag. Elaine assumed all would have brought pyjamas; she fancied Sylvia to be eyeing hers with scorn—or it might be the way she had got into them, avoiding nudity as she had always assumed one did. Now it occurred to her that might be something imbibed from her mother's convent-bred modesty; never, come to think of it, had she seen her naked—though she well recalled staring at her father in the bath and he had encouraged her to look; she supposed it was from his Leftist views on child-rearing, but she had felt awkward and that her mother would not approve... Then there was the morning—awful still in memory—when they were at The Quarry and she had opened the bathroom door to be confronted with Uncle Hilary's bare behind looming at eye-level, very large, and from beyond it his voice exclaiming, "Whoa back there!" She had closed the door, scurried away and for several days avoided him.

Such memories, with their charge of confused feeling, did not help as she lay, tense now and wondering if sleep would come—and if it did not, how she would endure the following day's more demanding climb. At length out of her misery she told herself she could surely pray; had not the Hebrew Psalmist spent nights sleepless in prayer and praise? "Thank you, Lord, for this day!" she began and entered on the accustomed roll-call of her family, to end with "Ian and all our friends here, our benefactors, our neighbours, our enemies...": the formula her grandmother had taught her. It occurred to her that the girl in the bunk opposite might be among the enemies, but even as she bethought her to pray for her, the day's exercise and mountain air prevailed. With succeeding climbs and purgations of wind, shower and sun—as well as the beers ritually downed with its sinking—she would find herself dropping easily into slumber and gaining in colour and appetite: even, she thought, in weight.

Moreover, Sylvia seemed to be attaching herself to another member of their party, causing Elaine to reproach herself again for her jealousy. Ian could hardly have been more attentive, and if he eyed her slowness deprecatingly, he took pleasure in helping her over rough places, laughing as he propelled her up steep inclines, leading her by the hand on treks through the valleys, making it plain she was his! And at least on the descents she could show herself the swifter, footing it nimbly over tussock and rock where his greater bulk lowered itself more heavily. At breakfast and at supper she would wait, alert for him to squeeze onto the hostel's bench beside her. Always after they made to turn in, he would draw her aside in the gathering darkness to claim the kisses from which she parted ever more reluctantly, confused by a carnality she half dreaded, half desired, and which reawakened the fear that this love might be drawing her away from her "real" vocation.

What if it was Sylvia God had in mind for Ian? Though she struggled against the thought, it would return to cause her agony, render her as though paralysed in will, unable to let him go—or rather send him away: thought to horrify and that could not be entertained! It might be sinful—surely, by the Church's teachings *was* sinful, this encroaching fleshly passion; then how to disentangle it from what might, what must be good: from love? It might or might not be leading her astray and down a fatal path, yet she seemed determined—even fated—to have him...

"Have him!" Elaine shied from the crude phrase, for it had been

Aunt Magda's one confidence as to Uncle Hilary's and her court-ship—if that could be the term for two people one would suppose so little romantic! Those had been her aunt's words: "*I told myself I must have him!*" No more—nothing about how that compulsion had issued in a forbidden union, never blessed with children, about which Elaine had heard mutterings... The cases were different, of course, Ian and she both without married tie, and yet... What, a voice would argue, if hers was to be the expiation for an entail—her mother's family, her mother herself, her aunts, grandparents, those behind them...? Aunt Freda knew a monk who had taken on the vocation in reparation for his parents' troubled marriage. Had any-one made restitution for the crossed marriage that to all accounts had been her grandparents'—the offspring of which had all gone off into rebellion at some time, and one into suicide...

Aunt Freda, too, failing to find a husband, had visited a convent to test whether she had a vocation. And, as she put it, had been put off by the sight of the sisters sewing felt flowers! What struck in that was that she assumed the freedom to find what might seem such a small and personal matter decisive: freedom Elaine half envied and felt her aunt had from having grown up Catholic. But was it right? Could *you* decide? Suppose it was God's will for you to make felt flowers! You presumably could pray while you did so; she recalled her answer to Ian on that walk by the river when she had first shocked him with talk of a nunnery.

No, and no again. She, Elaine, was not the first to stand on the threshold with the choice before her—the choice of renunciation as exemplified in those lives of saints of which she already could heart-ily wish to be in ignorance! Though a bitterness from which flesh must shrink appalled, yet was flesh to refuse the God who called to sacrifice and a higher fulfilment? Yet again, *could* she renounce Ian? Ought she even to contemplate dealing him a blow he had pleaded with her not to deliver? And she had reassured him! It would be a betrayal; she must not, could *not*.

At some point there came to her Veronica's dream not long after her own birth; her mother had more than once related it, with linger-ing intimation of the horror from which she had awoken. "Elaine was inside, shut in; I was outside, unable to get in to her..." Aunt Agnes had understood: it was the Church. But could "it" also have been the convent! Looking back, it was plain that her redoubtable aunt had systematically attempted to warn her niece off the lures of both: always disparaging her own schooling, lending her books: *I Leap over the Wall, Frost in May*... Could Aunt Agnes, that "good" schoolgirl, have felt the lure of the convent—to find it opposed by the lure of that "free love" she had proclaimed and practised? Was that the peculiar force driving her detestation of not merely her father's but her mother's cherished faith? Even if it were, what then? She Elaine, and Ian, they were not contemplating "free love"; how then should all that touch her? No, she must not—*must not*—think like that...!

Twice it happened during the long spells of slogging inseparable from their pursuit of the heights: him ahead, leading, her toiling in the rear: on the Glyders and, most frighteningly, on Crib Goch as they pressed toward the yet unseen summit, now in fitful sunshine: it was as though a shadow descended upon that beckoning mountain-scape; exalted as she saw it to be, she yet saw it as if absent, cut off from her—or as if she herself were unreal. And somehow this shadow would connect itself to those nights when the nun's image had arisen black before her; she recoiled from the half suppressed memory, struggled feebly against the perception, not invoking as cause the unwonted strenuousness, the release from the habitual round, the toll of contending emotions: far from connecting her experience to the "dark tunnel" to which Aunt Magda had likened her nervous break-down of long ago. "The valley of the shadow," this darkening of vision, menacing her with an Apollyon to fight: yet a delusion—as it must be and *must not* master her!

She would shake it off, but daylong it would return to prey on her, while she sought to hide her trouble; then it would be dispelled by day's ending, or under Ian's shepherding touch. Until at last they stood on Snowdon's peak and watched the massed clouds briefly part and re-part, as if revealing to the Pilgrim glimpses of a Promised Land. As body rested, so into the labouring mind came other ancient words:

"I will lift up mine eyes unto the hills
whence cometh my strength."
And Apollyon left her for that time.

X

Their return plunged Ian into preparation for exams and a posting he understood would be to a District Office in Northern Rhodesia's Copper Belt. Meantime he accompanied Elaine to a weekly session with Father Digby, with whom he was soon at ease in intellectual regions beyond her sure following; Ian's, she perceived, was an intellect adapted to theological inquiry, where her bent was toward meta-phor and poetry. The friar seemed to combine both gifts, governed by a prevailing asceticism. When she tried to express this to Ian he observed that it put one in mind of Plato's charioteer in the *Phaedrus* governing his two steeds—reviving her regrets about Greek.

But Father Digby was proving in himself an education. Once and timidly she raised with him the matter of vocation—to be met with a disconcerting silence, during which she was left undecided whether she was being taken either not seriously or too seriously for her com-fort. When the rejoinder came, it was what she least expected. Would she wish to live like some nuns he had recently visited, who maintained themselves by making sweetmeats? His evocation of the cloying atmosphere surrounding their premises had the effect of injecting a corrective of realism into her turbid imaginings. But he did not urge her to continue the studies she had all but abandoned. He must see the way the wind inevitably blew—as did she.

Immediately it was blowing towards Ian's college's May Ball—not Elaine's first, but being in the company of the man whose love she returned—Did she not?—it would surely be her best. An evening-gown had been Veronica's last couturial *rapprochement* with her daughter; between them they had concocted it, out of dramatic red and black organza over a flame art-taffeta, on Granddad's old sewing-machine. It had sufficed for three undergraduate years but now seemed to Elaine juvenile and outmoded. She purchased a Vogue pat-tern and swathes of the fashionable glazed cotton and borrowed Miss Browne's sewing-machine. Guiding the stuff between the whirring bobbin and needle was relief from tedious Library days: real material to be handled, smelled, enjoyed, not brain-matter to be juggled into something mustered as intelligence. For a week this engrossed her away from the youthful and ageing heads bent over strip-lit desks, from the feverish turning of pages and scratching of notes.

Ian too was chafing to plumb realer depths than what he ever felt to be Cambridge's superficial brilliance, and while this glamour still beckoned Elaine, she had begun to accept he was right. A yearning for a world not perhaps realer—Reading Plato was having its effect: rather more personal—renewed earlier notions of becoming a physi-cian: too late for that and a visit to the Careers Service about the pos-sibility of entering a Graduate Nursing programme confronted her with—this time—harsh realism: the course was long and demand-ing, like the work; had she not on their Welsh expedition compared her physique with Sylvia's?

She returned to the Library to consult the *Times Educational Sup-*

plement for positions in non-state schools not requiring a teacher's certification. Though with most of the girls at school she had declared she would not be a teacher, with him at her side the prospect changed. Why battle with discouragement to gain a further degree? Her tutor—from whom she must obtain a reference—the Principal herself—to whom she would offer to pay back that year's scholarship money—possessed no higher degree than would be hers by the lapse of a year or two and payment of five pounds: "M.A. (Bought)," they derided it, though Ian produced an explanation involving medieval and Scottish degrees.

On the afternoon of the Ball she lay attempting to compensate for shortage of sleep before she must bathe and lay the foundations of her attire. Evening found her arrayed in the blue-sprigged gown, curled, lipsticked, powdered, her strapped shoulders still bare of the mohair stole she had purchased against the uncertainties of early June: white, to match the long gloves and the acutely pointed shoes—their heels did not quite qualify as the fashionable "stiletto": being tall, she preferred them low. They had occasioned a struggle over extravagance: she might have worn her black-strapped sandals since only in the less demure dances would footwear show beneath trailing skirts. But the extravagance could be justified; the shoes would be kept for the wedding towards which she was being surely borne on that blowing wind...

Having still some time to wait, she had taken up Newman's *Grammar of Assent*, determined it should hold her attention. A ring at the front door—surely not him so early! Going to her window, she saw a florist's van, heard Miss Browne call up the stairs and soon was tripping carefully down them to receive the landlady's warm approbation—earned, as she became aware looking into the long glass that lightened the narrow hallway, by the demureness of her dress and wrap; the effect, she fancied—lipstick apart—a little nun-like: the colours those of the Virgin of virgins.

She returned to her room carrying a small box that must contain his favour: not a custom to which she had expected him to conform. Opening it she took out a card: "With my love, darling, Ian." Beneath folds of tissue-paper, nestled in ferny fronds, was a spray of deep red roses: a mere bud, a bloom unfurling, one more fully blown. She laid them to her shoulder, her breast, the stole, her hair before replacing them. He had written that he would wish her to be "as bright and beautiful as possible." She took up a casket of silver and cut glass; originally Grandma Rigg's, it had crowned her mother's dressing-table for as long as Elaine could remember, until presented on her twenty-first birthday to herself. From it she took an artificial rose and fixed its red into the sable fall of her hair; then her grandfather's corals that reached just round her throat, a gold-wire bangle given her by Aunt Jane, and finally—her Granny's gift—a silver brooch with which she fastened the live spray to the stole: her mirror showed it flaming red on white—like the heart below, she told herself. This heart, though, was not devoid of a small regret: a stiff black bag held comb, make-up, glasses, scented handkerchief; she had contemplated an array of satin pochettes but drawn back in favour of the shoes. That apart, she was ready and the frail glass of her happiness for the moment full. She had but to await him and his approval.

Both arrived duly with the taxi, into which he helped her, assuming an unpractised gallantry; she smiled inwardly to see it triumph over the fierce Scottish forthrightness she admired but also a little feared in him. As the taxi set off he drew her to him, searching for her gloved hand and offering to her cheek one kiss accepted and returned, then they sat silent until they were arrived in front of that Great Gate from which medieval princes looked down on a brouhaha of turning vehicles and evening-suited gallants handing down dames, many as amply skirted as any those stones had looked on of old. They passed under an awning, crossed the Great Court, negotiated the narrow passage and low doorway that gave access to the Palladian world of arcades now brilliantly lit, under which couples were already treading the dance on parquet laid over the flagstones to orchestral strains wafting from under the great Wren Library that bounded the court's further end. All soon faded from Elaine's awareness, in which they alone were dancing in a fusion of night, lights, music and the scent of the hothouse flowers gracing every alcove, and though neither was much instructed in the art, his mass supported her pliancy, her arms completed the circle of his as they gave themselves to their unifying motion.

An hour, or was it two, might have passed in trance before they were ensconced in Ian's room, where he had prepared for them a collation of French bread and paté, black Greek olives, strawberries with a sharp yet creamy yoghurt—a post-war novelty he had discovered; it came from Bulgaria—and a light white wine: Champagne, he explained, would have had to be drunk now; this they could return to throughout the evening. Champagne, she knew, would be an extravagance he could ill afford and she approved his provision of the intimate and to her exotic feast.

Thereafter they strolled and danced and strolled again amid the Ball's varied appeals. Finally, as they stood by the water's edge where punts were drawn up ready for the traditional early morning expeditions to Grantchester, she said,

"I only hope I shall be able to stay awake for breakfast!"

He turned and drew her to him, stroking her hair as she rested against his shoulder, tense, trembling, feeling the life in her frame must pass into his, or pass away...

"Then, in case you can't, I must ask you now..."

He paused. She felt, rather than heard, the rough intake of his breath, as he her thrill of attention.

"Marry me, Elaine!"

She remained dumb, savouring the moment, taking it in, casting about for the right answer. He placed his hands on her shoulders, stepped back, looking into her upturned face, and almost groaned,

"Elaine, you must say Yes!"

Another pause and then, "Of course—I will!"

That "I will"—it seemed dragged from her as though *against* her will, but she had said it and, like Luther, knew she could no other—not that Luther's was the example to reassure! Ian's arms had crept round her back, his mouth was upon hers.

Thus when at length they were borne upon a sullen river-back, Ian's frame bending and straightening, rhythmically thrusting their craft upstream, for her there was no question of sleep, only a strained unbelief and again that experience of unreality, as though the inverted shades of dawn clouds—now rippling, now parting, ever encroaching—needed to be withstood. Withstand them she did until a misty sun rose, to disappear again as they breakfasted, by which time she was as though falling away into a dazed weariness she would still conceal from him. Cruel, that at what should be the summit of happiness she must feign the very joy in his embrace, as he left her to fall on her bed and know no more until awakened to a lowering noon.

PART VI

Epithalamial

(1961)

I

EDITH sat at the opened-down lid of that "bureau" (so she called it) that, unbeknown to her, her granddaughter had coveted in childhood. It stood in the upper-front room of the house she and Freda had moved to in the street adjoining the Kellers'. Accepted was that they had moved there for mutual advantage and support; stated was how nice it would be not to have to travel to meet; understood was that mother and sister wished to have part in the only family sprung from progeny of René and Edith: moreover that Veronica, as she found her husband increasingly difficult, felt the need of reinforcement. Understood too was that at some future date Veronica would be on hand to help Freda look after their mother.

They had been fortunate in finding this house going cheap because divided into two flats, the lower tenanted by a lady whose age was warrant it would not so remain for long; thus as Edith advanced in age they might descend to occupy the ground-floor, by which time Magda might wish to move into the upper: it would be her due since it was she who out of Hilary's legacy had enabled them to put down the deposit on their first house. That all this was providential nobody doubted, nor did anybody voice the question: What if their mother's oft-fluttering heart and a new tendency to breathlessness should carry her off untimely?

The sun of early September still penetrated part of the east-facing bow window, to lie placidly across the room. Edith was half listening for the latch-click of the garden gate and the footfall—light and springy, she hoped—of her granddaughter. Elaine had returned from honeymoon last evening and she did not doubt would, so soon as tactful towards her parents, seek out herself. Edith's mind was wandering between this expectation and her writing. Her post-War success had made way for two more historical novels set in Catholic times both English and French, with Catholic personages haply more sinner than saint. But by now tastes in fiction, led by proliferating television, had turned to a harsher realism. Her third book had sold poorly and her publisher declined the fourth, the unpromising hero of which was the second James, last Catholic King of England, only Catholic king of Great Britain. Resigned to her disappointment, and the succeeding year being her eightieth, she yet would not lay down her pen but embarked on what, even if not published, should be a legacy to her descendants: the long-projected, half fictionalized account of her own life and memories.

Liza it was had supplied her with the title, after Edith had again left René and descended with her brood upon her sister and the already stricken Cousin Leon. Already her marital crises had driven a wedge between herself and the sister she had always protected, adding, as Edith saw it, yet another unjust blow to her life's tally.

"You *are* a tragedy queen!" that sister had exclaimed. Well, Edith reflected, in the longer term that wounding utterance had helped prod her into acknowledgement of past errors; some forty years of clinging to the Faith had surely inculcated self-criticism, as well as a sense of the scale of ills suffered in what René justly accounted this "vale of tears." Ineptitude in dealing with situations and people had been excusable in the young thing who had flitted across half Europe eluding improper male advances.

Though the gossip and strictures of women she might have borne with less standing upon "reputation," yet now that tendency to self-dramatization that had not assisted her past self might be turned to better account. *Tragedy Queen*, set in late-Victorian London, would draw on "realism" enough from her and her mother's lives. She read of fiction's newly "existentialist" mode with recoil from such bleak cynicism, and it was in still romantic vein that her heroine's proper deprecations of the attentions of the Polish Count competed with musings on the contrasting fortunes of herself and the unwitting author of her title. "Title": the ambiguous word itself supplied a thread to her reverie; was it not a "title" the elder of Liza's daughters had married, whose only son, the second Sir Robert, was being groomed to enter Parliament! The younger daughter too, long after the affair with the unfortunate German Jew—He had not been heard of again—had achieved a very respectable marriage, her husband adopting her love-child.

One up, one down! In worldly terms, that was, for in heavenly only one failure counted and worldly failures might be even the prelude to success! She, who had set out to rise by her education, her refinement, not least by the beauty with which she had seemed—no, *been* blessed, for beauty too was God's gift—she had been brought—kept—low. Not even as in times of which she had been writing: times in which a penniless English governess, cast adrift from her native London, could need to borrow from her employers for shoes and clothing suited to a continental winter! For long she had had to strive against poverty and for respectability, for herself and her daughters. And son: she must not forget poor Leo. He had attempted to ease the struggle from off her shoulders when he joined the RAF—until his personal struggle—rooted all too probably in his parents'—had over-powered him… Would her book—would she at any point be able to face up to *that* chapter?

Today the question could be shelved, smacking as it did of stark winter. Today—she looked up at the window—seemed to herald the autumn of days she would be content to pass cast up at last in this semi-urban backwater, with Magdalen's allowance and Winifreda's income to supplement her pension and the royalties which had all but dried up.

If it were only the past! The past one could entrust to the mercy of God; but Winifreda and "pension" brought to mind that all inimical to peace at the last was the present, about which things must ever be not only thought but done. A pension was the need Winifreda was now struggling to secure, after so much trouble, first with her back and now this recent bout of brain-fever contracted while working for the London County Council, visiting families in the slums, many of them immigrants from the sub-continent where such diseases were endemic. And contagious: Edith had caught it and, from nursing them, Veronica had been so stricken as to be taken into hospital. But Edith's abiding grief was for the youngest daughter who never had married, never would have children—who had tried to substitute for this by making all poor children her own: a burden not even the strong could carry. Freda who in her former positions had been bright and capable, had changed tack, riding high on a zeal to do good—only to be discouraged by the frequently intransigent and ungrateful recipients of her good works, worn down by the frequent jealousies and self-opinion of her fellow-workers.

Neither had Agnes married, though she had come close to (Edith mentally put the word into quotation) "marry"-ing an older man who had divorced his wife on her account. She had been saved—in the view of the Catholics of the family (relieved—it almost seemed providentially—of the dilemma of committing mortal sin by attend-ing the wedding-ceremony or mortally offending both)—by his sud-den death.

"A judgment!" was Freda's view, but their mother, compassion for the grief of her not entirely estranged eldest daughter mingling with her own grief at the waywardness of that daughter's life, inclined rather to see this as yet another and tragic repeat instalment of the family history: of Magdalen, of her own dear mother. Albeit "Not so!" Winifreda had objected: "Agnes *led* Mr James into infidelity! Your father—as also Hilary—both had lost their wives to insanity!"

"You are right, dear," replied her mother, "And yet—It seems Mr James too had in some sense lost his wife—her affection, I mean. And—Can we make distinctions—in what according to Our Lord Himself is adultery?"

But now they had witnessed an undoubted, even though "mixed," Catholic marriage, that of Edith's precious granddaughter—who next week would be setting off for that unknown continent, Africa: how she would fear for and miss her! Yet how happy her conversion and her marriage should—did—make her! Each joy contained the seed of a sorrow, each flower concealed a sting; it was ever so! In Elaine the family returned to its Catholic heritage: that was answer to their prayers, not least René's. And through her that patrimony would be passed on. Not as he had prayed and longed for: not in his and his forefathers' name, but in names introduced through females no less of his line; it was as though God mocked the assumptions of patriarchy; they could rejoice in that—even while she could never but sorrow for the cutting-off of Leo's young manhood, of John's infancy... Yet to René's pretensions, God had answered "No—but Yes."

Elaine would bear children who would be Catholic; Edith trusted Ian for that, seeing him deeply in love with her dear child and the love returned—and her new-embraced Catholicism prized as perhaps a treasure could be only by one who has discovered it. Had Elaine been raised as Veronica—as also Ron—had promised, who knew but she might never have valued the Faith, have discarded it as had all Edith's brood as they emerged from childhood—Agnes, Magdalen, Leo—even for a time Winifreda...

Would it ever be so? Should one fear for Elaine's children in their turn? Children were Hope: Hope, ever depicted as a child, was a Virtue surpassed only by Charity, and Edith saw grounds for it. Things were stirring in the Church even before the old Pope died—in the wider Church and even in these lands cumbered with their insular brand of Reformation. There was to be a Council; the amazing old man—older than herself—now occupying the Chair of Peter, had thrown open that window in graphic token that the Church of the twentieth century was in need of fresh air: his Italian word for it, *aggiornamento*, was on Catholic lips the world over, and nowhere was that "fresh air" more needed than in the fog-bound island of which Newman's mentor, Dominic Barberi, had dreamed, impelling him to go forth and labour to re-root the Catholic Faith in England... Surely the wind of the Spirit was abroad and turning the mills of God...

With these more consoling thoughts, Edith bent again to her writing, unable entirely to dismiss the anticipation of her granddaughter's arrival and how things—things kept vague—would have gone for her. Not that she feared this honeymoon would have been as dismal as her own; yet it was often a precarious time and harbinger of weal or woe. She thought them sensible to have decided to spend it climbing mountains—all but unthinkable for a bride of her day, but surely a better antidote to marital anxieties than decorous excursions in a pony-trap along the Riviera, admiring Nature, not engaging with her. Travel by air, too, did away with long, self-conscious journeys by train; she recalled the thrill, some ten years previously, of seeing France, the Alps, Elba and the long coastline of Tuscany laid out below, of glimpsing the Colosseum and St Peter's as they descended to Rome... Elaine's first flight, late on her wedding-day, would have been into latitudes north enough, in late August, for visibility before her wedding-night descended...

Here Edith thrust from her speculation that the bride might by now be, in the French-derived euphemism of her day, "in an interesting condition." She hoped not; that could overwhelm a couple just when they had to adjust to life together, let alone to a new and very different country. But things had improved in that respect since her day; Elaine had referred to new advances in Birth Control that were acceptable to the Church and put a booklet on it into Edith's hands; she had been eager to know of any impending resolution to the stern moral ruling under which she and so many had suffered. Elaine would have been preparing herself—Ian too, she supposed; young people were so much more open as well as better informed nowadays, and the Church had—if reluctantly—recognized Prudence as a virtue in family-planning, rather than, as it had sometimes seemed, in every other department of life but that.

And there at last was the key in the front door below and soon the welcome voice from the stairway,

"Are you there, my Granny?"

"Elaine! Come on up, my darling."

Edith laid down her glasses with her pen and reached the landing as the dark head levelled with it and the dear face was upturned with an expression eager if...

"Or should I say Mrs Roody!" she jested, to dispel the mutual self-consciousness they banished with a silent hug. Then Edith stepped back to survey the returned bride: wearing trousers, of course, as girls did these days, and she'd left for her honeymoon in a blue "anorak," as they called it, just like his, and carrying a rucksack—how far from her

own shimmering alpaca and hat wreathed with roses, half a century
ago! But her Elaine—now Ian's Elaine, but still assuredly also hers—
looked well in trousers, being slim, not like some of the women one
saw, who surely if they could see themselves... Yet she was, Edith fancied, a little thinner: in sparkling health though and with, yes, that
touch of reserve, that self-awareness of the no-longer-virgin. But
assuredly not unhappy, was her conclusion, and she knew relief: all
would be well. She asked,

"Where is Ian?"

"Unpacking. Or rather re-packing. And phoning his people. He'll
come on after; he knows we want to be together a bit."

"He is very thoughtful and—I am very happy for you. And you
too are happy, I trust, my Elaine."

It was more statement than question and the answer was indirect.

"Yes, I am very fortunate in Ian, as you know, and we've had a
marvellous time. We hope our slides will be ready before we leave
and we can show you. We've bought a little viewer; a screen is better
but we must wait to buy that: arranging for the wedding-presents
and things we have already is quite enough..."

She was beginning to prattle on and Edith suspected was evading
something. Probing a little, she observed,

"So! I'm delighted for you, that everything is looking so rosy."

"Yes. Only..."

"Only what?" (keeping her tone light).

"Only—leaving you, of course, and here and—everything."

"And your parents, of course." (She had noticed the hesitation).

"Yes, though Mummy..."

"Yes? How is she taking it?"

"Well—You know, I'm a bit upset and I'd like to tell you. I mean,
I think it's better I'm leaving where she's concerned. She's just done
such a—such an odd thing, really. I mean, it's not a big thing compared with everything I—I'm so lucky to have, but... She sold my
wedding-dress!"

"Sold your wedding-dress?"

"Yes. She's just put in my hand eight guineas she got for it, adver-
tising in the local paper."

"You mean you hadn't *asked* her to sell it?"

"No, I never did. It never occurred to me—I mean, perhaps it
would have been a good idea, certainly not to take it with me to
Africa, and she probably didn't want it left with her, but I just hadn't
thought beyond wearing it for the wedding, and—I know it wasn't a
very grand one, but I was so pleased when Aunt Jane gave it to me;

she offered me two out of their business and I chose that one and I altered it a bit to fit me and—well, it was *my* wedding-dress and I didn't expect Mummy to get rid of it like that while I was on honeymoon, without asking me!"

"I see. So what did you say?"

"Nothing. I was taken aback, of course, when she gave me the money—a short while ago, just before I came on here—but I thought there was nothing I could do about it now, except *not* let her think she'd hurt me—not let it show! I just said 'Thank you,' as if she'd done what I wanted."

Edith grasped her to her, hugging her again and smoothing the dark hair as if she was still a little girl whose playmates had been teasing her.

"You did well, my precious, and—I'm very sorry. It does seem extraordinary of your mother, but..."

She was thinking rapidly and steering her granddaughter into the sitting-room with its stately upholstered chairs and its china-cabinet full of relics of Edith's own wedding-presents: odd cups and dishes left from Crown Derby and Limoges services, curious glazed jugs and vases that had delighted Elaine as a child... They seated themselves side by side on the so-called studio-couch that was Freda's bed by night, because the third bedroom of this upper flat was its kitchen.

"We must remember how ill your mother has been with this foreign disease. We think Winifreda caught it from her work among the Indian immigrants: 'encephalo' we call it; it's a long name that means it affects the brain-lining. I caught it too, as you know, and I still sometimes feel giddy. And your mother had it worse than either of us. She was hardly over it in time for your wedding; we did so hope and pray it would not spoil that!"

Elaine was remembering her visit to her mother in the Royal Free Hospital, said to have particular expertise in the rare disease. Only the one visit, for she had been teaching all week and had a longish journey to and from school, and marking and class-preparation every evening; it had been reasonable, she told herself, only to make the one journey by bus and tube to the hospital. Very reasonable, and at the time she had suppressed the thought that she was doing the least she could and really it was a token, as of course a daughter had to visit her mother when she was in hospital, and besides she had sent flowers... She had sat there talking brightly but miserably aware that she didn't know what to say and was literally unfeeling. And what she mustn't feel was that her illness was a sort of trump-card her mother had produced late on in this embattled year which she had looked on as a last chance to show her parents she wanted to be with them while she still could. Such an unhappy year! Even before Auntie Freda caught the infection, even worse had been her grandmother's heart failure when she, Elaine, had been with her. And it could have been her fault... No lack of feeling there, as she reflected, actually shuddering as she turned to the beloved figure, grown so visibly frailer...

"But I haven't asked how you've been, dear Granny; see how selfish I am! At least you've had no more of that hot weather we had earlier, that laid you so low."

"No, God be thanked! I thought I really would expire, from heat and breathlessness! Winifreda is getting the roof insulated, but it may be better to go away for July and August rather than for the winter months, as Doctor Baines recommended; he thought the sea air would help me, but it nearly killed me, as we well remember!"

"We should never have gone out on that bitterly cold day. I blame myself. I remember you said, lying there holding my hand, 'It doesn't matter if I die,' but I'd never have been able to forgive myself!"

Freda, after four failures, generating a full year's anxiety and discomfiture, had passed the driving-test and, with a contribution from Elaine's parents—neither of whom saw themselves as learning to manage a motor-vehicle—bought a small Hillman in which to perform errands on behalf of all. With this and with Edith advised a change from urban smog, she had installed their mother in a cottage on the Sussex coast and in touch with friends in nearby Angmering. The four sisters were to take turns at keeping her company and Elaine had been delighted to offer herself for Christmas; she had been feeling indignant, as well as humiliated, at receiving from her father (set on, she felt sure, by her mother) a letter upbraiding her for regularly spoiling their so-carefully planned Christmases; yet that insistence on a meticulous enactment, she felt, was at fault as much as she: the furniture to be polished, plate cleaned, cake decorated, and the tree—even now when there were no children to surprise with it! She would bear up awhile in anticipation of remembered joys—only to break down amid the ashes of anti-climax. How willingly too she would avoid it now, when the Midnight Mass she for the past years had attended with her Grandmother and Aunt was a more desolate prospect without them!

Christmas in the cottage with Granny and Auntie Freda had been snug and informal by comparison, and Midnight Mass in a converted Sussex barn not only redolent of four centuries of clandestine Masses but as near as possible of a Stable, being hung with greenery, its scent mingling with candles and incense, the altar spread as for the Birth. Next midday they had dined on fowl and pudding, then while they slept she had sat by a log-fire reading Leigh-Fermor's travels in Greece which Ian had had his parents send her, books being little obtainable in the Copper Belt.

Two days later Freda had returned to work, leaving Elaine in charge of her mother. That night snow had fallen. They had set out to walk to the shops some quarter of a mile away, but on the return Edith had felt faint and Elaine hardly supported her into the cottage. There she had collapsed on the couch while her alarmed granddaughter phoned a list of doctors to find one who could come at once; then phoned the priest from the barn-church, who arrived just as the doctor was leaving, having injected the patient with digitalis and given instructions for her further care.

After the priest too departed, Elaine had telephoned her mother, whom Aunt Magda had driven down, with Freda, that afternoon. By that time the snow had melted and Veronica, taking charge, had arranged for Magda to drive Elaine to stay with Freda's friends. It was the old story and she had gone dumbly and without protest, feeling packed off like the child she no longer was. After all, she expostulated with herself, lying sleepless in the strange bed, who was it had called the doctor, called the priest, tended her grandmother until their arrival? An hour passed that seemed two as her feelings mounted, then she had arisen to walk the mile down to the sea and follow the coast back to Ferring, her anxiety that her grandmother might be worse—might even have died—overcoming her fear of the deserted country roads, of the small creatures stirring in the eerie moonlight, of the wires humming overhead where she had to pass a row of pylons, of the shore wide and whitened and the hissing breakers defining the ghostly expanse of the sea.

When at last she had arrived, it was to a frosty reception from her mother, who was still up, for her thoughtlessness in increasing their burdens. Where did she imagine she was to sleep? She was permitted the couch by which she had so recently knelt in imploring tears. Freda and Magda, she comforted herself, realized how she felt, and Magda drove her mother home the next day, leaving her and Freda to nurse Edith and run the cottage.

All this Edith too recalled and in sympathy patted her granddaughter's newly ringed hand with hers so softly wrinkled, saying,

"You were so good and kind to me, both before and after my attack! I remember you sobbing by the bed when the priest was anointing me, which I'm sure helped me recover—both the anointing and the knowing how much it was going to mean to you. As well as, of course, the injection the doctor gave me. Well, here we are still, despite my lungs and heart and despite 'encephalo'! The doctor has insisted I give up smoking, and I have, which is a blessing, to finances as well as to health; how I wish your mother could manage it at last! And I recall you saying to me in the days after, when I had a bit of a relapse, 'Granny, you must see me married'—and now I have!"

She paused before resuming archly,

"And do you remember what I said then?"

"You said, 'Yes, and I must see a baby'!"

"And do you remember you said, 'You shall, if I have to fly it home for you!'"

She gave the bride a look which began as searching and ended in a shared smile.

"I think I'll need a little time to settle in to our new life first," Elaine demurred.

"Don't let it be too long! Remember the nuptial blessing I passed on to you and Ian: 'May you see your children's children, to the third and fourth generation.' You will be the carrier of that blessing—and Ian, of course."

"Yes. But, Granny..."

She never would have called her "Deedie," let alone "Edith," and in that appellation both felt her to be still her grandmother's child. Edith waited and after Elaine still hesitated, prompted gently,

"What is it, my darling? You can tell Granny!"

She was half expecting confidence as to an "interesting condition," or at least its early possibility.

"Yes. It's only—I mean, it *is* all right, isn't it, to wait a while before having a baby? I mean, we have to get settled in Rhodesia and it's all so new. We thought a year..."

For once Edith was nonplussed. Sympathy for her child, situated between the newness of her married state and the unknowns of her destination, contended with the desire to see that Nuptial Blessing of old fulfilled in the Catholic baptism of a child of her and René's line, and the consciousness that she had already eluded death the once. Weighing into that scale was the Church's teaching on the purposes and uses of marriage—and then there was one's duty, under the rubric of the Seven Spiritual Works of Mercy, to give good counsel to those requiring it. Rapidly balancing all out, she replied,

"I don't know, my darling, about waiting. Of course, it depends how... I'd say not more than a year, at most. But perhaps you should ask your Confessor."

Silence while she bethought her to add, hesitantly,

"Though I dare say I am the last person who should preach this, still, we are admonished to rely on the Grace of Marriage—and of all the Sacraments.

"Which reminds me," she added amid her granddaughter's continuing silence, "I am to give you the photographs Magdalen took with the new camera she bought especially for your wedding: did you know? They are actually in colour and you look so well in them—indeed we all do! And while you look at them, I'll get some coffee and biscuits ready for when Ian arrives. This evening we must all have a drink to celebrate."

II

Edith left Elaine to her perplexities and to the memories revived by Magda's wedding-photographs. Of Granny herself in the fox-fur and half-veil hat brought out for rare occasions, upstaging Ian's grandmother's tweediness; seated at table, Edith had quite charmed the dour Scot—of whom her grandson clearly was not fond—with lady-like confidences, leading on to explanations of the Catholic service courteously given and as courteously received. Of their mothers, hatted, of course: she awarded the palm to Veronica's blue-feathered number and grey suit over Ian's mother's matching green outfit, while in men's apparel Ron clearly must yield to the son of the Manse, Ian's father. He, in ensuring that his son should go to Cambridge provided with the tailored charcoal suit that became him well, had provided also for his wedding; while to go with that suit they two had chosen a tie of silver-grey. Her brothers, each in flannels and blazer, displayed their divergent taste in ties: Joe's college-striped, Leo's standing out as a bright red streak—despite their mother's pleas—against the more decorous tones of the other five. That both sons now overtopped Veronica must gratify her; and past the mortification she, Elaine, had felt—long past now—at realizing her brothers were coming to tower over her. Now she looked on their appearance with some pride: of even height, Joe dark, well built—he would pass muster anywhere!—Leo lighter, slenderer.

And wistfully she admired—central to them all—herself in the dress that would live on only in photograph and memory. Some bride unknown, unknowing, might treasure it—and yes, she must let it go; Granny saw that and indeed it was unimportant compared with what it symbolized: her marriage and the prospect of getting away from the tangles of her family...

That, though, came at the price of a heavier renunciation: parting with the one to whom she knew herself securely dear; but Granny, she felt, understood and accepted that price, as must she. Understanding implicit in the Nuptial Blessing Edith had taken it on herself to impart to them, there in the sacristy after the registrar had gathered up his book and departed. Yes Ian, of stock unbending before any but a sternly Calvinist God, had yielded to her grandmother's hastily muttered instruction to kneel before her with Elaine. Mother Church might withhold Mass and Nuptial Blessing from this child's "mixed" marriage, but Edith, assuming matriarchal authority, ensured they should not set forth on their journey unprovided.

"To the third and fourth generation." She, Elaine, was of the third; her grandmother's expressed hope was to see a fourth. Her grandfather had fallen in death well short of it; had he then failed to merit that blessing's fulfilment? To hold so might seem superstition, yet if God was a God of Justice, one should expect Him to show His judgment in people's lives. If all that had befallen poor Pawa had been for his admonition, that after all meant for his salvation! The God of Mercy had made it plain that He alone could judge—as she must remember in remembering what she felt as wrongs: today's matter of the wedding-dress, stimulating memories of the past year...

Of two teaching posts she had been offered on the strength of her Cambridge degree, the obvious choice had seemed the nearer, at that very Beale College to which Kitty had gone and from which she herself had been debarred. She could live at home and rent the back bedroom in lieu of another lodger; it might seem strange to rent from one's parents, but it was reasonable they should not be financially affected and better to pay them than persons unknown in lodgings which needed to be found. Reluctance to anticipate the coming break with home underlay these reasonings; of this she had been aware, but answered it with the consideration that this arrangement would establish her in a "grown-up" relationship to them. Finding rent, to which was added paying towards her food, had meant precious little over to save up for her wedding—as kind Auntie Jane had realized when she provided, besides a generous gift of linen, the wedding-dress...

Well, that had served its day and now was gone! Poring over the photos, Elaine contemplated it in record. Modest enough, despite its skirts of the new, shorter length, it had a fashionably high "mandarin" collar and the diaphanous sleeves veiled arms of a "skinniness"

Epithalamial

that made her self-conscious: engraved on memory from a class reading, long before, of *Lorna Doone*, was the cruel West-country saying:

'A maid with elbow sharp or knee
has crossed words two out of every three!'

She had felt her classmates' eyes to be upon her, the "skinny" one
among them, all of whose elbows emerged from their gym blouses
and summer dresses nicely rounded. She, the bad child of the family,
her frame a muted version of her mother's... It was unfair...
Nonetheless as a triumphant bride she had paid that visit to Uncle
Ben's workroom, had chosen that dress, and Aunt Jane had cut her
off a length of tulle for a veil; that she had still, with the circlet she
had contrived of artificial lilies-of-the-valley; also the now faded
bridal posy of carnations, red to match his single one... They had
thought it all through, managed everything without great outlay; her
mother had written from hospital to warn that they keep the numbers down, as her illness might require the expense of convalescence,
adding, "You won't want a wedding-cake, will you? It's such a business, having to cut it up and post it to people after you've left!"
Of course she had agreed; they would have had to plan thriftily in
any case and her mother's illness made a respectable pretext. Remarkably, it had been her father who had found a caterer with whom to
strike a Jewish bargain involving canapés, trifle and the inevitable
Sauternes in a commodious dining-hall. Aunt Magda, bless her, had
provided real champagne, and Uncle Ben been impressed enough to
take down the details with a view to the future wedding of Elaine's
still teenage cousin, Rachel. The almost legendary Uncle Izzy had
come, with his taciturn wife, who no doubt would report the event to
their wider family; it had seemed proper to Ron to invite his brother
and no doubt had been partly with an eye to "keeping his end up"
that he had wanted things done "properly" for *his* daughter. And she,
leaning on his grey-suited arm the length of the aisle where her parents too had exchanged marriage-vows, could feel he was proud of
her and it was his way of showing it.
Thus had a year of struggle, what with the unaccustomed duties
of schoolteacher, with illness and with rancour, climaxed happily.
She had discovered she could earn respect from her pupils—if for no
better claim than Ian's ring glinting on her hand! In that sunny back
room, when class-preparation and marking were done, she had spent
some happy hours reading over and over Ian's airmail letters, full of
love and eager anticipations, some crammed with sheets of an ongo-

ing journal for her to type on the machine Aunt Magda had presented them with—adding a generous cheque nearer to the Day. On
it too, and forcing herself to touch-type, she was slowly turning out
pages for the book he was writing—and with which she would help
him after she would join him in Northern Rhodesia.

There had been satisfaction, too, in times when they were almost
her childhood family again, the fraternal antagonisms largely outgrown. Joejoe, on his vacations from Durham, had the small room
that had been hers and at last the household had a separate dining
room, where Leo again slept the couple of times he was back. He had
gone to University College to do Law, but been in some sort of trouble about which their mother had been evasive; one was left guessing
it involved a girl, or money, or both, but whatever the case, he had
failed his year and lost his grant. For now he had found a job servic-
ing vehicles for the American Army in Germany. He was good at that
sort of thing and the money too was good and would enable him to
pay for a catch-up year if he could find a University to accept him.

All that had been a worry for Mummy and Daddy, and in addition Daddy had had some kind of trouble with his work. She had
not much noticed it at the time but it seemed some building had
collapsed and some journalists had fixed on him to blame; he said it
was the contractors' fault and his boss and the Council had stood by
him, but his name had been in the papers and she knew he felt the
injustice and it was part of his bitterness and ready anger these
days—while her mother seemed to have emerged from her illness
strengthened in determination to contain his outbursts. And Elaine's
own: she had to admit she was like her father in that—had been
since she could remember. Though looking back, she was beginning
to see it as not so much anger in her as a propensity to arouse anger
in her mother—only she would throttle it back into a contempt that
elicited guilt, with its despairing cry to be forgiven—to be loved as
her Granny loved her and enabled her to feel happy and good! All
this she had hidden, had had to hide from friends, from the teachers
who thought so well of her—even, in a way, from herself: ever hoping, vowing this would be the last time: she never would give way
again! Granny surely did know something of it, though her mother,
she thought, said little; perhaps she too pretended it away.

And though she had dared to suppose that, fully grown up—a
teacher, a lodger in their house, about to be married—she would at
last meet them on an adult footing, it was not to be. Elaine groaned
as the back-revolving kaleidoscope of memory brought up the year's
eruptions: emblematic among them a day... Just as in childhood,

she had run to her room to throw herself weeping on the bed. And this time her mother had come after and, it seemed in triumph, had flung open the door, flung words, words meant to wound, after:

"You should pray more, pray to control yourself!"

Words aimed, she realized, at her newly embraced faith, but that struck also at her new independence, for surely no *lodger* should have the room she rented violated in this way! Indeed Veronica, perhaps aware that she was letting down her guard, had withdrawn, closing the door with decision; she never would have so forgot herself as to slam it! That control was the secret of her mother's superiority, learned young in the maelstrom of her own family; she should remember that in her inclination to "judge"! And yet, since "judging" seemed inevitable if one was not to give up on making sense of things—and had not Father Digby said could be in a spirit of that charity of which Truth was a necessary part?—that family, while more turbulent than their own, had had a loving, suffering heart at its centre: her grandmother's heart! That control, her self-defence, would be what had endeared Veronica to her own father in contrast to the externations of her younger sister. Elaine writhed inwardly again, as she had for long after she had ceased bodily to writhe on that bed that was no longer in any sense *her* bed, because she rented it! Again she was reliving in memory the unforgettable occasion in childhood when her sobbing had become unstanchable...

And she *had* prayed: prayed and wept because she never managed to control herself as she wished and knew she should... Only on this most recent occasion the weeping *had* subsided and a never-before-experienced peace come over her as she sensed a presence in that room: let others dismiss it as imagined, as a "projection"; she had not doubted its reality. A Someone had stood by and consoled her, saying, "I am your Mother!" She would see it as the last of the "signs" around her Catholic conversion that had begun, less than two years since, with the sunset on the top of the bus...

The photos lay in Elaine's lap the while her mind went casting ever further back. Once—once only—she had made a bid—a pathetic bid—to run away from felt misery! Slipping out of the house under cover of darkness, but soon daunted and at a loss where to go: Mena's? Father Billings'? But she had shrunk from explaining herself even—or especially—to them and the whispering and scandal she imagined ensuing. They had found her an hour or two later, lying shivering under the apple-tree in the garden, her feeble gesture having failed miserably: had it been largely a gesture, her intention to arouse pity, rather than to flee the home that still spelled for her more good than ill? What it aroused in her mother was the glacial fury that was more withering than her father's sputtering blasts duly backing it up. Doubtless relieved she had not provoked gossip or worse publicity, they were determined to shame her into not so exposing them in future.

That running away, that pathetic, paltry token running away—it must have occurred after Granny moved out: otherwise she would have taken refuge with her. Surely no guilt or shame would have barred that refuge! She recalled evenings when she had paced up and down the road that led past the lighted windows of the Parsonage, unresolved whether to ring the bell and reveal her unhappiness to Father and Mrs Billings, who thought well of her; they might be sympathetic, or Father Billings would. But "Captain"? So his wife was known to her Guides, among whom Elaine was exemplary: a Patrol Leader and well on the way to First Class status. She would be letting herself down: unthinkable to go snivelling to her! They both thought a lot of Mummy too, their Catholic convert; they surely would not believe her at any fault! And her parents would be furious at the "exposure." Each time she had turned back with heavy feet and heavier heart...

And now the dress—which she *must* put out of her mind, as Granny counselled—was of a piece with the past year! *Could* her mother's brain-infection have caused her to think she, the happy bride, had asked her to sell it? Her illness had been over by then, had it not? Elaine wrestled with the "disloyal" thought that her mother had foreseen how her action could be attributed to her late illness: that seeing her daughter walk in bridal white to the very altar to which she had been led in the purple dress (detail Veronica's children had more than once heard), on the arm of him to whom she had herself been there married—altar and ritual of that selfsame Church she had since repudiated... Seeing too her daughter's more fortunate and easier path to that state she herself had had to struggle to attain with sacrifice of honour (as she would see it), even of Faith... *Could* one sacrifice Faith—even—or especially—for marriage? Had that been too much for her mother, impelling her to be rid of the dress left hanging in her house as if to remind her... Dress symbolic of virginity: lost in the one case, preserved—only, God, Ian and Elaine's Confessor knew how precariously—in the other! The daughter had long suspected her mother had never forgiven herself for the *faux pas* that had engendered herself—nor, it might be, forgiven her father...

Moreover, and before all that, had it been that rage, suppressed yet smouldering, had caused her mother to succumb—worse than either mother or sister—to the infection? Elaine's mind ranged back to the onset of those drawn-out months of being slowly torn from a home no longer hers: to another piece of bridal white—well, almost white, for it was tarnished with age: the small oblong of lace that had been her mother's First Communion veil, and she had been a fool to request it for her Confirmation in Westminster Cathedral, but female confirmands were expected to cover heads on which conse-crated hands would rest, as Auntie Freda had explained and said that her new mantilla, black and gold, would not do; unmarried women by custom wore white veils.

She had remembered the relic her mother—surprisingly—kept in a bottom drawer of the triple-mirrored dressing table. Not that she had been unaware of the delicacy of the request, or that it under-scored her rejection of that Establishment occasion on which she had played the chorus to her mother's more dramatic role. She sensed too—and must recognize that she herself had shared in the intent—that Auntie Freda saw in it a God-given prompt to her sister to ponder her capitulation to the Established Church, now some decade since. Aunt Magda would surely have opposed her asking for it; she had declined to attend the Confirmation out of regard for her sister's feelings. Yet she must surely approve Elaine's move, and fur-ther—as her niece had gleaned from her grandmother—understand all along the unhappinesses of her childhood home.

"Take it and keep it!" had been Veronica's strangled-seeming reply.

In the event her Catholic Confirmation had not turned out an occasion of much joy, which might seem the penalty for an impure heart—like so much that had gone awry in that forlorn gap between girlhood unsatisfied and womanhood scarce attained. If lack of for-bearance was in her mother a weakness, she must surely also accuse herself: as she had done, and always rushed to the Confessional as to the medicine to which she had looked forward ever since that day on the bus—if not longer… And she had found relief, certainly; yet been ever overtaken anew by the old evil. Her confusion of feelings and her longing for her absent lover's caresses formed further matter for Confession, along with the doubts, that would not be driven away, about her vocation—thankfully she had found a Confessor able to help her over those!

No doubt these trials had contributed to make her difficult to live with, perhaps to making her mother fall ill; her grandmother's reminder of her mother's health was timely and should plead for her. In the remoter past, the grimmest episodes had had a tendency to occur when Veronica annually gave up smoking for Lent. The household always seemed to breathe more easily when smoking was resumed at Easter—but by that Easter Veronica had already fallen ill.

Besides, Elaine could believe her mother had ever intended well. She could recall words of kindness in the early days when she had pined for Ian; at the time she had guessed Joejoe, with new parsonical authority, had urged tolerance as the best hope in the longer run of changing his sister in matter of religion. But when Elaine had ventured to write to her brother in his northern parish urging the strengths of the Catholic position—naively thinking it her duty to impart her new light—he had returned dusty answer. No doubt he would have seen it as an attempt to co-opt him against Veronica; there *had* been an element of that, and their mother would have heard of it and thought the same, and she, Elaine, had been foolish and to blame...

Joejoe, though, had risen to Christian magnanimity: had literally risen early on her wedding-morning, as had she, after little sleep, to walk to the early Mass that was to be her Nuptial Mass—as her grandmother's blessing was to be their Nuptial Blessing. As was proper, she had fallen to her knees to pray, then rising been aware of someone seating themselves beside her—and settling back found it to be her brother! Hearing her leave the house, Joe had risen to follow her—and she had to own the gesture of magnanimity typical of him. Even her mother... On the eve of her wedding Veronica had suddenly produced, from the drawer where it had lain in a sachet together with that rusty lace veil, the heavy silver chain bearing its engraved oval. Abruptly had said:

"You may as well have this!"

Elaine, surprised, had thanked her and worn it over the ill-fated wedding-dress and on her honeymoon since. She knew it for the Miraculous Medal and that it had significance for them both. And no, she must not be mean-spirited; now was the break with all that, the time for a new beginning, the "acceptable hour." Did she not believe that evil suffered opened on the potentiality for good? She must forgive. Only how did one forgive, she asked herself, not for the first time? Did it not need some approach, some recognition of wrong done and suffered, if only token? Or did one need only to understand...?

A ring at the door: Ian, now her husband! And sounding in her head as she hurried down the stairs, words her grandmother had more than once quoted, and she had pondered as to whether they could be right:

"To understand all is to pardon all."

PART VII

A Breaking World

(1961–1977)

I
(1961–1962)

OF THE Sister Muses, Mistress of Destiny is only Clio. History which—as though in compensation for ancestral buffetings—had failed with two World Wars to knock the descendants of Edith and René Lumley-Rigg off course, here intervened upon those of their line the Mother Country had spun off to captain her acquisitions overseas. When the Britain that emerged enfeebled from those cataclysms, her imperial pretensions abandoned, proceeded to the casting off of her African colonies, the young Roodys were left contemplating the closing down of the career Ian had anticipated for himself.

That facing-up he at first hoped to avoid by migrating easily to a Southern Rhodesia flourishing on as to the "white supremacy" to which it was subject. It even promised to be a propitious move. Immediately they had to settle into a mutual and sexually adjusted living, and she into life in the Copper Belt: nor was it long before the strains of the double adjustment were showing. To begin with, the heat was stifling even in their bungalow. And in its environs, the purlieus of the white community with their blinds and gyrating fans did not help tempers either within or abroad—where white women felt constrained to entertain and instruct her, and while she would fain have found one in whom she might somewhat confide, she only felt her feebleness must let down a formidable caste to which she did not by rights belong.

Then beyond this white enclave, the shanty-town of the Africans, and surrounding all, the "bush" with its legendary terrors... As the rainy season set in, she had begun to view herself rather as a poor swimmer flailing about in cross-currents of surging seas, when the bloody spots she eventually recognized as sign of threatened miscarriage were the first intimation that she was pregnant. She spent December and Christmas—their first married Christmas—between a settee and their bed, attempting to divert herself with what books Ian could lay hands on for her. He, only son of parents who clung to traditional roles, was uncomprehending of this women's business, altogether unversed in matters domestic and moreover had scarce been ill a day in his life. He would attempt to make her eat breakfast, but his eggs fried in oil nauseated her. After he left for the Kitwe Governmental station, a "boy" would come in to do the chores and provide for their supper. Elaine was grateful for domestic help she had not known since she was a child at Aunt Magda's and the yet more distant days when even Ron's salary must have stretched to paying a weekly "char" whom she dimly remembered. But Josiah's dishes too were distasteful to her and secretly she felt intimidated, hardly knowing how to talk to an African servant, let alone direct him.

At least her seclusion exempted her from the more officious enquiries on the part of the "me'm-sahibs," as Ian referred to them; but between this seclusion and her confused fears, her hold on reality seemed sometimes threatened; this he realized with dismay when one night he was awakened by her crying out and found her standing in the bungalow's front room, pointing with shaking hand at a pool of moonlight on the floor. He spoke sharply to her and led her back to bed, convinced she had sleep-walked. The next morning she recalled her panic with mortification but could not account for it.

None the less, by the time the rains were ending, it seemed the pregnancy was saved and, according to the attendant midwife, progressing normally, with Elaine again on her feet and preparing for herself such foods as she could stomach, for the sickness persisted. She was advised to avail herself of the weather and walk outdoors, but the child stirring within engendered new fears for its and her safety. She begged to return to England, and though Ian demurred at this further impediment to what he had envisioned as the even tenor of their days together, he in the end consented and found occasion to accompany her by air to Lusaka and see her onto the BOAC flight to London.

She would not know whether that move saved their child or rather precipitated an early birth, brought on by a couple more months of uneasy living amid the old covert antagonisms of home. One night late in May she was rushed in premature labour to a maternity ward and her and Ian's very small daughter started uncertainly on life in what they called an incubator, and with Freda standing godmother was christened by the names they had agreed: Anne Edith, for Ian's mother and Elaine's grandmother.

By the time Elaine herself was discharged—to return daily, when they would take milk from her and allow her increasingly to hold the wizened, groping thing—Ian arrived, having been granted compassionate leave. Battling despond as to how she ever would look after it, she had begun to put it to the breast and they took it home—her old home, where her mother produced a second-hand cradle and pram and generally took over while Elaine watched, humbled unless agitated to tears. A couple of weeks of anxiety over every breastfeeding, and half thankfully, half guiltily, she succumbed to her mother's urging, backed by Ian, that she let the child be bottle-fed.

This relieved the strain and sleeplessness, but Ian must return and the separation would seem to Elaine only endurable for the time it gave her to share Anne Edith with her second namesake, and her determination that by the time September should bring him again, the child should be thriving, perhaps even showing credible likeness to him. As vigour returned, timidly she would attempt to assume the mantle of authority to which, as Ian's letters urged, her maternity entitled her, but which she felt her elders reluctant to concede, her mother in particular standing on the ground of her undoubtedly greater experience. It was relief to pay a visit to Ely, where undercurrents remained under, not threatening to throw up whole nexuses of frustrated emotions.

In the remaining time she could withdraw from the tensions of a former home from which she felt herself still only semi-detached, to her grandmother's house. There, between counsels deemed "out of date," yet partaking of an inveterate wisdom and, spread daily over all asperities, the balm of a shared delight in the child's flowering, the time wore on to Ian's return and preparations for the young family's departure and new start. Much of those two months was passed at Ely, with excursions by car to Cambridge where were revisited old acquaintances, among them Brendan McNally, now a Research Fellow elect, and moving, it seemed, in sophisticated intellectual circles. He accompanied them to a tea with a Monsignor Hervé contemplating retirement and deprecating possible outcomes of the impending Vatican Council.

"I fear it as a conduit for Modernism to creep in, despite the no doubt best intentions of the Holy Father!" He smothered a less than clerical sigh in a vast damask napkin.

Brendan suspended the passage to his mouth of another cream-filled meringue.

"Surely, Monsignor, a Council of the Universal Church can never provide an *entrée* for the Old Enemy!"

"Alas—one has to ask oneself whether it is the Universal Church assembled in Rome, the Schism still not healed, the Orthodox there as observers merely—among many *de facto* heretics!"

"But surely, Monsignor, on that reading neither was the First Vatican Council a Council of the Universal Church, nor before that Trent nor..."

"Perish the thought that one should be forced to such a *reductio ad absurdum*! Very clearly that cannot be, for without Trent the Church would surely have dissolved into endless factions—as has happened with Protestantism. The very thing I fear from this Council—called in a spirit very different from Trent, and I fear a Modernist spirit!"

"Yet the Holy Father—in Italy they call him '*il papa buono*' and many think him a saint..."

"'Woe to you when all men speak well of you'..."

"Come, Monsignor; you cannot mean to imply..."

"My dear Brendan, much harm can be done by saints—out of their time and place—or out of their depth!"

"So the Holy Ghost may have made a mistake with this Pope?"

"It is the harder to say so, when clearly he is a good—even saintly—man. There have, as we know, been popes of whom it might more readily have been said!"

"Not, though, that have called Councils, surely! And if Councils may go astray, how do we distinguish the genuine?"

"This one has not even got under way!" protested Ian.

"True, and we can hope, and must pray. But if the Holy Father may be said to have erred, it is, I fear, in *not* asserting his own Infallibility! Since the Holy Ghost led his great predecessor into defining that, I would suppose the Church to have no further use for Councils."

"Yet," persisted Brendan, "The Holy Father can surely not be expected to reform the Church on his own: an old man, however holy, he surely will have need to consult his fellow bishops worldwide—which is what a Council *is*: the Pope in Council!"

Monsignor Hervé sighed again and flicking crumbs of meringue off his cassock, murmured:

"*Ubi Petrus, ibi Ecclesia*! But let us not tease our friends with these recondite matters; rather let them tell us of the Missionary Church in Africa..."

"You had Hervé over a barrel about this Council!" observed Ian after the Mugger had escorted them to the chapel, thence to the chaplaincy door.

"Over a barrel from his own winery: it was vintage Hervé!" Brendan agreed. "And it won't do, will it!"

"Does it shake your belief—your faith as a Catholic?"

Brendan shrugged.

"Probably not! One's faith survives so much… If anything, it shakes my faith in the old Mugger: dear old boy, and has an eye on me for a vocation!"

"As a priest? Wedded to celibacy?"

"As a priest, I presume, is how he sees it and certainly as wedded to celibacy. The celibacy bit troubles me least—hardly a ladies' man! And no such luck as you, my dear Ian!"

"Then it's the priesthood troubles you?"

"How about a lay-brother?" put in Elaine, having seen the glance heavenward from under his eyelids, Brendan's only response.

"Inconceivable, unless any order would have me as an hermit! More likely an old-fashioned bachelor don: no need to be in any description of Holy Orders for that, now that the C of E has found the good grace to retreat from monopolizing the 'Varsities. But let us leave speaking of my vexed possible futures."

There seemed indeed no more to be said. Over the next week or so, the three of them were solicitous to seek out the views of Father Digby. He, after a space for careful weighing, declared himself surprised by the notion of the forthcoming Council's possible incompleteness in view of the unresolved Great Schism. It being all unlike the Chaplain to risk a heterodox opinion, Father Digby could only suppose him unusually perturbed… Still, that it might be possible to make distinction between a valid Council of an incompletely Catholic Church and a truly Universal Council was an interesting idea. Trent, necessarily without the contribution of the East, clearly had been valid for Western Christendom; Nicaea was exemplarily an Universal and Ecumenical Council…

Elaine found Ian unexpectedly taken with the neatness of this distinction.

In late August they again flew south, Elaine mingling relief with regret on her grandmother's behalf. Ian, plied by Veronica and Freda with justifiable predictions of harm from the climate, had agreed to press for a more salubrious posting. Freda further urged they inquire of their "boy" for a woman attendant for both. This resulted in Josiah's sister agreeing to replace him until her own child should be weaned. Black Lucy—So did they refer to her, in private, having learned "black" was a blanket description Africans declined—proved all her worth, her own maternity providing example and encouragement and fostering a warmth that soon had Anne's parents at relative ease and the child smiling and gurgling to delight them all. That Christmas would provide the paradigm for all Christmas should have been and should be. Then as Spring approached, it was agreed mothers and babes would spend the coming dry season in the hill-country around Salisbury, where Ian would from time to time join them.

For long they would look back on those almost carefree months as perhaps the happiest of their joint life. The contrast with "home" was palpable and "I must never be left with them again!" Elaine declared, shuddering. "It's not that they don't *mean* well"—and her words reminded him of their first encounter—so long ago, it seemed:

"It's just that they're so—overbearing! Not Dad, of course, and he dotes on babies. And not Granny; she was so glad for us, bless her! She prayed that things would turn out well—and they did."

"But your mother!"

"Yes, she's always so sure of herself! Auntie Freda too, in a different way."

"You're afraid of them, aren't you?"

She was surprised but after a pause admitted,

"I suppose I am. My mother, anyway."

But as the sub-equatorial season began to spell departure, all sense of serenity was torn up on Elaine's realizing that she was again pregnant. Her dismay was compounded by dread of confessing this to Ian—yes, confessing, as though it were a sin! He had weathered that first surprise that had issued in Anne Edith; indeed of her he was become quite fond, though babies had been to him an unknown quantity, and both knew her advent, involving them in such inconvenience and even misery, meant things would not be the same again...

All he said was,

"I thought those temperature-charts were supposed to be reliable!"

But his face told her the looming cloud had descended on them both as she answered,

"They are. Only I'm not so regular and—we've taken chances. I'm sorry, but..."

"But what?"

The coldness of his tone brought tears and she burst out,

"You said... You did say, 'I want to make love to you, not to a piece of rubber'!"

"So I did. But we can't have this happening too often."

"I'm sorry," she had repeated, half facetiously, but he caught the bitterness. "I suppose you blame my religion!"

"No, not exactly. I'm even prepared to think your religion's right on this one—or would be in an ideal world."

It began again, the sickness and soon the blood. This time Elaine could hardly lie up and Ian's work was engrossing more of his time and attention. Then, as she was growing apprehensive about the impending move, the sickness suddenly ceased, at which she was wondering when the bleeding became more ominous. Lucy, come to be their mainstay and viewed as a paradoxically dark angel of the light her name betokened, was willing enough to have charge of child and household. A midwife visited—a white woman who opined that the foetus was no longer living; Elaine should return to normal life until a specialist visit should be arranged. Dismay would have rendered her unequal to following this advice, but next day the pangs began and came on in force, unstoppably. Before Ian, recalled by telephone, could arrive and take her by car to hospital, in agony and blood she delivered the lump that was to have been her—their—child: only she would not think of it in that way. Lucy was with her and confirmed it was dead; Elaine would not see "it." The next day came a doctor and checked her over, then the midwife again, who remarked,

"It's probably as well. Most foetuses that miscarry are deformed."

"Was this…?"

"It's too early to know: less than two months, you said."

"My little girl isn't—deformed. She *nearly* miscarried."

The woman only smiled. It would be absurd to ask what they had done with "it"—Was it him or her? They presumably wouldn't know, and neither did she want to—did she? Later that day Lucy returned from walking Anne Edith to hear sobbing from under the bedclothes where her mistress lay huddled in the dark.

"What matter, Missus?" she asked, superfluously but in genuine concern.

"Oh Lucy, the baby!"

"They things happen, Missus."

"Yes—but I never saw it! I—Do *you* know if it was a boy or girl?"

"No, Missus, but the dear Lord, he know."

With that consolation from the good Methodist Elaine had perforce and for now to be content; more she would never know, never see… That thing from which she had averted her eyes, now, when it was too late, laid claim on her: her child, even if deformed…

Ian seemed almost unmoved by it all and she began to suspect might even be relieved—Would she be relieved, once the horror had subsided? Was he asking himself that? He was so silent, so stoical, so—Scottish! What was it he had once written, in those letters, so full of ardour, so carefully preserved, from that time of such—so it seemed now—such happiness? About the Stoic's calm, about indulging in stubbornness of will—about pride! Should that have been a clue—and if so, to what end? His new-found responsibilities had, she supposed, steadied him. Perhaps too he had not realized the seri-ousness of her own commitment—to her late-found faith, to the maternal vocation that went with the choice of marriage—and that thus far had weighed so heavily against that brief and even then flickering happiness. After all, she had not realized it herself! She felt almost afraid, as if she had not known him before—and now she must not know either...

Shocked and grieving, Elaine longed again for England but that meant leaving for a life apart from Ian. On him she had come to rely. Too much rely? In the event it was Lucy who kept her and her exist-ing—no, her living—child, going on day by day, until with the English Spring they would have furlough and she be able to confide in her dear Granny, who would understand and assuage all. Nothing of the mishap should be communicated to their parents; her mother in particular might judge it a fitting outcome to her perverse return to the Church she had herself given up because of Contraception...

Whether or not Ian was relieved that another paternity was not thrust upon him, Anne Edith, emerging from what had seemed to him infantile passivity, was beginning to gain his attention: to rear herself at his elbow and demand a notice which he bestowed with shy amusement; still she seemed to him more a sprite than his daughter, nor could he know if she ever would seem otherwise. Nor could he not regret Elaine's interest being absorbed away from him, and the multiplication of her anxieties. He tried to be content, for his sense of justice told him the newcomer clearly had the more imperative need, but he felt his wife changed, or rather a new aspect of her had been revealed: the purposiveness, he told himself, of the female prepared to sacrifice self and all else for the welfare of its cub! He too looked for relief in the upcoming return to England.

Edith did not figure in his expectations. He considered Elaine over-adulatory of her grandmother: an intelligent woman, certainly, but manipulative, and on her own admission a failure in her own marriage. Though her husband had been, by all accounts, impossible, still... Ian, not given to psychologizing, doubted if to understand all was to pardon all. In his family-history there figured impossible and violent men with enduring, down-to-earth wives who contrived to rule them and to raise their children: not, admittedly, as conspicuous successes, but without the flights into the showier neuroses that fre-quently seemed to mark the English middle-class. His mother, prod-uct of such a household, had known to seek out a respectable, if dull, marriage and conform to its requirements, externally at least—and barring the one matter of a repeat childbearing.

That, of course, pointed up a difference. In Elaine's family there was the Catholicism to take into account, adding, he thought, a strain of hysteria all its own and which lent some credence to the received outlook of folk like his—who he acknowledged were a cause of it: bigots adhering like stranded limpets to their island ledge from off which British Protestantism had built its now shifting empire! Perhaps when it should have collapsed irretrievably, firmer bedrock might appear—re-appear, he supposed Elaine would have it, from a viewpoint of which, again, he owned the legitimacy.

"The rains descended and the floods came and the winds blew…" The words, familiar from church and school, could not but present themselves to such musings! For a while the house had stood firm, buttressed by America, its revolted offspring, returned like a condescending adolescent to rescue its beset parent from a tidal wave; its ebb-roar they were even now experiencing. And stepmother—however little loved—to that Indian subcontinent whose sons too had early on been marshalled to her support. And now that seeming rock had cracked almost literally in two—indeed in three; and across an ocean, here in British Africa, the sands were moving as under a stratum of brittle shale.

But now for shattered, though if reports were to be credited far from sobered, England they had again leave: leave for their love to re-grow, that had been torn into by the pregnancies with their diverse outcomes. Both pairs of parents professed themselves anxious to maintain contact with their first grandchild; both should be indulged. The child must, of course, be accustomed to them, and then full advantage should be taken so he and Elaine could, if not relive their first passion—To hinder that would be that crippling precaution not to incur a third pregnancy—yet, and in some sense he acknowledged higher, be for each other all in all. Thus should all wounds be healed.

So to Shepherd's Bush and on, with Anne Edith's burgeoning charms to delight both families and cause the undemonstrative Ely couple to warm some degrees toward a daughter-in-law they considered exotic and temperamental. Ian's mother seemed still surprised that he should engender a female—To Elaine he observed that she must be surprised she knew how to produce any offspring!—but failed to conceal her pleasure that the name given was her own, if frenchified by that final "e"; they had agreed "Ann" was too plain English. The young couple—even Ian—began to appreciate the dullness of the Ely house in comparison with Shepherd's Bush, and to be thankful there were fewer distractions, or in truth none except to walk their child by the well-named, lazily flowing Ouse; in the evenings to leave her securely sleeping while they repaired to a pub.

More tinged with unease was a visit they paid to the Cathedral: to him a mausoleum of a dead past, to her a monument to the persecution of her faith in the ravaged Lady Chapel in which Cromwell had stabled horses, in the empty slab recording that shrine of the Foundress which Henry had extirpated with all the rest. To that Foundress was dedicated the Catholic church where they attended Mass and could view, through a dingy glass, Etheldreda's withered and blackened hand, clandestinely preserved through Reformation and persecution. Elaine knelt and prayed before it—exaggeratedly, he felt, struggling with hereditary antipathy... Well might this saint have left the English an unwitting legacy in the corruption of her name: Audrey into "tawdry"! Had not that tawdry burned in the purging fires of Reform...

A bell tinkled announcing the Canon: the ancient rite—candles, incense, relics, monasteries... Henry's schism, Henry's greed and lust, had had the effect of sweeping all away. Plucked out of the debris had been the two religious houses which entitled the tyrant to be called "Founder" of Ian's college: Henry in place of the Pope—of God: "*Junker Heinrich will Gott sein*": hadn't even Luther said that.

Ian's mother went sometimes to the Cathedral services: to hear the choir, she said, and it seemed her faith was rather in the Englishness than in the Christianity of the national church, to which she clung more for its choral singing, its parish fetes and harvest festivals, the country-dances of her youth... Except once a year at Easter, when she would remain in her pew when her husband went up to take Communion—without ever having sought permission to cross over from the Kirk, as Elaine registered with amazement, remembering her mother's formal transition into that selfsame Church of England. Atavistically averse to their daughter-in-law's church, they attributed to it—not without justice, as Ian was sensible—the early arrival of their granddaughter and disapproved the timing as distinct from the outcome. At least his mother did, despite the tactful choice of name. She made no secret of her own feelings of repugnance to childbirth, which she had elected to undergo under anaesthetic, and had taken occasion to declare to her daughter-in-law, "I wanted to know nothing about it!"

"Your mother says her one piece of luck was that you were a boy!" Elaine added, reporting this to Ian.

"I know. I've heard it all a dozen times and more. Do you find that—shocking?"

"I suppose I do, though it seems to have been a common attitude in women at that time, or down to that time—perhaps at all times. At least it shows she—values you!"

"Yes. So much that she devoted all her efforts to ensuring I should turn out a gentleman—as she saw it."

"Not a bad aim, surely?"

"I said, 'as she saw it'; that is, the English convention of the gentleman: nice manners, club rules. I'd have expected you to think that pretty limited."

"Nice manners are—well, nice!"

"Do I take it that's a criticism?"

"Well, you know, women like that sort of thing."

"And I, you realize, set out to thwart that limited aim."

"I do realize."

This, being close to a rebuke, invited one of the clashes over values that experience already told her she would no more win than had his mother. She shifted her ground.

"Do you think she didn't want to risk—that she'd been lucky the once and..."

"I do think so—that she wouldn't risk inflicting femininity on another being!"

"A kind of self-hatred, you mean?"

"I'm afraid so."

"That's interesting. Because I'm sure my mother's the same!"

"And you? Are you sorry Anne Edith's not a boy?"

"No, I was so happy she was safely born at all and... Though if I'm honest, there was just that tinge of disappointment when they told me it was a girl—not a firstborn male! Perhaps because your mother might think her—it a come-down! But not only. Perhaps we women are all alike!"

"Only the women?"

"No, you're right. Because there's Pawa—and of course the Jewish side; for them it's still important... But generally in society it's far less important now that..."

"So it's cultural."

"You mean—Christianity?"

"It could be. How about your Church—or for that matter the Anglicans! They claim that we are all equally children of God, but only ordain men!"

"But Ian, that's not the sort of equality..."

"Oh, I know the argument, but it still leaves women looking somehow lacking! After all, you only have to look at St Paul!"

"'Wives obey your husbands.' You surely have no objection to that!"

"If you think that, you don't know me."

"Sorry, Ian, I was being frivolous. Just like a woman, in fact! I know the feminists go on about Paul, but I thought it was cultural; I mean, in the ancient world women were married in their 'teens and usually illiterate, not educated as we are. And St Paul also says, 'In Christ there is neither male nor female.' That must have seemed quite revolutionary."

"It's taken a long time for the revolution to take effect!"

"That's true, but—'A thousand ages in Thy sight...' Meaning, what *is* a long time? Isn't it arguable that that revolution is what made way, eventually, for the emancipation of women, specifically in Christian cultures?"

"Post-Enlightenment, anyway. I'm thinking it has more to do with inventions like cars and guns and washing-machines. To say nothing of 'The Pill.'"

"Oh Ian! But really that's what I'm saying, that the seed was there, if you like, in St Paul, but could only flourish in favourable soil—like the seed in the Gospel, really. After all, it's still not in full flower—equality, I mean. Don't you think there's something in that?"

"There could be."

There they left it, with Elaine beginning to understand better her husband's genesis in the lonely child, reading insatiably to escape the dreariness of home, biding his time to gratify a besetting restlessness.

On points of conflict between Ian and his mother, his father said as little as he was wont to say on any topic, having long ago lit on this as the best recipe for a quiet life, but that it was likely he would have welcomed a daughter appeared in a shy tenderness toward the new young creature, this Anne Edith. There was a lot in names, Elaine reflected; the older English "Ann" suited Ian's mother, rather as Edith suited her grandmother. Who, she knew, rejoiced like Simeon in the Temple to have beheld this new generation that in all but name would carry forward her husband's house and more importantly, please God, his—their—Faith. Roody, she had observed, was from Rood, the Cross, auguring fulfilment of a promise.

II

(1963)

Elaine eased her legs over the edge of the bed and bent forward warily to pull on her shoes. Then she would only need coat and scarf when Auntie Freda arrived to take her home—or rather away, for home was now, of course, in the Copper Belt with Ian, who had returned there, leaving her in London in hope of avoiding another miscarriage. Which had now happened, two days ago, or was it three; there had been the "D-and-C," as they called the scraping out of her womb, and what with the anaesthetic and everything she tended to lose track of the days.

It had happened despite the attempts to lie up, firstly in Cambridge where they had settled and begun to enjoy their leave, and—when that proved too difficult even with home-help—in Ely, before the inevitable return to her old home. There her parents had undertaken the main care of Anne Edith; they had not been told of her previous miscarriage, yet Elaine could not but feel guiltily she was burdening them as a result of her own fecklessness. Besides, she feared the prising away of her child, too young to accept a mother "too ill" to pick her up...

Despite all this and the pills and the sickness and finally the admission to this London Women's Hospital, it had happened again: the agony, the despair, the blood, as unstoppably it came away, her and Ian's baby in the making, and there was nothing she could do. Except pray, and she had done that for the past two months she had known herself to be again pregnant so soon after the first miscarriage. Too soon: they should have been more careful. They had known they were taking a risk, that blossom-laden day of an English May, so contrasting with the climatic rigours of their new abode. When they returned to the flat they were renting, after punting on the Backs, she in her fuchsia-pink dress... They had the flat to themselves while Anne Edith was in the charge of a mother for whose child they performed the like weekly service. This was their "afternoon off," their only chance... Had it even been in part the risk that had made that love-making so poignantly sweet...?

"Hallo, my pet!"

In the doorway, as though to censure erotic memory, loomed Auntie Freda in her long Burberry, silk scarf at the neck; both would be sales or second-hand "snips": Freda, like Veronica, cared how she dressed, but unlike Veronica eschewed "cheap" substitutes for tradition-tested fabrics and brands. Freda knew quality when she saw it and was a consummate bargain-spotter. Now her broad face under the felt hat and greying hair proffered a smile of sympathy as she advanced to embrace her niece.

"My poor pet! How are you, my darling?"

"Better. Not too bad."

"You look a little pale. Not surprising, losing all that... We must make sure you have some tonic, or I know, a bottle or two of good red wine! So, are you all packed up? I'll help you on with your coat and here are the chocs you asked for to give the nurses. I gather they have been very good."

"They have. Much better than in that dreadful Maternity Hospital in Cambridge!"

"That used to be a barracks—still is, from your account: the worser sort of wards still are run like barracks; it's a hangover from Flo Nightingale and the Crimea—guarantees certain standards at the cost of the human element: charity Protestant-style—after this poor land had been robbed of its monastic hospices by the Reformation! Anyway, I imagine it was better than where you live these days. There you didn't even get taken into hospital."

"No. Now they've told me if I had—if they'd scraped me out then, it might not have happened this time."

"Well, this hospital is one of the best in the land and if even they weren't able to save... What a shame, my poor Elaine! Don't cry, pet; you did everything you knew and at least you do know you can get pregnant, which not everyone can—spinsters like me, to start with! I've known women, through my work, who started with miscarriages and ended with families, even big ones."

She lifted Elaine's case and led down the ward-corridor to the nursing-station. The smiling, not at all Nightingale-like sister accompanied them to Freda's car, chatting to her, approving the wine idea, recommending Australian Burgundy for its iron-content; Freda was saying they would buy a bottle just so soon as the off-license opened.

"Granny's dying to see you," she resumed, once she had her bearings along the Marylebone Road, "She's disappointed it won't be today. She even wondered about coming along, but we didn't want to risk her having one of her attacks. One invalid is enough and that's you for now, you poor dear! Not for long, I hope—though it will take a while for all those hormones to settle, I should imagine."

"Yes, so they've told me. In fact the doctor said to leave a year before starting—another baby. And I wonder; I'm not sure if the Church..."

"My pet," broke in her aunt hastily, "The Church—God—wants us to act on good advice—find out the sensible course, using the wits He gave us. Prudence, you know, is one of the Cardinal Virtues. That sounds like good advice to me, from someone qualified to give it. I have read that we should follow the advice of our doctors, second only to that of our confessors."

"But birth-control… I thought the Church was right about it. It was one of the things I agreed with…"

"The Church has thought much about this in modern times and, as I say, teaches prudence in the number and spacing of children. Only by methods that are—not unnatural, and give scope for God's will in what is, after all, a matter of life itself. Not of course that I can speak from experience, but it comes up in the course of my work, where some of my Mums—the Irish especially—are more generous than prudent, given their circumstances, poor dears! You'd best talk to Granny, who, as you know, had a hard time over this one."

Not "Mummy": Freda for all her closeness to her sister understood that Vee's daughter never had been able to confide in her on such matters: still less now that religion widened the breach between them.

After a pause, Elaine ventured again:

"One thing I *would* like to tell you, Auntie Freda, and ask what you think…"

"Yes, pet?"

"You said 'another baby' and—and it *is* a baby, or was. I mean, I didn't see it; I'm not sure I'd have wanted to. Anyway, I didn't dare to ask or—in fact, I didn't want—but—but I'd have liked to know if it was a boy or a girl—if that's possible—and—and it may have been alive, don't you think?"

"I don't know, pet. Hardly, I imagine, or not for long."

"But then I ought to have had it baptized—or done it myself, shouldn't I? And I only thought of that when it was too late. I expect they—just destroyed it. Burned it, like so much rubbish!"

Hearing the tremble in her niece's voice, Freda detached a hand from the steering wheel and patted her knee through overcoat and trousers.

"Don't, pet; please do *not* distress yourself when you've been through so much! You can't take responsibility for everything when it's you who are suffering. You don't even know it was alive and able to receive baptism. The one you lost in Africa wasn't, was it?"

"No. That had already died. There was nothing could be done. But I might have learned from that and—this one—I should at least have asked—or looked… But again I didn't want to know. I'm just a coward. I left it all to them, though it was *my* baby, and now... You won't mention this, or the—the one out there—to my parents, will you!"

"No, pet, though I think you underestimate their capacity for compassion, your mother's anyway, if it's her you're chiefly thinking of. Pet, you *must* not fret about this, but trust God who knows everything. You know, 'not a sparrow falls.' Much less a babe unborn!"

"I know, but that's the trouble! God sees, and He knows how I failed the test as—as its mother. You see: I don't even know if it's "he" or "she"! With the first there was some excuse, but—in fact I don't think I thought of either as a—as a person, not until it was too late."

"You *are* their mother, though you may not feel it: mother of both those little sparks snuffed out, we don't know why, but certainly through no fault of yours. You didn't know; you had no-one and no experience to guide you, plus you were suffering acutely. God understands all that better than we do, and is taking care of your little sparks—or sprites as I think of them. Sprites are spirits, you know."

"But they were unbaptized!"

"No-one can lose God through no fault of their own; we don't—can't—believe that! Just say a prayer of love and trust in your heavenly Father if these dismal thoughts come to you, darling. Remember, I am your godmother now, so you are to take notice of what I say."

"I will, and I do pray. I've been offering it all up for the Vatican Council. It opened, when I was lying up the first time."

"There's my good pet! Who knows how much grace that offering may have brought to the Church in these so important times! Troubled times, too, with the Communist persecution in Eastern Europe—poor Cardinal Mindszenty of Hungary a fugitive; they say he's in the American Embassy in Budapest. And poor Cardinal Wyszynski of Poland more or less a prisoner, I believe... But the devil does not have all the best tunes, as we see in this calling of the Council. Sad that dear Pope John died before he could see his *aggiornamento* bear fruit!"

"Perhaps he does see it."

"You are right, for he was a saint if anyone is in this life, and surely did Purgatory enough with his last illness! I should think he went straight to heaven, and it's only an earthly triumph he has missed—and that I am sure he was willing to forego. It seems Pope Paul is the man appointed to oversee his great opening up of the Church, which surely was due for it."

"And my mother—do you think she...?"

"My pet, God understands her as we cannot—though I can a little understand, as you cannot be expected to, the background to her—defection. In your mother's friend Winnie's case, who had lapsed even before she became your godmother—and not surprising, considering... I can only pass on to you what the priest who baptised you, and who knew Winnie—what I have seen to be true in her case and others, that 'The longest way round can be the shortest way home!'"

Elaine pondering this, they finished their journey in silence and she was welcomed back to her parents' house. Down the road Freda made tea and carried it, with thin slices of buttered bread and a dish of jam on a tray, to her mother, who was taking her afternoon rest with Spook, Freda's dainty tortoiseshell cat. Soon she was confiding what had been said in the car, and ended,

"I wonder if we ought not to have warned her to have the—the foetus baptized. I mean, we are her Catholic family and she herself has not had time to put on the mind of the Church. I did not say anything, of course, but I fear it is worrying her. Perhaps if we could take some of the onus, the blame..."

"I think to draw attention to it would risk worrying her more. For myself, I would not have supposed that a—a child would be living at barely three months of pregnancy. We used to consider 'quickening' as... Are you telling me it would be alive—moving, even—so early on?"

"Yes. I believe the heart beats almost from the start, and that can now be detected."

"Of course, in a *Catholic* hospital—a Catholic nurse would have baptized any child about to die. And who knows—a lot of nurses are Irish—the best ones, I always think: good Catholic girls who want to care for people and are willing to do it for small remuneration... But we don't know what happened to the—the mite, and you did quite right to speak as you did to poor little Elaine, who has suffered so, with Ian having to go back, and then there was that Cuban Missile business, which clearly frightened her with him away! Of course, to us, who have lived through so much... And then she seems to have been upset by some wretched doctor."

"Yes, the specialist made a domiciliary visit and saw something—a crucifix, or it may have been a rosary—and asked her if she was Catholic. He seemed to her to be making something of it."

"His words, she told me, were 'You're a Catholic and you want to keep the baby'—as if only a Catholic would worry about keeping a baby!"

"Yes, and she didn't understand that at all, until she was in his hospital and found abortions happening there."

"But it's against the law!"

"There's talk of changing the law. I expect this man, at the top of his profession, was pushing for that. Elaine found it all quite distressing, poor lamb! The woman in the next bed was having an abortion, for no apparent reason except that she reckoned she'd finished her family, and she was visited by the vicar, who just chatted with her, though Elaine supposed he must have known, or at least guessed why she was in. And there was she, desperate to keep her baby, poor child... I think she feels she might have said something to the woman, but didn't like to. Not that it would have changed things, as I told her, but she's inclined to blame herself for lacking courage to try."

"Very understandable in her situation. Everyone can't exercise heroic virtue; we should not expect it of ourselves, and there can be humility in recognizing that, as I shall point out to her if she says anything to me about it. It's a shame Ian has to be so far away, and of course is not a Catholic. But so much more is understood about these things—about fertility—than in my day."

"Hmm. Sometimes there seems *less* understanding, even if more knowledge! She gathered, from a nurse, I believe, that there was some disagreement as to the cause of these 'misses' between this man, who she felt was not well disposed to her, and his registrar, who she found more sympathetic and had suggested a different approach from his superior, but was overruled—actually in front of Elaine! She told me she woke up to find herself surrounded by medical personnel—students and such—and this Grand Panjandrum examining her—physically, in front of them, when she was scarcely awake! And actually contradicting the other man who now she thinks might have saved the—situation."

"I see. Well, nothing can be done about it now, alas! Besides, we don't know which of them was right."

"Nothing can be done about that, no. But in my view, she should consult a Catholic gynaecologist, if we can find one."

"That too is a good idea. I shall urge it on her. I hope to see more yet of my 'fourth generation' than the present little darling!"

"It may be Joejoe's child you see next. Elaine told me the Specialist advised her to wait at least a year before starting another baby."

"Indeed. Well, that is good advice, I expect, and I only hope they can follow it—together. I shall say something to that effect when I see my poor darling. Joshua has done well too; his fiancée sounds very—acceptable. Not, of course, Catholic; that was hardly to be expected."

"Far from it, I'm afraid: a C. of E. clergyman's daughter!"

"That may not necessarily be *so* far. Look at me, brought up a Methodist! I believe her father was a dean and might have been a bishop had he lived."

"Her mother, it seems, would have made a good Mrs Proudie! She objects to her daughter marrying someone as lowly as Joe—though one suspects Jewish is the real point!"

"It may be so, but clearly the girl herself has no such prejudices and I must say, when Joe brought her to see me, I thought her well bred—rather quiet…"

"Quiet, yes, but I had a feeling a lot goes on behind that demure smile. She was herself, you know, a student of Divinity, as they call their Theology—the Low Church, anyway, I believe. It seems Joe-Joe has given up on Vee's Anglo-Catholicism."

"Well, dear, we must pray; that is all. The ways of Providence are inscrutable and we none of us know how things may fall out. We have only to desire that God's Will be done despite all our clumsy failures: only to trust that He writes straight with us, His crooked pens!"

"You are right, dear Deedie, as ever; we must pray more assiduously for Vee to return and to bring the boys too with her, back to the Church in which they were baptized."

"Yes, she accepted that, even though she had lapsed by the time they were born. Father Grady, I recall, said it was strictly uncanonical where the parents did not undertake to rear them as Catholics, and he was stretching a point because he knew me and our family… And Ron was present, even though Veronica was not. I am convinced Ron has had a certain yearning to be a Catholic, but of course his origins have stood in the way, and then, alas, Veronica… I worry about them these days; he often seems so—discontented."

"Downright disagreeable, you mean!"

"Well, I know, dear, you never did see eye-to-eye—on politics, especially, and we know he can be very dogmatic."

"And obsessive: I notice him frequently washing his hands. I know Jews do that ritually and are very scrupulous about hygiene, but really—he'll get up for it even in the middle of a meal…! And *always* listening to the wireless, the News especially: forever putting it on. You remember when Elaine was studying she used to come round here to get away from it."

"Yes, I sometimes wonder what the effect of the War—and all the revelations after—those camps: unbelievably dreadful things—what effect that had on him… I have heard, or read, that Jews today feel guilty for surviving, so perhaps one can understand…"

"Again you are right, Mumsie, and as a Jew who's tried to throw it over, married a Christian—and we remember the trouble there was over that; his brother still keeps his distance…"

"Latterly, we hear, he has suffered some kind of breakdown."

"Yes, and been hospitalized. I suppose we should feel sorry for him, but…"

"Yes, we should pray for his recovery, even though he has slighted Veronica and his own brother: or rather more especially on that account; after all, we are bidden to love our enemies…"

"Dear Deedie, you are right as ever, though your charity I'm afraid goes against my grain! I just feel people who behave as he has have it coming to them: breakdown or illness of some kind!"

"It may be so, dear, and we are all, alas, liable… But no-one is unredeemable. In his case, he will have acted on what he takes to be principle, which may even have been hard for him. As ever, God must be the judge."

"All I know is it's hard on Vee to have to contend with such a difficult husband, without Ron's brother doing his bit to build up Ron's guilt over his marriage to a gentile!"

"It may be more that Ron is a disappointed man, I fear. His writing never came to much. He had the gift, I think, but not enough education."

"Not enough drive, rather. He had the same education as you: a grammar-school…"

"It seems he did not know how to make the best of it. I did pass my Oxford Senior—you see I'm still proud of that!—but I had my dear mother and even, up until then, my poor father behind me. It was about then that things started to go wrong for us—or at least that the wrong came to light… Ron's people were immigrants and not very literate, I would suppose."

"His brother went to University and became a solicitor; not that that has prevented him breaking down—rather helped to cause it, I'd say, and with my social-worker's hat on, I would diagnose there a failure in parenting such as we commonly find in immigrant families—and not only immigrant—when they attempt to break out of a lower societal status. Commonly the children are emotionally deprived and…"

"My dear, children being what you call emotionally deprived is not confined to immigrants, nor to the lower orders. Look at poor Winston Churchill! They say that Lady Clementine has to manage him…"

"Well, if all did as well as he—*and* she! But you are right, Mumsie, as ever; only having status and money has a wonderfully cushioning effect! That apart, it all comes down to the mothers—like you, you dear Deedie!"

"My dear, as you know, I have often failed."

"You never failed me!"

Edith in her private thought sometimes wondered if she had not failed this daughter too in some way. Magda, she knew, detected in Freda ambivalence, as she called it, towards marriage and mother-hood and in her new-chosen profession an attempt to compensate for that inhibition. But was Magda herself qualified to make such a judgement. She had hardly succeeded in the matter of marriage. Yet hers and Hilary's had been a peaceful marriage—anyway union— and his death had afflicted her almost inconsolably. Whereas the most incontestably married of her four had landed up with a mal-content of a husband. Money, of course, made a difference: still, Veronica's circumstances were not straitened as had oftentimes been her own: Ron was a steady earner and Veronica, her sisters some-times observed, made too much of a point of economy: less thrift might make for more happiness.

She only said,

"I am glad you can say that, dearest Freda—though I fear it is more than I deserve and I bear responsibility for much I have since struggled to undo. But, alas, we are left with the results of our fail-ings and can only make amends by patience—and prayer: prayer for grace—the grace to love!"

Her earnest tone had sunk almost to a whisper. Freda rose to place a kiss on her mother's still residually brown, though thinning, hair, then resuming her seat exclaimed,

"Yes, love! Self-sacrificing love—maternal love not least: you gave us all that, whatever else befell! And I do wonder—We know little of Ron's mother. No doubt she was hard-working, but also hardened, I would guess: inhibited, anyway. As I would say her daughter Jane is."

"It may be so, my dear; Vee took me with her to visit Mrs Keller just the once—for the decencies, you know—and that I think would have been my impression. Of course her husband had died, and she had no great reason to welcome me. But you are right, it all comes down to the mothers—only backing them they need the fathers' support."

"Yes, and not just financial support but emotional—and you, you poor Deedie, had little enough of either, and still…"

"I had my own mother for most of those years who, thank God, was the best of mothers—and how I long to see her loving face again and in a better world!"

Taking her mother's softly wrinkled hands into her own capacious ones, Freda leaned over to kiss her on the cheek, then sat stroking a hand in silence until she resumed:

"Well, it seems likely Ron did not have the—the foundations, emotional as well as educational, to achieve all they may have hoped for, and we may now see his brother falling by the wayside! I know in Jewish families more is expected of the eldest son and maybe that at least has been in Ron's favour; I mean it may be as well that he was indolent, dreaming that things could come easily and complaining when they haven't, instead of working himself into a breakdown. Even so, it has been hard on Vee!"

"I have somewhat wondered at his apparent lack of interest in the new Jewish state they are setting up in Palestine. Veronica is quite enthusiastic about it and I almost believe would go if he would."

"Yes, and then she could become Jewish next move!" exclaimed Veronica's sister, adding, "No, Mumsie; she won't—and happily he won't either! Though you're right; she's positively starry-eyed about this Ben Gurion! We know they did think of emigrating to Canada, where at least they have friends from the old WEA days. But even that was a move too far for Ron! No, he'll stay put, if only to enjoy the largesse of the Left, for which he has campaigned and which is really his religion—but it's as much about envy as a zeal for justice! Of course," she added, "Magda votes Labour too, and she's well off; I can respect that."

"Yes, Magdalen is a little quixotic there—and Agnes has become quite militantly Liberal, which might seem a contradiction but I suppose it's again in reaction to her father, as they've always been the anti-Catholic Party. Labour, after all, get the Irish vote. We know Cardinal Manning was a champion of the dockers, and our new Cardinal too is…"

"He wouldn't have championed the things the Left did in the Civil War, crucifying priests, raping nuns… To people like Ron, all the atrocities were from the Nationalist side. And that was before Hitler—before the War, anyway."

"Yes, before *that* War—but after the one before, which you do not remember! And now that we have had more wars involving us—anyway the Americans; we seem to have been able to stay out of this latest in Vietnam, which from reports is as dreadful in its own way… I wonder if there can ever in human history have been a time without war! Even in the Pax Romana—the time of Our Lord's birth, when 'the whole world was at peace,' as Saint Luke says: even then there were probably tribal wars in lands hardly known to the Romans. But now the whole globe is known to us and every local war becomes our concern..."

"Yes, all working up to Armageddon, if we are to believe the Scriptures! And the Cold War still close enough to home: poor little Elaine was frightened by that Bay of Pigs stand-off, with Ian so far away... At least Ron ought to be able to get a glimmer of understanding that all righteousness is not of the Left! I gather from Vee his brother-in-law has given up Communism—even he couldn't stomach Stalin in the end! No, I know Ron was never a Communist—perhaps that's why he can cling to his Socialism so absolutely—but he seems even more prejudiced..."

"I agree, my dear; we know Ron is not open to reason on some subjects, Christianity included, I fear. But as ever, we cannot judge. It is a pity he is not closer to his children, Leo in particular, though I'd say Joejoe too is more dutiful than affectionate."

"And Elaine? As a little thing she was quite attached to her father; it was touching to watch!"

"Yes, I fear he has repulsed Elaine in ways we have seen over the years. And Veronica has—unintentionally, I'm sure—abetted that. I have always sensed she felt uneasy toward the child whose origins were—somewhat irregular. She has been more indulgent of her boys."

"Vee *always* preferred men. I've heard her as good as say she wished she *was* one! She has said it to Elaine, too, which struck the child—she must have been just into her 'teens—very much at the time, and she told me—like other distresses which she did not confide in them."

"Again, my dear, we all have our weaknesses, and our blindnesses. Veronica has always been very fond of you and also, I'd say, of me."

"As we all are, Mumsie darling!"

"Well, some more than others. You most, perhaps."

Again her daughter's arms were round her, her kiss planted on the lined brow.

"How would I not be, when I owe my life to you twice over? But Vee is only less devoted than me."

"As is natural and right when she has her own family. Then Magda, I own, has been very good to me, though I never did quite understand her; she is more like her father."

"And Agnes last?"

"It seems to go up in order of age, does it not? Or down. I think I would have to say Agnes *is* the most—detached from me. Not that she has not been supportive too, financially as in other ways, but it is noticeable that she lives as far off as is possible in London and has resisted suggestions to install a telephone. How much simpler it would have been if she had been able to ring us herself when she was laid up last Spring, or when burglars went through her bungalow and she lost so much—just about everything of value to her!"

"You know, Mumsie, I do wonder if it was not Providential, them making off with those carved boxes poor Leo brought from India and her boss's letters in them. I mean, he was married and..."

Edith sighed, more perhaps for the relics of her lost eldest son than adulterous letters to her eldest daughter. Leo's letters to her reposed in just such a carved box, which she occasionally opened almost furtively, but never brought herself to peruse the contents. She had left instructions these were to be placed unread in her coffin. She hesitated, then,

"Poor Agnes! Again, we cannot, may not judge. It does seem as though evils—sins—have effects through the generations, a chain of ills that binds those who come after. Like those Greek plays you girls used to read."

"Like the House of Atreus!"

"Maybe. It may be the pagans had already observed this—this entail within families, this chain binding us, with its origins in our first parents, in Original Sin. My parents—and behind them who knows what—what tragedies! Your parents, René and me; René's parents, as we know. 'Not for nothing is this life called a vale of tears': I recall him saying that oftentimes, poor René! Then Veronica. And Ron—We can guess at some of the 'tears' that lie behind him! As for Agnes—it is to be hoped she might come to reconsider her attitude to the Church and to God: the two may not necessarily be synonymous, or not in her case... Again, we must continue to pray. It takes Grace to break the chain, to 'bend the stubborn heart and will,' as the hymn puts it."

"The beautiful Sequence for Pentecost—one of my great favourites! 'Stubborn heart and will' does describe our Agnes and her attitude to the Church! We know that Grace has to be received and God does not force us to accept Him. Even Our Lord could work few miracles in his own country, where they had Him in contempt..."

"What you say is true, no doubt, dear, and it is a mystery how any of us can receive Grace—can be saved, in fact. I was taught that it takes 'prevenient Grace' to dispose us to receive Grace..."

"But never against our will—not if that will *will* not 'bend'! Of course, God must make every allowance, as it were, Who knows everything, Who alone can judge..."

"*Tout comprendre est tout pardonner,*" murmured her mother, as if to herself, but Freda caught it.

"'To understand all is to pardon all'—I know you're still fond of that saying, Mumsie dear, despite all we've seen... And no doubt there's something in it. I still wonder, though—Hitler and the Nazis we were talking about just now, who we've talked about in the past—at Magda's, as I remember: only then we only suspected and now we know what they were doing—to Jews and others—Catholics too, like that Polish priest who gave his life for another man's in the starvation cell... And the consequences reaching on, even into our own family, in Ron and who knows... Can one really say...?"

"That they can be understood by the All-Understanding, and so pardoned? My dear, I agree it seems improbable to us. And yet in the mystery of salvation—I can suppose Father Kolbe, dying slowly among his desperate cell-mates, praying with them, calming them, as I have read—that he prayed for forgiveness for his enemies—as did Our Lord Himself, also dying slowly and painfully, and jeered at and mocked..."

"'Father, forgive them; they know not what they do.' And we can suppose that they did not know they were crucifying God Himself, but in their minds were merely carrying out a routine punishment, even if Pilate and the High Priests had stretched a few points to suit their convenience! Our Lord said those who handed Him over to Pilate 'had the greater sin'—which was not to say Pilate was sinless. But those who enslaved, starved, tortured, murdered countless men, women, children even—may still be doing so in Russia—though they say since Stalin's death things have improved there—Can we suppose they do not know what they do?"

"Indeed, I agree it offends against all our ideas of justice. And yet... It is not given us to know or to judge—not ultimately, that is; earthly judges have, of course, the responsibility, and have exercised it on those wretched men—where they did not pre-empt justice by taking their own lives."

"I, at least, can only suppose they—Hitler, Stalin, those responsible; I agree we cannot judge precisely who they are—I believe them to be in Hell: that very Hell they created for so many, only without end, whereas their victims at least could escape it in death. That is their very just desserts!"

"I believe you are right, dear: just desserts! Yet Shakespeare seems to me very Christian when he makes Hamlet say that in that case

THE CHAIN

'Which of us shall 'scape whipping?' Certainly we believe there is
Hell, whether or not anyone is in it—apart from the Devil himself,
in whom too Catholics believe: certainly I do, seeing his work so
plain in smaller matters as in great... As for Agnes, I think one *can*
'understand,' at least up to a point. We know she never has looked
back since her early decision to leave the Church, which..."

Freda broke in on her mother with a disconsolate sigh.

"Yes, forever talking, never listening, and you can hear the animus
in so much of what she says! Nowadays it's her Liberal causes, political and also more widely—or narrowly: women's rights and equal
pay, and above all birth-control... Well, I'm all for equal pay, of
course, but..."

Another sigh, in which Edith joined, adding,

"Her intransigence, I fear, is a revolt against poor René's narrow-
ness of outlook—and my failure to manage him better: to love him
better, it may—no it must be! Nonetheless and with all these failures, here we are: you and I practising Catholics, as is Magda and
now Elaine, and her child baptized and we hope and pray in time
other children... You and she especially are my consolation and I
have hope will bring me to heaven before too long. The others may
be won over in time; or it may be I have to answer for them in Purgatory—as perhaps must we all: at least Purgatory is a merciful doctrine, leaving less need for Hell, you might say."

Her daughter again embraced her silently before observing,

"It doesn't at present look as though either of the boys will return."

"Perhaps not, or not for a long time: not Joshua, anyway. Leo
might be nearer to—I almost said to salvation, but I do not suppose
that C. of E. clergymen cannot be saved if they truly know no better—as clearly Joshua does not at this point; I only mean that
Leo..."

"I know: the black sheep, the repentant sinner, like Saint Augustine. Did you ever find out what exactly did happen?"

"I did not. Only that poor Leo failed a year and lost his grant. If
there was anything further, Veronica has been reticent about it."

"Is it because there has been an abortion...?"

"I sincerely hope not—though alas, who am I to talk! I was myself
tempted, as you know..."

"Temptation is not sin. Our Lord Himself was tempted and you
only inquired... In those days less was known about the child in the
womb's development..."

"You are right, dear, and let us leave me aside. Veronica, I know, is
very against abortion. You recall that young woman, her lodger who

became—entangled, with her boss, and Veronica suspected had her baby aborted. She was very shocked."

"I still wonder. Why did young Leo push off to Germany?"

"So far as I know, because he needed to earn until he could get another University to admit him. After all, he is working again for a degree, so is trying to make good, despite having to give up thought of being a lawyer."

"It would be well if he would give up thought of being a Lothario!" exclaimed Leo's aunt with warmth, "Or even if there hasn't been an abortion, there will be before he's through! Young people these days are ceasing to wait to get hitched before—I mean, just look how the girls dress! These so-called miniskirts: positively asking for trouble!"

"I know, dear, and as I learned, and I'm sure you and your sisters did, it's women who must take care to restrain men. Though she does not say anything, I believe Leo's—proceedings—are a worry and a sorrow to his mother—and to his father, who perhaps has failed to control him or inspire him to better courses. I believe that is one reason for Ron's moroseness these days—not, I agree, the only one. It is sad, but we live by Hope. There is always dear Elaine, poor little Elaine! We must pray for them all, or I must—pray continually; it is what one can do as one becomes old and increasingly housebound, alas! I shall pray that Leo meets the right young woman and settles down; a good wife is the dear Lord's medicine for restless young men. And you who are his godmother can pray, even though you are burdened with your job, my poor Winifreda!"

Freda sighed again and rose.

"Yes, and I must get on now. And first and foremost I must feed my little cat, waiting so patiently while we talk on! Come along, Spookle darling…"

III

(1964)

"I do wonder how things are going upstairs. Should we take tea up to them do you think?"

Veronica, uncharacteristically flustered, had in her own kitchen yielded organization to her sister, content for once to ply tea-towels and, in tandem with a silent Ron, cause stacks of plates and other crockery to grow from the new formica he had with much toil and trouble attached to the top of the old kitchen table. Freda had diverted some of the cups and saucers to a tray and, having filled the largest teapot, was replacing the kettle on the gas burner.

"That's a good idea," she answered her sister. "We need to get *her* out of here and on her way! When you've finished, Elaine pet, will you take it up? I think you're the best person in the circs."

Elaine was at the sink, a bibbed apron replacing the jacket of her Spring suit, one rubber-gloved hand wielding a mop, the other alternately plunged into a bowl in the white porcelain depths and surfacing to hold each item under a running tap. Now she tipped out the suds, mopped the bowl round, wiped the gloves on the apron and removed them, then resumed the chequered jacket from the back of a chair, feeling again a pride in its smartness and its economy; she had made her suit herself on the electric Singer machine that had been her parents' wedding-gift and had remained in their house as unusable in Africa.

"Let us know the lie of the land," her aunt bade as she placed two filled cups on a smaller tray and handed it to Elaine, adding,

"I shouldn't say much, though."

"I shan't."

Elaine carried the tray upstairs, tapped on the door of her parents' bedroom and hearing a muted "Come in!," entered to find Deborah, now her sister-in-law, seated by the bed still wearing the white frock and demure "picture" hat in which she had that day walked unaccompanied to Father Billings' altar.

"We thought you'd like some tea."

"Oh, how kind! Mother," Deborah continued in her habitually low and controlled tone, "Joe's sister has brought us tea!"

The bundle of tweeds and lisle stockings on the bed sighed, stirred slightly, grunted.

"Do sit up, Mother, and have your tea; you'll need it before driving back. Thank you, Elaine, and please thank your Mother, won't you."

Embarrassed, each avoiding the other's eyes... Elaine quietly closed the door and returned downstairs. She was nervous of this collected young woman whose praises had been hymned by brother and mother as a paradigm of the good order and good works which went with a degree in Pastoral Theology recently exercised in Hospital Visiting. Deborah was pretty too: an English blend of compactness of figure and delicacy of colouring very different from Elaine herself or for that matter her mother or grandmother, all darkhaired and slender: different, too, from the towering, exuberant aunts; and Elaine already felt her weaknesses appraised as by an expert: her insomnia, her hovering anxiety, the proneness to out-bursts she shared with her father… A couple of years older than the twins, Deborah could be the daughter her mother might have wished…

"Well?" demanded Veronica, so soon as her daughter regained the kitchen.

"She was just lying there, quiet enough, and I think will be leaving soon."

"I should hope so: making all this scene—and after saying she wouldn't come to her own daughter's wedding!"

"I think you'd better prepare to see her off, Vee," said Freda, still taking charge. "*Noblesse oblige* and all that—Show her *we* know how to behave correctly!"

"I expect you're right," said her sister reluctantly, "Shall we, Ron?"

"Catch me!" was her husband's response. "The only send-off I want to give her is a flea in the ear! *She* should have been *giving* this do, not leaving it to them—which of course means to us: washing her hands of it and then turning up to stage her hysterics: doing her best to muck it up for everyone!"

He stared round to see how his sister-in-law was taking this pro-vocatively vernacular outburst but, the bride's mother having for once produced harmony in their views, Freda contented herself with remarking crisply,

"All the more reason not to let her!"

"I'll just pop upstairs and make myself tidy," Veronica was saying, "A nuisance I can't use my own room, but there's a glass in the lodger's."

She hurried out. Ron put things away assiduously for a few min-utes, intermittently drinking noisily from his teacup to cover his uncertainty as he listened for developments in the hall. Finally he said,

"I could go and give Joe a hand with getting off—the Reverend Joe I suppose I should call him: fine profession for a Jew's son!"

Though he spoke banteringly, they were, as often these days, uncomfortably alive to an edge of malice. He left abruptly, which was as well, thought Elaine, and felt the air more breathable; while he was there, there was always the threat of a run-in with Freda, and she would be caught in the middle. It made her mother edgy, too—as if she hadn't had enough today; and here she was returning, hav-ing combed her hair, powdered the elongated patrician nose that contrasted with her husband's fleshy one, refreshed her lipstick. She joined them at the table and they sipped their tea, listening for the cue for Veronica to sally forth into the hall. Freda took out her cigarettes and opened the packet.

"Give me one, dear," her sister coaxed.

Freda waved the packet in her direction.

"I thought you'd given up!"

"I had, for Lent, as I do every year—and every year something comes along to start me off again. This year I even got by Easter, but now all this…"

"Well, I certainly can't talk; it's all that gets me by some days, with my cases and… Mother's done amazingly, giving up after all these years, but she doesn't have that daily pressure—not now—and of course, with her heart and the breathless attacks, the doctor insisted."

She drew smoke in, exhaled it in a cloud and remarked complacently,

"I expect it's bad for all of us! You don't smoke, do you, Pet?"

"Not since the night before *my* wedding! You remember, Mother?" (She had dropped "Mummy" in favour of "Mother" these days, though she felt it unwelcome.) "You invited the neighbours in and I had two—my last, I knew they would be. Ian would not have stood for it, and of course he was right; it isn't good for you."

"Least of all for your pocket," said Freda, tilting up her head to watch the wreathing blue curlicues. "You'll be the wealthier for not smoking. As for healthier—I'm past caring, I'm afraid. Life is such, I have to have 'em."

Elaine was about to change the subject when they heard steps on the stairs. Veronica stubbed out her cigarette and left the kitchen—"to speed the unwanted guest," as her sister observed drily. When she returned, it was with her new daughter.

"Have some more tea, Deb?"

"Thank you, Vee, and may I take one out to Joe, when he's seen off Mother? He spotted a tyre was down and is seeing to it for her. He's very forgiving!"

A pause as they considered whether to applaud the magnanimous Joshua would be to censure the offender. Deborah laughed drily:

"And then we must be leaving. Joe's all changed and the beauty of this outfit is I don't have to have separate going-away clothes—just put on my jacket."

Elaine and Freda had further noted that "Vee," the latter with disapproval, the former marvelling: she had attempted calling her parents by their first names, to be indignantly repulsed.

"*I* was married in purple," Veronica was remarking. "They say it's unlucky, but it was my best frock and I didn't care for any fuss. We were poor enough!"

Elaine, while wondering if her mother remembered *her* wedding-dress, tried to ignore a feeling this was aimed at her and what her parents considered the unwarrantably good income Ian made. Soon all trooped out to wave off the bridal couple in Joe's Morris Minor—purchased cheap and done up by himself lovingly, among the other vehicles he sold on; he appeared to have inherited Pawa's "engineer's thumb." Working in a garage during his University vacations, he had put aside enough for the down payment on a small house they would rent out to supplement their income. They were to be housed by the parish in the northern city where he would gain experience of his calling, where too Deb was to be employed as a part-time parish worker and take a course in Counselling. They had everything mapped out.

Ron broke cover from his refuge in the front room, where the radio drowned out unwanted sounds from the hall while he kept an eye on developments beyond the bow window that fronted each and every of The Crescent's "semi"s. Leo stood bantering with his twin and, the happy pair once settled in the car, ducked out of sight to affix the "Just Married!" notice he had been concealing, together with an old boot, to the rear registration-plate. Amid forced cheers and vigorous arm-waves, Joe drove off, then stopped the car some thirty yards down the road and emerged grinning and waving to detach the appendages and throw them in their direction. His twin, flinging up head and arms, staggered in a brief pantomime of violent passion. Joe clapped mockingly, jumped back in and slammed the door, to depart at full throttle. Returning from retrieving his spurned decorations, Leo saw his brother-in-law striding toward them down The Crescent. Holding open the garden gate, he called,

"Ian! You've been missing all the fun! Not deliberately, surely!"

They walked together to the front door.

"Your Aunt Magda wanted to show me some Colonial prints."

"Ah! The print-pretext: an old one! Well, you're just in time for another round of tea. Eh, Mum?"—seeing her emerge from the kitchen.

"You make it, Leo; I've about had enough! And your father…"

"Ian will look after him, won't you, Ian? He likes talking to you. Pick something we can all agree on without any hysteria. Like the Russian Revolution!"

He opened the door to the front room and peered round at Ron huddled disconsolately on the "studio-couch."

"Cheer up, Dad! The reverend son is well and truly spliced and I alone remain, the un-reverend—or is it ir-reverend? Afraid I'd have let the old baggage go with her flat tyre and chance it—but that's what it is to be Christian! Well and I'll be on my solitary way soon! Meantime, here's the man who relieved you of your daughter!"

"Uh. Sit down, Ian."

"Sister, you come with me and we'll bring them their tea."

Closing the door, Leo preceded Elaine to the kitchen, to find their mother slumped on a stool at the formica-topped table, taut, almost shaking. She raised her face from her hands to exclaim,

"That insufferable woman! I could murder her!"

"Too late for that, Mum!" laughed her son.

"Just as well!"

"Tell you what," Leo added helpfully, "Break a few plates! Here's a stack—take 'em out and throw 'em at the wall!"

"Don't be..." began his mother, but Elaine was chiming in:

"Why not, for goodness' sake! Let's do as Leo says!"

Hilarity was communicating itself between brother and sister, suddenly united by the "splicing" of their sibling and the chagrin they sensed this occasioned in their mother. Elaine lifted half a dozen plates off the pile and followed Leo as he propelled Veronica protesting through the outer door and round the corner of the house into the back garden, where he pressed a plate into her half-willing hands and hurled another against the house-wall with a satisfying crash. Elaine, shouting and laughing applause, did likewise.

"Pretend it's her, Mum!" called Leo in ungrammatical glee. Veronica's bony arm emerged from the sleeve of the sheeny grey rayon dress she had bought at C.&A. for the wedding. She hesitated, then stumbling forward flung the plate. It fell short of the wall and smashed on the concrete at its base.

"Harder, Mum!" yelled Leo, handing her another plate, while Elaine applauded. This one reached its goal and Veronica's arm fell back limp beneath the grey folds.

"No more! Pick up the pieces and don't tell your father or he'll have a fit!"

Leo watched laughing as the women scrabbled up the sherds and Elaine fetched newspaper to conceal them in the zinc dustbin.

"Don't you feel better?" he demanded.

"Well, maybe—a momentary madness: you two egged me on."

"Nonsense! Our new kindred drove you to it! Anyway, do you a power of good! Now, where's that tea?"

"I'll make it," said his sister. "You go and relieve Ian."

"Why? Better employ him while he's here. You too. Fact is, nobody knows what to do with Dad these days."

"Yes, Elaine, you might make a point of talking to your father for the short time you are here," her mother interjected. "As for me, I'm going up the road to have mine with Freda and Deedie if she's awake. We'll hardly need supper, I should think; anyway, there are enough leftovers. I leave it to you, Elaine."

"That's it; make the married women work: take their responsibilities seriously!"

Having made Elaine smile through the discomfiture her mother seemed adept at provoking, Leo added,

"I'll go in if you'll join us with the tea. We'll let Our Mum recover in peace!"

He gave his mother a bear-hug and saw she too was grateful. Then he repaired to the sitting-room, where he was acting as irritant in discussion of the Labour Manifesto when Elaine brought in tea and further slices of the bridal-cake the couple had contrived out of their limited resources to offer their guests as culmination to cheeses and wine. She had learned to steer clear of political discussion. An under-graduate flutter with the Liberal Party had succumbed to finding in Ian a Socialism less dogmatic than her father's, nor had her embrac-ing of their Church inclined her to Edith's staunch or Freda's more ardent Conservatism. In any case, these days she never found much to say to her father, into whose gathering eloquence against the class-enemy Leo eventually broke.

"How about we all go out for a drink?"

"I'm sure I've drunk enough," from Elaine.

"I'll stay in for your mother," from Ron.

"But I need some air," Elaine continued, "Tell you what, I'll go over and fetch Mother for you."

Ron grunted assent. All sensed he was obliging his wife's return, who would prefer to stay with Freda and Edith. So would Elaine, and momentarily fearing the young men would offer to do the errand for her, was grateful to Ian, who understood and observed,

"We can collect you on our way back. It'll be dark by then."

"Don't you want a walk, Dad?" asked Leo.

"No thanks. I'd rather read."

He hardly did read these days, they knew, or only the papers: the old *News Chronicle* and occasionally the *Sunday Times* so he could talk about books.

"We can have a sing-song this evening, Dad, before these two leave tomorrow. You still sing, don't you, Sister? And Ian, how about you? It's a family tradition, you know."

"I'll try. My family never sang—only a few Scottish songs and hymns when my grandparents were alive. Music-Hall's about my level, but I'll need some lubricating first."

"Precisely what we're off for now. Tell Mum she's expected to play for us once we're well lubricated."

"That was a brain-wave of mine," he bragged happily as the two set out to walk the mile to the pub. "Last resort for family harmony: 'Blest pair of sirens' and all that tosh; we did Milton at school: insufferable bugger! Dad's actually rather musical. Pity it was never worked on! I took up the French horn at school: bloody hard work that was! But I like to sing and I seem to have inherited Dad's voice— maybe something too from our grandfather; the frightful Pawa seems to have had one for church stuff—and comic opera."

"Was he so frightful? Elaine seems to have had time for him."

"Yes, she can remember him, which Joe and I hardly can. But the received opinion is he was frightful—Agnes', of course, and Freda tends to confirm it, though she's hampered by Christian considerations. Joe is decidedly of their party, at any rate of Agnes', putting all the family ills squarely down to the Catholicism—though in his case from a C of E perspective."

"I thought it was that his mother was a martinet?"

"Pawa's? Yes. But a Catholic martinet, so same applies so far as Joe's concerned. Seems she drove her hubby to drink and then disowned him."

"He was Catholic too?"

"True. Else she'd not have married him, not in those days."

"Something rather similar happened back in my family—the god-fearing Protestant branch! The demon drink…"

"Ah yes, it was of that generation—teamed with the demon of respectable marriage to wreak destruction!"

If this was provocation, Ian ignored it.

"At all events, without your grandfather and *his* parents, Elaine would not have existed—nor would you!"

"True. Nor Joe nor any of the above: rum isn't it! But since we find ourselves existing, we should make the most of it. That's my view. Not Joe's, nor Elaine's, I'd guess."

"In a way, yes, it would be Elaine's—in a different way."

"Going back to Joe, he was probably frightened of the Pawa from early on; we were all a bit—well, in awe: a larger-than-life figure! And Joe was nervous as a boy; it might have been the War, though it doesn't seem to have affected me that way. Plus he managed to fall downstairs when we were only two and was concussed; makes you wonder—poor old Joe! Not to mention Mum, who's probably never recovered from the guilt of it! He must have got a hold on it at school—being nervous, I mean: put on a tough, don't-mess-with-me air; I rather admire him for that. But in a way, I think he's played the part ever since."

"He must have, to get to where he is. Having to preach and set a good example and so on. Does he have to sing too?"

"Not if he can help it! Joe's like Mum, without a singing voice, though I gather he had to do some intoning as part of his training—probably helped to make him Low Church. Mum brought us up High: same as Rome without the inconveniences, as she saw it."

"Was Elaine nervous too? She still…"

"I suppose. Not the same as Joe, though. She would just break out—or down—and of course not sleep. Yes, I would think she was quite—unsure of herself, underneath."

"She is musical—though she's not made much of it."

"Music's probably a good indicator, if you're a psychologist. I remember before we got the piano, she used to take lessons on the cheap from old Miss Penny—We called her Moneypenny: not much of a Bond girl, though! Did good works at the church, so Elaine was allowed to practise twice a week in the church hall. Well, the Moneypenny decided it would be a nice return if she played hymns for the Sunday School. Our Elaine would stop practising if anyone came into the room, so she was in a blue funk and cried off—to obbligatos of ingratitude! And it didn't help that she managed to pass the Moneypenny's bosom friend in the street—a quavering creature she'd reduced to near-imbecility by sharing a house with her, and God knows what else done! Where was I?"

"Elaine passing this lady in the street and not recognizing her."

"Yes, well, you wouldn't, she was such a mouse—or hamster: her one memorable feature was her sticking-out teeth! Anyway, it gave excuse for another shindy. Elaine hated wearing her glasses outside, as Our Mum, on the receiving end, tried to explain, but Penny was loth to be deprived of her bit of spinsterly triumph… What is it about virgins—elderly ones, I mean; young and tender they're delightful, of course! Isn't there something in the Bible? About pride?"

"I don't—don't know it that well, I'm afraid! There is in Augustine."

"Really? Bit of a lad that one, wasn't he? Still, that's in his favour! Anyway, in the end it was Mum who took up the piano again, which is something of a blessing as she can accompany Dad. Politics and singing is about all that brings him out these days: you might say the one thing he can't resist is the sound of his own voice! A small price to pay if it stops him going psycho!"

"Aren't you being a bit hard? I find him quite reasonable to talk to…"

"With you he is; he's living up to you. With us it's different. That's what families do to you—so be warned, I say! I'm in no hurry to bring it on myself."

"There was talk of you getting married."

"Yes, talk—too much of it! She was under age—and a bit of an heiress: industrialist father deceased. And an ogre of a guardian, who happened to be one of my Law professors—I met her when he threw a party for us poor sods. He cut up rough, accusing me of all sorts of iniquity."

"Falsely?"

"Yes, unless hoping to marry where there's 'brass' is in itself iniquity, or hoping not merely to live but to live well, and without the interminable grind that was the Law. Chemistry is a doddle by comparison, but there's little enough prospect in it and prospects are what I needed—still do. *She* was willing—and willing to let me plan some investments I could have swung for us to do my bit; surprisingly, perhaps, she trusted me! And I wouldn't have let her down."

"And won't she still be willing?"

"No. She's been warned off. As have I—making two of us thought unworthy to marry into the self-regarding Establishment! And Dad knows it's because of him! No wonder that woman made him—react! Turning up like that, after…"

"Perhaps she had second thoughts."

"Realizing she'd lost out, d'you mean? My dear Ian—you're too Christian charitable! Like my brother, in fact, who will end up taking her to his bosom! Makes *me* think I had a lucky break *not* getting a supercilious British bat for a mother-in-law! Mind you, in my case…"

"Elaine thought there might have been a—pregnancy?"

"An abortion, you mean. That was dear Aunt Freda's construction. Well, there might have been, I suppose, though I took precautions… And if I had—put a bun in the oven, I would be the last to hear of it. She disappeared behind a wall of silence. Funny, isn't it: people like me seem liable to make—mistakes, while people like you and Elaine… I mean, I'm sorry about the miscarriages."

"Yes, we could have done without them. You realize it's made Elaine very sensitive—about abortion, especially."

"Yes, and of course the Catholicism doesn't help—never did in our family, according to my brother: can't think why my sister's become so wedded to it. Joe's convinced it's to spite Mother, but I've the impression she genuinely believes it."

"She does, and abortion is an added reason now. She quotes your Aunt Magda on the Catholic Church being the only body to stand up for the unborn…"

"Yes, well, I can see the point and I certainly hope that in my case—though if there was, it would have been very early days, which surely makes a difference. Wouldn't Elaine agree with that?"

"No. She'd say every human life is a human being."

"And that's where these people who stand on principle leave me behind! I'm not particularly fond of babies—find them rather repulsive, in fact—but I might draw the line at anything you could recognize as human. You have to weigh up the various damages: that's life, bloody awful though it is, for which I suppose we have to thank God, if He exists."

"Elaine would say we have to thank, or rather blame, the Fall: Augustine's view."

"Ah, him again! Takes one to know one: sinners, you know!"

"She'd say we're all sinners. As does Augustine."

"Well, there you have it: guilt! That's why Our Mum gave up the Catholicism: guilt over contraception and Hell if you don't repent! Mind you, it's at least consistent, unlike the C. of E., letting you off the hook all the time… Seems to me if you expect heavenly rewards, you should accept to suffer for them; it's only fair. I don't believe and so I don't accept, but I ask, what's the point of religion if it makes no difference to what we do now? Best settle for honest self-interest. Wouldn't you agree?"

"I'm not sure. I tend to see both sides of the God-question."

"So which do you come down on?"

"Neither, though I think the proposition 'God exists' may have more to be said for it than its contrary. Or anyway than is often allowed."

"Fair enough; I'm an agnostic too. So's Dad. I'd have expected Elaine to side with him, but women, you know… Joe, of course, sided with Mum. Poor old Joe, he's had it now: become solid-respectable: wouldn't suit yours truly! And I will say she's stood by him, unlike my—Mind you, she was younger… But a bishop's daughter—or did the old man die a mere dean? Either way, not bad for a son of Aaron Keller! You know the rhyme?

'The Lord said unto Moses
"The Jews shall have long noses,

All excepting Aaron
And he shall have a square 'un!'"

Our Mum thinks that's really humorous!"
"You don't, I gather."
"Oh, one can be too po-faced about these things. I did think it
went a bit far when she made up the rhyme about Dad's brother, the
egregious Izzy, who we've only seen the once—but then he'd been
particularly nasty to her before washing his kosher hands of Dad and
her."
"I've not heard this rhyme."
"No? Of course you and Elaine are always away in the Dark Continent—sensible you!"
"How…?" Ian began, but Leo was already chanting, to the mel-
ody of the Battle Hymn of the Republic:

"'Poor old Izzy-wizzy, he is in the loony-bin;
he's getting ever so loo-oony; that's why they put him in!'

There's more, but that gives the flavour."
"And your father? It does seem a bit—well, looking down on…
Does he think it's funny?"
"He seems to. But then he always falls in with what Our Mum
thinks—that's what Joe calls her these days; he's become a right
Northerner has Our Joe! Dad thinks what Mum thinks except for
religion; after all, she condescended to marry him! And you've got it!
The Lumley-Riggs were some cuts above the Kellers—even though
they made a hash of the dress-trade and Grandfather Keller, had he
lived, might have taught them a thing or two!"
"Being themselves in a ghetto may have helped!"
"A Catholic ghetto, you mean? Yes, that—and then there was Leo,
my namesake uncle making away with himself—quite fresh, that
was—to give the Pawa pause, who otherwise might have cut up
more… Anyway, one way and another Our Mum didn't have a great
deal of choice, and she stooped to marry Dad—odd word: she's
always had a thing about stooping!"
"Yes, I gather she used to go on at Elaine about 'stooping'! Any-
way, I'm glad she did marry your father!"
"I'm glad you're glad. Because if they'd had abortion in those days,
I suppose Elaine might not have been born."
"That's probably true for not a few people. Or for all of us. If
Elaine hadn't been born, perhaps neither would you."

"You're so right! But as things are, and as I said, it would be positively ungrateful not to make the most of it, don't you agree?"

"Yes—in a sense: an opportunity not to be missed, so to speak. Only for what? And grateful to whom?"

"God knows! Let's say Destiny. Leave God to Joe and wife!"

"And to my wife?"

"Why not, if it makes her happy! I can see my sister never had much chance to blossom; first there was the War and then there was never any money and Dad fed up about it and Mum making a positive virtue of scrimping and Joe and me coming along to stand in her light—don't you think?"

"Perhaps. I can tell you what my mother said the first time she met yours. When they visited after we were engaged. The first thing she said after we left was, 'Anyone can see who's the favourite in *that* family!'"

"Not me, I take it!"

"No."

"I suppose that's why Elaine had to shine at her own thing—make her own light to stand in. And she made it to Cambridge. Joe and I never aspired beyond redbrick. So—she's had her—her opportunities: with you, too—and for all I know she may have been quite a girl!"

"She was—is!"

Leo's half-amused glance at Ian showed him the Scot was not about to divulge more. He sensed a something more pain than embarrassment. Happily they had reached the pub.

IV

(1968)

"Of course, you came for your grandmother's funeral, not my birthday!"

Having alerted his hearers to his intention to discomfit them, Ron went on in the same bland tone:

"But I'm honoured you were able—also willing to stay!"

"I'm very glad to be here, Dad," Elaine mumbled; then, recognizing in herself stirrings of an anger she must control or it would throw her off balance, she attempted to maintain her ground under a guise of neutrality: stance to which her confessors had been leading her, and supplemented latterly by such books of psychology as she could lay hands on. She said,

"It was very good of Ian to let me come and be left with Anne."

"Of course, we should have liked to see her."

Again Elaine felt herself cringe inwardly, again attempted to parry.

"I know, but it's full fare now...," ending lamely,

"And she'd be quite a handful!"

"Young children don't adapt well to travel," put in Freda from across the Keller sitting room where she had had Leo bring in an upright chair from the dining-room, because of her back. Ignoring her brother-in-law's just audible snort and impatient gesture, she went on,

"*Such* a grace for dear Granny to live to see and bless your little Anne Edith! It gave her so much joy!"

"Oh, I know!" Elaine exclaimed, then was dumb, wondering how they could speak so lightly of what to her was loss she still could not compass. Her grandmother—who was their mother! Auntie Freda had brought her her breakfast tray in bed as usual that morning when she had sat up and "just glazed over and died," as Freda told it, with her holding her hands and repeating steadily, "Into thy hands, O Lord, I commend my spirit. Lord Jesus, receive my soul!" Then had closed the eyes and pulled up the sheet and gone to phone the doctor and the priest, who had come and anointed the still warm body—You didn't know when the soul left it, but in any case Edith had been to Mass and Communion the morning before, not knowing she was receiving her Viaticum... The priest had said that at the funeral, how Edith was as well prepared as any soul. And how she had often admitted her fear of dying—Her family knew that was because she felt she had failed as wife and mother—but in the event she had been spared the knowledge of her near end, and how merciful that showed God and like a Shepherd...

Edith's other fear had been of being buried before life had left her body, and so, by her particular request and in accordance with old custom, had been laid out over two nights in the church where Elaine had arrived just in time to bid the corpse farewell. The sight of the coffin lowered into the ground had almost undone the effect of the priest's words of comfort... But here and now it was her father's special day and, cautious of joining too readily in her aunt's effusiveness, she added hastily,

"You will have other chances, Dad—but I shan't see her again..." Adding, "In this life," so as not to be utterly deficient in the proclaiming of the Faith, for of course she held that her dear Granny was or would soon be in heaven and a participant in all she had loved in this life: anything else was unthinkable—but also unthinkable to try to intimate this to Ron now. He, however, following the unspoken thought, remarked with heavy signification:

"*That's* as may be!"

All inadequate, too, to express her sense of loss: this crowning bereavement hard upon the other! For once again she had miscarried, out there in Salisbury, with Ian now employed by the hateful Smith regime—though even if that lasted, they would not stay long; he was working in all his spare time for the Doctorate that would enable him to seek an academic post somewhere—she hoped back in Britain. Otherwise, would they ever settle? Or would he be ever restless, a rolling stone as she by now suspected…?

That had been nearly six months ago, and this time she knew "it" had been a boy, for he had lived long enough to be baptized and named Benedict, which was the name of the African priest who had seen to all; again she had hardly wanted to know, certainly not to see. But she could take comfort that this third casualty was surely a little angel in heaven, saved in Christ from all taint of mankind's heritage of sin: indeed, better than an angel, as the Church taught, and much better than a "sprite," as Aunt Freda had called Benedict's precursors: "sprite" might be the same word as "spirit"; to Elaine it implied less than Christian. But God, as her confessor affirmed, could not be unfair, and she now thought of the baptism of Benedict as standing for them all and placing them under that saint's protection.

She returned to the banal present on hearing her mother remark, "Mother saw two more great-grandchildren after Anne!"

"And very fine ones too!" Joe was entering the room carrying his year-old daughter, leading her three-year brother. "Aren't you, Abby? Aren't you, Sin?"

"I do think, Joe dear," remonstrated his mother, "You shouldn't shorten St John's name in that way! He'll soon understand what it means!"

"He'll be wiser than his Dad, then!" In the tone bordering on unctuousness Joe had perfected since being ordained, he went on, "Outmoded medieval concept!" (with a glance at his sister), "We don't recognize it, do we, children! You might as well object to my shortening Abigail to Abby!"

"*Both* outmoded medieval concepts!" This from Ron, not to be outdone by his "reverend" son. "Sin and Abbeys: not unconnected, one could say—eh, Elaine?"

Elaine was silent, though her thoughts were again taking off: Original Sin… washed away in baptism… Benedict… abbeys…

"Perhaps 'sin' is less poetic than abbeys!" Freda put in, attempting a clumsy tact on her niece's behalf; then, bethinking her, on her sister's, to steer the conversation away from further collision,

"Talking of poetry, Vee, dear, have they seen your beautiful gift to Ron? Do show them, Ron!"

"I already have."

"Dad unwrapped his presents at breakfast," issued from a heavily bearded, be-jeaned and be-sandalled Leo, in exaggeratedly patient tones as of one making allowances for imbeciles. His aunt was not to be put off.

"Do they know how you laboured, day and even night, to type out every last one of Ron's poems and make them into that beautiful book, stitching the cover, too: *such* a labour of love! And with your job to do on top of everything!"

Her tone had ended up accusatory, but all knew it was not simply that the Kellers needed the money; all they had to spend it on these days was doing up the house, in which they persisted with maximum economy and no little friction; it was work in which Ron acquiesced while he hated it, but for which neither of them wanted to employ anyone who could possibly be done without; only if the roof leaked or a pipe burst would builder or plumber be admitted. Fortunately the mortgage had been paid off before Ron came down with this circulatory problem that meant his foot went numb so he could not travel to work as before. He had been able to transfer his pension and himself to a humdrum part-time position; found for him courtesy of his old poet-friend, in the town hall a short bus-ride away. He complained of missing the long journey by tube, when he could read the paper; it was the stairs he could no longer negotiate and the hurrying crowds. His wife, soon experiencing as irksome the extra hours spent daily with a morose husband, had found herself a clerical position at the local hospital, requiring late shifts. It put her, she said, "in touch with real people."

Now she acknowledged her sister's tribute with deprecatory brightness:

"Without the job I'd never have revived my typing-skills! I gave him a new hairbrush as well—for what hair he has left, poor Ron!—but the pittance I earn wouldn't run to much and I don't see spending Ron's earnings on his birthday-present, so I made the best of my poor skill. Of course, it's Ron's poetry that makes it what it is!"

An instant more of tension, then relief as Ron responded to this demonstration, as effusive as anyone remembered to have heard from Veronica. Both no doubt were being assisted by the Cointreau that was Magda's gift—because Ron, she had long believed, liked it, and he had not brought himself to tell her, after the third or fourth bottle had been received with thanks, that what he really liked was cherry-brandy, like his mother had made in far-off days in Robert Street on the other side of London.

"It is indeed a priceless gift: a gift without price, my dear!"

This in a tone of mock gallantry—and whether irony was intended was overlooked in the general consciousness that this was the closest he was like to come to seeing his poems published. A pause, broken by the slow tones of Ron's brother-in-law:

"Well? Aren't *we* to see it?"

"I didn't know poetry was your cup of tea, Ben!"

Saying "I'll fetch it," Veronica quickly left the room and "Perhaps not," Ben began, but Jane, alive to currents of acrimony: Cointreau too rendering her uncharacteristically forward, broke in to champion her husband:

"Ben read a lot in the army—poetry and things. He brought back these little books, small enough for the men to keep in their pockets and really nice, with leather covers and the titles in gold letters: Keats, Shelley…"

"He sent me a Shelley…" Elaine was beginning, but,

"'O wild west wind, thou breath of autumn's being!'" declaimed Ron, suddenly animated, and stopped.

"Go on, Dad!" urged Leo.

"'Thou, from whose unseen presence the leaves dead
…like ghosts from an enchanter fleeing…' That's all I can remember."

"'Yellow and black and hectic red,
pestilence-stricken multitude…'" came, unexpected and unwelcome, from Ben.

"Well I'm damned! Go on!," Ron challenged.

"I can't."

"Yes you can, Ben," persevered his wife. "Say that bit about the Mediterranean you liked so much when you were out there in Italy."

"Don't remind me!"

Taciturnity had overcome the ex-soldier. He seldom spoke of those years, but his wife ventured on:

"Ben was changed by the War. It was three months before he could sleep in a bed again—just had a mattress on the floor…"

Her boldness tailed into their silence; they had heard this before and all wondered about Ben's war-experiences.

"Changed your politics, too, didn't it, Ben?" Ron challenged; then to the room at large: "Can you believe it? On our last visit I found Ben reading the 'Daily Express'"!

"Surely not, Uncle!" from Joe in vicarage tone of mock reproof. "The Beaverbrook Press? You old capitalist!"

"I think I'm capable of making allowances!"—imperturbably from Ben,

"And you forget we have a business to build up!" from Jane. "It's easy to be snooty when you don't *need* to depend on what you call capitalism!"

"Now we're down to brass!" from Leo. "And let's leave it for another occasion! Give us the 'Grecian Urn,' Dad," he urged again.

His father hesitated, muttered,

"Can't remember it these days!"

"Yes you can. 'Thou still unravish'd bride of quietness…'"

"Perhaps not suitable…," came in hushed remonstrance from his wife, returning at that moment with in hand her gift: a wad of quarto pages painfully stitched into plastic covers pinked at the edges.

"Don't be absurd, Vron!" Ron's hiss of exasperation was audible. "They're all grown up now, and the youngsters too young… Anyway" (capitulating to his wife's warning head-shake) "I can't go on—except the end, of course." His voice from truculent became on the instant declamatory:

"'Beauty is Truth, Truth Beauty; that is all
Ye know on earth and all ye need to know!'"

His relations applauded tepidly, finding his sudden fervour embarrassing. No-one supposed those lines might in some way be true of the Ron they knew, avid after what passed for knowledge and withal opinionated, assertive.

"The 'Nightingale,'" persisted Leo, knowing this would be irresistible; Ron would break into its opening lines uninvited and regularly enough for his family to regard it as an irritating peculiarity rather than a *cri-de-coeur*. But the communal sigh was inward as they braced themselves to hear out his histrionic, word-perfect recitation.

"'My heart aches and a drowsy numbness pains
My sense as though of hemlock I had drunk…'"

Applause again, the last line scarce ended—and the performer, with a hasty gesture as dashing tears from his eyes or sweat from his brow, cleared his throat and sat silent, taking occasional sips of Cointreau while they made admiring noises over the book of his poems, from which no-one asked him to read.

"Tea-time!" interposed Veronica, judging poetry had gone on long enough. "I've made you a cake, you know."

"Before that I have an announcement to make," said her husband. This was unscripted and the portentous tone was of one nerving himself to an unwelcome duty. All fell silent as he cleared his throat, except for his wife, who began,

"Oh Ron, not now!"

And on any other day would have prevailed, but he made another gesture, as brushing her aside.

"Vron here already knows, of course, but I want it known to everybody, *especially* our children! I have been making my Will."

He paused impressively, and long enough that Joe was impelled to break the tension.

"Go on, Dad. We're listening."

"There's plenty of time! Even though I'm sixty, and threescore and ten are the years of a man's life as the Bible tells us—the Jewish Bible, note, which brings me to the main point: not what you might suppose, as I've little enough to leave apart from this house that I've sweated to pay off, and that of course goes to Vron here, assuming she outlives me. Everything else, nearly, has gone on educating my children, so they could provide for themselves and for their families in due course, and by now all of you are better placed than ever I was" (glancing round almost fiercely at them): "Elaine married to Ian, who earns pretty well, I should judge; Joe a vicar now and won't ever have a mortgage on his vicarage—even if it is in the slums, which are no worse than those I came from—and besides has something put aside from his various deals, plus a careful wife" (with a facetious bow in his daughter-in-law's direction). "I dare say," he added for good measure, "you both have better expectations than could ever have come from such as me! Then Leo: not anxious, we all know, to encumber himself with a wife and kids, but seems to have a talent for dealing in properties: can't imagine how he finances it, but that's his business and it seems a good spec. Or should we come right out and say 'speculation,' eh, Leo?"

"Nothing so exotic," parried his son imperturbably. "Just one or two adroit transactions and you're off! Even a single man has to live."

"A teacher's salary, surely, is ample for a single man!" put in Freda admonishingly. "When I was in Child Care…"

"I think we'll finish what *I* have to say, if you *don't* mind…," began her brother-in-law with pointed emphasis and ignoring her annoyed flounce, while Leo went on regardless of them both,

"I may hope one day 'to wive,' even if not in such a hurry as Joe and Ian here! And maybe 'whoe'er she be—that not impossible she'—See, I know English Literature too, poor Chemist as I am!—maybe someone will have me the more gladly if I'm richer than a mere pedagogue—and I shouldn't blame her, being a realist myself. I might even pay my way back into the Law before it's too late."

"A lawyer in the family *would* have come in handy!" (Again Ron's daughter felt herself quail inwardly at his tone of heavy irony, which appeared not to touch the brother at whom it was levelled.)

"And you had your chance so far as I'm concerned," went on their father, "But it's something you have to stick at. Like my dear brother Izzy—'busy Izzy,' we called him, and too busy to come today, though he was invited. Too rich, too, no doubt..."

"Ron, he's not been well," began his wife in her reasoning tone.

"I know, Vee, he's been depressed, and not surprising! You might think a visit to his brother should cheer him up, but the truth is he's too *frumm* to associate with my family! Which brings me to the point, which is that I consulted a young chap in the Town Clerk's department: a fellow Jew and he put me in touch with this liberal rabbi, and I went to have a talk with him. Very helpful: didn't make any problem about my family, and so I've arranged with him for my funeral. I just want you all to know that that's how it's to be. It's in my will: a liberal Jewish service and cremation at Kensal Green."

He paused to savour the embarrassed silence in which his family registered, with differing emotions, his message that they were not to have him at the last. Finally he added:

"Is that clear, Joshua?"

A deep and deliberate "Yes, Dad," from the new vicar.

"Leo?"

"Sure, Dad"—heartily.

Elaine's faltering "Yes" was half lost in a decided "Quite right too!" from Agnes, unable to keep silent any longer.

"Of course, dear," concluded Veronica, whom he would not have presumed to interrogate in so public a manner but who felt the need to set her seal on matters. "But we hope it won't be for many a year. And now let me get the tea."

Nimbly she again quit the room as her husband flung after her,

"It probably will be, with these palpitations and pains I get and this cursed numbness!"

Frustrated he turned to the assembled roomful.

"My parents both died in their fifties, in their sleep—lucky them! I've done better than them, reaching sixty—or worse, depending on your point of view. After all, what is there to look forward to at my age?"

This produced silence, until,

"Much, surely, to give thanks for," began Joshua nervously, seemingly mindful of his calling.

"Thanks? To who?—or I *should* say 'To whom'? To my parents, who no doubt did their best but couldn't do much—wouldn't have known *what* to do, and anyway are gone? To you children for putting up with me and letting me launch you on your various paths? To God, d'you mean?" He stared belligerently at Joshua. "*Prove* to me there's a God and I'll thank Him—though God knows for what!"

"Grandchildren?" suggested unexpectedly Leo, while "Life!" came softly from Ron's daughter, which, if he heard, he chose to ignore, concentrating his fire on the younger twin.

"*Not* something *you* seem to care much for—and who knows but you're right! Enjoy your youth while you can, I say, before the 'hungry generations tread you down'!"

V

(1970)

"This doesn't seem such a bad place: a bit bare, but a room to yourself, at least."

Leo was first to speak, following his brother in and glancing round. Their sister seemed drawn and pale under the thin red dress and the arms protruding from the short sleeves—it was insufferably hot in here—were thinner than ever. She said,

"I know. I suppose I'm lucky. The ward is horrible; the two nights I was in it I couldn't sleep even with pills. Then this came vacant and they put me in here—but they'll probably turn me out any day if they reckon someone else needs it more. And I don't feel safe: can't lock the door—this morning another patient just walked in—woke me up."

"A man?"

"No, a strange woman called Geraldine, who seems to want to run me; what is it about me that everyone...? She says she's Catholic too, but—I don't trust her. She brought me a cup of tea, but I never asked her to do that and I was too drugged..."

"So. You have to get better and get out."

"I don't think I ever shall."

"Nonsense!" interposed Joshua. "Just don't go telling people you'll commit suicide."

"But I told them I *wouldn't*, that I'm Catholic and I never would, not even... They said—Dr McGinley says he's a Catholic too, though... Anyway, he said I couldn't say that. But I know I can, that that would be worse than anything..."

"How can you know?" from Leo and, from Joe:

"The doctor's the one who knows best."

"He doesn't know. I know because whatever I feel like, I know I have to endure it if that's the will of God, and even though I *feel* like suicide and can't help thinking of it as a way out—of everything, of what I'm enduring—that can't be God's will; it's a temptation of the devil, more likely. Anyway, I'd never have the guts to do it."

"So why do you feel like it? Why are you in here?"

"I don't know. Because I couldn't sleep and then I couldn't keep still, and I became afraid because I began to get these thoughts and I told my doctor. I wish I hadn't. I only did because the thought kept coming and was so—so horrible! But they were giving me all these pills that didn't seem to work and I was getting worse."

"So they sectioned you."

"Yes, when I wouldn't come in here because I wouldn't leave Anne. However bad I was, she needed me, and it was all right until Mother went. Only I know what it's doing to Anne."

"Nonsense!" began Joe, but Leo broke in:

"What do they say about that?"

"This horrible nurse they've assigned to me just said, 'Oh, it'll be the making of her!'—whatever that's supposed to mean, and as if it *could* be! Yesterday they brought her to visit, the neighbours she's with, who don't really want her, I know, but they're being paid; the woman actually came here and told me I had to pay them twenty pounds a week—implying I was trying to scrounge off them!"

"Did you tell her that?"

"I couldn't—couldn't put up a fight over anything; I still can't. I was just so taken aback. They run a church, some kind of sect... I suppose that's why; they know I'm Catholic and here I'm in the loony-bin, so they know my faith's no use to me—just what they want to think—and so they treat me with contempt."

"I'm sure," Joe began with vicarial emphasis, "It was nothing of the kind. They wanted to get things clear, as was only proper, so there'd be no awkwardness later. One mustn't always suppose..."

His brother interrupted: "Okay, Joe, we know. Go on, Elaine, about Anne."

"It was terrible—for her and for me. She was wearing one of their girls' cast-off dresses. It didn't fit and she looked—oh, so sad and

frightened, like a little waif. At only eight she can't begin to understand…"

"No—though she can understand you'll be out soon, that they're
making you better. By the way, how do *you* manage for clothes and
things?"

"Not very well. I came in in what I was wearing—slacks and
sweater. And I stayed in them. They'd told me to grab some things
when—when they carted me off—but there didn't seem any point in
dressing up. It's hard enough to dress at all!"

She shuddered at the memory: the ambulance arriving at the very
moment of Anne's return from school—to the spectacle of her
mother being led off between two uniformed men, in a state of distracted lamentation and wild pleading to which all seemed deaf. Her
most precious child! What tragic effects would be inscribed upon her
unformed soul that she, her mother, had been powerless to prevent!
The wickedness of it…!

Leo was saying,

"You look quite presentable now."

"Yes. After a few days my nurse went for me: I was to tidy myself
and dress smartly. For what, I thought, but I had to do something
and they took me home to fetch some things. Home! I don't have a
home and the flat looked dreadful—all shut up and no Anne—but
plenty of reminders of her. I brought this dress back and another one
and some shoes… I was in mortal fear of shock-treatment if they
decided I was too far gone. Several patients here have had it, some of
them several times; I don't know how they can submit to it, but I
suppose if you protest they drug you…"

"Electro-shock therapy is a recognized…" began Joe, but his twin
trod on his foot, occasioning a pause through which his sister interposed with a vehemence contrasting with her tone hitherto,

"Don't tell me! I've seen people who've had it and it terrifies me. I
know it's meant to dull—suffering, but I'd rather suffer than be
dulled. I value my brain!"

"So you decided to conform."

"Yes. It was like being back at school, being ordered to dress
properly, only if you didn't, there it was a matter of a detention or a
bad report; here they could attack your brain. So I managed to get
into tights and other equally absurd things. The worst was washing
my hair, over a bathtub with a jug, like Mother used to do: no
shower or dryer. It was just hard to do anything at all. It's a bit easier
now."

Joe cleared his throat preparatory to resuming control; it was a sound that always had irritated his sister, though she knew it was nervous really. In his most authoritative voice he began,

"I've—we've had a chat with Dr McGinley. He seems very competent and you do have to trust the professionals. He says once they've stabilized you, certain things will need to change."

"What?"

"Your present unsatisfactory situation, with Ian away and you not coping. More generally, your outlook. Better if you *could* cope."

"I shan't be able to with Ian always away."

"Then you must go out there and set up again with him."

"I can't—couldn't begin to organize it! Besides, he wants to leave. He *will* leave—when he's finished this Doctorate and found something—a position over here."

"He seems to be taking his time about it."

"These things take time!"

She would always defend Ian; was it only because to do so was to defend herself? Not her choice of him so much as her failure to stand up to his greater determination and drive. And he would do the same for her—for the abortive pregnancies that had put strain on the early years of their marriage, for her general timidity and clinging to rule. To each other they would always be loyal in the face of others. Yet the hint of criticism in her brother's words had set it in train. The marriage—the lifelong love they had flung themselves into, so recklessly all those years ago, so lightly as it now seemed: but no, not lightly for her, giving up her scholarship, her research, her chance… Aunt Freda had said it: these chances didn't come twice. Worse, perhaps giving up a "vocation"—even her salvation; for "What shall it profit a man to gain the whole world and lose his own soul?"

Oh, she had been over this ground so often, so why still churning it round? Marriage was not "the world"; a husband, Ian, was not; a child, Anne, was not… And yet… The vocation had never been tested; that at least she could have—no, *should* have done; that thought had haunted her these past months. And then she might have lost Ian, certainly wounded him, perhaps critically. Then had she done it for him? Assuredly not only, and she was not to be exonerated on grounds of selflessness; there had been too much self-love; some lines of Milton would recur, it seemed ominously:

"Or was too much of self-love mixed
Of constancy no root infixed
That either they love nothing or not long?"

Milton the misogynist... Dalila's treachery to Samson... Hers to Ian?

Joe, she distantly perceived, as her thoughts revolved through their familiar train, had spoken and she had answered something without quite knowing what. It seemed he was about to speak again when Leo silenced him with a nudge and a frown, and as if he sensed her distraction put in hastily,

"You know, you don't seem so bad, talking to us like this."

"No? Probably it's the pills they've got right at last. I think the ones my own doctor gave me actually made me worse..."

"Nonsense!" Joe was beginning, but Leo, disregarding him, went on:

"Apparently they've lifted the section now."

"Yes. I made them, and it's a relief. They can't force me into shock-treatment now."

Joshua, beginning to shake his head admonitorily, was hastily pre-empted by his brother.

"What do you mean, you made them?"

"A nurse—the staff-nurse actually; I wish she could have been mine instead of—She told me I had the right to appeal, only I would have to appear before a tribunal. I knew I must make myself, even though I didn't feel I could. But I must—for Anne. So I filled out a form she gave me. The tribunal would have been on Monday and all last week I kept thinking 'I can't go through with it' and I would have to withdraw. But then I would think of Anne and that I couldn't lose anything by trying... Just yesterday they told me they were lifting the section—so I feel I bluffed them!"

"Good for you!" That was Leo of course, while Joe said,

"And you said you couldn't fight!"

"I don't feel it was me. I really hadn't the strength. It was an answer to prayer. I hardly can pray these days, but I hold my rosary and think 'Please, help me!'"

"You don't need a rosary...," began Joe, but this time his brother interrupted with,

"Shut up, Joe! If the rosary helps her, why not? By the way," (to Elaine) "what do you do with yourself all day?"

"Not much. I can't do much; I've tried to read and write. Elspeth—that's the nice nurse—explained it's because I'm agitated—I can't concentrate. Most people watch television but I could hardly sit still and anyway I couldn't gawp at all that stuff; I've tried and I hate it: so—false! I go for walks in the grounds, though that's quite frightening: no-one else does, hardly, and there's a gypsy encampment in the fields nearby."

"And they let you, on your own?"

"Yes. At least no-one's said anything, thank God! Because if I couldn't get out that far, at least—if I couldn't get out of this atmosphere—get some fresh air and quiet and—and green—I really *would* go mad!"

"They shouldn't..." Joshua was beginning, but his twin hastily interposed,

"Well done, Sister! I'm sure that's the way to get better. What else do you do?"

"I do some exercises—every day I make myself go through with them. And they make us play silly games. Answering each other's questions; I don't know if it's meant to be therapy or just to fill in time. You can knit squares for blankets and I managed a couple."

She broke off, shuddering; those squares had a lurid afterlife.

"I'd thought there'd be 'occupational therapy,'" she resumed, "The sort of careers Miss Forster-Davis used to suggest girls trained for, that you didn't have to go to University for. You know, handicrafts— it turned out there was nothing like that; they said there used to be but I wouldn't be able to do it anyway. That made me feel more awful—if possible!"

Her vehemence produced another pause, until Leo continued,

"So now you can leave when you like!"

"Nonsense, Leo!" Joe began and "Yes, she can...," began his twin. With what seemed an effort Elaine broke in on them.

"They made me promise I would stay another week and then they'd see. Next Friday I should be out for the weekend and then on a day-basis, on Anne's school-days. I was able to tell her yesterday, and that helped a lot. Though I still don't know how I'll cope, now Mummy... I suppose Ian's mother—but she can't abide illness of any sort, let alone this!"

The mothers, that was it: the sins of the mothers! Her mother, grandmother, great-grandmother Edith, Grandma Rigg: mothers all the way back to Eve, "Mother of all the Living," who had sinned first! But the Chain had been broken, hadn't it—or if not, there *was* no Church, and what then did it matter? No Church, no vocation, no nunneries—no marriage, for that matter: do as you please! "*Ama et fac quod vis*: Love, and do as you will," Augustine had said that. But for him that "Ama" meant God! And then it all followed, all so logical: why could she not grasp it, as if it was some fantastical theory instead of the crux of her ordeal, her life...?

That time she was last at home—her old, childhood home, that was—when in the depths of her misery a Mother—God's Mother—

had seemed to come almost tangibly close to her. Was that a mystical experience? "Psychological," sceptics would say, but what did that tell you? Either way you looked at it, it had meaning. "Love was his meaning": that was Julian of Norwich. Love again—and w*as* there "meaning"? What *was* meaning? A word. Love too—a word. Word! *The* Word? "In Him was Life, and the Life was the Light of men." Love—Life—A Person? Three Persons…? Father, Son—and Love Their Spirit…?

Leo was saying,

"And Ian? Have you heard from him?"

"Yes, twice. He phoned and they fetched me."

"Won't he come?"

"He says he can't. He'd lose his job."

Those agonizing phone-calls: before they took her away, they had lasted an hour or even two, cost heaven knew what—and got nowhere, she thought. He couldn't understand what was wrong— just kept repeating she should be all right. But it was not as though it was only her. There was Anne, and that had brought the cruellest, most excruciating thoughts of all: Anne a "mistake" and she, Elaine, would have to leave her, or if that was not allowed—and she did not believe the Church would allow her to go and say, "I made a mistake; I should have been a nun; I want a second chance…" No, that was madness, and here, in this prison, this madhouse, at best dreary and at worst frightening, she had seen that, knew there was no way but forward, that there never was, that the Church would say that. "I have set my hand to the plough and will not look back": she had said that to herself when such thoughts ambushed her these past years. But of what use, if she could not in any case look after Anne—if that was the just consequence of her sins? Anne had not sinned, her revolted soul cried out—and it was as if pat on cue the Devil answered with that "The sins of the mothers…" Anne, too, inherited that entail, would be another link in the chain… Almost involuntarily she clutched at the solid silver chain round her neck, her mother's chain—her mother's grandmother's. The medal on it was hidden inside her dress: the Miraculous Medal of that Mother who finally had broken the chain from Eve…

Leo was speaking, catching at her attention. She seemed to return to a realer world.

"I thought Ian had decided to quit his job."

"He has—at the right time. Meanwhile, we have to live."

"But…"

"Oh, don't ask me!"

That was another thing. No-one should know what that horrible doctor had suggested: that if her husband wouldn't come it was because he had tired of her, had another woman... This she had denied fiercely, and "How do you know?" he had insisted, to which she had countered a feeble, "You don't know Ian." She could tell he thought she wasn't facing up to it, that any man away from his wife had to have another woman; he thought he knew it all—and of course her brothers thought so too, Joe anyway, with his faith in "professionals." Dr McGinley, who said he too was a Catholic—implying he knew it all, though probably he was in favour of this new law on abortion: so she guessed from the way he had asked if she had had one, because she had told of her miscarriages; when she was first admitted they had asked everything...

Miscarriages! Mis-takes! How many were "the result of a mistake"! Some that should have been born, some that should not? Her grandmother had seemed sometimes to have that view of her own history, only in her case faith issued in trust in God's Providence "writing straight with crooked pens." Her mother? As a fifth child, or was it sixth—what if she had not been born? Her mother had—for all her protestations—surely seen her, Elaine, in light of the fruit of her sin. Even Anne—Perhaps everyone was "the result of a mistake," all "the fruit of sin." After all, who could truly plan a new life? Unless God, in Whose terms perhaps no-one was "a mistake"—this the Church taught: all known by name, all precious. And only because God was God could it be so, and so beyond our reckoning...

She had begun again to pace up and down, turning on her heel at each side of the small room, as she had done nights before they brought her in here—and at first fiercely, out of indignation at them all, her brothers included. And they watched as if at a loss, even Joe, until her pace slackened with her thoughts and she halted, whereon Leo laid a hand on a thin arm and said in a kindly tone that arrested her; she had not heard it from him before:

"Sit down, Elaine. If Ian can't be here, we are. Only we must go soon; Barbara and I always go out on Saturday night and I can't let her down, but can I get you anything before I go?"

She sat almost dreamily as he repeated his question.

"Fruit... Yes, some fruit would be nice. The food here's mostly baked beans and stodge: worse than school!"

"Fruit, that's easy! I know where there's a supermarket; I'll just nip over in the car. You stay, Joe, till I come."

He left and "Yes, we must be going," Joe said after a silence. You could tell he felt uncomfortable; probably he thought she had brought all this on herself with embracing a faith that didn't help her now—and the worst of it was, surely someone of real faith couldn't fall into this pit from which there seemed no escape, only endless despair: like the poor creatures she had seen in the main part of this hospital, where Geraldine, that strange woman, had taken her, who seemed to know a lot of things and was in because she had taken an overdose, but *she* didn't seem depressed or anything, and it seemed almost as if she'd been sent—an unlikely Vergil conducting Dante round Hell's circles! And she, Elaine, had accepted to go along because—because Geraldine took her and it was something to do, but it had been so dreadful, those shattered men and women, some madly chattering, some—the worst—vacant in front of a television blaring away, and over it a male nurse yelling at one mute crone to eat up her plateful, ending by shovelling it into her drooling mouth... Elaine couldn't get it out of her mind all that day, saw it as foreboding her own ending, and now shuddered again; the figure—it hardly seemed that of a woman—had been wrapped in one of those garish blankets made of squares like the ones she had knitted...

Yet perhaps now she *could* conceive of going home, making supper for Anne, shopping even? Or would she collapse back as before?

"So Leo's still with the German girl?" she asked, to say something.

"Yes, we're in hopes they might decide to marry."

"Dad won't like that."

"If it's the price of Leo marrying, he may accept it. And we really can't go on blaming Germans who weren't even born."

"How's Auntie Freda?"

"She had the mastectomy. Successfully, they seem to think. Now she's having radiation-treatment."

"Does that mean it's spread?"

"Not necessarily, as I understand it. It may be just a precaution. At all events, she's having the best treatment, and thanks to Mum she was done with almost no delay."

Veronica, on receiving news of her sister's diagnosis, had left the flat her daughter was occupying in Cambridge and hastened to her. Learning it was a two-week wait for admission to Barts, she had called upon all possible contacts in their local hospital, where she was by now a valued auxiliary, until her determination got the wait reduced to two days.

It could not be helped about Elaine. Agnes, who in addition to having been psychoanalysed, knew about Depression from her work, had opined that Veronica's presence would have a calming effect on her daughter. Freda too had urged that she go, perceiving a providential occasion for the repairing of the relationship, perhaps opening the door for the return of the lost ewe to the fold. But her mother's presence had seemed to change little for Elaine; though for the duration it spared her acutest anxiety about her child, her sleeplessness and agitation seemed rather to worsen. Veronica might feel mortified, might tell herself her transferral to the more tangible affliction would spur Elaine to pull herself together and, in taking her daughter's welfare upon herself, be healed of this nebulous "neurasthenia" (adopting the jargon of her day).

But at the far limit of Elaine's outlook had opened a chasm towards the rim of which she had felt herself ineluctably sliding. Having somehow got Anne off to school on the morrow of her mother's departure, she had straightway phoned her doctor and begged for help—which had come only as this inexorable precipitating of them both into the abyss. The doctor, a fussy woman bent on discharging her obligations to the letter, had appeared at the house having made arrangements for Anne with the neighbouring family who were also patients at her surgery. So Freda's gain was loss to her and, worse, to her child, and "Loss, loss, loss!" her mind had kept intoning during the enforced drive to hospital and into that dreadful first night in the ward, until toward dawn it would come to her in the form of a refrain, a childhood memory from a story of the Grimms:

"Ach, lieber Augustin,
All'ist los, los, los!"

Only that wasn't quite it; and how came she to know it at all—in the language of the enemy with which she had become hardly and reluctantly acquainted? Somehow disembodied, it went revolving on for days in her fractured mind that would not concentrate where it had been wont. Augustine, and "Our hearts are restless...!" Hers plainly was, and mind failing (and how to rest at all, let alone in a God who seemed absent, irrelevant, anyway to have cast one off?). That text went working in her garbling memory, as occurred to her after Kitty, happening to phone her mother for her address and hearing the news of her, had driven the nearly one hundred miles to visit her here. Practical Kitty who would never have got herself into this mess in the first place, who these days appeared a determined feminist, certainly practising birth-control and to Elaine's chagrin defending defiantly abortion: Kitty who had let fall those words of Augustine all those years ago and—what a mixture of good and ill people were!—Kitty had been her only visitor until her brothers today. At the hospital, that was, for Auntie Freda had visited her at home and brought a letter from Magda, who was laid up with sciatica these days, lying heavy on her bed like a felled tree-trunk, reading, taking pain-killers by day, sleeping-pills at night—and they suspected too much gin. Then Freda too was felled; that was it, felled, fallen: same root. Uprooted tree-trunks—those who had been to her like sheltering oaks, falling one by one since her grandmother died, who had kept them all going—all except…

Leo burst through the door carrying a plastic carrier-bag in each hand, from which he drew forth to lay out on the bed apples, oranges, pears, bananas, grapes, a packet of dried figs…

"Leo, you shouldn't! I'll never eat all that; it'll only rot!," she protested.

"Then give away what you can't eat; it'll win you friends."

"You must let me pay for it."

"Don't be absurd! You know I'm filthy rich now—but not a miser as yet!"

"You're very generous!" She was half minded to kiss him, and Joe too, but instead said,

"By the way, I've not asked: how's Dad?"

"Loopier and loopier!" replied Leo grimacing, as perplexed how to describe their father's condition to one in hers; then added:

"Far worse than you!"

"What do you mean?"

"Won't go out of the house for days on end—mostly sits in front of the telly—says the police are looking for him; you'd think he's the one should be in here! But then he'll seem to get a handle on reality and one hopes is improving."

"What does he say about me?"

"He hardly says anything except about his ailments and other obsessions; the doctors say there's nothing organically wrong with him: somewhat high blood-pressure; they've put him on some pills and said he should exercise more—but he can't if he won't go out. Mum's got pretty tired of it, as you can imagine; she was quite pleased of the excuse to go to you, until Freda needed her. He can be pretty offensive if you try to reason with him—not usually to her, though—I think he's quite afraid of her: power of the female, you know! She's always put him down pretty sharp if he misbehaves."

"What rubbish you talk," interposed Joe hastily. "I reckon Our Mum's had a hard time most of her life one way and another and I'd like to think she could look forward to ageing serenely. She's fifty-six, still not over the menopause, and I don't like this tremor she's developed in her hand. I suggested she could play more for Dad, which used to cheer him up, but she says she hardly can these days. I find it distinctly worrying."

VI

(1977)

Ron Keller extruded a foot from under the bedclothes and twisted into a half-sitting position so he could ease the numb one out with his two hands. Then he sat rubbing it a while. She had left his clothes in tidy order on a chair near the bed, top-wear below under-wear, clean socks topmost; he reached for these, pulled them on, slid his feet onto the rug and eased himself out of his striped pyjama-bot-toms and into the long pants: "passion-killers" he used to call them in knowing jest, as if for one like him passion could never die. It had, for him as for other old men, barring a lucky few—and they, he seemed to have noticed, rarely among the circumcised…

He pulled his fly-fronts hurriedly over his genitals and did them up. Circumcision—he had long suspected those patriarchs prescribed it to chasten a man's proud fires before they could take hold. It might even be that it called down upon the Jews that contempt of the Gen-tile that led even to what was now being termed—evasively, Ron con-sidered—the Holocaust! Fires, ashes—cremation, to which his Will committed him at the end! The end—end of passion, of that love of which the poets sang as though it had *no* end: that eternal, erotic love he had sought and somehow missed… Passion meant suffering, too, or why was Christ's appalling death called his "passion"? Christ, a Jew, circumcised like him, he supposed, though they didn't show it on crucifixes, which always had loincloths. It had occurred to him before to doubt that Romans who nailed hands and feet were squeamish about their victim's decency, but it was a subject you couldn't raise with Vron or any of the Christians he knew. Circumcision was pretty unmentionable too, except among Jews referring to the ceremony by its Hebrew name, that "bris" which was to subdue the son of Israel to his birthright, the Covenant: already on the eighth day lay on him the yoke that should endure, written in his flesh while he lived… Bunkum of course, holy bunkum—poetic even—and you couldn't escape it, not at eight days old nor ever after. He, who had rebelled, thought to cast off that yoke, look where he was now! Mechanically he donned each further garment: vest, shirt, trousers, cardigan—*car-digan!* An old man's garment that, when it wasn't a woman's! She had chosen it for him, as she always had everything. Not his religion, though; he had kept that, or at least not sold it away.

Having lastly eased the numb foot into its shoe, Ron went to pee and wash his hands and face. Shaving could wait; there would be no-one to see him at least until lunchtime. He went limping down the stairs to the kitchen, knowing what he would find: his breakfast laid on the kitchen table, his pills counted out on the plate, the *Guardian* folded beside it—not much in the way of news these days, just the Unions stirring up trouble. He'd believed in the Unions once… Anyway, here all predictable, all made easy. She had brought him his tea before she left for early shift at the hospital; he wasn't hungry for cornflakes and milk and the pills did him no good, he was convinced. He was tired of being dictated to: first circumcised, finally controlled—if not actually poisoned, with what they were pleased to term his "medication"! No wonder he was no better after all these months, or was it years now: almost two, he rather thought, and even before that… What if he rebelled, let nature take the course that It might know best, if only people would leave one alone…

He stood and stared doubtfully at the pills: perhaps one should cut them out gradually, take only the yellow ones, or only the blue, or only one of each…

"To hell with it!" he said aloud and tipped the plateful into the Ideal boiler that warmed the kitchen this late November day and still provided their hot water, though she was planning central-heating, which would mean the house given over to plumbers and gas-fitters and endless trouble and expense…

Seeing the fire sunk low in the cast-iron bowels, Ron tipped a hodful of coke after the pills; stoking the boiler was a job she could hardly do now, certainly not in the morning before *her* pills had taken effect! Even though she'd had that brain-operation a year or two ago, or was it three? She'd been still under sixty or they wouldn't have done it, they said, opening up her head like that—trepanning they called it and it used to be done with a saw: the skull like so much timber! Ron shuddered, then shuddered again, recalling that had been so they could insert the probe—like a knitting-needle, they had explained—into the brain… Had it worked? Perhaps it had slowed things down, but the tremor in the hand had increased and now one foot was affected; she limped if she forgot her pills, as she tended to at weekends—so he would have to remind her, he sometimes suspected; then he would feel that was an unworthy thought when she was so brave and would point out it was providential they had one working pair each of hands and feet between them; no, he didn't think she was joking, though in his view it could rather be the work of an infernal jester.

He took up the glass of orange-juice waiting under the net cover weighted with green beads that had been her father's in that lair behind Oxford Street: his last home, poor devil! Ron had himself squeezed the oranges yesterday for both of them, because of course she couldn't, but she insisted fresh was best, for the vitamins. Much good vitamins did his foot or her hands! The juice of one orange less than half filled the glass; it occurred to him he could add gin from the bottle she kept for gin-and-orange when her sisters came—which he couldn't have because of the pills, but he wasn't having the pills today and a drink would help nerve him for what he wanted to do, which was to get out for once. He found the gin-bottle tucked away on the lowest shelf of the larder, topped up the orange-juice, hesitated, put the bottle to his lips; he was normally fastidious about saliva on things, but why not? Alcohol was germ-free and she would never know...

The raw spirit stung his throat; he gulped and hastily replaced lid and bottle, then took a long swig at the glass, feeling guilty, but again, why? Because he had always looked down on those wretches—Irishmen usually, anyway not usually Jews—who succumbed to drink; well, if they led the dog's life that was his these days, he could sympathize with them! Anyway, the odd drop was not a habit—only he'd better wash the glass out or she'd notice the smell—if she was back before him...

He was going out; of that he was sure, though he had yet to be sure where he wanted to go—only it must be far enough away that he didn't risk running into Freda doing her and their shopping! Fortunately she had that car, so buses were safe. The bus-stop might be a danger-point, but she would wait until after the rush-hour. If he left quickly now... After all, he'd been told he should exercise more...

He picked up the *Guardian* and went to take his coat and scarf from the hall wardrobe, his hat from its shelf: a cloth cap now, oddly like that his father had worn; fashions always seemed to come round and the trilby had gone out he couldn't remember how long ago: it seemed with detachable collars and they had gone out with the washing-machine, now "automatic," like the one under the draining-board, beside the boiler; they had bought it when she struggled to lift the wet clothes into the spinner of the old twin-tub...

It was bright outside after weeks of fog and dank. A bright day made one feel better but it still was November—his birth-month—and by the time he reached the bus-stop, Ron's chilled fingers made him aware he had forgotten his gloves. No going back now; he shoved his hands down into his overcoat pockets, in the depths of which he could feel his wallet and change-purse; she had expected he would pay the milkman and so left him with a little money: just as well! He stood back behind a group of yammering schoolboys with crested caps and satchels over their dark raincoats—poor blighters, with their swagger and bravado; they little knew what was coming to them! Being almost of his height, they would shield him from recognition by any of her acquaintance: "Oh Mrs Keller, I was so glad to see your poor husband at the bus-stop yesterday; the stay in hospital must have done him good!" Like hell it had!

The bus seemed long in coming, but he couldn't have just missed the last one or where had all these boys sprung from and the three or four expressionless and sexless adults who formed their unforgiving line-up just ahead of them and him? Ron checked his agitation, remembering a poem, his own; he had had it printed, at his own expense, with others in a booklet a few years ago: not one of his best, he thought, not lyrical, but not bad, rather modern; even reminiscent of Eliot. It began:

"It does not matter if I reach the bus
In time, or come too late..."

Well, a bus was arriving, the schoolboys all pushing forward in the face of identical frowns, oddly reminding Ron of another line from the same booklet:

"The timeless, deathless world of happy boys!"

He had titled that one "School Swimming Gala": he'd thought of it while watching Leo compete in one. Like many of his poems, it was about death really—he thought more Wilfrid Owen than Eliot: about "ghostly companies" of boys who would soon be dead...

He would have liked to follow these boys upstairs; he hadn't been on top of a bus in a long time, but he'd better not risk it with this cursed foot—though oddly that was feeling better; surely it couldn't be the lack of pills, or not yet. Was it then "psychological," as he thought that idiot doctor at the hospital had hinted: just like a woman to reduce you to infant status when she had no answer to your problem! The likeliest explanation was the gin; perhaps a drop of gin and orange to start the day was the way forward—Vron, though, would take some convincing...

Ron paid his fare and sat reading his paper in fair content all the way to Hammersmith Station where the route terminated. There he joined the queue at the ticket-office. But where was he going? Not to his sister's, or Vron would get to hear of it and set Freda to spy on him in her absence. No, he had known it all along, really; he wanted to go home, see Robert Street once more, where his father had his workroom and his brother sat to his studies of a Sunday, while he, Ron, trailed after his mother and sister on their rounds of the Jewish shops and neighbours in the dingy streets—streets, though, that for Succoth sprouted arbours hung with greenery and fruits, where the great Night of Pesach was announced by the odour of chicken soup simmering in every kitchen...

"Stepney Green," he said to the clerk at the window, extracting his wallet. It contained only a five-pound note; he delved in the other pocket for the change-purse, in which was some small change and three round pounds—So the new coins had come to be called: clever that; showed the English still had a feel for their language. He would get rid of the coins, not add to them with change from the fiver: the less weight to be carried the better if his foot started acting up. He had not asked for a return ticket, but he let the seconds in which he might have changed that pass: no need to make an ass of himself; he would have enough for his fare back.

It does not matter if I miss the bus,
and the way back; if I never arrive
It will not matter...,

That was how the last verse of his poem began, picking up from the first: recapitulation it was called. The first verse, he remembered, ended how

'no-one cares
whether I am worried, ill, or desperate.'

He often was those things—or had been; what Ron remarked now was how easily he negotiated the stairs to the platform, at which a train was already standing—and no trouble finding a seat; that was why he had always come to the terminus on his daily journey to work, because even by Shepherds Bush there could be only standing-room. He should have brought something to eat; he was beginning to feel hungry.

The train started and was soon rattling through the tunnel, filling up at each stop until "Move away fro' de doors, pleeze!" the guards were shouting, who these days were West Indians; otherwise it was none too different from how it always had been on this Underground which was the circulatory system of the capital, carrying him, Ron Keller, under its heart to where he had been born—as most of *them* had not! Ron was pleased with the metaphor and the reflections it entrained. The *Guardian* forgotten, he settled back much at his ease, watching it all, tasting the superiority of a Londoner born, identifying with the city he loved: its people much better dressed these days, though the young women—of whom there were decidedly more among the passengers—surely were cold in those miniskirts that so shocked Freda and to a lesser extent Vron—with whom of course he agreed, though away from them he found he could make allowances for the young minxes! The men were mostly taller than him—better fed, it might be, though he could certainly not fault his mother's cooking; you might have supposed it was Vron's family who would be malnourished, considering... Jews, it seemed, were disadvantaged in height as in most things that counted: misfortunes they hid under the claim to be the Chosen People and to suffer on behalf of humanity: "vicariously," that was the word and briefly he wondered if it related to "vicar," which Joe had become—fine profession for a Jew's son!

Everyone, too, seemed in more of a hurry. And younger; of course many would not have been born when he was young and some must be younger than his children—whose world had turned out so different from his, from whom in differing ways he had become alienated... It was like in his poems. And in other poets; had not Keats said it all? "Hungry generations tread thee down"; they did indeed! Then "Getting and spending we lay waste our powers": who had said that? He had the rather clever notion that whoever it was meant "begetting" but could only hint at it because the Victorian Age suppressed sex—until that was put paid to by Lawrence...

Some half hour on, past Liverpool Street, the crowds had thinned again and Ron's fellow-passengers had become decidedly shabbier and in the main dark-skinned, plus he was beginning to feel less well: not so much hungry now as light-headed, dizzy almost, but he must keep going. At Stepney Green he would find a café; he supposed there still were cafés, or did these immigrants only run take-aways and curry-houses? No matter; one of their interminable corner-shops would suffice for a drink of something and a bite. How different from his young days, when youngsters like him had friends all up and down the streets their own kind tenanted—and honest tenants they were in the main, keeping their houses trim from Sabbath to Sabbath, plus a painful Spring-cleaning for Pesach: not like...

He glanced doubtfully at the half-dozen assorted mutes who shared the carriage with him: four males of varyingly sombre hue, two females, one middle-aged and sallow under a headscarf, one younger and black, with dangling earrings. The poor always started in the East End; that was a given of London life. But could one imagine these people moving into the suburbs: to Golders Green, now colonized by the grandchildren of those Jews among whom he had grown up? To Edgware, where Jane and Ben now inhabited a spacious semi with double garage? One or two aspiring Indians had attained to Shepherds Bush, where he and Vron had been content enough to settle... From dealings with these immigrants throughout his latter years working for Hackney Council, Ron viewed them as wedded to overcrowded tenements and unsanitary ways.

The train drew in to Stepney Green and he alighted with some difficulty now; his foot was playing up again and his head felt swimmy. By the time he had negotiated his way onto the street he realized there was scarce a white face to be seen—far less one you could suppose Jewish. He must stand out; he should have known— just hadn't realized how far things had gone! But there was a café of sorts, quite close to the station. Ron almost staggered into it and slumped in a chair.

"Yo all right, ol' man?" inquired a male voice. A white apron behind the counter contrasted with a dusky face above it.

"Yes, all right," lied Ron. "I'll have a tea, please, and one of those." He indicated the sandwiches the man was making.

"Cheese-tomato or tuna-an'-lettuce."

"Cheese and tomato, please."

"Tha'll be one pound ten."

Ron produced the wallet and the five-pound note.

"Can't change that, man. Too early."

Ron produced the purse, but the change in it only amounted to six shillings and fourpence.

"It's all I've got," he began and as the man shrugged he ended,

"I'll just take the tea."

"Lily, a tea for this gen'lman" called the man with, Ron felt, offensive irony.

A fat female with complicated dark braids looped round her head appeared from behind the shop and Ron soon had his tea. He heaped two spoonfuls of sugar into it and felt somewhat better, though he was thinking it had all been a bit of a mistake; this world was no longer his and he was no longer sure he even wanted to see Robert Street, but he would change the note, buy something to eat…

He set out again, limping by now, to find he was less than sure of the way to Robert Street. Too much had changed since the bombing that he so well remembered—Could one ever forget? Moishe, his young cousin, had gone to bomb the Germans and ended "missing in action," his body never found… Kurt's family sucked into Auschwitz… Kurt himself, he believed, had gone to America. Behind them lurked Sammy Finckelstein, shot like a frightened rabbit… The history of his people… Faceless modern blocks looked down on a few remaining squat tenements; they made you dizzy. He would hate to live in one: better designed, no doubt, than the tenements—"pullulating"; that was the right word, like rabbits in a warren—with the families of these dark-faced men who were usually all you saw; their women presumably hardly went out: not surprising, really; you'd have to take the lift; did they have lifts? That was something he ought to know… The house in Robert Street had been old, small and dark, but it had been homely—a home for the five of them…

He'd have to ask someone the way there, but he was nervous. They would be anti-Semites, supporters of that murderous Arafat and his henchmen, hijackers of planes; they'd guess he was a Jew… A black man might be better, though Ron was nervous of them too. He was feeling like giving up on Robert Street, only he had come so far and might never—or would never?—see it again.

Some five minutes of painful loitering and there came towards him, emerging from a doorway up the street, a face a shade or two darker complexioned than his own—Cypriot perhaps? Ron summed up his small courage to stop the man and ask in his best manner—short of a "sir," which he felt to be out of place; besides, the man appeared quite young:

"Excuse me; can you direct me to Robert Street?"

The man stared down at him but seemed not unfriendly.

"What that, Mister? Robert Street? I not know that name. Wait; I ask."

He turned back and re-entered the building and Ron limped after him; his foot was becoming useless and he must sit down.

"She not know Robert Street. Must be a leetle way from here," began the man, returning to find Ron sitting on the doorstep.

"How far?"

"I dunno. Mebbe half mile, mebbe less. You okay, Mister?"

"A bit faint. I need…"

"A moment. I get you…"

Again he disappeared into the doorway and Ron heard him calling to someone. By the time he returned carrying a half-full glass, Ron had noticed an Underground sign on the next corner; he must have been going in a circle. He would give up on Robert Street, which, even if it still existed, would, he felt sure, be unrecognizable. If he could get to the station—rather if he could get down the steps—he might arrive home before Vron.

"Water?" he asked doubtfully, looking at the glass.

"Wait, I get you water. This raki. Do you good."

Encouraged by this morning's experiment with gin, and mildly curious about raki, Ron received the glass and downed the contents; they burned his throat but spread an instant warmth which might even make it to his foot. Handing the glass back he said hoarsely,

"Thank you, sir; very kind of you, and if I might have some water…"

The glass soon came back with water, which also Ron downed gratefully.

"I'm much obliged to you. Now I think I'll go home."

"Where you live?"

"Shepherd's Bush. I can get there on the train."

The other drew in his breath, shaking his head.

"You eaten?"

"Not really. I tried to buy a sandwich but I only had this five-pound note. They had no change."

That was foolish, he realized, to a stranger, in an area like this. Sure enough, the man responded,

"I change note for you."

Ron hesitated but knew he had small alternative.

"If you could perhaps buy me something to eat—then I can pay you for the raki!"

That seemed an inspiration: the best way to ensure the man would do his errand and return.

"Pie-shop not far; I go, come back soon. No need pay raki; my mother live there, give you."

"You are very good, but…"

"No worry!"

He was gone and yes, the warmth seemed to be penetrating that cursed foot; in fact he was sweating. He rose unsteadily to look after the man, see where he was taking his five pounds, which he would need for his train-fare; why hadn't he bought a return? No, the foot was still useless; he slumped back, overcome by the horror of the mess he had got himself into, imagining he could somehow pick up with his past. The past was past—just that; you could never get back, never go home. Only, a voice was mocking, wasn't that what he was about to do now, go back, out of this developing nightmare, to home, the familiar prison where Vron at least looked after him: back to her and Freda and the house with its endless round of trivial occupation and soon the plumbers and the gasmen and the world news, which was frightening enough if you thought about it, and their children's doings, who cared little for him or if they might have—his daughter anyway—it was too late...

Too late! "Forlorn: the very word is like a knell!" Only sickness and increasing incarceration awaited him now: "shades of the prison-house": how true! And if true for a gent like Wordsworth—or was it Tennyson?—either way, a national poet, studying at Cambridge, sowing wild oats like a lord, like Lord Byron: Tennyson too was a lord, or they made him one; Ron wasn't sure if Tennyson had sowed wild oats, though it was likely enough; Victorian men were all hypocrites! And Wordsworth had got all fired up by the French Revolution, but ended joining the Establishment:

"Just for a handful of silver he left us,
Just for a ribbon to stick in his coat."

Like that turncoat Ramsay Macdonald, going to Buckingham Palace in morning dress! Even Socialists did it. Englishmen did it; it was their Establishment, and in short, what hope for Aaron Keller, failed poet, son of an immigrant Jew and now drunk on a doorstep, a day's stubble on his jaws and no money unless that Levantine returned: "Levantine" was what Tennyson and Wordsworth would have called him...

He had raised his head to look for the man and at that moment another man passing by stopped and said,

"Well, if it ain't Mister Keller after all these years!"

This one was pale-skinned and Ron did not like the way he spoke and looked at him.

"How...? Who...?," he began, stuttering and trying to raise himself.

"Mister Keller!" repeated the man, with heavy emphasis on the "Mister." "I thought as you'd retired, like got out. You remember that matter of my premises that was declared unsafe like? Skinner's the name; remember me?"

Ron in his confusion remembered that he had been in trouble over something that had got into the papers, had been blamed—

unjustly: was that what this man was on about. His face and attitude showed alarming menace; if only his befriender would return quickly. With an effort he got on his feet.

"Don't know what you mean," he said feebly, "Wrong person…"

The man laughed ominously.

"You don' fool me! You's Mister Keller all right: remember you in court! And I's unfinished business wiv you arter all these years. You sit down, you hear me?"

He shoved Ron back onto the doorstep, whose startled cry of "Help!" brought a hand down like a clamp over his face. He was struggling feebly, attempting to bite the hand, when he heard, it seemed in the far distance, the voice of his Good Samaritan:

"Hey, what you do? This ol' man, I leave him here go buy pie for him hungry…"

"You mind your own business!" from the assailant. "I know this man: a Jew, ruining my business, and my family out on the street: what's that to him?"

Ron heard "What that to me!" from the other and the hand came off his face, when squinting upward he could see it high on the end of an arm, held in the grip of the taller, younger man.

"Here, old man, you take pie and five pound here; they no change, I buy… You," turning to the assailant, "bugger off or I call copper in next street!"

"Okay, okay, only he'd be best not come into these parts or there's others besides me…" He turned away and the other dropped the arm, whereon it made a grab at the fiver. As he broke into a run, the Levantine was on him roaring,

"You give back!"

Ron had resumed his cries of "Help!" and having dragged himself to his feet, started off down the street toward that station entrance. The hot pie lay in its bag, squashed by trampling feet.

"Stop there—you!" bellowed a new voice. Ron heard several shrill whistles and half turned to see the policeman running toward the wrestling pair, heard other voices of people appearing from doorways, a crowd collecting. He began to run for the Underground entrance; arrived, he grabbed the rail and lowered himself by hops from step to step, panting, panicking: Sammy Finckelstein stumbling among the trenches; kid-cousin Morrie ricocheting in his burning plane; Kurt's relatives herded into cattle-trucks; that was it: the Gestapo, after him as in his nightmares, catching up with him at last to arrest him; people shouting "Stop!" Which way to a train?

His heart was pounding above the roar in his ears as he burst through the nearest access to the track. Hands clutched at him as he stumbled blindly forward and over the edge, with a cry that was half a sob and a hand outstretched as to the mercy of that shining rail that went marching on its white porcelain sleepers. People surged along the platform as was heard the rumble of a train in the tunnel…

ENVOI

Understanding

A DECEMBER night and a different train rumbling through darkness: the express from Glasgow and amid its slumbering freight Ian Roody, with opposite him his wife, awake on her fibrillating bunk. To Elaine—as if the occasion of their journey were not forlorn enough—the darkened compartment, the disparate snorings of two of the occupants, the relentless noise and vibration of the wheels racing beneath them, all were become nigh intolerable and she would have to reach over to Ian and prod him awake if it went on much longer, or rather if she did not sleep again soon, which was the only exit possible, but the luminous dial of her watch showed it to be nearly three hours since she had succumbed—all too briefly—to her capsule of Nembutal: "End-it-all" she had heard it called in grim jest, but the jester could have had insight of her present state! Which was more than could be expected of Ian half-awake, whose settled view was that a person wanting to sleep had only to lie still and quiet; in barracks you couldn't put on the light to read or go padding about in search of drinks and biscuits as she did, nor would his parents have tolerated that; one just got on with it. To which Elaine would tartly reply that he was fortunate to have been the boy-child of his mother's wishes, or his parents might have had to live with pre-menstrual tension and suchlike female frailties.

But in tonight's circumstances Ian would surely rise above somnolence and even entrenched conviction to make allowance for her. If only she could creep in beside him, feel his warmth surround her, she might relax and sleep. But she could scarce turn over on her narrow bunk and he must fill his. Nor could she risk disturbing the other passengers. Nothing for it but just to go on and on with the rhythm of the revolving wheels…

The children—though she must get out of the habit of regarding Anne as a child; she had turned fifteen and might have had charge of three-year-old Johnny: not that that would have been right even if there had not been school on Monday. They were lucky to have Caitlin, a lass from the Isles and a Catholic to boot; the two girls got on well, the elder mitigating Anne's seriousness, so reminiscent to Elaine of her own girlhood. It had enabled her to finish her Master's in Psychology, and that not only had marked a watershed in her life but appeared to have cleared the way for Johnny after a decade of trying and two further miscarriages. Her confusions and tensions largely resolved, she had found herself more decisive in dealing with people—doctors, teachers: she'd known what to expect from the Nursery School they'd—she'd—selected for Johnny. From which Caitlin would be fetching him at midday: had it not all worked out—or been worked out? A year ago they would have had to take Johnny with them by air and leave him with his Roody grandparents; you couldn't take a toddler on a train like this, nor to a funeral. By Monday evening they'd be home again, with all this behind them, and life would carry on—wouldn't it?

Almost certainly Johnny would not remember his grandfather. She saw again that fleeting moment of their last visit to her old home at New Year; she was glad they had gone, that her last memory of her father was not that dreadful ward where they had visited him on their first journey up to Stirling... Ian had put the three of them into a minicab for Shepherds Bush before himself going on by air to take possession of the University house they were currently renting. So it had been in Joe's company she had to go to visit their father—their mother too, because the hospital had specially requested she spend some days in with him. Veronica had taken this to mean they knew he could not do without her; that was perhaps true, but Elaine, from her newly clinical outlook, suspected that they wished to observe her parents' interactions.

Yes, her interest in Psychology—awakened by motherhood, even before her own breakdown (though she should not use so unprofessional a term for it)—had changed much. Sessions with an analytic psychiatrist had led to her entry on the part-time Master's course, that to her current training in family therapy—all instilling a new self-confidence; she reflected that by now she could even note with a detached amusement the studied ignoring of these developments by her relations—more especially those who held themselves to be the already qualified. With Aunt Freda, retired early with intractable back-pain from her years spent striving to love and serve indigent children, often in despite of those children's parents and even of her superiors, it was easier to master one's feeling of being snubbed: harder with a Deborah these days dedicated to "planning" the very sorts of families Freda had attempted to succour, and viewing Joe's sister's Church as perversely holding back well-meaning interferences in the habits of a wider indigent world! Did she, Elaine, lean too much on her grandmother's maxim of old, telling herself that even if full understanding could not excuse, it at least might mitigate blame? Blame for what? Ultimately for that opening up to a spiritual death worse even than the ever-mounting slaughter...

Uneasily she would conclude it might; yet anger at banal prejudices and assumptions contrary to that Truth to Whose service all knowledge and all skills were rightly to be ordered—this was justified; this she must hold onto like Ariadne's Clue, or risk another collapse and disorientation mental if not physical. Body and soul were inextricably intertwined, as the insights of Freud only confirmed: his variegated successors, scientifically trained, seldom professing faith in God, bearing witness to this very Catholic truth... Those aggressions dismissed or laughed at in the infant, that sexuality deprecated or sentimentalized in the child: all, to the synthesizing mind, only fleshed out what Paul, what after him Augustine, had pointed to as humanity's "original" and besetting flaw: that unerring entail that Aeschylus, that Sophocles had dramatized, even to a shadowing of divine Redemption. Confounding their citizen audiences—with pity, yes, but also fearful recognition...

And in seeming confirmation of this opening perspective, a thread from Ariadne's Clue had been handed her: her mother reporting her specialist's opinion that her spreading tremor originated in the brain-infection that had prostrated her—so signally beyond its effects on Freda or even their aged mother—during those unhappy months between Elaine's adhering to the Church Veronica had cast off and marriage in that same Church, before that same altar, where her parents had pledged themselves—where she too, their child, had been present unseen... This inference had shed sudden illumination, as from a lantern hitherto kept shuttered by that dread of "judging"—and judging a parent! It had met with instant denial from her sister-in-law; Deborah, no fool, well perceived the implication—was it deduction or induction; she would ask Ian: either way, it could not be "proved"; but then could anything—ultimately—unless we had ground to stand on: ground that only the Faith as handed down—that universal *traditio* enshrined in the Church built on the Rock that was Christ and then Peter and his successors—could supply! This she had seen; this she had been shown—and why to her, this awed glimpse into the slow-grinding mills of God? The answer lay hid in that universal Providence, recognized from ancient times, within Whose awful workings she could believe the "merits" of her Catholic ancestors won for her, their descendant, that return and that role. As if instinctively Elaine felt for the silver chain around her neck, the chain her mother had handed on to her, having received it from her father, he from his mother. Her fingers closed on the medal hanging from it...

Why her and not—so far, at least—her brothers? Because she had been the unseen witness of her parents' vows? Because Pawa had taken her to be his spiritual child? Because the female was more open to divine promptings—so it would appear from the lives of Our Lady and many a woman saint, Catherine Labouré among them! That "Song of Songs" of Solomon the Wise had been allegorised to show just this: the soul as a bride, receptive to God even as brides—as she to Ian. Would Ian in time become receptive? Would that too be in virtue of her passing on the grace won by those patient ancestors? Be all as might be, and overcoming doubt and reluctance, she had opened eyes to that lantern ray, that glimmer of a fear-full illumination! Christ had come for this, bringing light—better, breaking that adamantine Chain that descended inexorably through humanity, through the psyche as through its frail flesh: Christ the Good Drover, prodding homeward the straying and recalcitrant, all who, like the Apostle Paul, kicked against the goad! Each metaphor expressed in part His Truth, which no metaphor would exhaust. "The longest way round is the shortest way home," Freda had once said of her sister's adoption of the Established Church, viewed as a "low road" to the mountain of Sion. Then would this her mother's more—in every sense—indolent way at some point rejoin that steeper, narrower path that led one by and to the Rock? If so, would it be in Veronica's lifetime? For one could continue kicking: continue on that long way round, still suffering the goad, becoming even numb to it! Then God, who would not force anyone, but who could not be defeated, would have to find another way...

Relations with brother and brother's wife had become minimal by mute if not quite mutual consent as, continuing to view her as perversely keeping alive his family's hereditary faith, they set themselves to ward it from their household. Even materially: in his northern parish they could be seen, by adroit mortgages and purchases, to be building up a local stronghold of familiars and adherents to their low-church version of Christianity, even as that shifted toward ever greater secularity; Joe's sister could not but be reminded of Black Pussy's fortifications about the dust-doomed diamond mines! Into this fastness they had welcomed Deborah's mother, diagnosed with terminal cancer; Joejoe, resolutely overlooking her slighting of his suitability to marry her daughter, had with exemplarity "turned the other cheek"—as was like him! Foreseeably she would make way for his mother: Elaine, acquiescent by upbringing, could accept that she would not even be consulted, thankful to be spared an undertaking God knew would be beyond her to sustain, effectively yielding to Deborah her position as daughter.

Her mother, she supposed, would be taking her widowhood without great regret; of a late violent strain in Ron's comportment towards his wife they had heard from Freda, who had informed the doctor, fearing her enfeebled sister in actual danger of attack by her deranged husband. That had clinched Ron's admission to an institution, for observation, they said. And that her father's mind was indeed unhinged she had experienced for herself, visiting him last August on her way up to join Ian in Glasgow, accompanied by Joe and throttling back her shock at the emaciated figure brought to them sullenly out of the ward... They had been told he was refusing to eat or to speak: was that because of their mother's presence? To them he had spoken some few, half coherent words; but when they had urged him to eat and get well, had made a snarling, clawing motion in their direction: gesture pathetic in its impotence, its childishness, but still it frightened, seeming to his daughter to represent the culmination of their relationship, of her parents' marriage, of the house that seemed to be falling on and all about them. But she would not recoil from him and endeavouring to stand her ground, grasped for her new "psychological" understanding.

"We're not afraid of you, Dad," she had tried, or rather lied, wanting to believe him in need of reassurance he was not dangerous, not noxious... But immediate was the inner recoil of fear, here mitigated by the hospital setting, which she felt of him in his moods ever since—when? Joe, with some idea of what to expect, Joe who had never shared this shrinking—had hardly spoken beyond a formal greeting, ignored by Ron, after which her brother had stood back as though to watch the effect on Elaine.

And so they had left, she dry-eyed, for from the time of her own "breakdown" nothing could move her to tears, and already things seemed as if running downhill, as with the motion of this train, on an appointed course to perdition. Only now did a new thought occur to her and fight for space with and against those churning wheels: that there in that institution, that ward with its guardians and its bars to freedom, their father had withdrawn into the self-inflicted condition of the Camps...

If her mother had regrets, it would be for this outcome of her marriage, this seeming undoing of love. Had there been love? She, who

should have been their "love-child," supposed there had been: assuredly on his part, even if she could recall scant evidence of it—anyway
not now on this headlong, rattling ride—"to the death" kept occur-
ring to her. What, oddly, she did recall was something Anne, laughing uncertainly, had told her Granny had said on their visit en route
to Stirling, her mother already facing Ron's as well as her own decline,
but "I'm as tough as old boots!" she had repeated to the child, in
apparent jest—so the proverbial true word was ever spoken!—and
perhaps intended be relayed to her daughter, that child's mother?

When then had her mother taken refuge within that leathern carapace? Before it was called into service in the struggle against straitened means, against history's and War's particular menaces and the
alterations effected in her husband: this interior toughness and self-
reliance, under the decorous exterior ("I'm vain, I know!"—in tones
her daughter recalled as complacent, from her mother sitting in
front of the triple mirror).

Whatever the explanation, she ought, she supposed, to feel sorry
for her mother: she surely did—as for anyone facing physical
decline; then why did even that "natural" response seem so hardly
won from her? Was it again the long-assumed guilt of the bad,
unloving daughter? Again, from the submerged pool of childhood,
came a recollection: her mother—in what context she did not recall,
but showing, it might seem, some apprehension of their failing relationship—pronouncing in her all-knowing manner, "One is not
required to like, but to love..."

As for the guilt, it had been challenged by her psychiatrist in
almost his first observation, having invited her childhood memories.

"Your mother's a cold fish!"

Shocking, as much for its dismissive tone—of her mother!—as for
its revelatory power. It had brought back that chill November day,
the two of them waiting at the bus stop...

"Oh, Mummy, you're all *goosy!*"

The icy response—and now,

"Your mother's a cold fish!"

Shocking because up to that point she could suppose her father,
with his moods and furies, the culprit, not her always-right mother.
A "cold fish"—under a leathern carapace! And whence that frigid-
ity—that "carbon-dioxide ice" that would strike to convey her ill-
repressed anger! Who knew? There was the pre-history: the daughter's own conception and birth, following on her mother's loss in her
brother—and his Greek-hero friend...

She would continue—perhaps ever—to suffer the backwash of

that "guilt" that had taken her to the psychiatrist, yet a seed of illumination had been sown: the slow beginnings of a change in the light in which she would view her early self. There was danger, of course, and one must not excuse oneself too readily; she perhaps should feel guilt at *not* feeling—or was that the so-called "guilt-trap" again? Better to rely on sober judgment—or, better, on the folk-wisdom mercy of her grandmother's favourite saying: "To understand all..." Even she could understand something of the genesis of that carapace of her mother's putting-on—and if even she, then how much more God...! Feeling must go hand-in-hand with understanding: she at least could feel she *ought* to feel; the casuists would say that might be enough—this she could imagine Ian remarking half-sardonically, as also that it doubtless could all be put down to Original Sin!

In that Ian appeared to believe, even if in nothing else much! How many years—sixteen, seventeen?—since Father Digby had told her he had given as grounds for the "dispensation" for her marriage to a non-Catholic that there was hope of Ian's conversion? Adding, "I don't want you to think it a *near* hope!" It might have been nearer if she had been a better wife, a more saintly Catholic—or was that "guilt" again? Latterly it seemed relations with Ian had been complicated by her becoming less reliant on him; he was used to making the decisions and both were easily roused. Ian surely harboured comparable resentments, and the thorns must be worn, indeed must bind them the closer, if Father Digby's words were one day to be fulfilled. The old passions of her childhood now formed matter to take repeatedly to Confession—and whether that was guilt or "guilt" one could not be sure, but at least sometimes it seemed her confessors thought the latter...

But her father—he who should be the object of her thoughts and memories on this last ride on his behalf! Her grandmother had long since confided in her their early hopes for Ron's conversion, before the Nazis and the War had wrought on his as on others' souls; well, eternal blame must rest where Justice decree it lie. Evil, as Christians must believe, was not inexorable in its effects, nor would be final...; the long-dead Englishwoman's utterance came to her: "Sin is behovely, but all shall be well." Evil would be *ex*orable—expunged by prayer; she could, she must, pray—hardly though prayer might come to her: pray for her father—why did her mind habitually veer away from the so simple "my father," that expression never seeming to fit their relationship? It might be the "my" more than the "father"; after all, everyone perforce had been fathered, and she had called him "Dad"—perhaps not with the same half-patronising ease with which her brothers used the term… "My Dad," which in school-friends had implied an enviable closeness, even possessiveness? She thought she might have used it in imitation of them—and as it were in hope; but "Dad," certainly, and "Hullo, Dad," she had said again that last time she would see him—alive. Recoiling from the final seeing she anticipated today, she resuscitated that last meeting, thankful it left her with a happier last memory of him than that encounter in the mental hospital. There they had diagnosed him as having suffered probably a series of minor strokes; from there, at first briefly and sedated, he had been gradually for lengthening periods discharged…

"Hullo, Dad!"

She had bent to place the inevitable kiss on the bald pate bowed in the armchair, had caught a grudging "Hullo!" from scarce-moving lips.

"Have you had a good Christmas?"

No reply. She was going to have to work at this.

"We've been at Ian's parents' in Ely. Pretty dull there but they managed a tree for the children, and Ian and I got to Midnight Mass. Now we're on our way back to Stirling. You remember? Ian has a Lectureship there, in the University."

A pair of grunts that might or might not mean he remembered. She had drawn Johnny to her side, where he was retreating behind her skirt and from this protection had stuck a finger in his mouth while he stared at his grandparent, whom clearly it would be impossible to get him to kiss.

"Dad, you've not seen Johnny since he was a baby. Hasn't he grown?"

Another pair of grunts, then, surprising her, "He's grown!"

And momentarily Ron had looked up. At the same moment his wife spoke:

"Ron, do take some notice of the child!"

Herself uncomfortably aware of her mother's eyes on them… Veronica continuing,

"We think he's like you, you know!"

"Poor bugger!"

Annoy expressed by a tongue-click, his wife moving decidedly out of the room, door shutting… The child had escaped to where Freda was ostentatiously clacking the cards at Patience, willing to divert him onto watching her game. She had real enough empathy for children—lasting, as Ian had remarked, just so long as they remained young…

Standing on awkwardly by Ron's chair, at last venturing:

"It's good you're out of that dreadful hospital, Dad! You must come and see us up in Stirling whenever you feel like it—just so soon as we're settled."

She had thought animation passed in a faint wave over his slumped figure, then,

"I can't—can't go anywhere."

"Yes, Dad, you will be able. We can come and fetch you and you can stay for as long as you like."

That wouldn't be easy, but she would contrive it somehow; Ian would not refuse. Even now God might give a new beginning—if only her father would give the word...

Waiting in suspense until Ron stirred again, bending to catch his hoarse whisper:

"I can't. Your mother..."

That seemed all, he withdrawing again, leaving her grasping at what seemed a half-clue to his malady.

"I'll arrange it with Mother; it'll be good for her too to have a break..."

Spoken without conviction and tailing off; seeing in the rigidity of his face it would not happen: sensing him bent on enduring a chosen path to its end.

But after all he had lifted his head to look her in the face as he uttered distinctly words that would be the last she would hear from him:

"I can't go—against your mother!"

So spoke the son of that Abe Keller who had vented his wrath on his own head rather than on his wife's. In that too spoke son of all the patriarchs back to their father Israel. In those words she saw their position as it had always been: between her and him, her mother...

Shortly after, Ron rose to leave, when the child's heedless path crossed his to the door. She saw Johnny stop short and stare up at his grandfather, doubtful finger again in mouth. Whereon her father raised a hand to place it in a brief caress that was like a blessing on the dark curls of his grandson. Then he passed silently out of the room.

The memory of that visit was consolation to Elaine, borne tense into morning on her shaking berth, bemused still by the tragedy of her father's end as they had been able to reconstruct it from inquest, autopsy and the police. Yesterday, with all prepared for their departure, she had found time to dig out of the boxes awaiting unpacking in the stark basement of their latest home a slim booklet he had had printed at his own expense and presented on their last furlough—inside the yellow paper cover "for Elaine and Ian" in his flowing hand and the signature he had practised with the flourishing "R" and "K": "Ronald Keller"; he had taken to using "Ronald" as *nom-de-plume*. Attached to it with a rubber band was the quarterly magazine in which one of those poems had first appeared and that he had sent to them in Rhodesia: it was that among his poems which most directly referred to herself—with, she had felt, an ambivalence which complicated her reception of it.

Now it was with remorse that she could see in that poem an opening on a love she had long discounted: in its sense of loss, ostensibly in those things that had physically separated father and daughter—her marriage and removal abroad—but surely standing for less material obstacles, and in truth it could have been a plea, his writing of it, his sending it, his bringing it to her notice: a plea to which she had been deaf, allowing herself to see in it only bad faith. Worse, he had invited criticism of the subsequent collection—and as she recalled she had responded with strictures born of her superior education, she who had "sat in on Leavis": but it had been a book of her father's, a seminal book by Leavis' own teacher, had acted like spur to her bent for poetry and its criticism. Book and shared passion that might have formed a bond... She would beg that book of her mother as a memorial and reminder. For it was too late—had already been too late when some intuition below the level of her will had prompted the gesture uttered in her parents' sitting-room. Too late, too, his response: the poems had seemed to her to refer to her mother's restraining of his excesses and his rage; now she would read them with new eyes—if she dared re-read them. Oddly it occurred to her he might have arranged the poems so as to obscure their meaning. Shakespeare seemingly had so sequenced his Sonnets to obscure their already riddling references to great matters and persons. Comparison wholly incongruous? At their best, her father's verses held a power of feeling, a directness that surely characterized the Bard's youth; that cryptic proto-sonnet with its concluding couplet thought to encode the family name of his Ann—her on whom he too had begotten a daughter ere they were well wed: her of whom he would seem to have tired, yet who, judging from his plays, remained the lodestar of his wanderings, waiting for him, enduring much, until finally he had returned, full of honours and remorse, to pass his last years with her and their surviving children.

A happy ending—so much happier than her parents' endings! Yet were not also scattered among Ron's poems lines invoking an old love staled by custom, tedium, recalcitrance: still in memory smouldering, yet never quite re-kindled—was that because her mother's heart had become enclosed into all those cares and chores that preoccupied her and were a constant among his themes? Their union had been based, as Elaine had long understood, in a double self-interest—yet so was many another marriage—perhaps all marriages—yes, including hers to Ian—and yet one saw—or thought one saw—that love and life-long fidelity could flower upon that soil...

Who could more than surmise another's heart—or even one's own? Her now assiduous practice of Confession should be a bid for self-knowledge, yet did it do more for her beyond that initial glow of the justified that faded with repetition of one's sins? Her response—or lack of it—was what regarded her! No perception then, no acknowledgement—least of all to him—that some turns of phrase might not have disgraced Shakespeare! She had been deaf to the plea implicit in the small triumph of his published poem, closed to his reaching out to her in what he might have hoped, late on, they could share.

And answering her chagrin were other voices, asking if it was not always so with a death, that people became conscious of their failings toward the departed one? But a father! "Honour thy father and thy mother"! Her grandfather had written that in Aunt Magda's book, as her mother had told her: her mother who had once pronounced with striking vehemence on that surely grandest of Shakespeare's plays, *King Lear:* how unbelievable Regan's and Goneril's treatment of their father, how in a daughter unnatural! Behind this judgment lay her mother's "conflicted"—the word emerged from her own late studies—*conflicted* feelings about her own father: King Lear as she, Elaine, had even then perceived him: tragic figure, great and flawed, bestriding the rooftops of a too-literally blasted city, tramping a "Circus" laid to waste by the storms of War! Lear-like he had antagonized his daughters—wife and son too—all but one: only this Cordelia would go on to transgress his dearest wishes, deserting his Church for its supplanter, derailing his remaining hope for his family's continuing Catholic heritage! And yet—and beyond his reasonable hope—that hope had been given fresh scope in her, his granddaughter: "another girl," conceived out of wedlock by a Jewish father, yet his goddaughter; he had put himself forward to take her to himself! Was that the bond, spiritual albeit unconscious, held her attached to this larger-than-life Pawa, in opposition to her brothers who, scarce remembering him, accepted uncritically—Joe at least— the denunciations of Agnes, the resigned grievances of Freda, supplementing their mother's more tempered account? And Magda? From her one would hear nothing injurious. Improbable though it might once have seemed, had Magda proved Pawa's Cordelia?

And behind Pawa *his* father: had Pawa "honoured" Austin Rigg? "Dear Papa and Mama," the schoolboy letters preserved in his album uniformly began, and continued dutiful: no hint of criticism of either parent that could have been regarded as sin by him as by the schoolmasters who vetted the letters; therein lay the virtue of such unyielding standing upon the Church's teaching, on that wisdom inherited from Israel—there was the striking passage prescribed for the Feast of the Holy Family at each New Year. Pawa might have struggled with his "natural" feelings, have brought them to Confession as a fault. Pawa's father, the "meek" Austin Rigg, too, might have brought to Confession the suppressed anger and fear inspired by his wife, with whom lay the chief fault, so family lore held; yet that too could be known only to God, in Whose eyes—of this alone we could be sure—struggle was significant merit and met with Grace.

"That thy days may be long in the land the Lord your God gives to you." Her father had fallen—literally fallen in death—just short of those Biblical threescore-and-ten that Pawa had reached, as *his* father had not and neither had that other grandfather, named for the Patriarch of patriarchs, who was just as much her grandfather as Pawa had been—no, *was*—though she had not known him. But who only yesterday had become a less shadowy figure since she had read among the poems one titled "To My Father": its theme Avram Keller's moderation in ruling his children with his "frowns fiercer than his punishments"; it appeared her father saw him as a model and a restraint on his anger—his here confessed "rage"—with his own children: she had feared that simmering rage that both encouraged and resented her attainments and prospects, that turned up too in other poems and other contexts, providing glimpses into the encroaching paranoia that had finally unhinged him.

Finally? The last poem in the book, titled "A Prayer," strikingly opened and closed with address to God as "Father, Sire"! Old-Testament surely, and probably in the image of Avram Keller, yet the prayer thus enclosed was for "charity," for "understanding"—of those who repelled its author, who kindled that rage that under one aspect was a rage against injustice. It asked for the writer "one memorial"—At this time how not to be struck by that?—to be known for that charity and that understanding. And if these he had not achieved, or not in her memories of him, it was much to know he had aspired to, even prayed for them. God Himself had told us to aspire and to pray for virtue; that was the Catholic faith and further could none of us attain without grace—nor indeed that far. Her father in that final utterance would appear to have cast himself upon that Grace. She could at least be glad she had made him that offer at their last meeting, even in the expectation it would be refused; yet made it she had, and if it was a case of the wind being tempered to the shorn lamb, of God's mercy not putting her to the test, it might be it had held out to him some assurance of a daughter's concern, even love. The rest must be left to that mercy that understood all. The book of his poems remained to remind and to reproach her; yet as if from a further distance there echoed insistently in her mind the sentence her grandmother had made her own: she had used to wonder how far it might be true and speak for man as for God:

"To understand all is to pardon all."

She had attended only the one funeral, seen only that one dear body: her grandmother's, laid out in its coffin for burial beside her husband in the Catholically consecrated ground of that same cemetery to which she was now on her way with grimmer apprehensions. Then she had shed tears, yet all about was seemly: the hushed church, Christ's Real Presence announced by the red glow suspended above the altar before which the beloved one reposed, the features so familiar yet relaxed and, as through a waxen imaging of life seeming to speak to her of ultimate reunion. How different might be the sight of one she felt she scarce had known to love, and following his harrowing exit from life in that flight to which the Cypriot and other witnesses had testified at inquest—like nothing so much as the panicked last flight of a hunted animal! In the unknown and fearful space of a crematorium, would peace be able to be read in *his* features—and if not reunion, some final reconciliation?

That his violent end had not disfigured him she knew, for it had been given out not suicide but a massive stroke. The out-flung hand had not reached to the fatal rail; the driver had seen and braked; the oncoming train had stopped just short. Tragic though her father's death had been, not for that was Elaine afraid to look on him.

She might have been spared this apprehension, which kept her waking until the carriage window grew grey and she saw Ian heave over in his bunk, when she stretched out a hand tentatively to touch him. He took and stroked and kissed it; she could know he understood at least in part and so relaxed into a dreaming sleep until roused by the shout of the guard folding away the bunks and Ian's hand now on her shoulder.

She would not look on her father's face again, and could not know if it was more relief or deprivation that, with all-British distaste for the business of death, the coffin had been shut and secured in place on the crematorium bier as they took their places in the chapel. Fortunately, as it was a Liberal service, she and Ian could be side by side, and there was even a light-hearted moment, fastening the *yarmulka* onto his springy hair with her hairgrip, as she saw Uncle Ben and others had done; her brothers' incipient baldness appeared to support theirs unaided. Her mother wore a black hat, as did Aunt Jane, whose face under its brim betrayed sporadic tears—while she herself had resurrected the small black pill-box she had worn for Joe's wedding all that time ago: hats had gone out in the meantime and the then-bride Deborah's head stood out for its fairness; on it was perched a millinery token scarcely more than a black ribbon. By contrast Auntie Freda, from a certain drawer of relics and tissue-papers, had produced their mother's black mantilla: veil that would figure in her niece's memory as symbolic when, a bare year after, her aunt would succumb to secondary bone-cancer.

Aunt Agnes was absent, being now in a nursing home. The one time Elaine had visited her, she had been grateful for Ian's presence; her aunt had lost none of her spirit, though reduced to glaring defiantly over a fringing white beard which she would not allow anyone to shave or pluck, and insisting she be addressed via an ear-trumpet; they had fitted her with a hearing-aid but she refused to wear it, loudly maintaining the trumpet was better—if people would only speak up.

Aunt Magda, though, had pulled on a pair of slacks, a cardigan and a raincoat and got off the bed where she spent much of these days reading, to be driven hither by Leo together with Barbara, his German fiancée.

Into the dimness of the crematorium chapel the unknown rabbi, an obscurely suited figure, began reading: his texts, mostly familiar, rolling from his mouth in the Yiddishly-tinged accent he shared with the deceased's relatives—not, though, with her father; his fine tonal sense must have filtered it out—to disperse somewhere above the subdued heads, their ever-dying plea for reassurance intermingling with lament. To begin with Elaine could catch at significant-seeming verses as the threnody swept along; the psalm itself provided the metaphor:

"You sweep men away; they are like a dream, like grass which springs up in the morning: in the morning it flourishes and is renewed; in the evening it fades and withers…

"Whether our days be many or few, how little we achieve by our labours…

"Teach us to number our days, that we may gain an understanding heart."

But it was as though gradually the crematorium's chill spread itself between her and the words that spoke of comfort: of faithfulness, righteousness, trust, of rest in an eternal home; she had not thought Jews believed in that, or her father seemingly had not: how was it all relevant to his life, his belligerence declining into sullenness lit by manic flashes, his pitiful ending? She kept her eyes on the print of the booklet, skipping over its pages to keep up with the reader until the final heading caught her attention: "Kaddish"; this she understood to be the prayer read in her father's assembled family upon the news of his "marrying out," and meant to mark his death in their eyes. And yet a paean of praise, ending in petition:

"May the Most High, source of perfect peace, grant peace to us, to Israel and to all mankind, and let us say: Amen…

"Be comforted, be comforted, my people, says your God."

Then the coffin began its programmed slide through the doors beyond which its freight would shortly be reduced to a little ash— after its dressing of flowers had succumbed to the first blast: one must resist thinking it a waste of so costly a wreath as they had sent—only to be exempted, after all, from the decay a day or two more must bring… "The grass withereth and the flower fadeth." Was it better a corpse be reduced to ash in the breath of a furnace or be food for worms? Did it matter if indeed, and whatever it might mean, "The Spirit of God remains"?

After it was over, a dazed Elaine took Magda's left arm, the right being required for the stick on which her aunt contrived to support her bulky six-feet haltingly upright as she made her way to where her nephew was to bring the car. There would be room for Elaine also, Ian having accepted to go in Freda's car with his mother-in-law and listen to them opine past one another: Freda that a German daughter-in-law would have been a bitter pill for Ron to swallow and it was perhaps merciful…, Veronica that Barbara was a nice girl and you couldn't keep on blaming…

"Aunt Magda," began Elaine hesitantly as they waited at the kerb-side.

"Yes, dear Elaine."

"My father… Did you think he believed in God?"

"My dear Elaine, I cannot know, but I can well suppose he did."
Words well meant from one she trusted to look straight at things
with that painterly eye, but how answering to her anguish?

"I mean—he is all right, isn't he?"

...and his body being even then consumed, emitted into the air
they breathed... What *could* her aunt answer?

What indeed but simple enough words when they came:

"Why, yes, dear Elaine. He was a good man, was he not? He followed the light he had?"

"I suppose so. Yes."

There could be no more to say; only to trust it was so. Whether
Aaron Keller had or had not so followed she could never know—not
in this life: it was among the things without end one could not
know, like whether pardon was an uncovenanted gift or attended on
God's understanding—only God did not "understand"; men might
or might not understand: God *knew*—or none knew and the sands
shifted under whatever house men thought to build. One could have
Faith—in the Covenant that was Christ the Rock.

Then what had become of that onrush of what she had taken for
Faith? As it was written in those same Hebrew psalms: "Your young
men shall see visions..." Was her and the world's weariness, its
encroaching blandness, in part effect of "The Council," as averred by
some Catholics of the stauncher sort? That Councils eroded the
Catholic Faith to which that Faith held them integral might seem
illogical. What, then, was happening to the world she had thought
hers, the world of her aunts, her grandmother, grandfather, his
ancestors, the "recusants," the old cry, "Blood of the martyrs, seed of
the Church!": world that had prayed, suffered and bled for England's
conversion as once for Rome's? History, as well as geography, had
corralled English and Irish Catholics away from Continental fashions of thought, for both good and ill; were the "secular" tendencies
that had overtaken their Protestant countrymen in the centuries following the Reformation now belatedly overtaking them also? And to
end up where? In the sands, surely! Newman had seen the danger,
had retreated to the Rock...

Yet surely all were at least agreed that Truth was what mattered.
Or were they? Were all agreed what Truth meant, or could, should
mean? "'What is truth?' said jesting Pilate": this she recalled from
long ago, taking down that slim volume of Bacon's Essays from her
parents' bookcase... One of those Essays began like that and she
could not remember how continued, but Bacon would have had his
reasons for scorning the immutability that distinguished Truth by

that capital letter. Like Caiaphas, who "had the greater sin" than the cynical (and scarce "jesting") Pilate of that Roman world on which the Light was due to break—in beams of blood...

"And the darkness comprehended it not," nor ever would: that darkness of Original Sin already brooding over the whole of ancient history, from the House of Atreus to the Fall of Rome: that struggle against the light that Augustine chronicled—that you could trace on through the Reformation to the Fall of a greater but shorter-lived Empire. Yet all the while the Light shined: only the discerning of it depended on Grace, on God. Had she not once asked Father Digby if we could *know* we were in the State of Grace—and been chagrined when he replied—as of course he must—that we could not but must live by Hope. Faith the Rock and Hope built onto it; Sin pervading, Grace abounding; through all time darkness, yet pierced by that Light that was "to enlighten the Gentiles and to be the glory of Thy people Israel"! Light that would prevail: that was the Catholic Faith, what it meant—for her, for Ian, their children, her father, grandmother, all of them, all peoples, countless billions, sons of Adam, daughters of Eve... The human brain—hers here and now, flagging before the common mystery, must yield itself up...

Never quite. Over succeeding weeks and months that teetering brain would return to a measure of rest, though still went nagging on things part-remembered: voices she would wrestle to take hold of: voices that would resolve into the voice of Father Digby, perhaps on that occasion when she had asked him about Grace, perhaps on more than one occasion: either way speaking to this sublunary world... Those voices coalescing as she recalled them though could not recall their context...

"In this life everything is as it is and we are not deceived. Our business here... our busy-ness wherewith to busy us... that business is twofold. To strive to discern the things of God that lie beyond the present—that lie beyond Creation, even as God is Beyond Creation... Otherwise to content ourselves to walk, albeit in darkness... Until the Day allotted."

About the Author

Born a Londoner, Anna Thérèse Rist read Classics and English at Newnham College, Cambridge. On marriage to John Michael Rist, she joined him in Canada, where she taught Classics at St Michael's College, University of Toronto, later turning her attention to Hellenistic poetry, and studying for her M.Ed (Toronto). As an associate editor of the *Canadian Catholic Review*, she worked from Britain and also Tuscany, where acquisition of a farmhouse provided material for *We Etruscans* (Lutterworth 2007). She played critic to many of her husband's books on Philosophy while herself producing *The Mimiambs of Herodas* (Bloomsbury 2016), and *Festival and Ferial* (Kaufman Publishing 2014).